the cottoncrest curse

A NOVEL

Michael H. Rubin

LOUISIANA STATE UNIVERSITY PRESS

BATON ROUGE

Published by Louisiana State University Press
Copyright © 2014 by Michael H. Rubin
All rights reserved
Manufactured in the United States of America
First printing

Designer: Laura Roubique Gleason
Typeface: Whitman
Printer and binder: Maple Press

LIBRARY OF CONGRESS CATALOGING-IN-PUBLICATION DATA

Rubin, Michael H., 1950–
  The Cottoncrest curse : a novel / Michael H. Rubin.
    pages cm
  ISBN 978-0-8071-5618-6 (hardcover : alk. paper) — ISBN 978-0-8071-5619-3
(pdf) — ISBN 978-0-8071-5620-9 (epub) — ISBN 978-0-8071-5621-6 (mobi)
  1. Curses—Fiction. 2. Prophecies—Fiction. 3. Historic buildings—Louisiana—
Fiction. 4. Murder—Fiction. I. Title.
  PS3618.U297C68 2014
  813'.6—dc23

                          2013041472

To Ayan,
whose love, creativity, and support
make this book (and everything else) possible

Acknowledgments

Many people have given me guidance and encouragement. Marc Staenberg's continuing enthusiasm and assistance have been invaluable, Michael Adams read early drafts of the manuscript and gave many helpful comments, and the late Les Phillabaum's confidence in the novel buoyed me. Special thanks to Frank Maraist and Brenda Bertrand for their assistance with Cajun French phrases and to Rabbi Harold Robinson and Dr. David Ackerman, Director of the Mandel Center for Jewish Education, for their assistance with the Hebrew and Yiddish. I appreciate all of their advice, and any errors that remain, whether in English, French, Hebrew, or Yiddish, are purely my own.

But most of all, I cannot acknowledge enough the contributions of my wife, Ayan. She worked on and refined the characters and plot lines with me in the daily discussions we had during our many, many early-morning walks, she tirelessly edited and reedited every draft, and she devised the name of the novel. This book is the result of her efforts as much as my own.

the cottoncrest curse

PROLOGUE

Today

Nobody blanched as she described the gruesome event. They were captivated.

"It happened right up here," said the docent, a thick-waisted woman in an antebellum costume complete with lace collar, crinoline skirt, and double petticoats. The tour group, which had been wilting while standing outside Cottoncrest in the intense Louisiana heat and humidity, gratefully jammed into the wide hallway that ran through the center of the massive plantation home.

The docent signaled to the tourists to follow her as she ascended the curved interior staircase. "The main house has been restored—y'all come up single file, please—has been restored to how it looked in the 1890s, when Colonel Judge Augustine Chastaine, the son of the original owner, lived here."

The docent paused, her back to the wall, carefully avoiding an area near the banister. "This is what y'all came to see, right here. Where the most notorious murder-suicide in Louisiana occurred. One step below where I'm standing. As you come up the stairs behind me, look . . . but don't walk . . . on these Plexiglas panels. This is where the Colonel Judge brutally slit the throat of his beautiful young wife, Rebecca, and then took his own life. Their intermingled blood soaked the wood, permanently discoloring it. Think of the tremendous amount of blood there must have been!

"But the deaths of Augustine and Rebecca Chastaine weren't the start of the famous Cottoncrest curse. And they weren't the end of it either."

1893

He had just finished cutting her throat. He had done it so swiftly that she hadn't had time to make a sound. With pleasure he had felt his long blade slice through the muscles of her neck and throat, scrape against her spine, and cut into the bone. He was still holding her from behind as her head flopped backward onto his shoulder, coating his shirt with blood.

He let her body slide onto the stairs from the landing as the blood poured out of her once-beautiful neck. Her head, held onto her body only by a bit of spine and a few shreds of flesh, fell to one side and, with a thud, hit one of the fluted white balusters that held up the handrail. Her dark hair became a sullen red sponge. Her blue dress turned crimson. The steps became bloody pools.

He paused to admire his handiwork in the blue moonlight glow that filtered in through an upper window. He lit a match and checked his shoes to make sure there was no blood on them. His shirt was soaked with Rebecca's blood, but his shoes were clean.

He let the knife slide from his grasp and fall beside her body. It clattered as it hit the staircase. Then he reached for his pistol.

✠ ✠ ✠

Jenny did not dare open the door leading into the central hallway at the foot of the stairs. Although it was dark, she did not want to light a candle. Not yet. In the hallway outside the door, the glow might be seen through the gap between the bottom of the door and the wooden floor.

Her heart was pounding. She had heard the noise clearly. A gunshot.

Jenny had been at the foot of Little Miss's bed, checking on her. Little

Miss was sleeping soundly, oblivious to everything, as only the very young and very old can be when they retreat to their interior world. The gunshot did not disturb Little Miss.

Jenny pressed her ear against the door. Though she thought she had heard muffled noises after the gunshot, she could have been mistaken. There was silence now, broken only by the sound of crickets drifting in through the late-night air. It was almost as quiet as the meals that the Colonel Judge and Rebecca shared, where the only sounds were the clinking of silverware on porcelain plates. For the last few months, the Colonel Judge and Rebecca seemed to speak to each other only when absolutely necessary. They were like two wary creatures forced to coexist in the same cage.

No noise at all came from the hallway. Not the rustling of Rebecca's white linen petticoats or the delicate clicking of her narrow shoes on the wooden floor. Not the tapping of the Colonel Judge's cane as he limped along.

Jenny waited a good while before daring to open the door a crack. She could see no movement in the hall.

Cautiously, she moved to the foot of the stairs. She looked up toward the second-story landing. It was worse than she feared. She jammed her knuckles into her mouth. She could not allow herself to scream, although that was what she wanted to do.

In the faint fingers of moonlight that crept into the hallway through the large windows, she could see dark splotches spreading from a few steps below the landing, crawling down the stairs, and dripping over the edges.

Blood. Blood pouring from two bodies.

It was the Colonel Judge. He must have shot himself. Just like his father. But this was worse. It was not only his blood. It was Rebecca's too. Both dead.

Jenny had no choice. She closed the door and hurried down a side passageway to the back staircase. Let Little Miss continue to sleep in her first-floor bedroom. Jenny had to reach the other two on the second floor. They would wake up soon, and if she didn't act quickly, it would be too late.

1961

Hank Matthews sat on a lawn chair in the shade of an oak tree, near the huge sign he had erected. The words IMPEACH EARL WARREN were printed in letters five feet high, clearly visible three quarters of a mile away to all who passed up and down the highway skirting the edge of what used to be the second section of sugarcane fields.

Fucking right, Hank Matthews thought, that a Supreme Court lawsuit trying to put blacks in the classroom would be called Brown.

Brown versus Board of Education. Browns and blacks and all the other colors that weren't white. Fuck 'em all.

Petit Rouge Parish wasn't going to do anything different than it had been doing for the last fifty years, and no fool court was going to change that.

Washington, D.C., was far away. Things here were invisible from there.

Yet the sign next to the white mansion was not meant to be invisible. It was meant to be seen. Everyone could spot it looming above the overgrown fields sprouting spindly bull thistle and ugly Johnson grass.

Hank Matthews loved his old, rambling Cottoncrest mansion, even though it badly needed a paint job. Even though at least eleven of the forty columns that marched around the veranda were cracked and broken. Even though the front steps were sagging and the once-elegant wallpaper was turning dark with mildew. Even though weeds had long since overtaken the gardens and tendrils of poison ivy had climbed over the fences and up into the branches of the oak trees.

He had bought it to prove something. To himself. To the community. To flaunt in their faces what he had become.

He had wanted to share it all with his family. But Sylvia had died ten years ago, and his twin boys, Brett and Beau, had long since moved away. They wouldn't talk to him. They blamed him for their mother's death.

But that wasn't the result of any curse. It was just damned bad luck. And you made your own luck. Made it by working hard. And now here he was, president of the Citizens' Council and three-term member of the school board. Hell, he could be elected at the snap of his fingers to the Petit Rouge Parish Police Jury if he wanted.

He looked over with pride at the large Confederate flag hanging from the twelve-foot pole he had nailed to the frieze above the second floor. The flag told them damn fool northern meddlers that there was not going to be any meddling here. Not on his property. Not in his parish.

He knew he shouldn't have let that big-nosed, curly-headed kid onto the property. He had had a premonition. The kid had Jew written all over him, from his horn-rimmed glasses to his fancy words to the file folder he carried under his arm. Not only Jew, but northern Jew, the worst kind. Obvious from the moment the kid had opened his mouth.

Damn. Shouldn't have let him on the property. Shouldn't have listened to him. Shouldn't have let him open that folder and reveal its contents.

Well, they'll have something to talk about now, won't they? They'll say it was all a part of the Cottoncrest curse. But they'll never know the truth.

Hank took another long look at his house, leaned back in his lawn chair, and put the double barrels of his shotgun in his mouth. Stretching out his right hand, he pulled the trigger.

Today

The old man and the teenage girl were sitting on a bench in the herb garden. They hadn't followed the rest of those who had traveled more than an hour by bus from New Orleans to tour the beautiful antebellum home that bordered the Mississippi River.

"Sit here a minute with me in the shade. There's no need to go into the big house just yet. There'll be plenty of time to tour Cottoncrest later this afternoon, before the bus leaves.

"As I was saying, the question is not how Jake Gold, your great-great-grandfather, got to be called the Cajun Jew. That's the easy part. And the question is not how a boy who grew up in Russia speaking no English came to Louisiana and then ended up marrying New Yorker Roz Levison, who herself had come from Poland.

"I know you think you know the answers, but the answers you'll give are the simple ones your parents told you—simple answers that sufficed when you were younger. But the simple answer is as dry as a week-old loaf of French bread.

"The real question is how did Grandpapa Jake get mixed up with the Cottoncrest curse? Now that you're older than Jake was when he left Russia, you deserve to know his full story."

PART I

1893

Chapter 1

The sun cut through the scraggly pine tree, its green needles pointing aimlessly in every direction. Not much shade here around the small cabins on the edge of the Cottoncrest plantation. Perhaps a thick cloud would pass by. No matter. Concentrate on business.

Jake turned the wheel of his grinding stone, pumping the levers at his feet, and reached down for another knife. "Mrs. Brady," he said, "I can get these good and sharp, but sometime you ought to try a really fine-quality blade, one that won't rust, one that will hold its edge without having to be sharpened every time I pass through."

He spit on the whetstone and pumped harder, sparks flying as he painstakingly ground away, removing uneven sections that were barely visible, honing the edge of the dull metal to a gleaming point that, when he finished, would be fine enough to cut a strand of hair. That was the selling point. It always got their attention. He would politely ask the lady for a strand of her hair, and while she held it in her hand, dangling in the wind, he would take the sharpened knife and slice it in half.

Of course, given the knives most of his customers had, they'd be dull again in a few weeks. But more and more of them were starting to buy the Freimer blades he sold. German made with exquisite precision, they held their fine-honed edge far longer than the knives the locals used.

Even after his customers bought a Freimer blade, they still would use their old knives. Yet when they saw how his retained a keen edge while their knives quickly dulled, they were all the more anxious for him to come around. To visit. To sharpen once again their old blades.

When he was sharpening, there was plenty of time to talk. And when there was time to talk, there was time to sell. Pans. Pots. Needles and thread. Rough loom fabric and pieces of fine lace. A few yards of French silk taffeta. Cotton silk printed to look like brocade. Less-expensive weaves with bouquets of bluebells, roses, and tulips scattered among pale stripes the color of spring leaves. Percale-weight toile with cherry-red wreaths and garlands. Even a few scraps of velvet and tapestry fabric, perfect for cuffs or collars. You had to ease into it, however. Let the customer ask. Don't push. If you did it right, the customers sold themselves, and then they even thanked you.

Mona Brady worked the butter churn with slow, even motions. Her thin calico dress was damp with perspiration from her efforts. It was early October, and the first cold snap had not yet occurred, although the weather at this time of year could change abruptly.

Mona was worrying silently about all of her problems. Tee Ray and the kids were out in the fields, but the crop wasn't going to yield much. They'd never get out of debt at the Cottoncrest store. Tee Ray and the kids wouldn't be back until late, and then they'd be hungry. Got to get the butter ready, then shell the peas and make the cornbread. And the garden still had to be weeded.

"Oh, Mr. Gold, we can't afford none of your fancy blades."

Without looking up from his work, Jake responded, "I'm not trying to sell you a knife, Mrs. Brady. No, not at all. I just want you to try one. Hold one in your hand. Cut something with it. Of course, you need to save your money. These are tough times."

Mona Brady thought about what he was saying. He was right. She had to save her money. Of course, there wouldn't be any harm in just trying out one of the Peddler Man's knives. Just to see how it cuts.

Today

Chapter 2

"Even though your great-great-grandfather's death certificate read 'Jake Gold,' that's not the name he was born with.

"Yaakov Gurevich. Now, *that* was a name. Jake remade his name, just as he remade himself. Yaakov Gurevich. Jacob Goldenes. Jacques Giraudoux. Jake remade himself time and time again.

"Jake used to say that it was all the blood that drove him from Russia. The blood from the cattle. The blood from the chickens. The blood from the sheep. The blood from the Jews.

"Jake—or Yaakov, as he was known then—grew up in a small village not too far from Bialystok. Yaakov's father was a *shochet,* a butcher. The job of a butcher was critical to the life of a Jewish community back in those days. The laws of *kashrut* had to be observed strictly if you were to keep a kosher home, and of course, everyone kept a kosher home.

"Now, your mother and father have never kept kosher. I know they serve shrimp at parties and order lobster bisque at those fancy restaurants, so you've never been to a kosher butcher. *Kashrut* requires that not only the death of the animal be as painless and quick as possible but also that the blood be drained.

"After being quickly killed, *shechitah,* with a single knife stroke across the windpipe and the esophagus, right through the jugular, the animal is hung head down so that as much blood as possible will drain from its body. The cutting must be as quick and as painless as possible for the animal, and the laws of *kashrut* require that the knife be sharpened each time it is used.

"The *shochet* carries out a *bedikah*—an examination—to make sure that there is no defect in the animal, for a defect, such as missing or defective organs or broken or fractured bones, will prevent the animal from being declared kosher.

9

"You know why the blood is drained? It's in the Torah, right in Leviticus. You know the phrase, he that eats any blood, 'his soul will be cut off from his people'? You don't know it? Well, it's there. Look it up. Not only does the blood have to be drained, but the remaining blood has to be drawn out, either by salting or roasting it over an open flame.

"Little Yaakov was intimately involved in the process. He helped tie up the animals. He held them so that his father could kill them. Every morning and evening he used buckets to help his father clean up the blood that came from that day's butchering.

"As a little boy, Yaakov learned the laws of *kashrut* and all the tools and methods of a *shochet*. How could he not, living in that house? But he didn't like to kill the animals, and he didn't like all the blood. He much preferred to work with his father's customers, the ones who brought their cows or sheep or chickens in for butchering, or with the ones who came to buy a cut of meat for a family meal or a chicken for a Shabbat dinner.

"So, Yaakov became adept at negotiating with customers. He was smart. When he was ten and eleven, he could figure all the angles. He instinctively knew when to push for a higher price, when to give in to an offer, and what goods to take in exchange for the butchering job. In fact, Yaakov was so good at negotiating that sometimes he helped his Uncle Avram out at the tailor shop. While Yaakov's father dealt only with other Jews, Avram had not only Jews but also Cossacks as customers.

"Yaakov had a quick mind and a quick ear. Yaakov didn't 'sound Jewish' when he spoke Russian. He could talk to peasants like a peasant and to Cossack officers with the accent of one raised in a Cossack home. For his classmates he would mimic the rebbe's talks in Hebrew. That always got him into trouble, for the rebbe would walk in and find the boys laughing at Yaakov's antics rather than studying. Even at home, Yaakov was a chameleon. His sisters would hear their mother calling them to stop lounging around the garden and come into the house immediately to complete their chores. Once inside, however, they would find that it was only Yaakov, who, with pitch-perfect intonation, had fooled them.

"But all of Yaakov's accents couldn't protect him in Russia. After Czar Alexander II's assassination in 1881, Russia was beset by increasing political and financial problems. Czar Alexander III's solution was simple—blame the Jews. The pogroms began. Their intensity increased. Over 150 Jewish settlements were set on fire. Yaakov's family was right to be worried. The village down the road had been attacked, the women raped, houses and businesses destroyed. Jews weren't safe anywhere.

"Not only were individual Jews at risk; the entire Jewish culture was in jeopardy. The Czar had reinstituted compulsory military service for Jewish boys. Starting at ages ten or eleven, the boys were forcibly taken away and put into the army. Cantonists, they were called. Cantonists were lost to their family for a long, long time—a minimum of twenty years. But they were also lost to their religion. Conversion to Russian Orthodoxy was 'strongly suggested' by their superiors, and their superiors' suggestions were the law.

"You've heard of Moshe, haven't you? Yaakov's older brother? No? That's all right. With no children of his own, Moshe Goldfarb is just a memory. Part of my memory and now part of yours. Moshe had left years earlier to escape being a Cantonist.

"Growing up outside of Bialystok, Yaakov never knew Moshe. Moshe had been gone since Yaakov was six months old. Yaakov's older twin sisters, Beruriah and Leah, still grieved over Moshe's absence even as they shed tears of joy with their mother when, once or twice a year, they would get a short letter, written in Moshe's spidery handwriting, that somehow made it to them from New York. He was fine, Moshe would write, and there would be American money folded carefully into the letter, money that they couldn't spend but that they knew was being sent for Yaakov.

"Can you imagine how difficult it must have been for Yaakov's parents to have sent one son away, knowing that they would never see him again, only to be confronted with having to do it again with their youngest son, their baby, a son who could take over the business and was so adept at handling their customers and even the Cossacks who went to Uncle Avram's?

"The Cantonist crusade would be coming to the village shortly. The pogroms were heating up. Only recently, in the fields outside the village, a young rabbi had been attacked and his head split open with a scythe. He had stumbled into the synagogue, blood pouring from his wounds. He had lost an ear. Yaakov's father and uncle had helped the young rabbi out, bandaging his wounds, hiding him for the night.

"The danger was upon them. Yaakov's parents knew that there was no time to waste.

"Yaakov always said that it was blood that drove him from Russia. It seems strange, doesn't it, that it was blood in Louisiana that ensnared him."

1893

Chapter 3

"It's the curse, ain't it, Raifer? The curse that done 'em in."

Deputy Bucky Starner, sweat dripping from his forehead onto the fine rug on the upper landing and mingling with the drying pools of blood, was looking at the bodies with a combination of fear and excitement. Fear that the curse was real. Excitement because this was the biggest thing that had happened in Petit Rouge Parish in his lifetime.

Bucky had been happy last year when the Sheriff hired him, even though his friends had made fun of the way he proudly wore his badge on a shirt so encrusted with sweat and mud and grime that it seemed to have a life of its own. But now Bucky's friends were going to know that he was someone important. He would be someone people came up to talk with. To listen to. All because he had seen the bodies, had seen the blood of the curse.

Sheriff Raifer Jackson made no comment. That boy was green and naive. But the boy did as he was asked. If only he didn't run his damn fool mouth off.

Raifer stood silently next to Bucky. The bodies sprawled below them on the curved staircase. Colonel Judge Chastaine's hand held the pistol clasped tightly in a death grip, finger on the trigger. The Colonel Judge had blown his brains out after he had viciously slit her throat. The Colonel Judge couldn't have used the knife and held her and the cane at the same time; that's why the cane was a few feet away. He had left the cane on the landing, had done her in on the stairway, had thrown the knife away and pulled out the gun, and had then shot himself.

Maybe Bucky was right. Maybe the curse was to blame.

But did she expect to die? Was this a suicide pact, or was it something else? Was there a look of fear in her face?

"Bucky, go down a few steps and turn her head where I can see it; I want to see what her face looked like."

"Raifer, she was beautiful. You know that. Everyone knew that. We all saw her. Do you really want to look at her all dead and everythin'? And I'm gonna mess up my boots with all that blood. It's spread all over everywhere."

"Bucky, it's a fine time for you to start worrying about your boots." For the first time today Raifer smiled. Bucky's boots were cracked, one heel partially broken off, and they hadn't seen boot black since Bucky's daddy bought them years ago, before wearing them in and wearing them down, before handing them off to his son to replace an even worse pair that Bucky had been wearing.

"Get on down there and move that hair aside and turn her face so that I can see her expression."

Bucky complied. Raifer was not only his boss, but also the toughest man in the parish. And the fairest.

Bucky carefully picked his way down the staircase, but with each step drying blood coated his shoes and left splotchy marks on the few portions of the carpet runner that were not already soaked. There was no easy way to do this, with her body sprawled the way it was, with the Colonel Judge's body on top of hers and her head lodged against the banister.

Bucky gave up trying to keep his boots out of the blood. Planting one foot on a lower stair and one on an upper stair, he straddled her body, her dress nestling against his trousers. Trying to avert his eyes from the scene and the Colonel Judge's rigid gaze looking blankly through him, Bucky reached down and grabbed a handful of her hair. Gently lifting her head, Bucky turned it so Raifer on the upper landing could see her face.

The head was easy to turn.

Too easy.

Bucky gave a yell and fell backward, her hair still in his hands. Lifting her head had completely separated it from her body.

Too frightened and shocked to let go, Bucky held her hair in his grasp as he tumbled down the stairs, her skull bouncing against the wall at the end of the tether of tresses in his fist.

Chapter 4

"You all right there?"

"Yeah, Raifer. It just startled me a tad, that's all." Bucky was sitting on the edge of the veranda, his heart continuing to pound, the glass of water that Jenny had brought him half drained.

Jenny had retreated back into the house to care for Little Miss, who was being confined to her first-floor room and who still hadn't been told anything about what had happened in the house last night. Surely the Sheriff wouldn't think of entering Little Miss's bedroom and disturbing her in the slightest, but Jenny closed the door behind her, just to be sure.

Raifer could see that although Bucky tried to act calm, his right foot, encased in the bloody boot, was tapping constantly on the top step and his face was still pale.

"Tell you what. Why don't you stay here and keep an eye out to prevent anyone from coming in while I finish up what I have to do inside."

"Good idea," Bucky agreed with relief.

Raifer walked through the large front doors and examined the bloody head lying on the floor at the foot of the stairs. The cut that had severed her neck was cleanly made. There were no ragged edges except below the nape where Bucky had twisted. No ragged lines evidencing a sawing motion. The Colonel Judge had done this in a single stroke.

How the old man could have held Rebecca, who was almost forty years his junior, while he did the cutting was puzzling. Why didn't she break free of his grasp? Did she allow the Colonel Judge to do this? What was her final thought?

Raifer took a rag Jenny had gotten for him and wiped the blood off the face. There was no way to tell what Rebecca had been thinking.

Her nose was broken and squashed to one side. One eye was partially out of its socket. When Bucky fell down the stairs, her head had been smashed numerous times, as the bloody blotches on the wall paid witness.

Raifer walked up the long, curving staircase to examine the headless body on which the Colonel Judge's body rested. She was wearing a crinoline hoopskirt and double petticoats under a silk brocade dress. Here and there, where the blood had not completely soaked through and turned everything shades of crimson, he could see the color of the fabric. White petticoats. Blue dress. Her left wrist, twisted at an odd angle to the torso, was encircled with a silver bracelet. Her shoes were still laced. The blood had drained from her body, coating the staircase. Her legs, now visible with the hoopskirt askew and the petticoats awry, were a porcelain white, as perfect as if sculpted by the finest artist.

Raifer shook his head as he climbed up the few remaining steps to the landing. What a tremendous waste. When the Colonel Judge had brought Rebecca home, after their wedding in Philadelphia, he had given the most elaborate reception and feast in her honor—a grand infare—the likes of which had never been seen in this part of the state.

The Colonel Judge had achieved his goal. People came from as far away as New Orleans. Some arrived in their fancy carriages, which required that they make the three-day journey up the River Road on the east bank of the Mississippi River, then take a ferry to the west bank to cross over to Petit Rouge Parish. Others, emerging from their grand staterooms aboard one of the few fashionable paddle wheelers that were still plying the Mississippi, were greeted by Marcus and the other boys at the dock in front of Cottoncrest. No shabby riverboats for these people; they traveled only in the grandest of style, as was befitting the great gathering and their host.

Handwoven rugs from the Continent, rum from Saint Domingue, wine from France, new silverware from England. All had been brought in, boat by boat, coming from the port in New Orleans. Cattle and pigs had been slaughtered for the feast. Hunters were paid to bring in ducks and deer and turkey. The kitchen staff was not big enough to handle it all. House servants from the neighboring plantations had been lent to Cottoncrest to assist. Elaborate desserts were prepared, from ornate cakes to custards and pies to mousses served in multicolored miniature baskets woven from the candied peels of lemons and oranges. Old Marcus had supervised it all behind the scenes.

Raifer remembered the evening well. How could he not? It was only four years ago. The staircase and landing were garlanded with roses. The fragrance of flowers and perfume was everywhere. He remembered his first sight of Rebecca, a glittering presence among women dressed in their most elegant attire and wearing their most expensive jewelry. She outshone them all.

Raifer, whose Sunday best clothes were clearly inferior to the fine tailoring sported by the other guests, had stood in a corner near the front door. He knew he had been invited because of his office as sheriff; otherwise, he would never have been asked by the Colonel Judge to attend. His family background was not grand enough.

While the crowd mingled and talked, while the men smoked and drank, while the married women gossiped and the young girls demurely flirted with the young men, a string quartet had played excerpts from French operas by Berlioz, Gounod, Bizet, Offenbach, and Saint-Saëns. Then the conversations slowly quieted. Voices became whispers. Although the main hall was vast, it was not large enough to hold all the guests who now crowded into it from the veranda and the side rooms.

Raifer had squeezed further into the corner to make room for the others as they all craned for a look at Rebecca at the top of the landing.

She was the most striking woman he had ever seen.

Her dark tresses cascaded down onto her pale shoulders. Her skin was perfection. There were whispers in the crowd about her regal bearing, her fine features, and her charming smile. Some said that as she came down the stairs, she looked like a goddess descending to earth from the heavens. But these comments were weak specifics; it was the entirety of Rebecca that was too beautiful to capture in words.

She had come step by delicate step down the staircase on the Colonel Judge's arm. His eyes had beamed, betraying his pride and pleasure, although no smile could be seen beneath the thick white mustache and beard.

Rebecca and the Colonel Judge had passed the point at which her headless torso now lay and had reached the bottom of the stairs into the welcoming arms of their guests.

Raifer stood at the top of the landing and looked down the bloody staircase. Where there had once been life and joy, there was now only death. The Cottoncrest curse is what everyone will say was the cause. It seemed to Raifer that they might be right.

Raifer walked down a few steps to examine the body of the Colonel Judge more carefully. Afterward he would call Marcus and allow the boys to clean up as best they could.

He bent down to look again at the pistol. It was only then that he noticed something strange about it.

From a crack in the door downstairs leading to Little Miss's bedroom, Jenny peeked out at the head on the hallway floor, at the two bodies on the stairs, at the quarts of blood everywhere, and at the Sheriff bending over the Colonel Judge. She had no tears. She had learned long ago that it was dangerous to show white folks any emotion but joy. If she had sorrows enough for one tear, she had sorrows enough for an ocean. But there was no time for that now.

The two of them had to be protected. It was what Rebecca would have wanted.

Chapter 5

As he pushed his cart down the road toward the bayou, Jake felt very satisfied. The last two days had gone better than he expected.

Why, just this morning Mrs. Brady not only had gotten three blades sharpened and traded a nice raccoon skin for two yards of gingham; she also had given him a third down in cash on the Freimer knife. That covered his cost of the knife; the remaining payments would be pure profit. It also guaranteed two more trips to Mrs. Brady's, and each time she undoubtedly would purchase something else.

That's the way to do it. *Honik oifen tsung.* Honey on the tongue. That's what Uncle Avram used to tell him in Yiddish in the tailor shop. Make the customer happy, and the customer will make you happy.

Jake looked up at the sky—about another hour until noon. If he kept up this pace, he'd hit the bayou, head south, and be in Lamou by four, leaving plenty of time to do some selling and some trading.

Although there were long walks between stops, Jake far preferred this rural and untamed country to the docks at Hamburg and Paris or the East Side of New York. It reminded him, in some strange way, of home.

Of course, there was no snow, no mountains, no fir trees, and no Jews out here. Yet it was just like what his father and Uncle Avram had wanted their village to be. A quiet place, where you could raise a family, where you could smell the fresh air and own land, where you could be free from looking over your shoulder in fear, free from wondering whether the Cossack you fitted for a new shirt today would come stone you tonight, free from wondering whether the Czar would take your children away and destroy your family and your religion.

This Louisiana had many things that his father and Uncle Avram would appreciate. Here you could earn a living. Here you could buy land. Here there was no one to tell you that Jews weren't allowed to do this or to do that.

Of course, out in this countryside, unlike in New York or even in New Orleans, they had never seen a Jew. That meant that Jake could do anything he wanted, could be just like anyone else. He wasn't Yaakov the Jew. He was Jake Gold, the Peddler Man. Jake Gold, a good, short American name. He was just like many others in Louisiana—a man who could speak more than one language, who had come here to make his own way, who would be judged on what he did.

Moshe! His brother had not one but two Jewish names. Here in America Moshe could have any name he wanted, but he chose Moshe Goldfarb. With a name like that, you knew he was Jewish before he walked in the door. Of course, Moshe would probably never leave New York a second time, and he was never coming south again. Not now at least, not after what he had been through.

Moshe loved New York, however, and he was happy to stay there from now on. Moshe loved the crowds and the bustle. He loved living in his sixth-floor walkup on Mott Street. He loved the nightlong card games and the days filled with trading. He loved being on the streets and being able to conduct business in nothing but Yiddish.

Jake remembered the first time he had walked down Mott Street toward the tenement where Moshe lived, where Moshe was going to let him live. It was a Saturday afternoon. Moshe had carried the little bag that contained all of Jake's belongings, the bag he had bought in Paris before sailing. Moshe had just met him at the ferry that brought Jake from Ellis Island.

For three long days, from early in the morning until late in the evening, Moshe had waited at the ferry landing. He had been worried, Moshe had told him as they walked, that Jake would not clear customs, that something would be found wrong, that Jake would be sent back. Moshe had written to him to put a white slip of paper in his hatband and that Moshe would do the same. That way they could spot each other.

Jake had no way of contacting Moshe while the customs officials kept him sitting on hard benches in that long, high-ceilinged building on Ellis Island. It was not until that Saturday afternoon, after being questioned time after time, after being poked and prodded by doctors for a whole day, shuffled from one area to the next, and after being cooped up in a packed dormitory for two nights and waiting in long lines to be served strange food on metal plates, that he had at last arrived and found, amidst the sea of hats, the one with the white piece of paper and the face underneath that looked like a twin to his sister Beruriah.

Yet Moshe was years older than Beruriah, and it was Leah and Beruriah who were the twins, although they were far from identical. Where Leah was outwardly emotional, Beruriah was coolly logical. Beruriah was taller by a head, with a more fulsome figure. Beruriah had a rounded face and hair the color of the finest black ink, hair that naturally curled and twisted into ringlets the few times she let it down at night before carefully combing it out and braiding it back onto her head, held in place with a mass of cleverly hidden pins. Unlike Beruriah, Leah, with her finely chiseled features, with her pale skin, with red hair brightly luminous as the setting sun, stood out from all the other Jewish girls in the village.

How Jake had wished that Beruriah and Leah and his mother and father and Uncle Avram had been with him to see this marvelous city through which Moshe wove with such practiced skill. Hamburg had been crowded, but at least Jake—Jacob Goldenes as he was known there—could understand what was being said. Yiddish was similar to German, and he was able to pick up German quickly. Paris, where he went by Jacques Giraudoux, was harder. It was more difficult to get his tongue around French pronunciation, although the intonation he absorbed readily, so that when at last he started to speak the language, he did not sound as if he had been in the country only six months. And besides, in Hamburg and Paris there were lots of Jews and lots of Russians. He had no problem getting what he needed.

But here in New York, they spoke so quickly! Their tone was so flat and nasal. Jake had started to pick up some English on the boat over, but the English he had heard sounded nothing like the English that now engulfed them as they walked arm in arm toward Moshe's apartment.

And the Jews! In Paris and Hamburg the Jews had their special places where they lived and worked, but you seldom saw them out on the main streets in huge groups. But as Jake and Moshe had approached the East Side, on the sidewalks and in every door there were Jews. Hundreds of Jews. Thousands of Jews. Tens of thousands of Jews! Signs in Hebrew above shop doors. Signs in Yiddish. Jews with tables on the street filled with goods, piled so high that Jake had been sure each was richer than the next. Jews crowding around the tables, touching the wares, comparing. So much to sell! So much to buy! So many Jews and so much negotiating over prices in Yiddish and Russian and German and Polish and other languages that Jake barely recognized. So much money changing hands. And on the Sabbath!

They had been walking past one corner on the way from the ferry to Moshe's—it was almost five o'clock, and already the streets were filling with shadows from the tall buildings six or seven stories high, one after the other—when a whistle blew and hundreds of girls poured out onto the street from the nearby brick buildings. Jake recalled, with a smile at how little he knew then, that he had turned to Moshe and said in Yiddish, feeling a mixture of lust at all the women and astonishment at the sight, "Isn't it wonderful, Moshe, that there are so many good Jewish girls here who have spent the whole day in these enormous shuls and who only now are coming home for Havdalah?"

Moshe had turned to him and said with a straight face, "So true, so true. You should be so lucky as to worship in one of those shuls. They're open from early in the morning until late at night every day."

It was only later that Jake had found out that those brick buildings were not synagogues at all but, rather, garment factories.

There were no Jewish girls here in the Louisiana countryside, and those in New Orleans hadn't appealed to him. He would have time soon enough to find a wife. First, however, he would build his wealth and protect what he already had.

Jake paused to wipe his brow and look in the cart. He checked his inventory, especially the Freimer knives, which were his highest-profit item. If he could do what he anticipated, if he could trade for them profitably, it would be at least another week before he would have to go back to pick up what he had hidden at Cottoncrest.

Chapter 6

The pistol in the Colonel Judge's hand was old and rusty. Raifer hadn't noticed that fact the first time he had looked at the scene, but now that he was bent over the old man's body, he could clearly see it was not like any weapon the Colonel Judge kept.

The Colonel Judge had been meticulous. If you went to see him in his court chambers, his desk was always clean. He kept in front of him only the one thing he was working on at the moment. As soon as he was finished, the documents were filed away. His inkstand was always filled, his blotter always fresh. Even as times grew harder, even as the Colonel Judge had to cut back on farming and sell off some of the cattle, he had kept the house at Cottoncrest in the finest condition. The fence around the garden always looked as if it had been freshly whitewashed, with no tinge of green from the rain dripping off the leaves of the oaks and magnolias. The veranda was swept clean each morning. The windows and mirrors were washed and the furniture dusted daily. Before Rebecca had arrived and taken over supervision of the house, Marcus had been kept busy. Everything had to be up to the Colonel Judge's standards.

The Colonel Judge's special pride was his military collection. He had mounted, over the mantel of the great fireplace in the sitting room, his father's sword, pistols, and rifles. The General's arms were always kept polished, seemingly ready to be taken down and used in battle on a moment's notice.

After the Colonel Judge had gone hunting, he would clean his guns himself while Marcus chopped off the feet and removed the feathers from the ducks or turkeys the Colonel Judge had downed with expert aim. Then, the guns would go back into the gun case in the wall of the study.

This revolver in the Colonel Judge's hand did not look like the kind of weapon the Colonel Judge would have kept.

Why would the Colonel Judge use a rusty gun to kill himself? It was not an ordinary revolver. It was not a Colt or a Derringer. It was an unusual design. It had a cylinder that held nine shots, not the usual six. It looked like the .36-caliber bullet you'd use with a Colt wouldn't be big enough. What type of bullet did the Colonel Judge use to kill himself?

The revolver had two barrels, a normal-sized one and another one, underneath, larger in diameter. The larger one, however, hadn't been used in years; it was jammed with dirt and grime and crusty mud. Why had the Colonel Judge not cleaned the pistol to make sure it would fire properly?

Raifer examined the loading lever. It flipped up, and the accumulated rust made it difficult to work. This, too, was an unusual design. If it stuck, the piston could be shoved into the cylinder, and the pistol would jam when you got ready to cock it for the next shot. Why use a revolver that had a chance of misfiring?

The Colonel Judge's body lay across Rebecca's back. Raifer grabbed the wide, mahogany banister to steady himself as he squatted down awkwardly to get a close look at the Colonel Judge's face. The bullet had clearly entered the skull at the left temple; there were burn marks there. His eyes were open in a fixed gaze. Blood—his and Rebecca's— stained his white beard and mustache and his once carefully combed mane of white hair. His right ear rested on Rebecca's lower back as if he were listening to something. Carefully and very gingerly, Raifer picked up the Colonel Judge's head to look at the right temple and stared long and hard at the blood-covered head in his grasp.

Raifer returned the Colonel Judge's head to Rebecca's lower back. Let them have one more time together, even in death.

Maybe the Cottoncrest curse was worse than people said, or else there was something very, very strange going on here that had nothing to do with a curse.

Chapter 7

"First I buy needles and thread and two, yes two thimbles for my Jeanne Marie. That should be enough, I think. But now you tell me," Trosclaire Thibodeaux was saying in French, "that this knife, she is one beautiful piece of work and that she could slice through anything like it was butter. I think you are fooling me, no?"

Although Jake had no problem understanding the French spoken in New Orleans—his time in Paris had equipped him to converse fluently enough—the French that the Acadians spoke had taken some getting used to. They had a different intonation, a different pronunciation, and a slew of different ways of saying things. It was as if they had been separated from everything French for 150 years and had developed their own vocabulary and way of speaking.

But of course, they really had been separated, first in Canada and now here. The British had driven their grandparents from Port-Royal and Halifax in Nova Scotia, which was then called Acadia. Some had gone to Saint Domingue and then to New Orleans and finally to here. Others had been sent to Virginia and then Britain and then, courtesy of Spanish transport ships, to New Orleans.

But no matter what their route, the high French in New Orleans looked down their noses on these Acadians. The high French considered the Acadians coarse and uneducated. The Acadians had callused hands and sunburned faces. They lived in the swamps and ate anything they could catch or shoot. Crustaceans that lived in the mud of ditches. Old alligator gar, fish too ugly to even look at. Catfish with their protruding lips and stinging, fleshy whiskers. Even alligators and possums and armadillos.

But Jake liked the Acadians. They were openhearted. They were sharp traders. They had a sense of humor like his Uncle Avram's—they told stories on themselves and told stories about how they got the best of others, who never even realized they had been taken advantage of.

Jake appreciated the Acadians, and the Acadians reciprocated. They appreciated this wiry little man with a grip like iron. They liked the Peddler Man who spoke an interesting form of French, who, the more he visited them, the better they could understand him. Maybe it was because the Peddler Man was just getting better in speaking the way they spoke.

The Acadians liked the fact that Jake would come on foot, pushing his wooden cart filled with interesting things, things that they couldn't get any other way. They liked the fact that he would joke with them and haggle with them and trade with them, and then, when they had finished their business, he would stay and talk. Jake did not run off like those American traders who were only interested in seeing how fast they could get from one place to the next, or like those nasty Germans who fought over every penny, or like those highbrowed New Orleanians who spoke as if they still lived in Paris, going to Versailles for parties, and ignoring the fact that the Bastille had fallen more than a hundred years earlier and that Napoleon had died in exile in 1821, more than seventy years ago.

"I speak only the truth about my goods," Jake replied in French. "If you want to use your knife, the one you bought off that American trader last year that I've had to sharpen twice for you since then, you go should do only that. Why would I try to change your mind when you clearly know what you like? Since you are happy with your American knife, I'll simply put this one, with its fine wooden handle and blade so sharp it would cleave an apple in two and allow you to hold it together so that no one could see the cut, back into my cart."

The customer was always right. Jake took the Freimer knife and slowly turned back toward his cart. No need to hurry. The longer he took, the better.

"You turn your back on me before I finish, no?"

Jake paused, his hand above the cart.

"I think you are becoming just like those American traders. Too quick. No wonder those American women are like ice. Their men do not know how to satisfy them. Too quick with everything, yes?"

Jake slowly turned back around, the Freimer knife still in his hand.

"I think you are already like those Americans say the Acadians are— too slow. If you do everything as slowly as you do business, your wife must fall asleep on you before you begin, no?"

Trosclaire laughed loudly, his open mouth showing his five remaining teeth. "My wife, Aimee, and I have eleven children to show that I am not too slow!"

Jake responded with a grin, "That does not prove you are not too slow. It only proves that you have a wife who is very, very patient."

Trosclaire reached under his rocking chair and retrieved a thick jug with a wooden stopper. He took a swig and, wiping his mouth with his sleeve, handed it to Jake. "My wife, she is patient so that she can enjoy everything. And I give her plenty to enjoy, I guarantee. You try this, my friend, and see if it does not make you enjoy life more."

Jake stepped up onto the narrow porch and lifted the jug to his lips. If a customer offered you a drink, you knew you had a sale assured. The fiery liquid burned his gullet, but the reaction he showed was one of complete satisfaction. Humor the customer at every turn.

"How are you going to prove to me that this knife, she is all that you say she is?"

Jake shrugged his shoulders, as if he were puzzled. "That is a good question. What would you suggest?"

Trosclaire stood up, the old cane rocking chair creaking. Jake could see that two slats on the chair were broken, but Trosclaire didn't mind it, any more than he minded the fact that several boards in the porch were missing.

Trosclaire put his hands on his hips, looking out over the bayou, its brown water barely moving downstream, its surface broken here and there by an occasional fish feeding near the surface or a snake slowly swimming across to the reedy shore. "You are the man who wants to make the sale of this knife, which you haven't even told me the price of yet, so she must be expensive, and you want me to tell *you* how to prove what you want to sell me is good?"

Jake turned toward the bayou to look in the same direction as Trosclaire and remained quiet. Let the customer convince himself.

"A *boucherie* for a *cochon de lait,* I think. That, my friend, would be a good test."

Jake nodded in agreement.

"And I think," Trosclaire added, pulling a plug of tobacco out of his pocket and sticking it in his jaw, "you should have the honor. About your knife, I think, myself, she cuts like a dog's leg. You say no? You should show me how this knife, how she cuts so easily that the pig will not even squeal.

From Trosclaire's viewpoint, Jake's face showed nothing but agreement.

But, inside, Jake didn't like it at all. He was going to make the sale, that was certain, but pigs were not kosher. They did not have cloven hooves. They did not chew their cud. There was no way to slaughter a non-kosher animal to make its meat kosher.

And Jake did not want to kill again.

Chapter 8

Dr. François Cailleteau flicked the ash from his cigar. When Bucky came into town to get him and dragged him away from his afternoon appointments, he hadn't been happy. But, he had ridden out here. Raifer wouldn't have disturbed him if it hadn't been important, and anyway, it had been more than a year since he had been out to Cottoncrest.

The ride from town had been long, and Dr. François Cailleteau found that the older he got, the less he liked to travel. He was getting too fat, and it was now difficult to get up on the rig. The road from Parteblanc to Cottoncrest was even more rutted than he had remembered, and his excess flesh rubbed uncomfortably against his clothing as the wooden wheels jolted along. Now that he was here at Cottoncrest, he was out of breath from his journey. A damn shame, he thought, that now even riding in a buggy was exhausting.

At Raifer's instruction Marcus and the other boys had taken the bodies out of the house, had laid them out on boards set up on sawhorses in the barn, and had covered them with sheets. Rebecca's head had been put in a wooden bucket set next to her body. The bucket also was covered with a sheet.

The boys were mopping up the staircase and landing. It had to be done, and it kept them away from the barn. Raifer had given them specific instructions on what to do. They didn't understand why he wanted it done in a certain way, but they nodded their heads and went to work.

The sharecroppers had come out of the sugarcane fields up to the big house to ask questions, but Raifer had told them only that the Colonel Judge and his wife were dead, that he'd have more information for them later. Although they already knew from Marcus that the curse had hit again, they were not going to cross the Sheriff. They retreated from the big house and congregated in small groups under the row of oak trees that lined the wide plantation entrance from the dock on the Mississippi River to the house, speculating on the curse and how Little Miss would take the deaths and what it all meant for their future.

As Dr. Cailleteau leaned against the rough walls of the stable, the flab of his neck pouring over his collar and partially obscuring the top of his tie, Raifer lifted the sheets off the bodies. The Colonel Judge's lifeless face was staring straight up at the barn ceiling high above them. Rebecca's full, shapely breasts pointed toward the floor, resting against the board, the stays at the back of her dress still tightly laced. She was heavier than she once was, and little mountains of the now unyielding flesh lumped beneath the bloody fabric. The afternoon sun, playing between the cracks in the wall and filtering through the hay in the upper loft, cast a yellow glow on the small of her back where the Colonel Judge's head had rested.

Despite Rebecca's bloody clothes and headless torso, and despite the fatal wounds to his friend's head, Dr. Cailleteau did not flinch. While serving in the Confederate army, he had seen worse. He had tripped on body parts blown off in battle as he tried to get to survivors writhing in agony. He had taken his scalpel and removed bullets from the stomachs and groins of soldiers while his orderly sat on their chests to keep them still, while assistants put tourniquets on the stubs of arms that had been blown off. More times than he cared to count, he had taken his saw and amputated a trooper's leg to save his life, the soldier screaming in pain as he was held down by those who were gagging from the gangrene's stench.

Dr. Cailleteau reached down and closed his friend's sightless eyes. "Well, Raifer, I don't know why you called me out here. If you want me to pronounce them dead, then that's easy."

Dr. Cailleteau threw the stump of his cigar onto the dirt floor of the barn, ground the remaining glow out with the heel of his boot, and pulled another cheroot from the vest that covered his ample stomach. He took a match out of his pocket, struck it on the rough wood of the board on which the Colonel Judge's body lay, and lit the cigar, his sixth of the day. "In my opinion they're dead."

Bucky started to smirk with amusement. The doctor always had a dry wit. Then Bucky caught Raifer's glare, and the smirk vanished.

"What I want to know," said Raifer, "is exactly how this happened."

Despite Raifer's harsh look, Bucky couldn't resist. He was going to prove to Raifer and the doctor that he was someone important, that he was someone smart, that he had been thinking carefully about things. He would show them both.

"I mean, it's clear, ain't it, Doc? The Colonel Judge slit her throat there on the stairs and then lay down on her back, all sad-like because he did it. Maybe he even hugged her, but she was dead already. And then he shot himself. It's the curse, ain't it. The curse came true again."

Raifer's eyes drilled into Bucky, trying to catch his attention. That boy just couldn't keep his mouth from flapping.

Dr. Cailleteau took the cigar out of his mouth and exhaled a large cloud of smoke. "They found him lying on top of her? Well, Bucky, since you got this figured out already, why don't you tell me how he did it?"

Raifer let the boy yap some more. The Doc was just leading him on. Let the Doc have his fun, and then we'll get on with it.

Bucky felt a swell of pride. The Doc was relying on him. Wait 'til he told his friends!

"The way I figure it," Bucky began, his hands carving the air with emphasis, "he had this here knife what we found." Bucky's hand now grabbed an invisible knife. "He takes the knife, and he cuts her throat just like you scythe down a stalk of cane. WHOOSH."

Bucky swung his invisible knife through the air, his arm extended, his elbow locked.

"She's dead, you see, the minute her throat is cut."

Bucky, now pretending to be Rebecca, fell dramatically to the barn floor. From the floor he looked up at Dr. Cailleteau. "Dead. She's here dead and bleeding. The blood is gushin' out all over the place."

Bucky then got back on his feet and carelessly dusted himself off, leaving bits of hay stuck in his hair and on his shirt.

"Then the Colonel Judge, he's sorry he did it. He killed her in anger or maybe a jealous rage. I mean, he was so old and she was so young. Or maybe because he was going crazy. Old people get like that sometimes, you know."

Raifer knew that Bucky was getting himself in deeper and deeper. To Bucky, anyone older than thirty was ancient. Bucky wasn't stopping to think that the Doc was older than the Colonel Judge.

"Anyway," Bucky continued, "he's now sorry, so very sorry, seeing her all dead and everything."

Bucky was now fully engaged in his story. He fell to one knee. "So, he kneels down on the stair to see if maybe she's still alive."

Bucky, as the Colonel Judge, vigorously shook the invisible body of Rebecca until it was whipping like cane stalks in a bad storm. He then laid her invisible body back onto the floor and raised his arms above his head, pouted his lips, and assumed an exaggerated expression of woe. "She is dead! She is dead! My loving wife is dead! What have I done?"

Looking up at Dr. Cailleteau, he dropped his pretended wailing and said, matter-of-factly, "He can't stand it. He must hug her once more."

Bucky became the Colonel Judge again bending over Rebecca. "He puts his head down on her back, giving her one last hug. She's face down on the stairs, so he hugs her back . . . he don't hug her head, because he has cut her neck all up and it's too bloody, so he hugs her right here."

Bucky reached out and grabbed a feed bag that was hanging on the stall and placed it on the floor. "The small of her back. Right here."

Then Bucky laid down on his stomach, his face turned sideways on the feed bag. "He takes his pistol, and he puts it to his forehead . . ."

Bucky took an invisible pistol and, pointing it down onto his forehead and the floor below, pulled the trigger. "BANG!" The invisible bullet went through Bucky's forehead, heading toward the feed bag and the barn floor.

He stood back up and dusted himself off again. There was still hay in his hair, and now bits of feed were stuck on his collar and on his cheek.

"And that's the way it was done!" he said proudly.

Dr. Cailleteau waited a full minute before responding. He took a couple of puffs on his cigar. He leaned back against a stall door. Finally, he turned to Raifer and said, in his usual slow and deliberate manner, "And to think, Bucky figured that out all on his own."

Raifer just waited. Let the Doc continue to have his fun.

Dr. Cailleteau looked over at Bucky. "You may have a real future, Bucky. If not in keeping the peace with a badge, then in one of those riverboat performing troupes that come through here on the way to New Orleans. Have you ever thought of doing that?"

Thought about it. Oh, he had thought about it. On his long rides through the back roads of Petit Rouge Parish, riverboats were something that filled his mind. He had never been on one, but he had imagined what it would be like. He would steam up and down the river. He would see New Orleans and Baton Rouge and Natchez and places so far away you could only dream about them. He would be in those plays they did with the fancy ladies. He would save a beautiful girl from a villain every night, and they would thank him and bless him, and the audiences would applaud. He would be famous.

Raifer saw Bucky getting worked up again. Before the boy had a chance to speak and run his fool mouth off some more, Raifer intervened. "Doc, just take a look at the Colonel Judge and tell me what you think."

Dr. Cailleteau groaned as he shifted his massive bulk and walked over to the board where the Colonel Judge's body lay. Clenching the cigar in his teeth and puffing away as he worked, he put his fat hands, with short, squat fingers that moved with amazing deftness, on the Colonel Judge's cheeks and turned the now-stiff body back and forth to examine both sides of the head.

A small bullet hole was in the left temple. Powder burns were on the skin, and hints of blue powder could be seen in the Colonel Judge's white hair near the hole.

On the rear right side of the cranium there was a large hole. Bits of brain could be seen through the skin that had partially peeled back, revealing the skull underneath. Blood had congealed in the hole, had hardened, and was turning black.

Dr. Cailleteau shook his head in resignation. All his friends were dying or dead. And now Augustine, ten years his junior, was gone. Augustine had shot himself in precisely the same way as his father had. First the father, now the son. Maybe there really was a curse.

Chapter 9

Trosclaire Thibodeaux had built a large fire next to a trench he had dug. They still had an hour or more until it died down enough to start cooking; they needed a good bed of white-hot ashes. In the meantime he had hung the big pot, full of bayou water, over the fire. The dry hickory that Trosclaire had pulled out of the woods would burn hotter than the soft pine.

Aimee was returning home with the children in the late afternoon's light. She was coming up the road carrying two of them. A small baby was cradled in one arm. A larger toddler, his rear cupped in the crook of the other arm, hugged her neck. Five more straggled behind her, none of them older than seven or eight. Some held buckets filled with wild blackberries and mint. Others had long willow branches, tied in bundles on their backs, to be used later to weave baskets for Jeanne Marie.

Jake and Trosclaire were on the porch, Trosclaire in the old rocking chair, Jake leaning up against the front wall of the small two-room cabin. Coming down the bayou in a pirogue were the four oldest children. The shallow-bottomed boat, carved out of the trunk of a tree, barely made a sound as it skimmed along. One quick movement by any of the occupants, one wrong shift, and the pirogue would overturn. But the children had grown up on the bayou. The two boys, ten and eleven years old, were paddling with quiet expertise. The two girls, their thin skirts gathered around them, held large baskets of flopping fish in their laps.

"Tonight, my friend," Trosclaire said in French to Jake, "we are going to have ourselves some feast. Aimee, she make a pie with those blackberries. Just look at my children bringing a mess of sacolet and brim. If they had caught any more, that pirogue, she would groan like a muskrat

34

in a trap and then break and sink to the bottom of the bayou. And you, you are going to show me that your knife, something that you want to ask me too much for, is worth paying a penny more than I paid for this American one."

Trosclaire took the heavy blade, the one Jake had again sharpened free for him a few minutes earlier, and threw it expertly at a nearby pine tree. It hit its mark and buried itself two inches deep in the gray, crusty bark.

That was a sign, Jake knew, that he could delay the *boucherie* no longer. The children were unloading the pirogue and bringing the fish up to the house. The feast would begin late at night, and the *cochon de lait* would start soon, and there was still the boiling to do.

Jake and Trosclaire went to the pen on the side of the house. Trosclaire picked up one of the larger suckling pigs, pulling it away from its mother's teat, and handed it to Jake.

Jake put a large bucket under the ledge of the porch and, holding the squiggling pig tightly, walked up on the porch. It must have weighed more than fifty pounds, but Jake handled it easily. He placed the pig between his knees, squeezing it firmly with his legs so that it couldn't move.

Jake pulled a large Freimer knife with a ten-inch blade out of his belt and, reaching down, grabbed the squealing pig's snout and pulled it up, stretching the neck taut. With one practiced stroke he cut the pig's neck, severing the jugular vein and the nerves of the backbone.

It was perfect. One cut. The pig never felt any pain.

Jake tilted the pig's body so that the blood would drain into the bucket below.

Trosclaire was amazed. "That knife, she is as sharp as you say. But you have almost cut off her head! What kind of *boucherie* is this? It is no way to prepare for a *cochon de lait*."

Chapter 10

The sharecroppers were still under the trees when Marcus came out of the house, another bucket of bloody cloths in his hand. Marcus already had used up all the old sheets. His wife, Sally, was doing her best to rinse them out as quickly as possible in the big old tub on the side of the kitchen. She ran them up and down the washboard, the suds from the lye soap turning a bright pink.

Marcus left the bloody sheets on the wooden pallet next to the washtub, where the brown soil had taken on a reddish tinge. He took some of the damp sheets that Sally had finished off the clothesline. He put these sheets in a bucket and headed back into the house. At this rate it would take until dark to mop up all the blood that had coated the stairs and dripped down the walls onto the hallway floor below. Tomorrow's daylight coming through the east windows would let them see clearly what remained to be done. But who would give the instructions? Where would he and Sally go? Would they have a place to live?

Marcus had been with the Colonel Judge long before he had that title. The General had bought him for Mr. Augustine when Mr. Augustine was just turning into a man. Marcus had been with Mr. Augustine in the days when a white ocean of cotton blanketed the plantation as far as the eye could see. Marcus had been with him when the cotton bales, stacked as high as four men, were on the shore waiting to be loaded onto the riverboats that used to line up in front of Cottoncrest.

Marcus had been with Mr. Augustine when the General left, before the fighting. Marcus had followed Mr. Augustine into the camps. Marcus had saddled his horse and polished his sword and cleaned his guns and washed and pressed his uniforms. Marcus had been with Mr. Augustine at the siege of Port Hudson, when Mr. Augustine had been made a colonel. And from that point on it was never "Mr. Augustine" anymore. It was "Colonel."

Marcus had been back at the campground when the Colonel's horse was shot out from under him and the Colonel himself was captured. At that time Marcus had thought his world had ended.

But it had not. Marcus had survived, and the Colonel had survived, although just barely. When after the war, the Colonel had returned to Cottoncrest from the Union prison at Camp Butler in Illinois, he was like a ghost. In fact, to the General, Augustine had long ago become a ghost, which is why the General . . . but that was the start of the curse, wasn't it.

When the Colonel had finally come back to Cottoncrest, his ribs showed through his thin cotton shirt, his face was gaunt, his chest hollow, and he walked with a limp that never left him, the old bullet still in his left thigh.

Marcus had made it this far. The good Lord had granted him a strong body. He was older than the Colonel Judge and had outlived him. He would do what he always had done. He would live today and let tomorrow take care of itself.

On his way back into the big house, Marcus passed by the sharecroppers. They had been counting. This was his sixth trip. Six buckets of bloody sheets. How much blood had there been? It was obvious the curse had hit again. The Colonel Judge had killed himself. And the curse was getting worse. Miss Rebecca was dead too. Who would run the plantation? Who would honor their crop pledges? Who would market the sugarcane now that the Colonel Judge, who had handled all the financing for them, was gone?

Some of the sharecroppers glanced upward as the sun headed toward the western horizon, the October sky the blue of well-worn Union uniforms, now absent for almost a decade since President Rutherford P. Hayes pulled the troops out and ended Reconstruction.

Some Reconstruction it had turned out to be. Times were now worse than ever. And even if they harvested their crops, the sharecroppers worried that they would not raise enough to pay off the money owed for the goods they had bought during the season at the Cottoncrest plantation store—the salt and flour, the hoes, scythes, and plows, and the seed for their personal gardens of corn and squash and beans.

There was hardly any wind. That was good.

Tomorrow would be a fine day. The entire plantation would be on fire.

Chapter 11

Trosclaire admired the way that Jake bled the suckling pig. You had to bleed it before cooking anyway, but why did he cut the throat so deep? All that was needed was a point in the knife in the jugular vein; let the pig squeal as it bled to death, and you'd preserve the head so that it would look right when presented.

Trosclaire tied the pig's hind feet together and then, slipping a stout branch under the rope, he and Jake lifted the pig and placed it into the big pot until it was fully covered, but only for a minute or two. After the skin had softened, they lifted it out and, propping the branch in a wooden rack that hung from the porch beams, they started scraping, Trosclaire with his American blade, retrieved from the pine tree, and Jake with his Freimer knife. They worked quickly, removing the hair and outermost layer of skin from the carcass while the skin was soft and hot.

Trosclaire noted that Jake worked far faster than he did, for the wiry man had no wasted motions. Jake's long, smooth strokes were just the right depth, neither cutting too deep and hitting the meat nor cutting too shallow, leaving hair and skin behind.

Trosclaire threw the bloody contents of the bucket on the ground behind the house. On the porch Jake was using his knife to slit the pig's stomach. The knife cut cleanly into the flesh, exposing the intestines and stomach.

Jake quickly scooped out the innards and then, swiftly but carefully so as not to damage the liver, removed the gall.

Trosclaire and Jake then went to the garden on the side of the cabin and dug up some shallots and picked some peppers and fall tomatoes. Trosclaire got some salt from the barrel he kept inside the front door. Together they filled the eviscerated animal with the seasonings, and Trosclaire bound up the stomach with some wire.

Jake and Trosclaire laid the pig into the trench next to the fire. Then Trosclaire shoveled the white-hot ashes over the pig.

"In a few hours, my friend, we will have ourselves some fine eating. A fitting tribute to my Jeanne Marie, no? She is most beautiful. Until then, what do you say we have ourselves some fine drinking and perhaps a game of bourée?"

"It is too fine a night," Jake responded, "to do anything other than sit out under the stars and enjoy a drink. Why don't we drink to Jeanne Marie?"

Jake didn't want to play cards anyway. He would let Trosclaire go on and on about Jeanne Marie, and he would pretend to listen attentively.

Beautiful women could be lovely. And beautiful women could be dangerous. His brother, Moshe, had been stupid. He had let himself be led on by a beautiful woman, and that had proven deadly. That's why Moshe could never come south again.

Chapter 12

"So, it's clear that the bullet went straight through," said Raifer, as Dr. Cailleteau set the Colonel Judge's head back down on the board. "But the question is, where is the bullet?"

"Damn it, Raifer, you didn't drag me all the way out here, away from my other patients, to ask me that question, did you?"

"No," Raifer replied, in his own quiet and determined way, "I asked you to help me dig that bullet out."

"Out of what? And why do you need that bullet anyway?"

"Well, if Bucky has got it right . . ."

Bucky, standing over near a stall, swelled with pride. Not only had Dr. Cailleteau asked him what happened, but now Raifer was relying on him too.

". . . then that bullet went right through his head and lodged in her back. Take out your scalpel and dig it out for me, if you don't mind."

Dr. Cailleteau, with a grunt, the vast folds of fat encasing his midsection bulging out under his vest, bent down and picked up his black bag. Placing it on the board next to the Colonel Judge's head, he reached inside and pulled out a scalpel. "Do it yourself. You don't need me for this. And I still don't understand why you need the bullet."

"No, you do it, Doc. Let me show you something." Raifer reached into the saddlebag that he had thrown over the top bar of a stall. "What do you make of this? Does this look like something that the Colonel Judge would have owned?"

Dr. Cailleteau took the rusty pistol that Raifer proffered. He gave it a quick glance and handed it back. "Not likely. It's a LeMat."

"It's a pistol, Doc," Bucky said. "Anyone can see that. It's not a mat or rug."

"It's a grapeshot revolver, Bucky," Dr. Cailleteau sighed with impa-

40

tience. "A black powder LeMat. General Beauregard had these made up in France and snuck past the blue-belly blockade. Didn't amount to much. They say it was a deal with his son-in-law. I don't know anyone who ever used a LeMat who didn't have trouble with it. Not rugged like a Colt. Not as small as a Derringer. Takes nine bullets in the cylinder rather than six, and it still isn't worth spit."

Handing the weapon back to Raifer, Dr. Cailleteau pulled out his handkerchief and wiped his hands to get rid of the rust stains that coated his palms. "Raifer, everyone knew that Augustine had been taught by the General, from the time he was a small boy, to care for all his arms. A cheap LeMat is not something Augustine would have owned. Even if this were his, Augustine would never have let a revolver get into such a condition. I mean, look at the second barrel. It's completely jammed with dirt and rust. Where did you find this anyway? Out in the yard? Had he thrown it out the window or something?"

"No, Doc. It was in his hand when we found him. This is the pistol that made that hole. At least I think it is this pistol. That's why I want to see the bullet."

Dr. Cailleteau picked up the LeMat with his handkerchief. It had a long narrow barrel and under it a shorter, fatter one everyone called the shotgun. The cylinder was oversized to hold nine bullets. But having nine bullets was not an advantage; it only made it heavier and more ungainly to use. The extra-long handle of the revolver made it difficult to aim. Dr. Cailleteau had never liked a LeMat. He had never used one in the war because of the firing problem. If you were too quick in cocking or if the pin in the cylinder got stuck, the pistol wouldn't fire.

From the size of the hole in his head, Augustine had shot himself with the smaller round. Why hadn't Augustine cleaned the shotgun barrel of the pistol and loaded it with a .65-caliber shell? That would have made a damn big hole pressed against your temple.

It didn't make any sense that Augustine would not have used the shotgun barrel, if he was going to use anything. Not after what had happened to the General.

When François Cailleteau was back from the war as a young doctor, he was just starting up his practice in Parteblanc and had been called from town to Cottoncrest. That was thirty years ago. Marcus had come on horseback, the steed heaving and snorting outside his door. Marcus had run inside, past the frightened white girl waiting to be seen, and breathlessly informed the doctor that he had to come quick—the General had shot himself.

François Cailleteau had dropped everything and, mounting his own horse, followed Marcus at a gallop all the way back to Cottoncrest. There he found the General barely clinging to life, gurgling and unable to speak. There was nothing he could do other than bandage up the General's head with roll after roll of torn sheets and gauze and tell the family he wouldn't last the night.

There was no question why the General had done it. It was the bad news.

The General always carried his combat pistol, even at Cottoncrest. It was a Whitney revolver, well made and sturdy, with the cylinder stamped with a coat of arms that seemed both English and American— a lion on one side, an eagle on the other.

The General had taken the Whitney and, placing its barrel in his mouth, had pulled the trigger too soon, or perhaps he had drunk too much bourbon before doing it. He had pointed the gun too far to the side, blowing off his left cheek, shattering his jaw, blinding him but not killing him. He tried to fire a second time to finish himself off, but he was in too much pain, and his hand obviously had been shaking, for he shot off his left ear.

When Augustine had found out about it after he returned home, he seemed inconsolable. He blamed all blue-bellies. And he blamed himself.

The General had acted too soon. Too abruptly. If only he had thought of his wife instead of his own grief. If only he had tried to live from one day to the next, he would eventually have found that the news was in error. If only he had possessed the faith to persevere instead of giving into despair. But the General hadn't, and he had died in agony.

After that, Augustine became even more careful and deliberate. Nothing was out of place. Nothing was left to chance. It had seemed to François Cailleteau, as he sat with Augustine on those many evenings out on the Cottoncrest veranda, that it was as if, by keeping the things in his life orderly, Augustine felt he could keep himself from the internal disorder and disarray into which his father had fallen.

But eventually Augustine had succumbed to both internal disorder and internal disarray. For more than a year now, Augustine had come to town only when he had to adjudicate the few court cases that arose from time to time, and then he would promptly leave. He had not received guests in his chambers. He had not paid the social visits he once did.

Augustine and Rebecca had retreated to Cottoncrest. Augustine used to travel to the Cotton Exchange in New Orleans to conduct his transactions, but for more than a year he had simply sent instructions in writing. Augustine and Rebecca used to host grand dinners, but since before last year's harvest, no one had been invited to the house. Internal disorder and disarray. Maybe it had consumed them both.

Maybe the old Greeks were right when they said that the four humors had to be kept in balance—the sanguine red of blood, the impassive green of phlegm, the rancorous yellow of choler, and the black bile of melancholy. If they were out of balance, then the soul would break.

"So you want to see the bullet, Raifer? It's clear from this small hole that he didn't use the shotgun barrel. Couldn't do it with this rusty old LeMat. After what happened to the General, seems to me that Augustine would have used something that he knew would do the job the first time, no mistakes. And he wouldn't have used anything that was not in pristine condition. Of course, the LeMat nine-cylinder takes a .40-caliber bullet rather than a .36-caliber like a Colt, but even so . . ."

"Doc, let's just see what kind of bullet he used. Go ahead and dig it out for me."

Dr. Cailleteau couldn't understand why Raifer was so insistent, but he picked up the scalpel and slowly walked around to the other side of the board, where Rebecca's body lay.

There was no way to tell from the dress, with the hardening blood clumping up around the laces, where the bullet had entered. Dr. Cailleteau sliced through the stays on the back of her dress and pushed the fabric aside. He cut through the waist cinch beneath the dress and pulled it back to reveal the gentle curve of her backbone and the soft rise of her posterior.

Her skin gleamed like alabaster. There was not a mark on it.

Dr. Cailleteau looked up at Raifer with puzzlement, and their eyes met.

"I thought," said Raifer, "that this might be the case. Now Doc, tell me one more thing. You knew the Colonel Judge longer than any of us. What hand did he write with?"

Dr. Cailleteau wiped the blade of his scalpel on his trousers and put it back into the black case. "Right hand, of course."

"Then how could he have done it?"

Dr. Cailleteau closed his case and sat down on a bale of hay, which, even though it was tightly bound, sagged under his weight. He took a long pull on his cigar and blew a vast cloud of smoke that drifted over the uncovered bodies. "Good question. Damned good question, Raifer."

"Bucky," Raifer commanded, "get back in that house and tell Marcus and the other boys I meant what I said. I want that place clean, and I want them to find that bullet. Probe the banisters and the staircase. Look at every wall. I want to know exactly where the Colonel Judge was when the shot was fired."

Chapter 13

The gathering for the *cochon de lait* had begun. More than thirty people were at Trosclaire Thibodeaux's house, resting on the porch, sitting on logs in the yard, standing near trees and talking.

Trosclaire's oldest daughter, who was not yet fifteen, was frying some of the fish she had carried home in her basket at the front of the pirogue. She had cleaned them expertly, covered them with a mixture of flour and cornmeal, and was placing them in a big pot of boiling lard. The reflection of the fire played on her face and hair, and it caught her eager smile aimed at the skinny boy who stood next to her. The boy, his thick dark hair jammed under an old hat, took every opportunity to brush against her arm and touch her elbow as he helped her with the frying.

Trosclaire took another swig from the jug and yelled from the porch. "Do not let the fish burn, Jeanne Marie."

Jeanne Marie just laughed. "Étienne, he is watching the fish almost as close as he is watching me!"

"But yes," her mother, Aimee, replied from her seat on a nearby log where she was shucking peas. "The *poudre de Perlainpainpain* sure worked on him, *cher.*"

Jake had understood everything Trosclaire and Jeanne Marie and Aimee had said in French until this last phrase. He looked questioningly at his host.

"Aimee, this man, who wants to sell us a knife sharper than the teeth of that old alligator in the bayou, does not know what a *poudre de Perlainpainpain* is."

An old woman who was sitting next to Aimee and helping her shuck the peas shook her head in disbelief and said to Jake, "How can you speak so well and not understand anything?"

Her face, a mass of deep wrinkles set in skin the color and texture of parchment, broke into a wide, toothless grin. "Are you a *loup-garou*, come to place us under a spell so that we will buy your needles and thimbles and fabrics?"

"Tante Odille," Aimee said, throwing a pea at her aunt, "if you think he is a *loup-garou*, then you'd better get some *gris-gris* before the moon gets any higher."

Jake called down from his perch on the porch. "I am no werewolf, but if you need a lucky charm to scare away a real *loup-garou*, then I think I have just what you need in my cart."

"See, my Aimee," the old woman said, "who was once my little Mimi who I held on my lap, you give that man a word, and he turns it into a way to sell you something. Besides, now I think he is too foolish to be a *loup-garou*. If he were a *loup-garou*, he would have in his cart some voodoo grease, and he would not use a big knife to do a *boucherie* and then sit and wait for his meat to be cooked. No, *cher*, he would bare his teeth and jump on a sheep and eat it down in one bite, yes?"

The small children who were trying to snatch pieces of the fried fish on the platter waiting to be handed out to the guests heard Tante Odille talking about sheep and started singing one of their nursery rhymes:

> *Mouton, Mouton, est ou tu vas?*
> *Passer l'abattoir.*
> *Quand tu reviens?*
> *Jamais . . . Baa!*

Jake understood it perfectly. Sheep, sheep, where are you going? To the slaughterhouse. When will you return? Never . . . Baa.

Just like Moshe would never return.

He and Moshe had left New York with such grand plans. The Cotton Exposition in New Orleans six years earlier, in the mid-1880s, had captured Moshe's imagination, and he couldn't stop talking about it. Countries from all over, he had said, had come to New Orleans to trade and sell. There was rum, coffee, cocoa, and dyes. There were oils and fruits. There were goods from Guatemala and Venezuela and Brazil. Mexico had built the filigreed and domed Alhambra Palace just for the occasion and filled it with display cases crammed with gold and silver from Chihuahua, Zacatecas, and Sinaloa. Lace in the Belgium exhibit, furniture in France's pavilion, machinery in Great Britain's arena, and strange and unusual items and food in the exhibits run by China, Japan, Russia, and Siam.

And the money that was flowing. Opening day expenses, Moshe had said, time and time again, were almost two million dollars. Who could imagine such a sum? And that was just the expenses for one day alone! And over seven thousand exhibitors!

The wonders that were to be seen, Moshe had said, time and time again, the wonders we missed. President Chester A. Arthur, sitting in Washington, D.C., had opened the fair by pressing a telegraph key. An electric railroad had been built specially for the Exposition and ran constantly three miles around its perimeter, ferrying attendees from gate to gate, from one remarkable sight to the next. The Pilcher organ, the biggest ever made, was the backdrop of the vast stage on which more than 150 musicians played under the huge seven-tiered chandelier whose gas lamps illuminated the entire area. Even the Liberty Bell had been brought from Philadelphia to New Orleans for the Exposition.

Moshe had read all about it. He had saved the old papers, folded neatly and pressed flat in a book. Just think, Moshe had said, if we had been in New Orleans then, think of all the trading and selling we could have done. But it's not too late. We can go, he had urged. We can still go to where the money is, where the woman flow as freely into your arms as wine flows into a glass, where a fortune can be made by two, like us, who are quick and smart.

"What is the matter, my friend, are your ears maybe sleeping while your eyes they are open?"

Jake looked up. Trosclaire was standing over him offering the jug.

"I said, will you do me the honor of drinking to my beautiful Jeanne Marie, who at the dawn will go to the church with Étienne for to be married, no?"

"Yes," Jake said, wiping away the memory of Moshe and the night they had hurriedly left New York and the girl there with the dark-red stain that had spread across the bodice of her dress. "Of course I will drink with you." He raised the jug high. "To Jeanne Marie and Étienne. May the love that brought them together be as lasting as the oaks that line the bayou."

After taking a drink from the jug, Jake added, "What God decrees, man cannot prevent." He said it in French, not Yiddish, although that was a phrase his mother often had used. *Vos Got tut basheren, ken kain mentsh nit farveren.*

He seldom spoke Yiddish these days. It was too dangerous.

Chapter 14

Marcus and the others were still cleaning. Although dusk had not yet settled, it had gotten so dark inside that candles had to be lit.

Sally had made sure that Marcus had not used the good beeswax candles. They were for special occasions, although with the Colonel Judge gone, when they would be used again no one could say. It did not matter, however. Sally knew that the Colonel Judge would have wanted them saved. So, she found some old spermaceti wax candles made from the oil of those whales they caught way up north. They were left over from the General's day. The Colonel Judge had ceased using them when he could purchase paraffin candles so cheaply, candles that were machine made with tightly plaited wicks that did not have to be snuffed and trimmed as the candle burned. And the best paraffin candles were brought to the Colonel Judge by that Peddler Man with the cart who came around so often.

The blood was now all mopped up. All that remained were the dark stains on the staircase and on the landing, stains that formed patches so dark they absorbed the flickering light. Marcus made sure that Cubit and Jordan double-checked for a bullet. It could have fallen on the floor and been pushed under a rug with all the commotion of the cleanup. It might have been bundled up in one of the sheets taken outside to be rinsed. It might have gone into a wall. But try as they might, searching around the wash bucket and the clothesline outside and the staircase and the first floor inside, no bullet could be located.

Marcus and Cubit had lifted up each carpet in the downstairs hallway one more time, and Marcus personally swept underneath and then examined the collection of dust, debris, and carpet lint. No bullet. Marcus had Cubit and Jordan walk up the staircase shoulder to shoulder looking at each step in front of them. No bullet. It was already too dark on the landing at the top of the stairs. That would have to wait until tomorrow.

After Marcus sent Cubit and Jordan to look again outside the front door and back and all around the garden and the washbasin, Marcus confided to Sally, now that the two of them were alone in the hallway.

"Woman, I'm gonna have to go out and tell Mr. Raifer there ain't no bullet here."

"You'll do no such thing, fool! Don't you go tellin' him there ain't no bullet. You don't know that. All you know is that you ain't found no bullet yet. What you go and tell him is that it's too dark to see good, what with the sun going down and all. That's the truth, and he gonna know it to be the truth. Then, if in the mornin' he wants to come and look for himself and decide that there ain't no bullet, then it's his decision, not yours. Don't you go givin' the white man anything but what you know. And all you know is that you ain't found a bullet yet."

Sally was right, as usual. Mr. Raifer and the others, they weren't like the Colonel Judge. Marcus would talk to the Colonel Judge, and even Miss Rebecca, without having to watch his tongue. Maybe in the last year, with them being in the house and not going out, with it just being them and him and Sally and Jenny and Little Miss and the others, he had forgotten all the caution he had spent a lifetime developing.

He didn't like Mr. Bucky anyway. Didn't like him coming around, bossing them. Oh, he wouldn't say anything to Mr. Bucky or even show what he thought. He never showed what he thought. Mr. Bucky was the law as much as Mr. Raifer. And what good was the law to him except to be something else to avoid.

Had the law helped Cubit's brother? No, he had been caught and beaten and strung up by those men in white sheets. Did the law do anything? No. All they did was cut poor Cubit's brother down and bring him home to be buried.

Had the law helped Jordan's daddy when the claim jumpers said that the land he had worked since after the war, the land he had bought with his sweat and toil, was theirs cause they had a piece of paper and he didn't? No. The law had told them to get off. If it weren't for the Colonel Judge, as poor as he was two years ago, letting Jordan and his daddy stay in one of the old slave cabins and work around the house and garden, if the Colonel Judge hadn't let them have half an acre to farm, well, who knows what would have happened? Sure, the Colonel Judge charged them a fifty share while he charged the white sharecroppers only a third, and then there was the furnish that had to be paid for at the commissary, the food and salt and supplies and all. But at least they got a roof over their heads at night and credit at the Cottoncrest plantation store to live.

But the law was no help. No help at all.

He'd tell Mr. Raifer only what he saw and what he didn't see. Let Mr. Raifer decide what it all meant.

Marcus walked out the back door toward the barn, and Sally followed, pulling the big handle and making sure the latch caught.

Jenny, peeking out from Little Miss's room, breathed a sigh of relief. Maybe they'd all be gone for the night. The sharecroppers already had left. Maybe the Sheriff and his deputy and the doctor from Parteblanc would leave soon also.

Jenny knew that she couldn't do what needed to be done until they were all gone, until the darkness of night covered her and prevented anyone from seeing where she was going.

Chapter 15

"Woe! Oh, awful woe! Oh, terrible woe! She is dead! She is dead! My loving wife is dead! What have I done?"

Bucky was now fully in character, and his arms waved wildly in the air. He added embellishments. He pulled at his hair. He rolled his eyes.

The crowd at the bar beat upon the tables and clinked their glasses against the liquor bottles in appreciation. They egged him on.

"Oh, where is your head, my darlin'? Where is your dear head? Gone! Gone! Gone!" Bucky, like a sea captain scanning the horizon and shielding his eyes from the bright sun, put his hand to his forehead and, squinting hard, looked this way and that.

"Hey, Bucky, didn't this take place at night? Are you afraid of all that glare from the half-moon?" The big sandy-haired man in the stained shirt and dirty trousers, whose forearms were as thick as Bucky's thigh and whose skin was as leathery as his voice, sat at a nearby table, drink in hand, enjoying the spectacle.

"Jimmy Joe," said his large, bearded companion in the next seat, "don't you think the reason he done lost that head is 'cause he couldn't keep it in his britches?"

They all had a good laugh.

Bucky ignored them and kept in character. "My darlin' wife. My young, beautiful wife, I must hug her once more." Bucky threw himself on the floor, hugging the sawdust.

Some of the men moved back to give Bucky more room. Bucky gathered up into a pile all the sawdust within reach and, pretending it was the small of her back, put his head down on it. The toe of Jimmy Joe's big boot, to which pieces of dry manure had stuck, was directly in front of him.

"Don't you want to hug my boot like you're huggin' that sawdust, Bucky? Hell, take a lick of it if you want to." Jimmy Joe lifted the toe of his boot and put it within inches of Bucky's face.

Bucky pretended not to notice. "Let me hug your dead body once more. Let me rest my head but a moment longer on your lovely back before I . . ."

As Bucky paused dramatically, embracing the sawdust, the bearded man spoke up. "Before I kiss your lovely ass."

Jimmy Joe laughed so hard he almost choked. "That's a good one, Forrest. And I bet her ass was real sweet! Hey, Bucky, you think the Colonel Judge got his fill of her ass?"

Now the entire bar was chuckling, but Bucky paid them no mind. They were appreciating his performance—that's what was important.

Bucky had seen a traveling medicine show once. They had done some Shakespeare and a bunch of other things he hadn't understood but had liked a whole lot. He knew that fancy words would carry the day.

"Now, I shall take thee, oh precious pistol, and with thee I put thee to my most sad . . . most sad, sad brow and thusly end my life . . . thusly."

Jimmy Joe interrupted again. "You ain't pointin' that finger at your brow, stupid! You're pointing above your ear."

Bucky broke character and sat up. "I'm almost finished here, Jimmy Joe. You got to let this language kind of wash over you. It's elevatin' language, don't you see?"

Whiskey dribbled out of the corner of Forrest's mouth as he grinned at Bucky's foolishness. Wiping his beard, Forrest said, "If we don't let him finish, Jimmy Joe, he's liable to go on all night."

Jimmy Joe motioned for Bucky to continue. Bucky put his head back down on the pile of sawdust and, making his right hand into a gun-like shape, shot himself in the temple. "BANG."

Bucky kicked his legs up in the air. He twitched. "I'm dyin'. I'm dyin'. I killed my wife, and now I have killed myself. Woe and tarnation. I am dead." He tried not to move. He tried to stare at the ceiling without blinking. He opened his mouth and let his tongue droop to one side, and he held it out as long as he could until saliva started drooling down his chin. Then he stood up and took a bow.

There was loud applause. It sounded so good to Bucky. It was what he had always dreamed of. He bowed again, even as the applause was dying down and coming to a halt. And, not content, he bowed once more, but by then the men were already talking among themselves.

A lanky man standing by the bar summoned Bucky over and handed him a glass. "Here, Bucky, have a drink. You done yourself proud."

Bucky gratefully took the glass, although the lanky man, his thinning hair drooping down long over his ears, did not offer to pay. Bucky knew better than to hesitate. This man was not to be messed with. He was shorter than the massive Jimmy Joe and fifty pounds lighter, but Jimmy Joe would never cross him. Forrest, with his thick beard and eyebrows, with his wild hair cascading off his head and sprouting out of his ears and off of his chest, deferred to Jimmy Joe and even more to this lanky man.

It was well that he did. The lanky man's emotions ran high, and his build was deceptive. His frame was as tightly wound as his temper, all sinew and meanness waiting to be sprung. Bucky reached into his pocket for a coin and put it on the scratched surface of the bar. Only after the bartender had picked up the coin did he pour Bucky a drink.

"Was that the way it really was, Bucky? He killed her and then he shot himself?"

"Sure was, Tee Ray. Dr. Cailleteau asked me what had happened, and when I showed him what I just showed y'all, well, I think that about says it all, don't it?"

"So, that's it, then? Another example of the curse? I guess Raifer figures his job is done."

"I think it's done, Tee Ray, but Raifer don't. For some reason we got to go back in the morning and look for a bullet. Raifer keeps asking questions about a bullet and something about what hand the Colonel Judge wrote with. I don't understand it at all. It's the curse, plain and simple. Anyone can see that."

Tee Ray was glad to keep Bucky talking. Bucky was right in saying that he didn't understand it at all. But Tee Ray understood it all too well.

It had better be the curse. In any case, there'd be hell to pay.

Chapter 16

"Monsieur Jake," Tante Odille chuckled as she pointed to the skinny boy next to Jeanne Marie, "for Étienne, what could he do once there was a *poudre de Perlainpainpain*, no?"

Étienne reddened and, embarrassed, turned his attention to the boiling lard, using the big wooden spoon to scoop up the now crispy fish that floated on the bubbling surface and place them on the large platter.

"Yes, Tante Odille," Jeanne Marie said, giving Étienne a teasing poke in his side. "It was all due to the *poudre de Perlainpainpain*. Oh, I was careful, and it took so long! First, to catch the thistle seeds. Three perfect seeds caught one after another. One for me, one for Étienne, and one for the two of us. They could not be picked. No. I had to wait until they floated in the wind. They had to be caught in the morning air, before the dew dries on the grass. Do you know how hard that is? To catch three perfect ones in a row? I take the three perfect ones that took me oh-so-long to catch, and I remove the down from the seeds ever so gently, so as not to bruise the seeds. I do not want to cause a bruise to my Étienne, no?"

Étienne pretended not to hear and dropped some more fish into the pot, but he acted too quickly. The lard sputtered from the extra moisture, and bits of it flew out of the pot, singeing Étienne's arm.

"Oh, my poor Étienne, maybe I was not as careful with removing the down as I thought." Jeanne Marie rubbed his arm where a little welt had formed.

"I take the three seeds, yes, and I dip them in honey, and then put them in a black thimble—the thimble, yes, she must be a black thimble—which I bury for three whole days under the house, under the floorboards where my bed is. It is so long, I think, but I do it, for it must be done right if I am to have my Étienne. After three days I take the seeds and mix them in the black thimble with three drops of bayou water that I have used to wash my face and three drops of honey. And Étienne, when you are not looking, I rub three drops of the *poudre de Perlainpainpain* on your shirt and on the trousers you had left on that tree when you were swimming in the bayou."

Étienne, who was trying to avoid the stares of all the smiling faces around him enjoying the story of how he was snared, looked even more embarrassed now that Jeanne Marie was telling everyone she had spied on him while he was swimming naked in the bayou.

"I rub the *poudre de Perlainpainpain* on your clothes, and, see how it happens, you are mine! It is all because of the *poudre de Perlainpainpain* in the black thimble."

Jeanne Marie paused and looked at Jake. "You have another black thimble in your cart, Monsieur Jake?"

Jake knew that tonight was going to be a grand night for business. "For you, Jeanne Marie, I have a special black thimble, and I shall give her to you as a wedding present."

Jeanne Marie gave a little yelp of joy. "I shall have my own black thimble! I shall not have to borrow Tante Odille's again! Étienne, we shall be so happy!" She grabbed Étienne by the hand and started to dance.

Some of the men, who had been sitting by the porch, pulled out their fiddles and began playing. Another one grabbed a metal washboard and, reaching into his pocket, pulled out two thimbles. Placing them on the thumbs of each hand and balancing the washboard between his knees, he provided the rhythm section.

Other couples joined Étienne and Jeanne Marie in dancing. They moved around the dusty ground barefoot, couple by couple in a large circle, two-stepping to the music.

"Come on, Trosclaire," one of the men yelled, "we need you."

Trosclaire went into the cabin and came out with a small accordion no bigger than a loaf of bread. The squeeze-box added depth to the music, and Trosclaire's fingers were a blur, for each button gave a different sound depending on whether the bellows were being pushed or pulled.

"A *fais-do-do!* We are going to dance all night, no?" Tante Odille took one of the seven-year-olds by the hand. The two of them enthusiastically joined the others, the old lady and the little boy moving gracefully with the music.

Chapter 17

"Sometimes I don't think you got half the sense God gave a horsefly. Lord, the way you rattle on to them white folks." Sally was sitting on the back steps with Marcus, the big door to the hallway closed behind them. The half-moon was hanging low, and the stars glistened in the clear October evening's sky.

"What was I to do? I had to answer Mr. Raifer's questions."

"Oh, there's ways of answering that don't say nothin', and there's ways of answering that tells all too much. You got too much of the too much and not enough of the nothin'!"

"Well, it ain't as if you and me hadn't talked about it first. You know that if I hadn't sent Cubit to go get Mr. Raifer first thing when we found those bodies, they'd be saying that us coloreds did it, and then there'd be hell to pay. No, you and me agreed, got to call the law in right away and let them handle it."

Sally huffed and raised her eyes to the night sky. "When I was a little girl, I used to look at the stars and pray and pray that one day I would be free. Free of a place where all the slaves I knew had whip scars on their backs. My Grandma tried to join up on that Underground Railroad, but she was caught. Old Marse, on that plantation we used to live on, had her drug back behind a mule, her hands tied, and in front of everyone he had the overseer whip her until she couldn't stand. Then that overseer took a knife that he had heated red-hot, and he poked her eye out, tellin' her, 'That's for lookin' to run away. You look to run away again, and you ain't gonna look no more.'"

Sally shook her head in dismay. "And now we're free, and what's it gotten us?"

Marcus put his arm around her fleshly shoulders. "Well, it got you me, didn't it?"

Sally shook out from under his arm. "Don't you start in with your sparkin' now. You know what I mean. The Colonel Judge is dead, and we ain't gonna have a home no more. And all you want to do is . . . well, it's foolishness, just plain foolishness, when we got this big problem in front of us."

"We always had this problem. At least for the last year. So, what was I to do? I think I did a good job of answering the questions Mr. Raifer asked without talkin' about that other problem even once."

"Well, I'll give that to you, but that ain't sayin' much, is it? Why did you have to go and talk about that peddler man?"

"I was only answering the questions Mr. Raifer asked. He said he knows that Miss Rebecca, she always like to dress fancy like, and she like nice things, but she ain't been into town in Parteblanc in months and months, and the Colonel Judge ain't been doin' nothin' but runnin' into court, doin' his business, and goin' home. He ain't invited no one out in the longest while, not even Dr. Cailleteau. He ain't been to New Orleans or Baton Rouge in the longest time, and yet somehow he still got them fancy cigars that he smokes while he's on the bench. So, where's he gettin' all the things he and Miss Rebecca needs? That's all he asked."

"And you got to go and answer him? Fool! You can't say you don't know? But no, you gone and done it now. You not only told him about that peddler man coming all the time here, but you told him about that peddler man speaking French to the Colonel Judge and Little Miss and English to Miss Rebecca and all."

"I don't see no harm in that. That's what he did."

"Sure he did. But you didn't have to go on about what they talked about. If I was asked, I would have said I don't know nothin' about what they was sayin'. But you, you gots to answer, don't you."

"But Mr. Raifer asked. What was I to do? He knows I speak French."

"But did you say they talked of this and that and then hush up? No. Did you say they talked about the weather and the crops and all and then hush up? No, not even then. Did you say they talked about politics and that there president who's come and gone and come back again, what's his name?"

"Grover Cleveland."

"Yes, him. You could have stopped there, but you didn't. You said that they talked about religion a lot. Well, that was like honey on a cow's teat, weren't it? Then Mr. Raifer asks you all about that. And you told him."

Jenny heard Sally going at Marcus good, but it hadn't disturbed Little Miss. She was sleeping soundly.

Jenny opened the French door from Little Miss's room and stepped out on the veranda that wrapped the house. She cautiously peeked around the front corner. No one was there. Jenny tiptoed to the back. Sally was still chewing on Marcus.

It was just as well that they didn't know where she was going. Sally was right. The less they knew, the safer they'd be.

Jenny took a deep breath and prepared herself. It was up to her now.

Chapter 18

Bucky was having a wonderful time. Tee Ray could not have been nicer. Tee Ray had just bought him another drink. Tee Ray wanted to hear all that Bucky had to say.

It had all happened just as Bucky had imagined, from the moment he and Raifer had gotten to Cottoncrest. He was famous because he had seen the dead Colonel Judge and all. He had been where the curse had hit and had seen what it had done. People wanted to listen to him. They wanted his opinion on everything. He had shown them. He had become a real somebody.

"Yessir, Tee Ray. Me and Raifer, we investigated real good. Once the Doc headed back to town, we stayed a while and questioned Cubit and Jacob, but they didn't know nothin'. And we talked to Sally, and she don't know nothin'. But Marcus, well, that's a different story, ain't it."

"Is that a fact, Bucky?" Tee Ray was solicitous.

Bucky could see that Tee Ray was hanging on his every word. Maybe the others weren't paying attention now, having gone back to their drinking and card games, but Tee Ray was still there with him, standing next to him at the bar. He could tell Tee Ray respected him for his investigation. "Fact for sure. We got Marcus talkin' good. Where was he during the night? What did he see? We all know that times is tough, but why is it that the Colonel Judge ain't had no one out and ain't had no wagons full of goods going to bring stuff to Miss Rebecca but the Colonel Judge always got fresh cigars? How did they get the stuff they needed all those months? Marcus, he told us everything. Everything!"

"And that," asked Tee Ray, "explained the curse?"

"Marcus explain the curse? I don't think so. How can anyone explain the curse? It just is. But Marcus, you see, did tell us that the only white man that the Colonel Judge had let come see him and Miss

Rebecca in the last year is that peddler man. You know who I'm talking about?"

"Yeah. Jake. The man with the cart."

"Right as gold specie. Jake, the Peddler Man. Did you know that he speaks French?"

"Well, I figured as much, all that time he spends peddling down in Lamou."

Bucky paused. He should have realized that everyone knew that the peddler walked a five-parish area, and that Lamou and the other Acadian villages were on his regular route. Of course Jake had to speak some French because a lot of those folks didn't speak English.

Bucky was not going to be deterred, however, and pressed on. "Maybe, but did you know *what* they talked about in French? He and the Colonel Judge?"

Tee Ray poured some more whiskey into Bucky's glass. "I don't speak no French, and you don't either. So, how was it that you know what they were talking about?"

That was more like it. Tee Ray needed him. Tee Ray needed to listen. Bucky would show Tee Ray. "We . . . Raifer and me . . . we questioned Marcus good. You know he speaks that French. Anyway, he said that they talked all about religion. Not just good Christian talk, no sir. They talked heaven and hell and lots of different religions. Religions that no respectable Christian could tolerate. The Colonel Judge had spent a lot of time at the Cotton Exposition when Cottoncrest was king of the cotton plantations, and he talked all about what he had learnt from them Chinese and Japanese and foreign folks about their religions, with lots of gods and no Christ or Virgin Mary. They were talking about how there could be so many religions and so many gods. 'Course, we all know that there ain't no god but Jesus, but them heathens don't know that. And then, Marcus said they even talked about . . ."

Bucky paused dramatically. He waited for Tee Ray to show the proper degree of anticipation. Tee Ray did. Bucky felt that he was really getting the hang of impressing people.

"Yes, Marcus said they even talked about those Jews what who killed Jesus. And you know what that Jake peddler told the Colonel Judge? Jake said he was a Jew and claimed that Jews didn't kill Jesus or use Christian blood in their ceremonies! Imagine that."

Tee Ray was glad he had let Bucky prattle on for the last half-hour. It had been worth it. It was perfect. Sure, it could have been a curse. But you don't need a curse if you have a Jew.

That's because Jews are cursed.

Chapter 19

The sky was clouding up by 10:00 a.m. It was going to rain by evening. If Jake didn't hurry, he was going to get soaked.

The wedding had been held at sunrise in Lamou's tiny Catholic church. The *cochon de lait* and *fais-do-do* had lasted all night, and everyone barely had time to get home, change into their church clothes, and walk to Sainte Clotilde sur le Rive before Father Séverin began. During the wedding itself, Father Séverin had talked about how love is perfect, like the perfect circle of the wedding ring, and how Jeanne Marie and Étienne were perfect for each other and would be bound until death by the perfect circle of Jesus's love.

Jake had been attentive throughout the service. When the congregation stood, he stood. When the congregation kneeled, he kneeled. He had let the Latin of the Mass wash over him. He was going to blend in wherever he was. Religion was something he never talked about to anyone. Anyone, that is, except the Colonel Judge, and the Colonel Judge knew how to keep a secret. And there were secrets to be kept.

After the church services he had offered his congratulations to the young bride and groom and to their families and started walking up the road, into the woods that surrounded the bayous, heading for the agricultural lands to the northeast. His cart, which had been half-empty before he had gotten to Lamou yesterday, was now full with the skins of deer, muskrat, beaver, and cougar. He had long snakeskins—brown water moccasins, black diamond rattlers, and the coral's red cross-bands bordered by yellow rings—all poisonous, all deadly, and all beautiful, stretched on boards and ready to be made into belts and purses and boots. It had been a full night of trading during the *cochon de lait*.

Jake knew that if his father were still alive, he would be appalled. A Jew slaughtering a pig and joining in the eating of it! If his father had known what Jake would do, would he have had second thoughts about sending him away? Would his father have thought that being an involuntary Cantonist was better than being an enthusiastic violator of many commandments, including the ones on keeping kosher?

Eating a pig was not the worst commandment that Jake had broken, but Jake liked what his sister Leah had whispered in his ear as he was leaving: *Az me est chazzer, zol men essen fetten.* If you're going to eat pork, let it be good and fat.

At the church the white of Jeanne Marie's dress and of the lace around her puffy sleeves and on her collar reminded Jake of the white lace on the petticoats of all the women on the train.

White lace. It always reminded him of trains. Maybe because it had been his first train ride. Even then, he liked being around women, but after that ride, trains always bothered him and lace always excited him.

Woman after woman in the cars on the train. Petticoat after petticoat. He was twelve, and they were hiding him in their vast petticoats. He was crouching down, hugging their legs, feeling the warmth of their skin and inhaling their odors. The Czar's soldiers were checking the trains, looking for those trying to escape being made Cantonists, and the women had taken pity on him and had hidden him. Mile after mile, hour after hour, he had stayed there, trying not to make a sound, trying to ignore the aching in his legs and back and trying not to move.

With each jolt of the train, he feared that he would be found. Each time he heard a footstep in the aisle, his heart beat so hard inside his little chest that he felt it could be heard above the constant rumble of the wheels. Each time the whistle blew, he knew it must be a signal to someone about his hiding. When the train stopped at stations or for water or coal, he held his breath and tried to curl up tightly under the petticoats, hoping against hope that the soldiers would not ask the women to stand or move to the next car. If the women moved, he would be captured. Then the train would start again, but the fear would not subside. Soldiers were still on the train, watching.

The women around him talked and talked. They kept up a constant stream of conversation to amuse themselves and to make the soldiers think nothing was amiss. They spoke softly in Russian of their sisters and their families. Jake's heart ached as he thought of Leah and Beruriah. The women shared stories about children and parents. Jake tried not to cry thinking about how he would never see his parents again.

And through it all, the train rumbled on, and Jake's fear continued. The closer they got to the border, the more fearful he became, for the risks were increasing. His tiny frame ached from being contorted in hiding. Would the soldiers find him? What would they do when the border guards got on the train? Would the women have to leave at that point, and what would he do then? Could all the women be trusted? Would one of them give him away?

The belching of the coal engine. The clacking of the metal wheels against the tracks. The creaking of the cars as the train rounded curves. Train noises and escape. And fear. And inner courage. For Jake they all were united somehow.

Chapter 20

Cooper was out in his garden, picking fall tomatoes and pinching the green, leafy suckers off the plants, when Jake rolled into Little Jerusalem. Cooper stopped, the muscles rippling in his massive arms as he held up a ripe tomato in his hand. "I've been done growin' the finest tomatoes you everest did see, Peddler Man. Sweet like a woman's kiss and moist as a woman as well."

Jake halted his cart and stopped to mop his brow. "It's as big a tomato as I think I ever saw, Cooper. And it's as red as the face of a white man telling a lie so big even he's embarrassed after saying it."

Cooper gave a big grin. "Could be. But since you seen my crop, then I believes you'll be wantin' to trade somethin' for such fine eatin' as this."

"Cooper, if I ate all that I traded for, I wouldn't have anything left to trade and wouldn't be able to buckle my belt, much less push this cart, except with my stomach."

Cooper's grin only got larger. He liked the Peddler Man, with his black curly hair cut close and his wiry little build. If the Peddler Man was getting any extra flesh on his bones, it had to be the thinningest flesh ever.

"If you don't eat, how you gonna push that cart of yours?" asked Rossy, coming out of the tiny cabin, holding a baby on her hip. "Cooper, ain't you gonna just *give* the Peddler Man one of your tomatoes?" She gave a sly smile to Cooper. "'Moist as a woman?' If you keep talkin' like that, you better get all your 'moist' from that tomato and don't come lookin' to get any from me."

It was always like this when Jake came to Little Jerusalem. Cooper would try to get him to trade for food, and eventually Cooper and the others would come up with something more substantial, and they would work something out and have a meal, for Cooper and Rossy and all the rest had no money.

It was a miracle the little community of Little Jerusalem was surviving at all. The Colonel Judge had told him all about it. Sixteen families sharing a half-section of land, 320 acres, acres that they had financed during the seventeen days in the mid-1870s when C. C. Antoine was the acting governor of Louisiana—the second black ever to hold that position in Louisiana and only because of the presence of carpetbagger blue-belly troops during Reconstruction. C. C. Antoine did things that the first black governor, Pinckney Benton Stewart Pinchback, could not.

P.B.S. Pinchback, the Colonel Judge had told him, had a white father and a black mother, and Pinchback could have passed for white had he wanted to, but he refused. When he was asked which race he more closely identified with and of which he was most proud, Pinchback said: "It is far more important to be evaluated by the worth of one's friends than measured by one's pedigree, for the former involves self-determination and mutual admiration, while the latter is a mere involuntary attribute. To deny one's pedigree would be as vain a folly as denying the sun to rise tomorrow; however, it should never be the cause to create or circumscribe a man's opportunities."

The Colonel Judge would quote it word for word because he had thought this was, as he said often, "the height of arrogance for an adulterous bastard of miscegenation." Of course, that was before . . . but by then it was hard for the Colonel Judge to change his ways.

Pinchback was one of many blacks, both former slaves and free men of color, who had been elected to the Louisiana legislature during Reconstruction. Pinchback had survived threats, taunts, and attempts on his life when he was elected to the state senate, and he had to fight all the way to the Supreme Court to retain the post as acting governor. But Pinchback, despite the success of his legal case, was kicked out of office in less than eight months.

C. C. Antoine, who, a few years later, served as acting governor, had seen what happened to Pinchback and had no illusions about what would happen to him as the second black to hold the state's highest office. The Colonel Judge was clear about what he thought about C. C. Antoine. Antoine, he used to say, used what little time he had in office to "issue proclamations that didn't do any damn good and did a lot of damn harm." Miss Rebecca would gently disagree, saying that C. C. Antoine used his time in office to make a difference.

Antoine had sold a portion of state land to some of the former slaves in Petit Rouge Parish. The mortgage was held by Comite River Bank, the only bank that had agreed to give loans to the former slaves because, for a short time, its board and employees were all former slaves. But they were ousted when Reconstruction ended.

Little Jerusalem had been formed along with other communities thanks to C. C. Antoine. Little Jerusalem was one of the last to survive, and it was surviving by the barest. The others had lost their lands because of legal title held by whites who could read and write and who "found" documents that voided the grants or because of the floods or because of the tough times, or a combination of all of these. Comite River Bank had closed, forced out of business by the hard times, and it looked as if it might be only a short while before the Little Jerusalem mortgage was bought for pennies on the dollar by some speculator who would foreclose and kick the families out.

Rossy came over to the cart and peered inside. "What you got there, Peddler Man, that you want to trade?" She handed the child to Jake as she picked through the top few layers. "Surely you don't 'spect us to trade for some old, dingy skins what got so many bullet holes in the deer and trap marks on the muskrat and beavers that ain't nobody gonna use them for nothin' but rags. And besides, if you want skins, why don't you ask Cooper here or Nimrod or Esau? They got squirrel and possum and coon skins so fine them ladies in New Orleans will be wantin' to wear them ev'ry day, and not just for go-to-meetin'."

The child was squirming in Jake's arms, reaching for her mother, but Jake could see that Rossy was warming up, ready to trade. Jake cooed and patted the baby, who calmed down again and nestled against his shoulder. Thanks to what had happened in Lamou, Jake had only a few trading items left in the bottom of the cart under all the skins. He checked the sky. To the west a dark line of clouds was forming. A thunderstorm could be headed their way. One never knew in Louisiana. It could rain like a waterfall on one side of a road, turning the fields into a muddy slough, while the other side would remain dusty, as if shut off behind an isinglass curtain.

"I'll tell you what," said Jake to Cooper and Rossy. "What do you say you let me sample one of your tomatoes? But I don't want a whole one, just a small piece."

"You want to take a bite out of my fine, plump tomato and hand it back to me? Rossy, I think that the Peddler Man is worser than a boll weevil that'll get in that cotton field and ruin it for ev'ryone."

"Cooper, have you ever known me to ruin anything?" Jake had picked his words carefully, gently adjusting the child on his shoulder. Cooper, isolated here in Little Jerusalem, would never know about what other things Jake had ruined. Jake had ruined many things. Like the girl in New York with the dark-red stain spreading across her blouse. "Now it just so happens that I have a knife here with a blade so sharp it will slice faster than a snapping turtle can snap. It slices so clean and so quick that you'd think it was voodoo."

Rossy looked uninterested, but Cooper's eye glimmered with anticipation.

"We don't need no fancy knife," said Rossy, digging down further in the cart. "We can't 'ford no fancy knife."

"Ah," said Jake, placing the child on top of a soft muskrat skin and pulling out a wide, thin box from the bottom of the cart, "of course you can't. But I see the quality of your stitching on your shawl there, and these are delicate stitches, each one identical to the next. My uncle was a tailor, and next to your shawl, his stitches looked like they were made by a blind man. Now, if you had a few yards of this new cotton fabric and some new needles and thread and a thimble—I've got them in pewter and porcelain and even black—then you might find you'd be making yourself a new outfit for church, or maybe you'd take just a yard and make a special dress for your beautiful daughter.

The baby, smiling and gurgling, was entranced by the feel of the downy muskrat.

"Come on, Peddler Man, let's go inside, and Cooper here will give you a tomato, and you'll show us this here fancy knife of yours, and maybe we'll show you some real skins so that you don't have to walk around sad because all you got is this stuff that looks like those men in Lamou took advantage of you."

Uncle Avram always said, *ven es gait gleich, vert men reich.* When things go right, you become rich. Things were going extremely right for

Jake. He had lucked into the *cochon de lait,* and now Rossy and Cooper were going to trade for even more skins.

Jake followed them around the back of the cabin, to a rickety lean-to shed, where he placed his cart. Coming toward them was Nimrod, bent over with age, being assisted by his son, Esau. Coming out of the fields, they had seen Jake talking to Cooper and Rossy. Esau's wife and the others would follow shortly. A few more hours here would be all that it would take.

By then the rain might arrive.

And afterward Jake would leave. He had to return to Cottoncrest. He needed to check on the two of them.

PART II

Today

Chapter 21

"Why your great-great-grandfather came to Louisiana in the first place seems strange. There he was, living with Moshe in New York City, in the midst of the fabulous 1890s, the time some called the Gilded Age, and it seemed as if they left, almost overnight, to come south at the worst possible time.

"Grandpapa Jake used to say he and Moshe had come because of the Cotton Exposition. But that had ended almost ten years earlier, and by the time they were heading toward New Orleans the South was in terrible shape.

"You've heard of the Great Depression? Good. That was started by the 1929 stock market crash and continued on through the 1930s. And why was it called the Great Depression? To distinguish it from 'the Depression,' which was what people called the calamity of the 1890s, the worst of it being in 1893. You mention the Depression at the time Grandpapa Jake was in Louisiana, and people knew all too well what it meant.

"While the rich in New York were living in the Gilded Age, the rest of the country, which had thought for sure things could not have gotten worse than they were during the Civil War, were finding out they had been wrong. Two decades after the fighting had stopped, the finances had stopped as well.

"The Depression of the early 1890s was a time of poverty and violence. Strikes. Deaths. Riots. Cotton prices fell so far that even the richest planters could barely scrap by.

"Storms hit in some years and droughts in the others. Crops were ruined. Little farms and big plantations were ruined. Lives were ruined.

"What's that? What did this have to do with Grandpapa Jake?

"Well, yes, I do run on, but I keep trying to figure out why Jake and

Moshe went down to Louisiana when they did, so quick like. It was the worst possible time.

"And I still don't know why Moshe never stayed in the South but came back up north before they ever got to New Orleans."

1893

Chapter 22

"I don't understand why we just couldn't get them darkies to do this!" Bucky was on his hands and knees, examining every square foot of the vast hallway that ran through the center of Cottoncrest, dividing the house in half.

"Because I told you to do it. That's why." Raifer was concentrating on the staircase, step by step. He was now halfway up and still had not found any signs of a bullet. They had thrown open both doors and all the windows to let as much light in as possible. They had worked their way around the walls of the hall, looking for a hole in the heavily patterned wallpaper or in the dark frames of the portraits that hung on long wires from the wide crown molding. That had taken them more than half an hour. Now they were doing the floor and stairs.

"I'm doin' it, ain't I?" Bucky responded. "But what's a bullet gonna prove anyway? Dead is dead. He shot himself. He had the gun in his hand."

"Bucky, you keep flapping your mouth, it's just likely to flap so much that we could use it to mill rice. Think about what you saw when we got here, and tell me exactly and without drama."

"Okay. She was dead. Face down on the stairs. Head almost cut off. His head was on her back. Gun in his hand. He had shot himself. Blood was everywhere. What could be clearer?"

Raifer had now reached the red-stained stairs. Despite all the wiping and washing that Marcus and Cubit and Jordan had done yesterday, the distinct odor of blood mingled with the smells of the wood and the damp cloying mustiness of mildew from the wallpaper. "Good. Now where had the bullet entered?"

"His temple. You saw that, Raifer. His temple." Bucky's knees were beginning to hurt, but he inched his way to the next section of floor.

"Think, Bucky. Which temple? Which way was his head lying on her back?"

Bucky paused a moment and sat with his back against the wall, to give his knees a rest. "His head was lyin' with his right ear down on her back, so that means he shot himself in the left temple."

Raifer looked out over the banister and saw Bucky sitting on the floor. "You can't think and work and talk at the same time?"

Bucky took the hint and started crawling again, pulling up the narrow oriental carpets and running his hands over the wood floor beneath, feeling for any holes. At each knot in the wood he paused, but the knots were shallow, filled with nothing but lint and dust. "He slits her throat, she dies. He drops his knife, and then he shoots himself in the left temple. We've been all over this. This is what I told you and Dr. Cailleteau yesterday. I seen it all and figured it out."

Raifer was now at the landing on his hands and knees. "Bucky, if you've figured this all out, then tell me how a man who is right-handed shoots himself straight through his head by putting the barrel to his left temple?"

Bucky called up, "Raifer, it's easy. Look."

Raifer stood up and looked down at his deputy in the hallway below.

Bucky, on his knees, straightened his back and took his right hand, and pointing his index finger like a gun, lifted it slowly to the side of his head. It was so obvious.

"No, Bucky. Remember. He shot himself in the *left* temple."

Bucky took his right hand and brought it around to the other side of his head. But now he had to twist his arm and wrist painfully to make the index finger point straight through. A puzzled look came over his face. "I don't understand. This don't make no sense."

"I agree. That's why I need you to keep looking."

Bucky bent over again, trying to figure it out. It must be all part of the curse. That's it. The curse explains everything because when you got a curse on a place, like Cottoncrest, anything is possible.

Raifer, crawling around the second-floor landing, had not gone but a few feet from the staircase when his hand felt a depression in the floor, something that could well have been just another deep knot in the wood. Up here, even with all the French doors open, the light was dimmer. Raifer took out his knife and probed in the knot. His blade struck something metallic. He rocked the knife back and forth to work it out. It was the mashed metal of a spent bullet, black with powder and blood.

Raifer was glad that he had found it and not Bucky. No need to tell Bucky. Not yet. Raifer had to have more time to work out the issues. Eventually, someone would get concerned. Eventually, someone would reveal himself. All he had to do was wait.

Raifer put the metal in his pocket, pulled a nearby rug over the spot, and pretended to keep on looking. Later, after he had sent Bucky on his way, there would be time to search the Colonel Judge's office here in the house.

⁂

Jenny was in Little Miss's bedroom. It had been a long night, and she had barely gotten back before Mr. Raifer arrived. Mr. Raifer had dismissed Marcus and Sally, but Jenny, hidden behind the door, had been listening to Bucky and Mr. Raifer.

They were bound to come down today and want to see Little Miss. Jenny was glad she had acted when she did.

Chapter 23

Tee Ray held a big torch and touched it to the ground again. It was so dry that flames rose up immediately. The fire spread from stalk to stalk. Billows of black smoke roiled upward.

To Tee Ray's right and left, as far as the eye could see, other men were doing the same. Forrest, his beard and hair wild in the updraft created by the flames, was walking and stooping every few steps to let his torch start another blaze. Jimmy Joe's huge muscular frame was already partially hidden from Tee Ray's view by the smoke. Another five or six men were now invisible, enveloped by the dark, smoldering clouds.

The flames moved inexorably through the field, jumping from one elongated leaf to the next, picking up speed as the fire grew. Low walls of red flame, silhouetted against a wall of black smoke, were sweeping through the brownish-green sugarcane.

Burning the field was necessary before the cane could be harvested. Burning stripped the foliage away, leaving only the thick, sugary stalk, a stalk so moist that it would not burn. The stalks were all that were important. The flames reduced leaves and brush and weeds in the field and made harvesting easier. It also drove out the rats and snakes.

It would take until nightfall for the fire to cross through all the cane—several thousand acres under cultivation at Cottoncrest in seven different fields—and burn itself out. At sunrise the next morning the sharecroppers would come with their scythes and cut the cane near the ground, just above the lowest nodules that protruded above the dirt. This year they were working on a ratoon crop, grown from the roots of last year's cane left in the ground after harvest. They could get perhaps one or two more years' crop from the roots, and then they would have to replant again.

The stalks would then be piled on wagons and taken to the mill, where the cane would be mashed by large machines to draw out its milky fluid. Tee Ray remembered well the days when slaves did not only the cutting but also the mashing, turning large mangles by hand to wring out the juice.

The slaves would work twenty-four hours a day, sometimes for a week or more, boiling the liquid so the sugar would crystallize properly. They'd stoke bagasse fires built with the dried, crushed stalks, keeping the liquid boiling in the huge iron pots large enough to hold ten men, stirring constantly with long wooden paddles to bring the impurities to the top. Adding slaked lime to the juice to settle out the dirt, they'd skim the brown froth and debris, removing it from the pot before it formed a blanket. When puckering began, when the bubbles and froth browned, they knew it was almost ready. Then, when hominy flop and hog eyes occurred, when the liquid boiled violently and unevenly, it would be put through the triple evaporators. Out would come the fine syrup and the thicker molasses and the thickest lacuite, more viscous than honey and twice as sweet.

Tee Ray started to walk back toward his house. The others could watch the fields as they burned the rest of the day. The cane breaks, the wide paths around thousands of acres of fields that they sharecropped, would keep the fires from spreading into the woods and neighboring pastures.

Watching the white men tend the fires to keep them low and cool so as not to harm the stalks, Tee Ray thought it a damn shame that coloreds weren't still doing this work. They were the ones who should be doing it. Hell, years ago it was an Orleans Parish nigger, that Norbert Rillieux, who liked to call himself "a free man of color" and who was all uppity, just because he was educated in Paris, who everyone said "invented" the triple-effect evaporator that was used now. But no darky could ever be that smart.

It doesn't matter, thought Tee Ray, what the coloreds did. It was the white men who made sugarcane king. It was De Boré who, right there in Audubon Park in New Orleans, figured out how to make a profit raising cane. It was white men who came up with a way to replace Otaheite and Creole with Louisiana Purple and Louisiana Striped varieties so that the infrequent frost wouldn't damage the crop.

But it was them blue-bellies, fighting for them niggers, what killed sugarcane. Where there used to be over a thousand plantations, there were now less than two hundred, and all of them, like Cottoncrest, were suffering. Oh, before he died, the Colonel Judge could put on a good face, but everyone knew hard times were upon him. The parties had ended. The sharecropping had expanded, and with more share-croppers farming the same fields, there was less for each to take home.

Niggers. That's who was to blame. And Jews too. Especially Judah P. Benjamin—all fancy with a middle initial and such. Once Jeff Davis and his ghostly looking vice president, Little Aleck, first let that Judah Jew become attorney general of the Confederacy, then secretary of war, then secretary of state, the Confederacy couldn't help but be cursed.

Jews and niggers. The northern Jews, with their newspapers and big words. The southern Jews, with their big noses and strange language that sounded as if they got too much phlegm. Tee Ray had never seen one before—that is, he hadn't known he had seen one until Bucky told him that the peddler was really a Jew—but he had heard tell what they were like. So what that Jake the peddler sounded normal and never spoke any Jew-strange language? That proved it all the more, didn't it? Jews were shifty and full of deceit. It was them what caused slavery to end, and now it was too expensive and time-consuming for small 'crop-pers like him to do the sugarcane processing by hand; 'croppers were relegated to taking their cane to centralized mills owned by the big plantation owners.

So, the plantation owner won again. He took a percentage of your crop. He took another percentage of your share of the syrup and molas-ses and lacuite. He took it even if he was your relative.

The niggers and the Jews had to pay. Tee Ray would make sure of it.

Chapter 24

It was damn unfair. That's what it was. Unfair.

Go look for this, Bucky. Go there, Bucky. Go get it for me, Bucky.

Here he was, having figured out what happened, having told it all to Raifer and Dr. Cailleteau, having everyone listening to him now, and what does Raifer do? Tell him to get back to Parteblanc and send a flimsy from town to New Orleans.

A lot of good a telegraph message was gonna do. Why couldn't it wait until this evening? Or tomorrow? What was the purpose of sending a flimsy to the Cotton Exchange to tell them of the Colonel Judge's death? They'd know soon enough. But Raifer said it had to be done. Something about the Colonel Judge's creditors having to know, him with no direct heirs or anything. Something about crop pledges and notes that may be due and all that kind of finance stuff.

Sending a flimsy. That's not a job for a deputy. A deputy should be investigating. Should be out there at Cottoncrest locking down the silverware and taking inventory to keep them former slaves from stealing the big house blind. Should be there with Raifer when he questioned all them others. Should be there to help out when Raifer talked to Little Miss.

But no. Go back, he said. Back to Parteblanc.

Bucky's horse, almost as thin and forlorn as its rider, moved slowly down the road. The smell of burning was everywhere. Wisps of dark smoke coasted across their path, sometimes obscuring their vision and then, just as abruptly when the wind changed, sweeping away, revealing the remaining thickly planted green cane, higher than a man's head, on either side of the road.

Occasionally, a rattler would slither out of the field and cross a few hundred feet ahead of them, moving rapidly to avoid the spreading fire.

Mice and rats scurried along, seeking refuge. Hawks hovered overhead, circling slowly, anticipating the feast to come as their prey was flushed from the shelter of the densely packed fields of cane.

The horse whinnied and shied. Bucky looked up. Coming out of a narrow cane break, thirty feet to his right, a man was walking with long strides toward the road, his long thin hair hanging from beneath his sweaty hat and its dirty brim.

"You give my horse a start, Tee Ray," Bucky called out.

The expression on Tee Ray's face was unsettling. The gap caused by the front tooth knocked out long ago in a fight was visible, and the lips seemed more a sneer than a grin. "Bucky, either you got to get a better horse or that horse got to get a better rider."

Bucky pulled the reins up, and his horse stopped. Bucky loosened his grip, and the horse started to graze on the grasses that ran along the edge of the field.

Tee Ray reached the road and turned down it. Bucky had thought that Tee Ray would stop and chat, but Tee Ray kept on ambling away. That was all right. Tee Ray would see how important Bucky was.

Bucky jerked the reins and the horse resisted, but the gag bits hurt its mouth. The horse reluctantly lifted its head and started moving again down the road toward the man ahead of them.

"You know, Tee Ray, ain't no white men seen them bodies 'cept Raifer and Dr. Cailleteau and me. I seen them again today, all waxy-like under the sheets. And did you know what Raifer and I been doin' all mornin'? Lookin' for bullets. That's right. Crawlin' around on our hands and knees like some darky scrubbin' the floor.

Tee Ray slowed his pace.

Bucky was proud. He knew what he had to say was interesting. Tee Ray was impressed with him, Bucky could tell.

"Is that a fact?"

"Fact, Tee Ray, fact. Raifer wants that bullet what the Colonel Judge shot himself with. For a souvenir, I bet. I mean, the curse made the Colonel Judge not only kill his wife—it made him do all kinds of strange things. Like, he didn't shoot himself like a normal man would. No sir. Got himself all twisted like. Like his arm and wrist were as twisted as his mind. Look, let me show you."

Bucky, sitting atop his horse, made a broad gesture of taking a gun out of his holster, forgetting that the Colonel Judge was not wearing a holster. But it made for a good effect. His forefinger cocked, Bucky raised his right hand to his right temple, and then he rolled his eyes. "My fate has been sealed. My darlin' wife is dead. Dead by my own bloody hand. And now I must be the agent of my own dee-mise."

Bucky was just getting started with his performance when a change in the wind brought smoke over the road. It was thick and obscured the sunlight.

Bucky started coughing as ashes caught in this throat. Bucky's horse frantically pawed the earth, looking for some way to escape. Burning embers smoldered in Bucky's hair, and his eyes were smarting.

"Get down off your damn horse before you break your neck and it breaks a leg!"

Gladly complying with Tee Ray's command, Bucky dismounted the increasingly terrified animal.

Tee Ray yanked the reins from Bucky's hand and, grabbing the throat latch of the bridle with a steely grip, led the horse slowly down the road. Bucky followed.

Eventually the wind shifted, the fire's dark smoke was now behind them, and the horse, now calmer, ceased resisting. The road finally exited the cane field, and the three of them, Tee Ray, Bucky, and the horse, continued on at a leisurely pace into the hardwood forest, the dark-green palmettos growing low and spreading their spiky fan leaves over the soil that was always damp or muddy and which, after the rains, was covered with several inches of water.

"They gonna bury the Colonel Judge and his wife soon?"

Bucky, his throat still raw from the smoke, blew gray-brown mucus out of his nose and wiped it on his muddy sleeves. This was good. Tee Ray wanted information that only Bucky could give. Tee Ray needed him.

"Don't know when, Tee Ray, but I guess soon. They got that plot where the General was buried, along with what was left of his other sons. But you know all about that. I guess that's where they're gonna put the Colonel Judge and his wife."

Tee Ray knew all too well about the plot. He knew his mother was not buried there. She was never allowed to be buried there, not that Tee Ray ever asked the Colonel Judge. His mother would not have wanted to be buried next to the General anyway. But that didn't matter. What did matter was that, if Raifer was looking for a bullet and if he had sent Bucky away, then Raifer must have found something. Or suspect something. Bucky, so anxious to please, could be very useful.

"Tell you what, Bucky. I think that your seeing the bodies is a good sign. An omen almost. You have described their deaths so perfect, it was almost like you could feel exactly what had happened."

Bucky straightened up and walked more proudly next to his horse. He knew his way of telling the story made all the difference. It made it real. Tee Ray had seen that. The others always listened to and respected Tee Ray. They followed him. Bucky knew that if Tee Ray told the others how good and real his story was, the others would respect him as well.

"You know, Bucky, I would like to see those bodies. Just once, before they're put in boxes and buried. To pay my last respects and all. After all, I sharecropped his land for years. It's the least I can do. Do you think you could take me to see them?"

Bucky thought about it, but only for a minute. What was the harm? If anyone deserved to see the body of the Colonel Judge, it was Tee Ray. The flimsy could wait. Raifer didn't want anyone else seeing the bodies, that seemed clear. Why else had he asked Cubit to start making coffins rather than getting old man Ganderson in town, who usually handled this for all the white families, to build a couple of coffins? Raifer wanted all the glory for himself. He wanted to be all-important. That wasn't fair.

Bucky figured he could leave his horse here, and he and Tee Ray could double back to the barn behind the big house, look at the bodies, and be back here in forty minutes. Raifer would never know. Then Tee Ray could tell the others how important and resourceful Bucky really was. Raifer was getting old. One day he'd have to stop being sheriff. With the help of Tee Ray and the others, Bucky would have that job for sure.

"Tee Ray, let me tie up the horse off the road, and you just follow me."

Chapter 25

The old lady sat in a wide, wooden rocking chair on the veranda. The shade from the tall columns, and from the protruding second-floor porch and the even higher eaves, shielded her from the intermittent sun that peeked through the gathering clouds. She could smell the rain coming. She could feel it. The change in humidity caused her joints to ache.

She sipped daintily from the coffee in the porcelain demitasse cup, thinking how nice it was that these two pleasant men had come to see her. The younger one seemed so friendly, even if he didn't speak the language. And the fat, bald man, who had made her open her mouth and had looked in her ears and who had asked her all kinds of foolish questions, seemed nice enough as well.

She held out her cup and the kind black woman, who seemed vaguely familiar, promptly refilled it.

Raifer had patiently waited until she had arisen and had dressed. He had waited until Dr. Cailleteau had examined her. The Doc, although he had grumbled about it, had driven out from town saying that he hadn't seen her in almost a year and this was probably as good a time as any, what with all that was happening, and he ought to be there anyway when Raifer questioned her, in case she needed medical help afterward.

It was now almost noon. She was attired, as she always was, in a dress with a high lace collar that encircled her narrow, patrician neck. Long sleeves with lace cuffs covered her bony arms. It was obvious by her slow movements when she came out onto the veranda, leaning heavily on Jenny's arm, that she was in constant pain. Despite her aches, however, she sat in the rocking chair with an enviably erect posture.

She had become far more fragile since Raifer had last seen her more than a year earlier. Her skin was as thin as the finest gossamer linen. Her high cheekbones, of which she always had been justly proud, now seemed bony protrusions threatening to burst through. Narrow cracks ran from her lips and extended like tiny spiderwebs above and below her mouth.

"It was very nice," Raifer began, "for you to see me today. You are looking quite well."

The old lady gave Raifer a pleasant, blank smile.

"The last time I was here, we had talked about the time Cottoncrest was being built. Do you remember that?"

The old lady's expression did not change. She sipped at her coffee and, holding the tiny cup in both hands, gazed out at the Mississippi River, which was just beyond the wide path of live oaks that lined the entrance to the big house. Now and then a large trunk of a tree or a broken limb would swirl by, pulled under and then popping up a hundred feet downstream, a captive of the brown, swirling water that stretched almost a mile wide at this point before curving south again.

"I told you, Mr. Raifer, like I told Dr. Cailleteau, she doesn't remember either of you. From day to day she doesn't remember me. She doesn't even remember English anymore. Only French. It's like she's lost somewhere in the past, and everything recent has disappeared from her like shadows being chased by the sun." Jenny stood dutifully beside the old lady. She didn't dare sit in the presence of the white men, especially the Sheriff and the only doctor in the parish. "Do you want me to translate for you?"

Raifer and Dr. Cailleteau could see for themselves that what Jenny and Sally and Marcus had all said was true.

Dr. Cailleteau had treated many patients who had the capacity to live but who just gave up, sliding into death rather than fighting it. For them the mind controlled the body; when the mind refused to struggle, the body ceased to function. And yet there were others who were completely different, where sometimes the body was able to go on but the mind was not. Ever since the death of three of her sons, thirty years earlier, Thérèse-Claire had been a changed woman, and the General's death had altered her permanently. She had become increasingly remote. Always the lady. Always gracious. But she had less and less to talk about and had more and more difficulty remembering names and events and faces. And now it had come to this, thirty years afterward.

Dr. Cailleteau had been on the battlefield, but when he had returned after the war the story became all too clear. It could all be traced to 1863, starting in April of that year. The General was home, recuperating from the injuries that had caused his leg to be amputated, when there had come the news from Charleston Harbor that at first had brought joy to the General and Thérèse-Claire. The Union's warships had been repulsed with the loss of only fourteen Confederates. Their oldest son was in command of a unit there, and they were proud, until the word came that he was one of the casualties.

Then, ten days later, over at Vermillion Bayou in Lafayette Parish, Major General Richard Taylor's Confederate forces were defeated by northern armies. In the retreat up the bayou, their second oldest son was killed.

As if that was not awful enough, starting in May 1863, there were more disasters for the South and for the Chastaine family. There had been the terrible battle at Plains Store, near Baton Rouge. Despite reinforcements being brought in, the Confederates were routed and had retreated to Port Hudson, leaving behind hundreds of dead, including her youngest son.

Then came two letters, six weeks apart. The first, from Augustine, let them know that, in leading his brigade, he had beaten back an attempted Union landing on the lower bluffs at Port Hudson and that he had been promoted to colonel. The second, in mid-July, had been hand delivered by a young orderly.

Thérèse-Claire had told François Cailleteau, on one of those long summer evenings on the veranda a few years later, that when the General had seen the orderly riding up to the big house under the arched oaks, his uniform immaculate, his posture rigid, that the General knew what was to come. The General did not even open the letter, sealed with red wax. He had handed it to his wife, Thérèse-Claire, who had read out loud the words Lieutenant Alden Reynard had written, declaring with sadness the news that he had to deliver. The Confederates had been forced to surrender Port Hudson. Only twenty-four hours before the surrender, Lieutenant Reynard himself, over his protests against being ordered from the field, had been sent out from Port Hudson in a regrettably unsuccessful effort to locate and bring in additional replacements. The morning before that order, his good friend Colonel Augustine Chastaine had led a troop of men against yet another attempted landing by Unionists at the foot of the bluffs near the bend in the river. Colonel Augustine Chastaine had fought valiantly and with great bravery against an overwhelming force. When last seen, Colonel Chastaine had been shot off his horse and was lying bleeding on the field of battle. After the Colonel had fallen, his men lost hope and retreated to the top of the bluffs. Due to the intense gunfire, the bodies of those who had fallen in that last charge could not be retrieved. Major General Franklin Gardner and the rest of the officers had been captured after the surrender, but, according to the best information, Colonel Chastaine was not with them, so it was beyond perchance that the Colonel had perished leading what all would remember as the most valiant efforts of a Confederate son. Lieutenant Reynard concluded his letter with the heartfelt hope that when the South emerged victorious from this conflict, as she must, Colonel Chastaine's efforts would be writ large among the mighty who had shown those cowardly bluebellies, who fired upon our brave soldiers from the safety of ships, what true heroism was.

It was then, while the southern armies were in retreat in Louisiana and while the New Orleans port on the Mississippi River was firmly in Union hands after the fall of Port Hudson, that her husband began his own retreat, a retreat into himself. Four sons, all dead. A daughter, long before that departed. For the General, it was a slow descent into an internal hell that finally overcame him.

After the General's death, Thérèse-Claire had continued her own withdrawal. Now it appeared to Dr. Cailleteau that her retreat was successful and permanent. She was locked in her past, in a safe time before war. Before children.

"Ask her if she knew of anyone who would want to cause the Colonel Judge harm."

"Mr. Raifer, do you really want me to do that? I haven't told her anything, and I don't want to upset her."

"Jenny, either you do it, or I'll ask Dr. Cailleteau to do it, and I think she's more comfortable with you. Just do as I say. Ask her had the Colonel Judge—had Augustine—had any problems with anyone lately."

"Yes sir, but it won't do any good."

"Don't you backtalk me. Just ask her."

"*La madame Thérèse-Claire, savez-vous si quelqu'un jamais a exprimé un souhait pour nuire M. Augustin?*"

The old lady looked puzzled, as if trying to recall something from the dim and distant past. Then she smiled once more, her cracked lips revealing a mouth filled with yellowing teeth, and, pointing at Dr. Cailleteau, said, "*Augustin. Cela'les un nom agréable. Je pense que j'a su une fois que quelqu'un a nommé Augustin. Est-ce que c'est cet homme?*"

She then turned back to look out at the river again.

Dr. Cailleteau leaned back in his chair and pulled out another cigar. She was in her own safe place. There was no hope for her to return to the present.

"Well?" demanded the Sheriff of Jenny.

"Mr. Raifer, all she said was 'Augustine. That's a nice name. I think I once knew someone named Augustine. Is that who this man is?'"

Chapter 26

"There they are, Tee Ray. See, I told you."

Tee Ray and Bucky had sidled around through the back door. The fields far behind the barn were now masked by the smoke, and if the wind shifted again, the soot-filled dark mass might even roll toward the house.

They were now standing over the boards that held the bodies, the sheets still in place, the cloth-covered bucket with Rebecca's head placed near her feet.

Tee Ray pulled back the white linen that covered the Colonel Judge. Flies buzzed around the body. Maggots were squirming in the nostrils.

They had closed the doors behind them, and the stale air inside was warm and heavy, the stench from rotting flesh filling the barn. "Bucky, you got gimp to bring me here, I give you that."

Bucky pulled himself up a little taller. To have Tee Ray compliment him on his courage made him proud.

"Why don't you go keep an eye out. I just want to have a look-see. I think I'm entitled to that."

Bucky knew that if anyone was entitled to gaze upon the Colonel Judge one last time, it was Tee Ray.

Bucky promptly went over to the door and peered through the slats where the wood had warped. He could see the big house a few hundred yards away and, north of that, paralleling the river, the fields where the fires would eventually reach.

As soon as Bucky's attention was directed outside, Tee Ray leaned over and stared hard at the lifeless man's face. No regal bearing now. No disdain for those he had treated as his lessers. As unworthies. No clever remarks to amuse those who came to his once-lavish parties. No more public embarrassment for those he refused to invite. No careful turns of phrases, all learned and full of fancy words, to confuse and confound. He was just another mass of dead flesh starting to putrefy, smelling so bad that even lavender water wouldn't mask the stench. Whatever soul he once had was long gone. Whatever fortune he once amassed was now for others to take.

Tee Ray gathered a mouthful of spit and let it drop on the Colonel Judge's cheek, the dampness making the maggots curl up. Serves him right. Dead was what the Colonel Judge should be. Just like his brothers were dead. Just like his father was dead. Just like Tee Ray's mother was dead.

Tee Ray then went over to Rebecca and lifted up the sheet. This was curious. Her body was face down on the wooden slab, or it would have been face down had she still had a face. Her dress had been cut open, revealing the soft curves of her pale, white back. The bloody, sliced fabric had stiffened, like the body.

They were all equal now. The Colonel Judge and his wife were no better than Tee Ray's mother. No better than Tee Ray's father. No better than Tee Ray.

Bucky gasped. Tee Ray looked up and dropped the sheet, whispering. "What is it?"

Bucky, as quietly as he could, approached the bodies. "It's one of them darkies. He's got a length of rope in his hands. And he's comin' our way."

"Perfect! We're gonna catch a nigger who's up to no good. Come on, Bucky. Up here."

Tee Ray scampered up the ladder to the hayloft, followed by Bucky. They moved to the back, under the low eaves, and waited.

The sound of footsteps scuffling along could be heard coming closer and closer. The front barn door opened, its hinges creaking, and fresh air cascaded in. They heard boots treading closer, stopping under the ladder next to the bodies. They heard the rustling of sheets being moved and of a man's heavy breathing. The man coughed; it was a deep raspy sound, like a dangerous creature far back in a hollow cave. He cleared his throat and continued moving the sheets.

Bucky cautiously dug into the hay, trying to get down to the loft's floor boards, trying to look through the knotholes and cracks. He could see the man's huge hands and what he was doing but not the man's face. All he caught were glimpses of a back of a muscular coal-dark black neck, thick and powerful, and a dusty hat. It was enough, however, for Bucky to know who he was.

"Cubit!" he whispered to Tee Ray. "He's using a knotted rope to measure the bodies!"

"Shhh!" Tee Ray said under his breath, pulling Bucky back and shoving him to one side. That boy sometimes didn't have the sense of a bedbug. At least bedbugs knew how to keep quiet and just do what had to be done.

As Bucky fell backward, his head hit something hard in the hay, but although it smarted, he bit his tongue.

"Six for him. Five-and-a-bit for her. Six for him. Five-and-a-bit for her." The sound of chanting drifted up to them from below. Cubit was working up a singsong method of remembering his measurements.

They heard the sheets being replaced and the heavy boots scuffling toward the door.

> Six for him. Tall and thin.
> Five-and-a-bit for her. That's the way she were.
> Six for him. Tall and thin.
> Five-and-a-bit for her. That's the way she were.

The barn door opened, and Cubit continued on, not shutting it. Anyone could see into the barn now.

When the chanting receded into the distance, Bucky reached back into the hay to see what he had hit. It couldn't have been a beam. Rubbing the back of his head with one hand and moving the hay aside with the other, Bucky said, in a hurt tone, "You didn't have to shove me so hard, Tee Ray."

"If you had known to keep your mouth shut and your eyes open, I wouldn't have had to do anything. If you're gonna be a law man, you gotta learn how to watch and wait until just the right time. You either got to make a spoon or spoil a horn, as they say."

"Oh, Tee Ray, I know enough to do lots of things right. Without me, you wouldn't be here at all. Besides, Cubit didn't hear us none. And yet you go and shove me into . . ."

Bucky stopped. His hand, digging in the hay for what his head had hit, had found something.

Bucky brushed away more hay. It was large and heavy.

Tee Ray came and joined him. Bending low under the eaves of the barn, they hoisted it up out of the coarse dried grass, bull thistle, dog fennel, jimsonweed, and Johnson grass.

It was a large wooden chest. It had handles on either end and two iron clasps on the front, each held firm with a heavy lock.

"This damn thing, Tee Ray, is as big as a tierce. Could probably hold more than a barrel, less than a hogshead. Looks like an overgrown hardtack box. But who the hell would want to drag this thing around, and why was it hidden up here?"

Tee Ray pointed to name etched into the side of the box. It read, "Prop. of J. Gold."

Chapter 27

"Jenny, you were in the house all night. Marcus and Sally have their own place out in the back, but you were in Little Miss's bedroom the whole time. So, you must have heard or seen something."

"No, Mr. Raifer. All the doors were closed. The door to the back hallway on the first floor leading to Little Miss's boudoir as well as Little Miss's door itself. All closed. I was just watching out for Little Miss. I saw nothing, and nothing is what I heard."

"Can't believe that, Jenny, with the commotion on the stairs and the gun going off."

"Honest, Mr. Raifer, if I'd had heard something or seen something, I'd have told you, just like Marcus told you about the Peddler Man."

Dr. Cailleteau rocked in the sturdy wooden chair that barely accommodated his ample girth, enjoying his cigar. The three of them were on the veranda, Jenny having served them lunch and helped Little Miss back to bed for her afternoon nap. Raifer was still sitting at the table, the few remnants of a meat pie that he had left turning brown and soggy from the gravy. Jenny was standing to one side, tray in hand, waiting on them.

"Marcus told us that Jake Gold, the Peddler Man, spoke French to Little Miss and the Colonel Judge."

"Yes sir. To them and to Miss Rebecca. They all spoke French most of the time, especially when Little Miss was around."

"You came from New Orleans, right?"

"Yes sir, the Colonel Judge hired me—it must be three years now—to watch over Little Miss. Sally couldn't do it any more once Little Miss stopped speaking English. And of course, Marcus couldn't take care of her, even though he speaks French, but then you know that."

François Cailleteau often marveled that even after all these years, everyone still referred to Thérèse-Claire as "Little Miss." François had been there after the war, when Augustine had made his way home and surprised his widowed mother, having been released from the prison at Camp Douglas near Chicago a month earlier. At that time, in 1865, she was already fifty-two years old, but the only name she had ever been called at Cottoncrest was Little Miss.

When the big house at Cottoncrest had been built by the General and Thérèse-Claire back in the 1830s, the General's mother, Catherine Chastaine, was still alive. It was a slave tradition to call the mistress of the house Old Miss, so even though Catherine was not the owner, she became Old Miss and Thérèse-Claire Little Miss. That name stuck, and Miss Catherine's death didn't change it, nor did Thérèse-Claire's advancing age, nor did the arrival of Rebecca a few years ago. No one had called her Thérèse-Claire again. Not her old friends and not the many visitors whom Augustine, as a long-confirmed bachelor after the war, used to bring to the plantation for extended visits. To everyone she was Little Miss.

It was strange, François thought. Perhaps her name, Little Miss, predestined her fate—a retreat of an old lady into the past.

"And you were here," Raifer continued in his questioning of Jenny, "serving, when the Peddler Man and Little Miss and the Colonel Judge and Miss Rebecca had their long conversations in French?"

"No sir. I was not needed. Marcus and Sally served, and I was able to get a few minutes' rest."

Raifer looked up at her sharply.

"I mean, sir, Little Miss needs lots of care all the time. So, the Colonel Judge let me have some time for myself when the Peddler Man was here. They would talk for hours, and though Little Miss might not be able to follow the conversation or might forget from one moment to the next what they had been talking about, she just loved to sit there and let the French language surround her. She loved anything that reminded her of the past, before all those bad times started happening. She was a first-generation Creole, you know, having come directly from Paris with her parents when she was very young, and she was once a great beauty, or so they say. I do know that when she looks at herself in the mirror, she often tells me, 'Créoles n'en meurent pas, ils sèchent.'"

Dr. Cailleteau took his cigar out of his mouth and flicked away the extended ash. "It's an old saying, Raifer, 'Creoles don't die, they just dry up.'" Dr. Cailleteau thought that Little Miss's saying this was probably a combination of her fear of her own mortality and her way of forcing herself not to remember, assuming that she had any memory left at all, of the terrible deaths that had torn asunder her family.

"It's a good thing in some ways, I think," Dr. Cailleteau said to Raifer, shifting his cigar from one side of his mouth to the other, "that her mind is lost somewhere in the distant past. That way, the Colonel Judge's death can't hurt her."

Jenny didn't say anything. She stood quietly, and no one looking at her would have thought she was doing anything but awaiting the next question from Raifer. But that was not the case at all. She knew that the Colonel Judge's death had changed everything. And sooner than she would like, the effects of the Colonel Judge's death would hurt Little Miss. But that couldn't be helped. Not now.

Chapter 28

"And where did you leave your horse?"

" 'Bout a mile and a half back, in the woods beyond the cane fields, Raifer."

Raifer was furious. Bucky and Tee Ray were standing below them on the ground under the oak trees, a shallow trench scraped through the brown winter grass right down into the dirt marking the path they made dragging the big trunk from the barn. Raifer was standing, hands on his hips, on the edge of the veranda. Dr. Cailleteau took the cup of coffee that Jenny was offering and waved her away, a signal for her to go inside.

"What's the matter with you, Bucky? You been drinking sack posset, putting wine in your milk? Has Tee Ray here been serving you calibogus, getting you full of rum and spruce beer? Didn't I tell you to get to Parteblanc and send that flimsy? Bucky, I don't think you have the sense God gave to a large rock, a small pebble, or even a tiny dornick."

"Now, don't be mad at him, Raifer. You got to give Bucky here credit. He done solved all your problems."

Raifer looked questioningly at Tee Ray. He didn't need any help, certainly not from Tee Ray.

"I mean, Bucky has gotten it all right, from the very first. He's been tellin' us all there was a curse, and now we know *what* the curse was, and we know *who* the curse was."

"And how, Tee Ray, do *we* know?"

"It's right here, Raifer," Bucky chirped up, "right here in this chest."

Raifer walked down the broad wooden steps and approached Bucky and Tee Ray. Bucky took one step backward, but Tee Ray simply reached down and pulled open the lid. "Raifer. Look at all this. This was hidden in the hayloft, just as Bucky said. We had to break the locks off with a sledgehammer, and it kind of ruined the front, but you can see all this stuff inside. It answers all the questions."

Dr. Cailleteau roused himself from the rocking chair on the veranda and, placing the coffee cup on the table, slowly moved down the stairs. Although they were made of stout cypress, they groaned under his weight.

"You see, Raifer," Bucky said, as Tee Ray started taking the contents out, layer by layer. "It says 'Prop. of J. Gold' on the side. That's the Jew Peddler what's been spending so much time here. Why would he go and hide this big chest way up in the hayloft? Had to hoist it up with ropes, I guess, to get it up there. And why here? Why hidden? Lookee. Just look."

Raifer could see clearly the treasures inside. Layer upon layer of fine skins. Months' worth of work for trappers and hunters. These would fetch a lot in New Orleans. They'd bring a small fortune if the trader had contacts up the river. They'd be even more valuable if someone could get them all the long way to New York by train. All those fancy women wanting to wear those fancy furs.

"That ain't all, though, Raifer. If that was all there was, it would be strange enough, but I done solved it, I did!"

Tee Ray let Bucky enjoy himself. Let Bucky take the credit. No one would believe that Bucky had solved anything, but as long as what had to be done got done, it didn't matter.

Bucky came around to the front of the chest and pulled off the bottom layer of skins, revealing a small roll of canvas tied tightly with a narrow strip of leather. "Open it up, Raifer. Go ahead. See what's inside!"

Raifer picked up the bundle and placed it on the ground. Kneeling next to it, he untied the leather binding and unrolled the canvas.

"See! What did I tell you! You were lookin' for a bullet, Raifer, and the more I thought about it, the more I figured there had to be a reason. And in talkin' to Tee-Ray . . ."

Raifer looked up at Tee Ray, whose mouth was bent into a grin. Raifer did not return the smile but maintained his steely demeanor. There was nothing that Bucky could have figured out on his own.

"You see, how could the Colonel Judge have done all that to Miss Rebecca and then shot himself in his left temple with his hand all twisted?

No, someone else must have done it, and the Colonel Judge came upon them and got himself shot. That's why there was no bullet in Miss Rebecca's back, where his head was. Someone must have put him on top of her. Which means that the bullet is probably still somewhere in the house. But who could have done this, 'specially with the Colonel Judge and Miss Rebecca all holed up in their house for almost a year, with not no one come to visit? No one, that is, 'cept the Jew. And look, this here's the proof!"

Bucky bent down and picked up one of the six gleaming knives that were now lined up on the unwrapped canvas. Two had four-inch blades, three had six-inch blades, and one had a ten-inch blade. Bucky picked up the biggest one. "See here, Raifer! Sharp as can be. Ain't nothin' it can't cut through, quick as you like, with nary any trouble at all." Bucky lightly drew the tip of the blade across the thick canvas, which parted easily, as if it always had consisted of two pieces.

"Let me see that," Dr. Cailleteau asked.

Bucky stood up and handed the knife to the doctor, who took it and used it to cut the end off of a fresh cigar he pulled out of his pocket.

"Damn clean cut, that I'll admit. Sharp as a fleam."

"A fleam?" asked Bucky.

"It's a small lancet," Dr. Cailleteau explained, "that we used in the war for bloodletting, sharp as could be so that when you were cut you hardly felt it."

"It proves it, though, don't it, Raifer," Tee Ray said, the sneering grin still on his face.

Jenny, looking out from behind the curtains of the second-floor window and listening to the men below, saw Tee Ray's expression, and it frightened her. On this man a grin was pure evil.

"The Jew," Tee Ray continued. "The Jew did it. He's the only one who comes here. He's the only one who has seen the Colonel Judge and Rebecca in the last year. He's the one, like Bucky has said, who was talking foolish religion and doubting our Lord Jesus."

Raifer shot an angry stare at Bucky. Bucky was revealing what Marcus had disclosed during an investigation. And the fact that he told Tee Ray was all the worse. Bucky would have to be dealt with. Later.

"He was the one who has the knives. He was here for blood. That's all them Jews want is blood, you know. Blood for their ceremonies and their bread and such."

"Bobbery and applesauce," Dr. Cailleteau said, deftly flipping the knife toward Tee Ray, where it landed right next to the toe of his boot, the blade sinking almost all the way to the haft in the dirt. "This isn't the kind of knife that killed the Colonel Judge. It was a regular old blade, honed sharp, but not a fancy knife like this."

Tee Ray turned to Bucky and asked, as if relying on Bucky to determine the answer, "You don't think the Jew was stupid enough to use his own knife, one that anyone could tell what was his, and then leave it for others to find, do you?"

Bucky thought a moment and then responded. "'Course not. He was clever. All them Jews think they're so smart, but they ain't smart enough for the likes of us. He done did it with a regular knife to make it look like he weren't involved. Just like a Jew to do that, isn't it?"

"Sounds right to me, Bucky," Tee Ray said with emphasis.

"More bobbery, Tee Ray," Dr. Cailleteau sighed. "I know that you put all these ideas into Bucky's head."

"I've 'bout had enough of you, Doc. Here we are, Bucky and me, tryin' to help Raifer find out who killed the Colonel Judge and all, and all you can do is insult me."

"Applesauce! Bucky said you told him you wanted to pay your last respects to the Colonel Judge. You didn't respect the Colonel Judge any more than he respected you. I guess this has nothing to do with degrees of consanguinity, does it?"

"Consan-what-tery?" Bucky blurted.

"Consanguinity," Dr. Cailleteau explained, "degrees of relationship." Bucky was confused. "I don't understand."

Raifer pulled the knife from the ground near Tee Ray's boot and started to wrap it up again with the others in the canvas. "Cousins. Relatives. Aunts. Uncles."

"Why don't you tell Bucky," Dr. Cailleteau said to Tee Ray.

"Ain't nothin' to tell," Tee Ray responded, walking over to Dr. Cailleteau and staring him straight in the eye with a cold expression. "Don't know what you're talkin' about, what with them big words and fancy ways."

"You don't scare me, Tee Ray," Dr. Cailleteau responded, moving a step forward. Dr. Cailleteau's huge stomach, protruding underneath the vast yards of his jacket, forced Tee Ray backward. "Now, why don't you tell Bucky what we all know. The Colonel Judge would never have let Cottoncrest fall to you."

Bucky's eyes opened wide. He looked at Tee Ray with admiration. "You got a chance to get Cottoncrest? How?"

"Anyone can see, Doc," Tee Ray said savagely, "that all that fat has gone to your brain. You're as crazy as Little Miss. It's clear that the Jew did it. He killed them. He cut Rebecca. He killed the Colonel Judge. He planned it all. Jews are like that. Scheming. Sneaky. Full of mysterious ways and secret languages. Well, he ain't gonna get away with it. Me and the others are going find him and bring him back so justice can be served."

Tee Ray turned to Raifer. "That's right, ain't it Raifer. When I bring him in, you got to hold him, and he's got to be tried. And then hung. Or maybe the hanging just ought to come first."

Upstairs, behind the curtain, Jenny heard it all. She thought she had solved all of their immediate troubles the other night. But now it was clear that other problems were looming. She had to find Marcus and Sally quickly. There wasn't much time.

Chapter 29

Marcus trudged down the road cautiously. He had been careful to slip out the back of the big house. Jenny and Sally were right. If anyone saw him, it would be all over.

It had been a good life. Not a great life, but a good life. No money, of course. Slaves didn't get money before the war, and even now, what was a house servant to expect? They got what they needed, as long as they stayed where they were. Credit at the Cottoncrest sharecropper store; of course, they had to shop there during the permitted time—a half-hour before the store opened for the white sharecroppers and only if they used the back door and didn't go inside. They also got a small cabin with a tin roof over their heads and a real wooden floor. That was something he and Sally really liked, that wooden floor. Plenty of food; there were always leftovers they could have after Sally had finished serving Little Miss and the Colonel Judge in the early years. And after Miss Rebecca came, she even made sure that Sally took back some of the sweets as well, to share not only with Marcus but also with Cubit and Jordan and their families.

But now all of that was over. After these many years on Cottoncrest, their time here was ending. Jenny was right. They had to get ready now to move. Tonight. The Knights were going to ride, and that meant nothing but trouble. But that wasn't the worst. No. The worst was that thing with the usufruct and all.

He hadn't understood it at first, and he made Jenny explain it to him three times before it began to sink in. He hadn't ever paid any attention before to what the law said about when people die. Didn't want to. The law never helped him, and he knew all he ever wanted to know about death anyway. He had seen more than enough. Sometimes it still haunted his dreams. That's why he hated foggy days and smoky fields.

But Jenny knew a lot about what the law said about when people die. She said that whether someone like the Colonel Judge had children or not, the law controlled what happened to what he owned. If you had children, Louisiana forced you to leave at least half, and sometimes more, to them. But if you don't have any children—if you can't have children or if you had them and they have disappeared and gone forever—then it goes to your nearest blood relative. If your momma is alive, as the Colonel Judge's was, then one fourth goes to her and the rest to your brothers or sisters, or if there are none of these, to your brothers' and sisters' children, and if there are none of these, to your nearest cousin.

This was all too confusing. Jenny said it all made sense, but it seemed just a waste of time. Who, but a few white people, would ever have enough after they died to worry about leaving anything but debts? But it got even more confusing. Jenny had said that the Colonel Judge really didn't own all of Cottoncrest anyway. Now, that didn't seem right. The Colonel Judge had been the General's only surviving son. He ran the plantation. He made all the decisions.

But Jenny said that the Colonel Judge only owned half. The other half was owned by Little Miss, and even the Colonel Judge's half was subject to what sounded like something dirty. "Usufruct," she said. Marcus made her pronounce it again and again before he got it right. Strange word. Meant something about Little Miss not only owning half of Cottoncrest on her own but her also having the right to use and live and get all the profits from the Colonel Judge's half as long as she was alive.

And now, whoever got the Colonel Judge's part was getting it subject to Little Miss's usufruct.

But with the Colonel Judge dead and with Little Miss not in any condition to make decisions about anything, who would take over the plantation? If Jenny wasn't there to feed and bathe and clothe Little Miss every day, Little Miss would forget to eat and would waste away, not that she wasn't already as thin and bony as Job's turkey.

Jenny had overheard young Mr. Bucky say something about Tee Ray having a chance to get Cottoncrest, and that would have been enough to raise the fear of the devil in anyone. But when Jenny heard Tee Ray telling the Sheriff that Tee Ray was going to look for the Jew Peddler man, well, that meant the Knights were going to ride. And if the Knights were going to ride, no one was safe.

That was why Marcus had to get to Little Jerusalem as soon as possible to warn Cooper and Rossy and Nimrod and Esau and the others before the Knights came riding down on them.

Jenny had told Marcus to get out to Little Jerusalem and then not to come back to Cottoncrest. Don't come back ever, she said. Even Sally had agreed, although there were a lot of tears. They would all meet up—Sally and Jenny and Marcus—at the spot they knew. Cubit and Jordan would get their kin out, and by tomorrow morning there would be no one left in the cabins near the big house.

The fact that Little Miss had to be left alone was terrible. But what they feared if they stayed was worse.

Marcus had walked almost three miles along the road that hugged the bank of the Mississippi River, although he was only a mile or so from Cottoncrest as the crow flies. The river twisted and turned and doubled back on itself in huge curves, some as long as a couple of miles, others longer. As Marcus passed the dirt road that cut west from the river through the cane fields, the road leading to the area where Tee Ray and the other sharecroppers' homes nestled against the woods, he moved quickly and cautiously. He didn't want to be caught by Tee Ray and the others. If they saw him out of the big house, there would be questions and trouble and not necessarily in that order.

The smoke from the burning cane fields drifted across the road, blocking Marcus's view even of his feet and causing him to choke. There were another two miles of fields along the river road still to go, for the Cottoncrest plantation ran for miles and miles along the river. Marcus slowed and felt his way, step by step, down the road. He bent over; the lower he got to the ground, the less dense the smoke was. He walked liked that, hunched over almost in half, for quite a ways.

He hated the smoke. He hated not seeing what was around him. It was like being back at Port Hudson after the Colonel Judge had left that day to lead what was the last charge before the surrender. Up on the bluff early in the morning, before daylight, they could see the outline of the yardarms of Farragut's steam frigates against the moonlit sky. As dawn began to break, they could make out the crews on the decks getting ready, the ships' cannons being elevated for shooting. They could see smaller boats being lowered on the far side of the ships, being loaded with men.

The Colonel Judge had sent Marcus down to the part of the Port Hudson bluff known as Fort Desperate, where Marcus was put to work with other slaves on repairing the earthworks. Every six feet they had sunk upright one stout timber. Jammed lengthwise against them, like the wall of a house, were ten tree trunks, one on top of the other. Row after row, one upright timber and then ten tree trunks. Behind the tree trunks they had piled the heavy clay earth of Port Hudson, five feet high and two feet thick. And whenever possible, they would offset one of the logs in the wall a bit so that they could dig a hole—a box twelve inches on a side—clear through the mound of clay.

Once the slaves had finished a section, most of the soldiers would stand behind the earthworks and fire down at the blue-bellies in the river. Others would kneel down in the mud, rest their rifles in the holes in the wall, and blast away at those below.

Every day for six weeks the positions were bombarded by the big cannons. You could stand behind the embankment on the bluff and see the billow of smoke from the ship's guns. The first one was always silent. Just a puff of smoke, and the ship would shutter, and little waves would move away from the boat in increasing circles. But no sound. Then you heard it. A rustle through the air, like a great bird. The rustle became a whistle, and then the boom of the cannon reached you, pounding the air so hard it hurt your ears and you could feel the sound in your stomach. Then the sickening crash of the cannonball and the crushing of timber earthworks and the crunching of bones and the screaming of those who had been hit.

And then blood and body parts and men dying all around you. Men dead and those who were soon to be dead and those in such agony only death would help them. And then you couldn't see anything, for you were keeping your head low, and the booms of the cannon and the crashing and the crushing was all around you, and then the smoke rose from the Union guns and from the Confederate guns, and all was noise and confusion and panic.

Marcus had hated it. Hated every minute of it. Hated it all the more because he had been there, waiting on the Colonel, serving him his meals in his tent, when Port Hudson had first been attacked. And what made it all the more hateful was that on the first day of what became a six-week siege, the Unionists who had led the attack on Port Hudson had been men like himself. The Corps d'Afrique, it was called. Organized by General Benjamin Butler in New Orleans to fight for their freedom, it was the first troop of slaves who were armed and permitted into battle. They had charged up the bluff on that first day of the siege, and they were beaten back viciously by those under the command of his own Augustine, not yet a colonel. His own master was resourceful and clever, and scores of bodies of black men in blue uniforms were left scattered on the mudflats below the Port Hudson bluffs. Bloated bodies that were a feast for the buzzards that coasted overhead in long, slow patterns. Bloodied bodies that were a warning to the rest of those on the Union boats who thought they could easily take this Confederate stronghold.

That evening the officers came to Augustine's tent to toast him. Marcus had served them all with a sinking feeling that he should be on the boats with the remainder of the Corps d'Afrique, not on this side of the line.

But there was no way to get there. No way to leave. Not in May or June or July of 1863, during the siege of Port Hudson. Not even though in January of that year Lincoln had issued the Emancipation Proclamation. He had been freed by Lincoln, and yet he was still a slave, serving his master in the Confederate army.

He couldn't leave Port Hudson when he wanted to then. Now that he was old and didn't want to leave Cottoncrest, he couldn't stay.

Marcus kept walking. Soon he'd reach the end of the plantation's fields, and then the marshy woods would begin. The sky was dark in the direction he was heading, south along the river road. A heavy rain was in progress a few miles ahead. He had to reach Little Jerusalem as soon as possible.

Chapter 30

The rainstorm, as was typical for Louisiana weather, had been both localized and torrential, its power concentrated in a small area. The low black clouds blanketed and darkened Little Jerusalem, but where Cottoncrest sat, there was blue sky smudged by the gray-brown smoke from the burning cane fields.

In Little Jerusalem they could smell the rain coming. The air grew heavy, the odor of the ground more distinct, the humidity palpable in the pleasant, late-October air. Before the storm swept through, the wind had whipped up, and the trees bent over. Then it roared past, lightning flashing and rolls of thunder pounding, the rain coming down hard and driven by the wind at an angle, liquid spears hurling viciously toward their targets.

When it seemed as if the torrent would carry them away, the rain stopped abruptly and the black sky rapidly retreated, heading south-west toward Lamou. In the short while that the storm had lingered, it had dropped several inches on Little Jerusalem. The bayou that ran nearby overflowed, and the road out front turned into a muddy, rutted stream. Yet to the north Cottoncrest remained dry, although gusts of wind could be seen shifting the smoke violently in one direction and then another.

Nimrod sat on a stool under the wide awning made by the tin roof, taking it all in. The shift in the weather caused his bones to ache, and he didn't like all the commotion and conversation anyway, even if he could have heard all the words. It was enough to watch God's work. Esau stuck his head out from time to time to check on his father.

Inside the small cabin water dripped down the sides of the walls through cracks in the tin roof and formed puddles on the dirt floor. But Rossy and Cooper paid it no attention, and therefore neither did

Jake, nor did the fifteen others who had crowded into the tiny one-room house.

They each had brought a tin cup and a spoon, along with a handful of fall vegetables, and they each placed their backyard garden offerings into the pot of possum stew. It was a celebration. The Peddler Man's arrival was always a treat. Cooper had taken the possum he had shot the night before and donated it for the stew. To have the Peddler Man stay for a meal in his house was a big honor, and it showed the others in Little Jerusalem how important he was.

Possum wasn't kosher any more than pork was, but that didn't stop Jake. He took out his own tin cup and, along with the others in the crowded cabin, waited patiently for Rossy to ladle out the thick brown stew and then ate heartily, even though he was still full from the *cochon de lait* and the wedding feast earlier that morning. His customer had offered it, and he wasn't going to offend his customer. Not by words. Not by deeds.

Uncle Avram had made that clear. Never offend. Ever. One day a huge Cossack had walked into Avram's shop and complained that a coat Avram had made was ill fitting and had torn. He showed Avram the sleeve that had separated. Avram looked at it carefully, examining it closely. He didn't say what he and Yaakov and the Cossack all knew. The sleeve hadn't separated at the seam. The fabric itself had been ripped by a branch or a nail or some careless action of the owner. But Avram merely nodded his head at the Cossack who towered over them, apologized abjectly, and offered to buy it back from the Cossack for what it cost, even though the coat was now well-worn and useless. The Cossack took the money and left, happy to have put another one over on another Jew, and when little Yaakov had started to ask his uncle why he had let the Cossack take advantage of him, Uncle Avram had leaned over, his long beard scratching against Yaakov's cheek, and whispered in his ear, "*Abi gezunt—dos leben ken men zich alain nemen.*" Be sure to stay healthy—you can kill yourself later.

The trading had gone exceptionally well. Every last item that Jake had left in his cart was now gone. Every scrap of fabric, every thimble, every spool of thread, and the last two knives, all traded away for furs for coats and trim and snakeskins for belts and shoes. Now the only things in the cart, besides his grindstone, were the goods to be sold to his contacts in New York. As soon as he could get back to New Orleans, he'd send a flimsy to New York. He'd set forth both the shipping date on the next steamer headed out into the Gulf of Mexico and up the East Coast and the date of delivery of the goods to Isaac Haber & Co., the brokerage firm he dealt with in New Orleans. That would be followed by a confirming flimsy from Isaac Haber that the goods had been delivered and were as represented. The New York contacts would wire him the money, and the whole process would start anew. Jake would buy new supplies and then begin his rounds again.

Moshe had set up the system upon his return to New York, and Moshe would get a cut of each transaction. That was as it should be. Moshe as an arranger—perfect. But Moshe as a partner—never again.

They had been just north of Natchez, and the crowd had already gathered around them on the boat. They had threatened to throw a rope around Moshe's neck and hang him from the balcony right then and there. A quick death was too good for him, others had argued. A lingering death was what he needed, to teach him and others like him a lesson. They wanted to keelhaul him behind the paddle wheeler, letting him drown while being towed downstream in the swirling current of the river.

The steamboat captain had intervened, gun in hand, to hold off the crowd. One of the crew patted down Moshe, looking for weapons, and they found one of the excellent knives Moshe and Jake sold strapped in a leather sheath against Moshe's calf, under his trouser leg. That almost did it. Even the captain was considering turning him over to the crowd. But they were nearing the turn to Natchez, and when they docked, the sheriff had been summoned, had come aboard, and had dragged Moshe off in handcuffs.

Too sharp, they had said. Too sharp and too quick.

Jake had taken almost all that he and Moshe had saved up to trade in New Orleans and had given it to the sheriff for Moshe's bail. Then, retaining only enough to get himself to New Orleans, Jake had given the remainder to Moshe to make his way inland up to Vicksburg and catch the next steamer north. All the bail was forfeited. Moshe's name was still on wanted posters in Mississippi and down into Louisiana and up into Arkansas. Moshe could never come south again.

But for Jake the South was now home. Here he could make a good living. A very good living.

Jake took another large spoonful of the possum stew. As soon as the meal was done, now that the skies had cleared, he would head back to Cottoncrest and check on them.

Chapter 31

Nimrod saw the lanky figure moving from out of the woods, across the road, toward the cabin. Although his eyesight was bad and he couldn't make out the man's features, Nimrod recognized the gait. The fact that the man was coming from the woods rather than down the road meant that he hadn't wanted to be seen coming to Little Jerusalem. And that meant trouble.

Taking his walking stick, Nimrod slowly and painfully started to make his way across the muddy yard, his bones creaking and the mud coating his bare feet. "Don't seem neighborly to be sneakin' up like that, do it?"

Marcus paused next to Nimrod and, giving his hand to his best friend since childhood, when they had been slaves together, led him to the large stump in the yard, where they both took a seat. Marcus picked up a small twig and started to scrape from his boots the thick mud he had picked up in his trek through the woods.

"Your clothes are soaked clean through," Nimrod said, his hand still resting for support on Marcus's shoulder. The water had penetrated Marcus's light coat and was dripping down onto Nimrod's wrist and arm. "Why you want to sit out here all wet like? Come on inside, and we'll get Rossy to dry you out. Got a good fire goin' and hot stew. You know what they's say about possum stew, don't you. Will cure what ails you, and gives you what you ain't got."

"No time, Nimrod. No time. You remember what it was like, back when, back when the Klan was roaming nightly?"

Nimrod didn't have to respond. Of course he remembered. He couldn't forget, even if he wanted to.

"It's gonna happen again, Nimrod. As bad—maybe worse—than before. The Colonel Judge is dead. Shot."

Nimrod turned with a start, his cataract-filled eyes gazing at Marcus with amazement. "Don't tell me . . . was it one of us?"

"Hell no! I think it's the curse. That's what I think. Done shot himself, just like the General. And kilt Miss Rebecca too."

Nimrod shook his head in dismay. "Black folks got no money, and when they got troubles, it's usually the troubles that others visit upon them. But white folks got money, and yet when white folks got troubles, it's the ones they bring upon themselves. Money and troubles just seem to go hand in hand. The curse, you say?"

Marcus nodded in agreement as he continued scraping the mud off his boots. "But Mr. Raifer don't think it's the curse, at least that's what I suspicion. And Tee Ray, he thinks the Peddler Man done it. Found the Peddler Man's trunk what he kept at the barn and found them fancy knives in it. Miss Rebecca, her head was cut almost clean off. Cut so clean it came off in Mr. Bucky's hands when he and Mr. Raifer were lookin' at everythin'. Blood everywhere. And her body up on the stairs and her head at the foot of it."

"Merciful Lord!"

"Tee Ray is gettin' the Knights together. They're comin' to look for the Peddler Man. And they're gonna be lookin' at all the places the Peddler Man visits. That means they're comin' here. And you know how they're gonna be, all liquored up and spoilin' for an argument. They ain't gonna take kindly to any answers they don't like, and that means nothin' but trouble. You got to warn everyone in Little Jerusalem to get ready."

"You can warn them yourself," Nimrod said, pointing with this thumb toward Cooper and Rossy's cabin. "A lot of them are in there, 'course, 'cept for Keith and Peggy. They never come to anything, but you know that. They just stay back there in their cabin in the woods, all by their lonesome. Anyway, the rest of them are there, along with the Peddler Man himself."

Marcus's eyes grew wide at this news. "Mr. Jake is here?" That wouldn't be good for Little Jerusalem at all. He stood up. "Then there really ain't much time. You stay here, old friend."

Marcus walked briskly to the cabin and, not bothering to knock, opened the door. The voices that started to rise in warm greeting quickly grew silent when they saw the expression on his face, one of grim determination and great sadness.

Marcus quickly told them what had happened, and the group immediately began to scatter, heading back to their homes to hide their few possessions and send their children and women into the woods for shelter and protection and to prepare themselves for the evil night that they knew awaited them.

Rossy picked up her baby in one hand and began to gather her belongings with the other. Cooper took down his gun from over the fireplace. He wasn't going to use the gun; it was a single-shot muzzle-loader, and it would not do him any good against the many riders who were coming, but it was his most valuable possession, and he had to hide it.

While Rossy and Cooper went about their tasks, Jake took Marcus out the back, under the shed where Jake's cart was parked. Jake's face betrayed no trace of emotion. *Di gantseh velt iz ful mit shaidim; treib zai chotsh fun zich arois,* he thought. The whole world is full of demons; you just exorcise them out of yourself. That he had learned from his father and his uncle. Never show your emotions to outsiders. "What can you tell me about them?"

"Horrible, Mr. Jake, just horrible. Me and Cubit and Jordan had to clean up afterwards. The awfullest sight. Part of his head blowed off and her head cut off."

"No, I mean . . . *them.* The others."

"Oh, them? They're safe. Jenny saw to that. But she didn't tell Sally or me nothin' more than that they're safe. The lessen that we know, the better, she said."

"How long do you think we have, Marcus?"

Marcus looked down at the cart. "Not enough time, Mr. Jake. Not enough. You've got to go, and go now. Get as far away as possible, and never come back."

"Never?"

"Not as long as Tee Ray is alive. You've got to leave for good. Don't you understand? We've all got to leave. By tomorrow morning there ain't gonna be none of us at Cottoncrest. Not Sally. Not Jenny. Not Cubit or Jordan or me. We'll all be gone. Disappeared. It's Emancipation time. Not like we thought it was gonna be. Don't know where we'll end up, but I think Jenny is headed back to New Orleans. All I know is we got to get away. And when they find all of us gone . . ."

He didn't have to complete the thought. Jake knew that Marcus and Jenny couldn't stay, and once they left, more disasters were bound to follow.

Jake wanted to ask Marcus more, but Rossy came out the back door, followed by Cooper. "What you gonna do, Peddler Man," Rossy inquired, "with all your goods? If'n the Knights are comin', you ain't safe either. Ain't no white man safe who trades with us and drinks and eats with us. And you can't take your cart. With all the mud on the road, you couldn't make time there even if you wanted to and had it to begin with."

Jake thought quickly. "Tell you what, Rossy. If you and Cooper can find some way to hide all this that's in the cart, I'll give you half of it. If I'm not back in a month for the other half, it's yours as well. All I want is for you to give me my knife back. I traded you the last one I had."

Rossy shifted the baby to her left shoulder and stuck out her right hand. "You got a deal, Peddler Man."

"One thing," Cooper added. "That cart. Everyone knows that cart. If your cart is found anywhere near Little Jerusalem, ain't none of us are gonna be safe."

"Break it up," Jake said, starting to unload the furs and handing them to Cooper. "Burn it. Destroy it. If I'm able to come back, I'll come back with another cart. And, if I'm not able to come back, it won't make any difference anyway."

Cooper took the armload of skins, piled more on, and walked back inside the cabin, his big muscles barely straining against the load.

Jake followed him, empty-handed. "Cooper, you can't keep these in here. If, as Marcus says, the Knights come, they're going to search everywhere, inside and out. It won't be safe for you or Rossy if these are found in your possession."

Cooper smiled. "Oh, there's ways." He took a shovel that rested against the fireplace, blackened from the ashes and coals that had been scooped out over the years, and, moving the table in the center of the small room, started digging in the hard dirt floor. The shovel only penetrated a couple of inches before there was a hollow thud. Cooper quickly shoveled away an area three feet wide and four feet long; underneath several inches of dirt were four rough wooden planks. Cooper pried up the planks with the shovel, revealing a hole lined with planks onto which had been nailed roofing tin so that the contents would remain dry. The hole was almost five feet deep.

"You can hide a lot here. Can hide a woman and child if need be. Have done it before, and I'll do it again if I have to."

"But where you gonna go, Peddler Man?" Rossy asked, coming back into the cabin with her baby, carrying more skins in the other arm. She handed them to Cooper, who was starting to lay his own pile into the hole. Then, reaching under the fireplace mantel, she dislodged a brick and pulled from the hollow behind it the knife Jake had traded to her earlier in the day. She looked at it longingly. "You ain't got no money. And when you leave here, you ain't gonna have nothin' to trade but this. How you gonna live?"

Jake just shrugged. He knew he was unlikely to see Rossy and Cooper again. "My people have a saying for this. *Tsum schlimazel darf men oych hobn mazel.*"

Cooper and Rossy looked puzzled. They turned to Marcus. "Is that French?"

"Ain't no French I ever spoke, and I've been speakin' it since I been born."

"No," said Jake, "not French. It means even for bad luck you need some luck."

"That," proclaimed Rossy, still holding the knife with a mixture of pride and resignation—pride of having been the owner of it, even temporarily, and resignation at having to give it up so soon—"don't make no sense either, and that was English."

"It means," Jake explained, "that things could always be worse." He took the knife from Rossy and, sticking it in his belt, turned to Marcus. "Look, if Jenny is coming to New Orleans, you tell her to meet me in two weeks time at the Lafayette Cemetery, after dark. If I make it, I'll go there every night, three nights in a row. I'll be there waiting for her. There are things we have to talk about."

"Well, no money. No cart. No nothin' to trade. And you gots to get far away. You're right, Peddler Man. Things for you can get worse," said Cooper from down in the hole.

"Cooper, you hand up that bearskin," Rossy commanded.

Cooper stood up, a thick bearskin in his hand. "What you want this for, Rossy? I got to get this all hidden. Don't got no time for you to go examin' the Peddler Man's goods."

Rossy grabbed the bearskin out of his hands and handed it to Jake. "All you said you wanted was your knife. Well, you better take this too. Your ol' coat ain't gonna do you much good if the temperature gonna go and drop. You'll freeze to death for sure."

Jake took the bearskin and opened his mouth to express his gratitude, but Rossy put her hands up in protest. "Hush. Don't say nothin'. Besides, I can't understand none of your sayings anyways, whether you're speaking that strange language or telling me what it means in English."

Marcus laughed. "A bearskin and a knife, and that's all he's got, and it came from you. Didn't know white men could get so poor." Marcus laughed again. "Rossy, it ain't only Mr. Jake's people that's got sayings. My people got a saying, too, that fits Mr. Jake. *La pauvrété n'est pas un déshonneur, mais c'est une fichue misère.*"

Now it was Jake's turn to laugh. "That's something *my* people might say!"

Rossy was indignant. "Marcus, it's bad enough when the Peddler Man starts in with his talk, and now you gots to throw French on top of that? The two of you! Speakin' things we don't understand. Marcus, I didn't think you'd be the one gettin' all high and mighty on us."

Marcus smiled gently at Rossy, patting the baby on the head. "It just means that poverty is not a sin, but it is a mighty inconvenience."

PART III

Today

Chapter 32

"I don't know why Grandpapa Jake came to Louisiana, but I do know why I came the first time. I was young, almost as young as you. The nation was in turmoil. President Kennedy was in the White House, and the Bay of Pigs invasion of Cuba had just happened and was a huge failure. In the meantime there had been twelve months of sit-ins all over the South. People were getting beaten up and arrested.

"There had to be a way to get blacks and whites together. There had to be a way to help bring the South to its senses. Here was something I could do personally that could make a difference. Here was something I could help with and not just study about in college.

"I made my way to Washington, D.C., and on May 4, 1961, after three days of training, I boarded a bus with five other whites and seven Negroes. I had just a tiny suitcase with two days' change of clothes, a toothbrush, a razor, and my most precious item safely hidden in the lining. The suitcase was small enough to fit in the overhead rack. All of us had been trained to travel light.

"We thought we were invincible, at least those of us on the buses who were white. We were going to expose the segregated interstate transportation facilities in the South and to overcome obstacles by the force of logical persuasion and peaceful protest.

How wrong we were. Our buses were stopped. Searched. Firebombed. We were pulled off and beaten up. White or black, it didn't make a difference. If you were on the bus, you were a target.

"Finally, in Alabama, the ride was shut down. The governor issued a proclamation telling all Freedom Riders to leave the state immediately.

"No more buses for the group I was with. Some of us were put on a plane and flown out. But me? I got on a train to New Orleans with a few others, and I held my suitcase in my lap all the way.

"It was 1961, but I found out that southern attitudes seemed to have changed little since 1896.

"Why 1896, you ask? That was the year the Supreme Court decided *Plessy versus Ferguson,* the famous 'separate-but-equal' case that was finally overruled by *Brown versus Board of Education* in 1954.

"The train we rode had a Whites Only and a Colored Only car. The train stopped at stations with Whites Only and Colored Only restrooms. The train had engineers who were white and porters who were black. And in 1896 *Plessy* had held that separating whites and blacks on trains was perfectly all right, as long as they were separate but equal.

"I'm ashamed to admit it, but in 1961, after having been cursed at and beaten up and driven out of Alabama, when riding that train, we sat in the white car all the way to New Orleans."

1893

Chapter 33

Dr. Cailleteau left Cottoncrest and headed northwest, back toward Parteblanc, his buggy squeaking with every slow step of his horse. The weather was changing. Soon the temperature would drop dramatically. Dr. Cailleteau could feel it coming. Underneath his vast folds of skin and fat, Dr. Cailleteau's joints ached with each jolt of the wooden wheels on the rutted road.

The air was full of odors. Ominous clouds to the south smelled of rain. The acrid smell of burning fields was everywhere. Strong wind gusts from the nearby thunderstorms gathered force and swept down in waves upon the burning fields, tossing the smoke in strange directions. Rain and smoke. The only thing missing was the smell of death; that was confined to the two bodies starting to rot in the Cottoncrest barn. The smell of death, however, had once filled his lungs every day, decades ago. The smell had remained on his hands and clothes, on his surgical knives and apron, on his boots and socks and hat. Death's odors had permeated him.

François Cailleteau had gotten to where he believed he could smell death coming. The war had done that for him. To him. Well, maybe not the smell of death itself but, rather, the smell of the fear of death.

From the time he spent in his gray uniform, his heavy canvas apron red with blood and covered with bits of human debris, he had learned that death could strike at any moment. From bullets. From cannons. From disease. From anywhere. He had seen it time and time again.

You could be hidden behind a thick redoubt and have it blown up in your face.

You could be kneeling down in the mud to tie your shoe, and a bullet would pierce your brain.

You could get scratched starting the late-evening's fire, and sepsis would set in, and your limbs would rot, and then your body would fail.

You could not have a mark on your limbs but start in with a hacking cough and not survive 'til dawn, gasping for each breath, your lungs clogged.

You could have survived another day's bombardment during the long siege and then choke to death on the bone of a baked rat caught in your throat as you hastily ate your first meal in two days, all the while glad that you had caught something to eat, even if it was only a rat feasting on the bodies of your dead comrades.

Death was everywhere, every hour of every day.

Young François Cailleteau, newly minted as a physician before Secession had been declared, his arms strong on a powerful torso, had walked the deep trenches at Port Hudson, tending to the wounded and comforting the others who were, as yet, uninjured but who cherished a kind word.

Young Dr. Cailleteau had found he could smell the fear of those who feared death. It covered them like a thick shroud. You could see it in their eyes—pupils dilating with a growing dread of the inevitable. Some were pimply-faced recruits, mere boys, their ill-fitting gray uniforms hanging limply on them, their Confederate caps pulled down tightly over hair crawling with lice. They had joined up, so sure of themselves and so ready for the glories of battle. Now they were shaken by days and days of bombardment, feeling certain that any moment would be their last. Others were married men, longing for their wives, desperately trying to survive just one more day and trying to hide their panic that they would not.

Then there were the injured and maimed. They cried in mortal agony, the mere act of inhaling bringing anguish with each breath. Dr. Cailleteau knew they were screaming not to be granted the release of dying but to be granted just a second more of life, no matter how terrible it was, no matter how wracked with pain they were, no matter that their guts were oozing out of their shirts and onto the ground, their limbs broken and missing.

And then there were those who squirmed under the saw and the fleam and the surgical knife. Hundreds of them. Maybe thousands. Dr. Cailleteau had lost count. Bilious fevers racked their bodies. Pus and blood ran from every natural orifice as well as the unnatural ones caused by their injuries. Even though he had doused their wounds with a decoction of red oak bark and water as an antiseptic, even though he had given them stramonium and nightshade to try to ease their pain after the amputations, even as they fell into a senseless stupor on the planks that served as surgical tables, the smell of the fear of death was on them as well.

Yet, there were others who seemed to know no fear. Perhaps they were the most foolish of all. They crawled through the rain of grapeshot as if it were a light spring sprinkle. They loaded their weapons with precision and speed, not with panicked haste. They ducked their heads when the earth flew from a cannonball's nearby crash, and not bothering to wipe the mud off of their faces, quickly raised up above the parapets to fire another shot at the enemy.

These were the men who created the smell of the fear of death in others. In the sailors attempting to assault Port Hudson, who did not believe that this small ragged band of southern farm boys could hold off Farragut's mighty fleet. In the blue-belly troops who now feared the hail of bullets and cannon fire coming from the bluffs of Port Hudson, high above the Mississippi River, that repulsed wave after wave of black Corps d'Afrique soldiers and white Union soldiers, even after day after day after day of constant bombardment.

These men, who created the fear of death in the enemy, also created the fear of death in their own comrades. Their fellow soldiers marveled at these men, at their seeming indestructibility. Standing beside them in the trenches or crouched low in the brush atop the bluff, their friends in dirty gray uniforms feared that they would die but these men would live.

Of course, these men who instilled the fear of death in others also fell and died, but they never believed they were going to die. They never believed it at all, until a bullet proved them wrong.

Dr. Cailleteau could see that Tee Ray Brady was like that. His mere presence caused weaker men to exude the smell of death. Tee Ray carried himself like a stalking creature of the night, full of guile and cunning, waiting to pounce on those who were helpless or frightened. Tee Ray wanted the panic of mortality to be cast over others as he strode by. That's why the Knights followed him.

Of course, to fear Tee Ray didn't mean that you had to respect him.

No one respected Tee Ray, except for the Knights. Not even Tee Ray's own family respected him, except Tee Ray's pleasant fool of a wife and his motley run of children.

No respect but plenty of fear. That's why, when Tee Ray and the Knights rode tonight, they would terrorize the countryside. And what would the upright citizens of the parish do? Nothing.

Tee Ray and Bucky's theory made sense, but it was a theory that Dr. Cailleteau realized Raifer had reached first and which Bucky, in his own slow way, had picked up. Cailleteau's old friend, right-handed Augustine Chastaine, couldn't have shot himself in the left temple, and he loved Rebecca so much, how could he harm her? Someone must have done them both in. And if someone did them in, then that someone would have to be found.

So, Raifer would let the Knights ride. He didn't have any good excuse not to. Once Tee Ray and Bucky had started talking about the peddler, Raifer couldn't very well not pursue it. A peddler with a knife was as good a place to start as anywhere. Raifer and Bucky certainly couldn't scour all of Petit Rouge Parish looking for the peddler.

All the argument and bobbery to the contrary, Tee Ray and the Knights could probably find the peddler faster than anyone, and whatever harm was done would have to be dealt with later.

Raifer had warned Tee Ray to do what he had to do but not to hurt anyone. Dr. Cailleteau doubted Tee Ray and the Knights would comply. And even if they did, all Raifer had said was don't harm anyone—he hadn't said don't harm anything. Tee Ray and the Knights would do some damage tonight, that was for sure.

Dr. Cailleteau looked up at the sky. The thunderstorms were curving away; they wouldn't reach Cottoncrest or Parteblanc, but the warmth in the air was gone, and a damp coolness descended.

The Louisiana weather in October could turn in a few hours. Dr. Cailleteau flicked the whip on his horse's haunches, and the creature picked up its pace. Dr. Cailleteau wanted to get back to his house and light a fire before it got too chilly. He'd crush some mint in a glass and add some sugar and bourbon and loosen his vest and pull off his shoes.

As his horse turned the bend in the road, Dr. François Cailleteau took one last look over his shoulder at Cottoncrest, whose white columns were silhouetted against the dark sky. He and Augustine Chastaine used to sit during the long winter evening hours in front of a fire in Cottoncrest's book-lined study, picking up a volume in Greek or Latin and reading to each other or talking in French, reminiscing about the past and commiserating about the present. But the one thing they never talked about was the war. That was too bitter a subject for both of them, and what could they possibly say to each other that would give solace?

Merely to have returned home alive was sometimes hell enough. It certainly had been that for Augustine Chastaine.

Chapter 34

He hit her in the head with the back of his hand. The blow was so strong it knocked her down to the floor of the small cabin.

She didn't whimper. She didn't cry. That would only make it worse. She wiped the blood from her split lip with the cuff of her blouse and started to get back up.

Just as she was almost erect, holding onto the mantel over the fireplace for support, he came at her again, swinging his big clenched fist toward her face.

She shut her eyes and waited for the blow. It caught her in the cheek, and she collapsed from the pain.

She lay there on the hard, rough floor, trying to ignore the stinging ache in her jaw and the ringing in her ears. She tried to remain motionless. Unresisting. Still. If she didn't fight back, if she didn't protest, if she did nothing, he would eventually stop.

The blood ran from the cut on her lip. She dared not raise her hand now to stem the flow. She could feel its warmth running down her chin and its salty taste in her mouth.

Tee Ray Brady took the knife she had handed him so proudly, only moments before, and, kneeling down, shook it in front of her face.

"Open your eyes! Open them, Mona, or I swear I'll pluck one out right now with this here Jew knife.

Mona Brady slowly opened her eyes and tried to show no emotion. No fright at the deadly blade that Tee Ray was flashing back and forth in the air, inches from her nose and cheek and forehead. No fear at the anger that contorted his face. No flinching at the little specks of spit that coursed from his lips and dampened her face as he yelled.

Tee Ray was working himself up, his face turning red, as he hit her again. "Buy all the thread and needles you want from that Jew Peddler.

Did I ever stop you? Did I ever say not to? No. But buy a knife from him? A knife as sharp as this? A knife you can't pay for all at once but got to have him come back and back again to collect on, only to sell you other *things*? Things you don't want and don't need. Things that don't bring nothing with them but trouble? You are as stupid as the day is long, woman! Got no more sense than a stalk of cane. Or a nigger. Why don't you leave the thinking to me? Women should open their legs and shut their mouths. A woman trying to think is worse than a nigger trying to act all uppity. Nothing but trouble, and you are trouble! Stupid and trouble. Just a piece of filthy manure. That's all you ever have been and that's all you ever will be!"

Tee Ray, his face now contorted in anger, bent over her prone body on the floor and, hitting her once more, screamed so loudly that her ears hurt. "A JEW KNIFE! IN MY HOUSE!!!"

She did not move. She remained limp. She tried not to blink. She tried not to think about her bloody lip and how it would swell up, or about her throbbing cheek and how it would show the dark bruise for weeks and how painful it would be to eat, or about her now-aching ribs, where his latest blow had landed. She let him rant and concentrated on his words, trying to understand his anger, trying to figure out how not to make him angry again.

A Jew knife? A Jew peddler? That's what Tee Ray had said. Who could know that Mr. Gold was a Jew? Jake Gold? That's a good, short American name. Didn't Jews have names that ended in things like *stein* or *berg,* like those rich New Orleans Jews Tee Ray was always talking about? Like Rothstein or Goldberg.

And Mr. Gold didn't have a long curved nose and a hunched back and a black skullcap that Tee Ray said all Jews had. Mr. Gold was nice looking—handsome in fact—with his short black hair and cheerful smile and clever hands that could thread a needle quickly and could sew a stitch as straight as the ones on a store-bought dress.

How was she to know he was a Jew? Of course, if she had known, she wouldn't have dealt with him at all.

Tee Ray had never said anything before. Tee Ray had known for years that Mr. Gold had come by the house whenever he was in the area. Tee Ray had never complained before when she bought needles and thread and fabric from Mr. Gold. His prices were fair, and he was nice to talk to. If Tee Ray had even given her any indication the peddler was a Jew, she would have shooed him away. But Tee Ray had said nothing until now.

Why was it, when he had come home for his horse and said he was going to ride with the Knights, that he got so angry? She had been saving the peddler's knife to give to Tee Ray as a special gift. Christmas was still two months away, and the chance of getting something unusual and useful for Tee Ray was difficult, even if they had the money to buy something. The Cottoncrest plantation commissary had only necessaries, and anything she bought there had to be put on the credit tab, which only reduced their crop share at the end of the year, and besides, Tee Ray did most of the buying there. Where else was she going to get something for him? He hardly ever allowed her to go to Parteblanc, where there was a dry goods store.

Mona had thought she had been doing the right thing, negotiating with Mr. Gold to pay for the knife over time through trade. She had done it all on her own. It had made her proud. Here was something she could do independently, without Tee Ray's help.

She had thought he would be happy that she had done this for him. She wanted to make him happy. She always tried to make him happy in every way she could think of. If he was happy, then he wasn't angry. And if he wasn't angry, he wouldn't beat her.

Mona had been hiding the knife, saving it for a Christmas present, but since the Knights hadn't ridden in several years, she knew today had to be an important time. You ought to give gifts when it's important to give them. That's what Mother Josie, Tee Ray's ma, used to say. "Give them," Mother Josie had said, "when people will appreciate them, because you never know when times will change or when people will change. People," she had said, "sometimes change all too quickly."

Mother Josie had been right. Maybe that was because she had seen people change too quickly toward her. Maybe it was because she knew that her son could change quickly himself, one minute sunny and bright as the early morning and the next moment furious as a thunderstorm. Maybe all these quick changes ran in the blood of Mother Josie's family.

Give gifts when people will appreciate them most. Mona Brady had been sure that Mother Josie was right. That's why Mona had thought

Tee Ray would appreciate the knife, when he was excited about riding with the Knights, when the knife could be useful to him.

So, after Tee Ray had saddled the horse, when he had come inside to get his gun, when she could see he was happy and excited, she had proudly unwrapped the knife from the scrap of fabric in which she had hidden it. She had handed the gleaming knife to him and told him, with a smile on her face, that she had gotten it specially just for him, for Christmas, from Mr. Gold all on her own, without spending any of his credit at the Cottoncrest commissary. She had told him, thinking that it would make him happy, that this was his Christmas present but that she was giving the knife to him now because she was sure he would find a good use for it tonight, when the Knights rode, because it was so sharp.

And that's when he hit her.

Mona stayed motionless on the floor even after Tee Ray, still yelling, knife in hand, rose up and went to the cabin door.

Tee Ray held the knife and thought about what to do. It was exactly like the ones he and Bucky had found in the trunk in the Cottoncrest barn. Bucky was coming to ride with the Knights. Bucky would recognize it. Bucky would talk. Couldn't keep his mouth shut if he wanted to.

Tee Ray went outside, leaving Mona lying on the floor. He had thought about getting his other pistol from the peg it hung on above the mantel, but the knife was more important. He crossed over the scraggly yard to the outhouse and opened the door. He used the point of the knife to pry into the wood; it cut deeply with little effort. It was a fine knife. It was a damn shame, but there was nothing to be done.

Tee Ray dropped the knife into the pit below, where it sank with a gurgle in the thick slosh of urine and feces.

Chapter 35

The late-afternoon sun setting in the west did not give much illumination to Jenny's tiny third-floor room, with its low ceiling and small window facing south. Jenny did not dare light a candle. Jenny's little window on the topmost floor of Cottoncrest could be seen for miles, and a candle would draw attention. She didn't need any attention. There would be enough attention tomorrow, when they found her and the others gone.

Jenny was trying to be as inconspicuous as possible, even though only she and Little Miss were in the house. The Sheriff had left a while ago, and Dr. Cailleteau had departed even earlier. Little Miss had been sleeping soundly, snoring, when Jenny had crept upstairs.

Jenny wrapped up the few belongings she planned to take, looking sadly at all the rest she had to leave behind. Her good dress? There was no room for that. Her Sunday church hat? No room. A second pair of shoes that Miss Rebecca had given her? The worn kid gloves with only a tiny hole in the left thumb that Miss Rebecca was going to discard until Jenny asked politely for them? The French books from the downstairs library that Miss Rebecca and the Colonel Judge let her read? No room for any of these.

Jenny pulled out her long, stiletto hairpins, the silver ones Rebecca had given her, and tied her hair back with a tignon. She looked one last time at the small quarters that had been her home for the past few years. Her high bed, its cypress frame holding a real moss-filled mattress, was the finest available. The cypress dresser with four deep drawers. The tiny mirror that Miss Rebecca had given her. The box with six spermaceti candles and the glass hurricane lantern into which they fit. These would be the things she would remember.

But these things had to be abandoned. Her life, Jenny realized, was one long road of abandonment, but then she never had expected anything else. Her father had abandoned her mother, but her mother had expected it and loved him nevertheless, even though he never again came to her New Orleans house on Rampart Street, even though he never came to see his daughter or even inquire about her.

Jenny's mother was not bitter about that, and her mother had told Jenny not to be bitter either. That's just the way things were. Planters' sons were like that. It had been like that since the days of the Quadroon Balls. Even during the war, a white boy could fall in love with a high yellow woman.

And it was love, true love, Jenny's mother had insisted, even though it could not last. Even though the planter's son had worn a Confederate uniform.

When New Orleans had been captured by Farragut and the planter's son was unable to escape the city, Jenny's mother had hidden her lover in the house on Rampart Street until the war was over.

Yet, after all that Jenny's mother had done for him, despite the fact that she loved him more than anything, when the war was over the planter's son left the house on Rampart Street to return home to Opelousas to marry some blonde-haired white girl.

Jenny's mother had not complained. The planter's son had left her the house, had signed it over to her. That was a sign, said Jenny's mother, of true love, even though he had abandoned Jenny's mother while she was pregnant. The planter's son also had left her some money. It was enough money for Jenny's mother to start a small business, a school for young Negro girls to teach them to read the French they spoke, to teach them to read English as well, to prepare them for the freedom that they now had.

When Jenny's mother abandoned her, leaving her for the blissful peace of death after being wracked by the fever and by consumption, Jenny had tried to continue the school, but it became harder and harder. When Reconstruction ended, when the northerners left, the whites in New Orleans made clear what they had long believed but which they couldn't act on while the carpetbaggers were in control. The whites did not want the "coloreds" educated. The Vigilance Committee first warned her, and when she didn't halt her school, they warned her a second time. There was no third warning. The house on Rampart Street was burned, and Jenny was lucky to escape with her life.

Louis had been kind to her. He let her work in his office and sleep in the back room at night. She helped him with his legal papers, carefully inscribing each word with a quill pen into the big folio-sized books so that he would have a copy of what he was filing with the court. She wrote out the translations of passages from the books of the French legal commentators, like Planiol and Aubry et Rau, so that the new judges, the ones who didn't speak French, could see what they had said about the civil law issues that Louis was handling. She helped him proofread the newspaper articles he was editing.

But Louis couldn't pay her, and she couldn't live in the back of his office forever. She was glad that Louis had found out from James Walker, a white lawyer, that the Colonel Judge was looking for someone to help care for Little Miss, someone who wouldn't mind moving to Cottoncrest, someone who could speak and read French and keep Little Miss occupied and dress her and wash her and be her constant companion. Someone who was young and strong.

It was a perfect job for Jenny. It gave her an escape from the oppressive oversight of the Vigilance Committee. It gave her a way to start a new life.

Jenny could not have known when she first came to Cottoncrest how close she would become with Miss Rebecca. Jenny became her support. Jenny became her confidante. Eventually, the two of them became like close friends. Almost like . . . well, not like sisters, not with all their differences, not with Miss Rebecca married to the Colonel Judge, not with Jenny being the Colonel Judge's employee.

But now Miss Rebecca had abandoned her. Not voluntarily. Not peacefully. Not without great pain. But abandoned, nonetheless.

It was not for the Colonel Judge that Jenny had done what she had done, although the Colonel Judge was nice in his own formal, ancient way. It was for Miss Rebecca and for Miss Rebecca alone. In her memory. In her honor. It had been dangerous, but it had to be done.

Now that it was accomplished, there was nothing left for her here. Not with both the Colonel Judge and Miss Rebecca dead. Someone else would have to take care of Little Miss. Besides, tomorrow morning, or even this evening, Little Miss would not remember who Jenny was, would not recognize her face even though she had seen it thousands of times over the last few years, hour after hour, day after day.

Jenny adjusted her tignon, tucking the loose strands of her hair underneath the kerchief, and glanced out the window. Far away, past the haze of smoke lingering over the cane fields, she could see the sharecroppers' homes. She could see men on horseback riding up to Tee Ray's cabin. It was not even dark, and already they were gathering.

Jenny stared at the figures, miles away in the distance. They were dismounting. They were milling about. They were talking. They were climbing back up on their horses. They were starting to ride. They headed east down the long dirt path from Tee Ray's and the other sharecroppers' cabins toward the Mississippi River, and once they reached the river road, they split into two groups. One group headed south, toward Little Jerusalem and, beyond that, Lamou. The other group was riding north, toward the Cottoncrest big house.

Jenny knew they would come looking for the fine bourbon that the Colonel Judge had kept. They would drink their fill and steal the rest. Then they'd probably head back south, toward Little Jerusalem. Jenny was glad she had sent Marcus ahead to warn Nimrod and the others.

The horsemen headed her way were picking up speed. The wind shifted, and the smoke from the burning fields blocked her view of the riders.

There was no time left. Jenny cinched the blanket, into which she had rolled the few things she was bringing, firmly into the small of her back and over her hips with her belt. It held only a blouse, a skirt, and her hairpins. She put on her cloak and shut the door of her room behind her for the last time and ran down the three flights of servants' quarters stairs and out into the back.

Sally, in her cabin, was waiting for her, wearing a thin jacket over the only sweater she owned, a bundle already tied on her back.

The two women, one young, one old, walked hand and hand up the road to the north. They walked away from Cottoncrest, not looking back. There was nothing back there that they wanted to see.

Chapter 36

Marcus raised his arm toward the northern horizon, in the direction of Cottoncrest. Jake, the bearskin over his shoulders, looked up and saw what Marcus was pointing at. It was worse than either of them had feared, and it had come faster than they thought.

Jake and Marcus were standing on the porch of Cooper and Rossy's cabin, and they could see horsemen, ten or more, riding their way at a fast gallop. They were riding along a high ridge next to the Mississippi River. The fast-moving images below the darkening sky were silhouetted against a reddish glow. The horsemen were rounding a large bend in the river to the north of Little Jerusalem. Behind them there was a curtain of spiraling flames and smoke rising from the burning cane fields. The vast Cottoncrest cane fields came within a mile of Little Jerusalem. The riders would be here, at this rate, in less than fifteen minutes.

"Got no time to lose, Mr. Jake," Marcus said, a trace of panic in his deep voice. "ROSSY," he yelled, "COOPER. GET OUT NOW. GET ALL THE OTHERS. THE KNIGHTS ARE COMING!!"

Rossy emerged from the cabin, still in the process of wrapping her daughter in a blanket. The temperature was falling. It was going to be a cold night. She started toward the woods. The inhabitants of Little Jerusalem, hearing Marcus's frantic voice, ran out of their homes and, holding children by the hand, followed Rossy. They moved quickly and quietly through the muddy yards seeking the safety of the woods.

Marcus looked around, doing a quick head count. Two were missing. Marcus ran toward Nimrod's cabin and pounded on the door. "ESAU. NIMROD. YOU'VE GOT TO LEAVE RIGHT AWAY!"

Nimrod came to the door and started toward the woods, but his pace was halting. Esau tried to hurry Nimrod, but the old man was stiff and in pain, and try as he might, he could not walk as quickly as Esau wanted. Cooper, halfway to the woods, looked over his shoulder and, spotting Esau's efforts, urged Rossy, who was clinging to their child, to go on ahead.

"It's hurryin' time, Nimrod," Cooper said, running back to the old man and his son. "We can't leave you behind. You're gonna travel in style, like some fancy person. I heard that in the olden days, them Egyptian pharaohs what enslaved the Israelites had people carry them everyplace they went. Four men or more would haul them in some type of contraption, walkin' all the way, so that ol' Pharaoh's feet never touched the soil. Well, consider yourself tonight an Egyptian pharaoh, 'cept without the contraption."

With that Cooper, his big muscles flexing, picked up the old man as easily as a baby and, cradling him in his arms, started at a slow, loping pace to catch up with Rossy, who already had disappeared into the woods.

"What about y'all?" Esau asked Marcus and Jake.

"We're going to stand and fight," Jake said, pulling out the ten-inch Freimer blade. "I'm not afraid. I've run enough in my life. Halfway across Russia. Halfway across a continent. I don't want to run anymore."

"Mr. Jake . . . ," Marcus said, clearing his throat.

"That's all right, Marcus. You go. You save yourself."

"You don't understand, Mr. Jake. They got them long rifles. They'll shoot you down from a hundred yards off, and you won't do no one no good. Not yourself and not the ones in Little Jerusalem and the ones you want to see. We got to do something else. We're gonna start up the road to the north, you and me."

Turning to Esau, Marcus explained, "If the Knights get here and find everyone gone, they'll head for the woods, and none of you will be safe, for they'll catch you before you reach the safety of the marsh, but if they see us first, then . . ."

Marcus didn't have to say anything else. Jake understood what Marcus was doing. The riders, if they caught anyone from Little Jerusalem, might whip them or kill them. The only way to save Little Jerusalem was to have the riders follow him and Marcus, and to do that, they'd have to head directly toward the horsemen.

Esau nodded. He understood that Marcus and Jake were going to risk their lives to save everyone in Little Jerusalem. "We'll be at Keith and Peggy's. No horse can make it through the marsh to their house, and no one knows where they live except us. We'll be all right. I just hope that Keith and Peggy don't have a fit when they see all of us coming. You know how they keep to themselves and hate any visitors, much less crowds."

Esau turned toward the woods. Once he had disappeared behind the trees, Marcus and Jake walked quickly to the road and turned north, toward the riders. The horsemen, as they came around the bend in the river in a few minutes, would spot them.

Chapter 37

As he urged his horse on, Bucky's hair flew in all directions. His hat had been blown off by the combination of fast gallop and the strong winds that continued to whip at the flames in the sugarcane fields, but Bucky was not about to pause to retrieve it. Bucky rode with abandon, digging his spurs into the horseflesh.

Bucky was right behind Tee Ray, who was riding a gray roan mare. The two of them were thirty yards ahead of the rest of the group. Bucky was glad that Jimmy Joe and Forrest had led one group of the Knights up to Cottoncrest to pick up "provisions." This way, Bucky would be right with Tee Ray and the lead Knights as they pursued the peddler. The Knights hadn't ridden in years, but now they were riding again, and Bucky was with them. He was not a Knight, but Bucky knew that when they finished, they would make him one.

Bucky was sure that by the time Jimmy Joe and Forrest and their crew had caught up with them, Bucky and Tee Ray would already have the peddler in hand. Bucky had a set of handcuffs latched on his belt, and he had an extra length of rope in his saddlebag. When they caught the peddler, he was going to be ready.

Bucky had it all planned out. He would leap off his horse, gun drawn, and confront the villain. "I arrest you," he would say, in a loud, clear voice, letting Tee Ray and all the rest know he was fearless, "for the cold-blooded, heartless murder of Colonel Judge Augustine Chastaine and Rebecca Chastaine. I arrest you," he would declare, louder still, "in the name of the law and all that is righteous and holy in Petit Rouge Parish."

Bucky knew that, at the sound of his voice, the peddler would lose all hope. The peddler would cower. Bucky would point his gun at the quaking peddler and hold out his handcuffs. "Put these on," Bucky would snarl, "you miserable, godless heathen." The peddler would drop to his knees and beg forgiveness, but Bucky's face would show no emotion, and his heart would be stone. "Put these on and rise to your feet," Bucky would declare. "You shall be well tried and convicted, and then you shall hang, and we shall all be witness. Verily." The *verily* would be a nice touch, Bucky thought. He would say it sternly, like those fancy actors on the steamboats. It would add a sense of drama to the event and make it memorable. Bucky knew that when he had finished with his speech, the peddler would be reduced to helpless tears, and the others, especially Tee Ray, would not help but be impressed.

Then, after the peddler had put on the handcuffs and Bucky had made sure that they were snug, Bucky would slide his rope around the peddler's waist and through the handcuffs so that the peddler could not escape, and then Bucky would tie the rope to his saddle horn and triumphantly lead the riders back to the courthouse in Parteblanc, the peddler jogging behind, trying not to fall so as to be dragged by the rope. There Raifer would book the peddler into jail, and Bucky would go to the bar to tell the waiting crowds how he and he alone had made the arrest.

Then they would respect him. Then they would know that Bucky was meant for great things.

"UP AHEAD," yelled Tee Ray.

Bucky was startled. He had been so deep in thought his gaze had wandered out over the river and not on the road. There, a mile ahead of them, running north up the river road alongside the burning cane fields, were two men on foot. One black, in a short coat. One white, in a long fur coat.

"IT'S NIGGER MARCUS AND THE JEW NIGGER LOVER!" Tee Ray screamed. He whipped his horse and rushed down the ridge toward the road.

Bucky and the others whooped and urged their horses on, following Tee Ray's lead, racing toward the two retreating figures.

Chapter 38

"NOW," yelled Marcus with urgency, as the Knights came down the ridge, whipping their horses into a frenzied gallop.

Marcus and Jake turned due west, away from the river, and ran at full speed, toward the smoke and flames, into the cane fields.

The sugarcane, with stalks as thick as heavy clubs, was densely packed. Moving through the field was difficult. The sugarcane formed a forest of unyielding plants in row after wide row. The leafy tops towered a foot or more above their heads, and the sticky stalks clung to their clothing. Shoots had sprouted up between the rows, and Marcus and Jake had to push their way through the bamboo-like foliage.

The smoke hung over their heads in spots; in others it enveloped them in a choking cloud. Marcus pulled out a handkerchief and covered his nose and mouth, and Jake followed suit.

Deeper and deeper they plunged into the field. The rain had made the soft delta dirt a sea of mud, but still the fire blazed on. They could hear the pounding of horses' hooves behind them, and ahead they heard the crackling of the fire. Marcus and Jake could feel the heat as one long sugarcane leaf after another was burned away, leaving only charred but intact stalks.

Marcus moved with remarkable speed across and through the high furrows, sliding on the mud, pushing aside a stiff curtain of plants here, ducking low there to avoid the roiling smoke. Jake stayed close behind him.

The sweet smell of burning cane foliage was everywhere, mixed in with the acrid smoke. The leaves were sharp and could cut you if you were not careful. The ashes fell around them, and embers drifted down like a storm of red snow, stinging whenever they found skin. The smoke penetrated their handkerchiefs and filled their lungs. Their mouths were dry. Their throats ached.

Still they pressed onward. As they wove their way through the field, sometimes Marcus would step to one side to let a large snake slither by. Jake could hear the scurrying of panicked mice and rats trying to outrun the fire destroying their homes. Occasionally, two or three rodents would dart across Jake's path and sometimes across his boots.

Farther and farther they pushed into the field. Now the smoke was so dense they could hardly see. Marcus bent low and kept moving, sometimes on his hands and knees in the mud, but always moving. Jake had tied the bearskin that Rossy had given him around his neck like a cloak, but now it was dragging in the mud. Nothing to do about that now. He pushed it onto his back and crawled along behind Marcus. Their pants were soaked and heavy, now coated with the wet alluvial soil, but as long as they stayed low near the furrows, the smoke was not that bad. The leaves were near the top of the plants, and that was where the flames were concentrated. Only when a downdraft hit, or when the wind shifted, did the smoke curl along the dirt, rolling toward them in thick billows, only to swoop up and away again, leaving them coughing and spitting up black phlegm.

"DAMN!!" Tee Ray exclaimed, his horse rearing on the muddy road. The gray roan was not about to enter the burning fields. Its nostrils were distended in fear, and no amount of beating from Tee Ray's whip or prodding from his sharp spurs would compel the horse forward. Again and again, Tee Ray flayed the roan's haunches, drawing blood, and the horse reared high into the air in anguish and distress. Tee Ray simply yanked the reins harder and, beating the horse over the head with the whip, forced it back down.

The wind shifted. The smoke and embers now swirled around all the riders. Bucky raised his hands to his face to wipe his stinging eyes, and the moment his horse felt the reins go slack, it reared up. Bucky slid backward in his saddle, dropping the reins completely and grasping for the saddle horn. The reins fell to the ground. The horse, frantically pawing the earth, started bucking.

Bucky was bounced out of the saddle and came down hard upon it again. He groaned with anguish as his groin crushed down on the stiff leather. The horse reared again, and when it came back down, it lowered its head. Bucky, who had been hanging on to the saddle horn, now slid clear over it, over the horse's mane, and onto the ground, tangling in the reins. As Bucky fell over the horse's head, it reared up one more time, and now the reins looped themselves around Bucky's neck and arms. The horse's hooves came perilously close to Bucky's head, and Bucky tried to move away, but this only caused the reins to wrap around him more firmly. Feeling the reins entangled, the horse furiously flung its head up and down, trying to free itself, and started backing up, dragging Bucky along while the reins formed a leather noose that tightened around Bucky's neck. Bucky couldn't get his arms free. The horse was now in full terror mode, and it tried to jerk free, all the while backing up with increasing speed. Bucky's face was turning blue as he was dragged through the mud.

Tee Ray jumped off his horse. With his right hand he reached into his waistband and pulled out a short, rusty knife and, sawing at the reins, finally cut them. At the same time, with his left hand he roughly grabbed the bridle of Bucky's horse, holding on with an unyielding grip until the horse quieted down.

Bucky lay there in the ruts in the road, still entangled in the cut reins, gasping for breath.

Tee Ray shook his head in disgust at the sight. "Bucky, I'm gonna glue your seat to that damn saddle if you can't stay on it."

Bucky slowly unwound the reins from his neck and arms and stood up. Mud from the road coated his already dirty outfit and matted down his hair. Thick gobs of it dripped off the knees of his pants and clung to his boots. "Thanks, Tee Ray, it was just . . ."

Tee Ray didn't even bother to listen. He swung his foot in the stirrup and climbed back up on his horse, considering the situation. The other eight Knights, high in their saddles, gathered around him, their horses obedient now that the wind had shifted yet again and the smoke around them had cleared.

"This is what we're gonna do," Tee Ray announced. "Ain't no way that we can ride into that burning field, and followin' them on foot is just plain foolish. They could be anywhere in there. "Morgan," he said, pointing to one of the Knights, "you ride up this road toward Cottoncrest. When you spot Jimmy Joe and Forrest, tell them what happened.

Y'all divide into three groups. One group needs to ride each cane break, one needs to go to the back of the cultivations—back where we first set the fires—and patrol there, and the third needs to head back down this way. They can't stay in those fields all night; the smoke will get to them and force them out. You know, I think Marcus was going to try to sneak the Jew Peddler back to Cottoncrest to pick up his things and all them Jew knives. Well, they don't know that Raifer's got his whole chest of stuff and has taken it back to Parteblanc as evidence, but even so, they sure as hell now ain't gonna go to Cottoncrest, not with us out here. So, where can they go? They gotta go south. That leaves Little Jerusalem. And after that, Lamou."

A nasty grin crawled across Tee Ray's face. "Come on, boys, we're gonna have some fun in Little Jerusalem. Gonna whip up on some niggers tonight."

Chapter 39

"I don't know how you did it. I been scared ever since it happened. When we found the Colonel Judge and Miss Rebecca, my skin was crawlin' like crawfish dumped in a boilin' pot, and my wits were as fidgety as a grasshopper, and yet there you was, calm as calm could be, doin' what had to be done, tellin' me and Marcus and Cubit and Jordan what had to be done. You was right. Everything you said. The things had to be moved right then. We did it. The room had to be rearranged before dawn. We did it. And all the while, you was out there in the middle of the night, traipsing who knows where to get them safe. How you stayed so collected, I don't rightly know."

Sally walked slightly behind Jenny as they moved north along the river road, the soft rush of the Mississippi River in their ears. To the west the sky was red from the setting sun. To the south the sky was red from the fire in the cane fields. But ahead of them the sky was already dark. That was good. It was safer for them in the dark.

"It was you that stayed so collected when all this started, Sally. If it hadn't been for you, Rebecca would have been dead long before. Yet there you were, calmly telling all of us what to do."

Sally brushed off the compliment. "That's nothin', nothin' at all. Weren't anythin' I hadn't done lots and lots of time before. But you? No one has ever done somethin' like that."

"When you come right down to it, neither one of us had a choice." Jenny readjusted her cloak as the temperature continued to drop. "We both did what had to be done because not to do it would have been worse."

"Well, when I do what I usually do, I just get myself started and follow on through. But the other night I had the conniptions. My stomach was all tight like. And ain't none of us got no sleep, but at least we had things to do. Unlike you, at least we could stay in and around the big house, haulin' the stuff down the back stairs and breakin' it up and buryin' it, like you said. Ain't none of that won't ever be found. But you was up all night and gots to have traveled miles and miles before you got back. Must've half-run on your way back, from the looks of you. Yet, you got cleaned up so quick and seemed so calm that by the time Mr. Raifer and Mr. Bucky came out, you looked like you hadn't gone any farther than from Little Miss's room. 'Course, I don't want you to tell me where you went. Don't ever want to know that."

"No, you don't. That's the only way you and Marcus will be safe. What you never know you can't reveal."

"Lord, I was worried that if Marcus talked any longer to Mr. Raifer, he was goin' let somethin' about them slip for sure. You were right that we all gots to leave. It's for our own safety. And for their safety as well."

Chapter 40

"Hell, Tee Ray, there ain't no one here and ain't no one been here for a long time. Don't know how these niggers live—don't got hardly nothin' in their cabins. Nothin' worth takin' anyways."

Jimmy Joe, his sandy hair blowing in the gusty wind, stalked out of Cooper and Rossy's cabin, a half-empty bottle of the Colonel Judge's bourbon in his hand. He paused to take another drink and then passed the bottle up to Forrest, who was sitting high on his horse, his saddlebags bulging with bottles. He knew that there were children who lived in Little Jerusalem, but there weren't no sign of them either. No toys. No blankets. No cribs. Hell, he had it up to here with children anyway, what with Maylene whining all the time about wanting to have kids. And now they had one, and what difference did it make? That kid was whining all the time, just like Maylene. It was like they was related. Sometimes he wished that the baby and Maylene both would just go away.

"Just like Cottoncrest, Tee Ray," Forrest said, wiping his beard on his sleeve after taking a swig and passing the bottle on to the next rider. "The niggers done flee'd. What did we tell you. Ain't no one was at Cottoncrest when we got there 'cept Little Miss, and she was just kind of dozin' in her chair in her room. None of them darkies around at all. They all had left the big house and are now prob'ly doin' whatever darkies do when they think ain't no one watchin'. So, we just 'freed' these here bourbon and whiskey bottles that the Colonel Judge ain't got no more use for, just like you asked us to."

Tee Ray rode his gray roan slowly around Little Jerusalem. The other men remained on their horses and waited for him to finish, not daring to do anything until he gave the instructions. To pass the time, they passed the bottle among themselves, each taking a sip and handing it to the next one.

The bottle finally reached Bucky, who brought it to his lips and, tilting it up too far, overfilled his mouth. The bourbon spilled out over the corners of his lips. Bucky tried to swallow quickly to keep the rest in, but it was too much. He began to choke, and the rest spewed out of his mouth. The other riders backed their horses quickly out of the way to keep from getting sprayed.

"Can't keep your seat in the saddle, and can't keep your liquor in your mouth, Bucky," Jimmy Joe said with disgust. "Tell you what, you just stay on your horse far from me 'cause I got no interest in seeing what you can't keep in your pants."

Forrest and the others laughed loudly.

Too loudly, Bucky thought. He'd still show them. They'd learn to respect him.

Tee Ray, hearing the laughter, came riding up, holding his old rifle. He wished he had taken his other pistol as well, but now it was too late. "Shut your gaps and stop callyhotting! Are you so liquored up from elbow crookin' that you can't see what's goin' on?"

"Them darkies are long gone, Tee Ray. We can see that."

"Jimmy Joe," Tee Ray shot angrily back at the huge, sandy-haired man whose forearms were as big as Tee Ray's thighs, "you don't see nothin'. Look over here."

Tee Ray pointed to the hoes and rakes on the muddy ground. "Ain't no farmer, even a nigger farmer, just leaves their tools on their ground to rust, not with the rain that passed through here. And look at this garden. It was being tended to. Them tools ain't rusty, and they ain't muddy. Jimmy Joe, I know you got muscles, so why don't you use some of them to open your eyes. Come on. What do you see here?"

Jimmy Joe didn't need Tee Ray to be larkin' on him, but he took it anyway. There was plenty of liquor in his saddlebag for later on to forget his problems.

Jimmy Joe squinted hard in the dimming light at the spot on the ground where Tee Ray was pointing. "Mud. Lots of mud, Tee Ray. Deep ruts and stuff filled with water. That's what I see."

Tee Ray, rifle still in hand, jumped off his horse, throwing the reins to Forrest to hold. "Your eyes ain't connected with your brain, Jimmy Joe? What's caused the ruts? Them is the ruts of a cart or a wagon. And them's fresh ruts. So, where's the wagon? And where's what was in the wagon? You said you looked in this cabin?" Tee Ray turned his back on Jimmy Joe and the others and walked into Cooper and Rossy's home.

Jimmy Joe slowly dismounted and, pushing down his anger, followed Tee Ray. Bucky, now seeing his tormentor, Jimmy Joe, brought to earth, dismounted as well. Bucky was not going to miss what else Tee Ray might say to the big man.

Inside the cabin was dark. It smelled of sweat and stench and old grease. The smoke and steam from too many meals had permeated the walls, giving off a slightly rancid odor. And although it smelled just like Tee Ray's own cabin, to Tee Ray it didn't smell the same at all. To Tee Ray, all the smells of Little Jerusalem were the smells of niggers.

Tee Ray lit a match and looked around for a candle. There was none. A forlorn-looking mattress lay on a crude bed frame in the corner. Tee Ray took his knife from his belt and made a long slash though the mattress ticking and, reaching inside, pulled out a handful of dried moss. He threw the mattress on the floor in the center of the room, on top of the loose dirt, and lit the moss that was spilling out. A small fire erupted, throwing off a musty smell but little illumination. Gray smoke curled through the cabin, drifting out the door and spiraling up the chimney.

"See, I told you, Tee Ray. Ain't nothin' here. No food. No candles. Nothin'." Jimmy Joe kicked at the rough-hewn table. A leg broke off, and the table fell to one side and hit the floor with a hollow thud, loose dirt flying.

"I see it, Tee Ray, I see it," Bucky called out excitedly. "Jimmy Joe didn't see it, but I do!"

Jimmy Joe glared at Bucky. "What do you see? Empty cabin. Dirt floor."

"It may be a dirt floor, but look, it ain't all as empty as it seems." Bucky strode over to the fireplace. He ran his hand over the top of the mantel. "Look at what I see'd. No dust. Someone was livin' here, takin' good care of this place."

Jimmy Joe spit, the glob landing next to Bucky's boots. "'Course they was livin' here at some point, but they was takin' good care of what?

Of dirt? What did they eat? Dirt? Not that niggers won't, you know. They'll eat almost anything."

Bucky bent down and, with his own small knife, cut into a corner of the mattress lying in the dirt. He pulled out some moss and, going over to the fireplace, kicked some of the thick ashes to one side and laid the moss down in the center and started blowing on it. After less than a minute the moss began to smolder. Bucky blew several times more, and the moss burst into flames.

"They was here, Jimmy Joe, see? Hot coals. It ain't been that long since they done left. They must've taken that cart, what ruts Tee Ray done found, and moved it out with all their goods into the woods." Bucky was proud. He had shown Jimmy Joe how smart he was, and he knew that Tee Ray couldn't help but be impressed.

Tee Ray motioned to the bed frame and the upside-down table. "When even Bucky can figure this out, Jimmy Joe, why don't we leave the heavy thinkin' to him and the heavy bustin' up to you."

Jimmy Joe nodded, gritting his teeth. He didn't like Tee Ray's tone of voice, but he was good at busting up things, and he felt like doing it now. He lifted up a big foot and brought it crashing down on the bed frame, cracking one of the sides. He lifted up the rough planking that formed the headboard and smashed it against the stout logs that comprised the cabin's walls. Then he broke up the table and tossed it into the fireplace.

Tee Ray, followed by Bucky and Jimmy Joe, emerged from Cooper and Rossy's cabin, the smoldering mattress beginning to die down and the broken table in the fireplace beginning to flame up.

"Don't y'all see?" Tee Ray proclaimed to the horsemen who had gathered outside the cabin. "We rode fast here from the cane fields. Ain't no way that the Jew Peddler Man and that nigger Marcus with him could've beat us. Yet, Little Jerusalem here is empty, and the niggers here can't have left more than an hour ago."

Tee Ray remounted the gray roan. "Someone must have told them that the Knights were ridin' tonight. Well, let 'em flee. Let 'em be scared of us. They got a right to be scared 'cause the Knights ride for right."

"THE KNIGHTS RIDE FOR RIGHT," a chorus of voices echoed back loudly. It was their motto. The Knights of the White Camellia rode for right, for what was right was white, and what was white was right.

The Ku Klux Klan Act was supposed to have put an end to the Klan and masked riders, but the Knights of the White Camellia didn't need masks. Petit Rouge Parish was so small that everyone knew everyone else's horses anyway. A masked rider could be easily identified by his steed. The Knights of the White Camellia rode unmasked and unopposed.

"What we're gonna do is to make an example of whoever warned these niggers," snarled Tee Ray. The horseman yelled their approval.

"When we catch him, we're gonna whip him so hard that even his own mother wouldn't know him to give him shelter in a hurricane." The horsemen roared again. Forrest pulled out another full bottle from his saddlebag, took a drink, and passed it to Tee Ray.

Tee Ray drank deeply and, deliberately bypassing Jimmy Joe, handed the bottle on to Bucky. Jimmy Joe looked away to hide his disgust. Bucky! Ain't no way that Tee Ray was gonna get his hands on the bottles in Jimmy Joe's saddlebag now.

Bucky carefully took a drink and, smiling broadly as it went down his gullet, took another.

"That's the way, Bucky," congratulated Tee Ray. "You're drinkin' like a real man. Now, Bucky, I think you're ready. You want to be a Knight?"

A Knight? Tee Ray was inviting him to be a Knight? In front of all the others. Tee Ray had honored him mightily.

"The Knights ride for right," Bucky replied in as forceful a manner as he could muster, dropping his voice down an octave to try to sound more forceful, like Raifer. "You know, in my official position as an official officer of the law, I'm always for right, Tee Ray." Then he added, a little too hurriedly, with more gratitude than he intended to show, "I'd be right proud to be a Knight and proud to ride for right."

"Proud is the right feelin' to have," said Tee Ray, tapping Bucky on the shoulder with his rifle, " 'cause I so declare that you are now a Knight of the Camellia of the First Order."

A Knight of the First Order! Bucky could barely restrain the grin that kept creeping to his lips. First Order. That was appropriate. Bucky should be first among all the others. After all, hadn't he shown, time and time again, that he was invaluable? Hadn't he shown Tee Ray and the others how he could see things that others couldn't, like a moment ago when he had spotted, as Jimmy Joe kicked over the table, a glow in the ashes caused by the draft? He could figure out things others couldn't. He was important.

Tee Ray didn't tell Bucky that the Knights had thirty-two orders and that the First Order was the lowest rung. "Bucky, since you patrol as official Petite Rouge deputy out here in Little Jerusalem, you know who lives where, right?"

"Right," Bucky said proudly. Already they were depending on him.

"Whose cabin is this?" Tee Ray inquired, pointing his rifle toward the one with the open door and the smoldering mattress.

"That's Cooper's."

"Where's old Nimrod's place?"

Bucky lifted his arm to show them.

"Then, Bucky, as your first order of business as a Member of the First Order of the Knights of Camellia, you're gonna lead us in making an example of old Nimrod and his takin' his people away so that you, an official officer, can't question them about the Jew Peddler murderer. You're gonna show Nimrod and the rest of those niggers they can't mess with the law and they can't mess with the Knights, right?"

"Right," Bucky responded promptly. It had to be an important task for Tee Ray to ask him, instead of any of the others, to do it.

"Come on then," Tee Ray said, urging his roan toward Nimrod's house. "You get to start the fire. Let's burn that nigger Nimrod's cabin to the ground."

Chapter 41

Keith stood, gun in hand, barring the way. He had moved out into the swamp beyond the woods because he and Peggy wanted to be left alone. They wanted to be someplace where they didn't have to talk to anyone but each other. They wanted to be someplace where small children didn't taunt them. About the way that he walked. About the way that he spoke. About the way that Peggy talked.

"NO!" he said, raising up his gun.

"You know me," the old man said, leaning a thick branch that Cooper had found for him to use as a cane. "Nimrod. You recognize me, don't you, Keith?"

Keith peered hard at the old man's face. "Yes." Keith spoke slowly. Deliberately. He was always that way, as if thinking about what to say and then speaking it was difficult for him. Which it was.

"And you know Esau and Cooper and Rossy and the rest of us, don't you?"

Keith looked slowly from face to face. ". . . Yes."

"There are bad times right now, Keith. The Knights are riding, and we've had to leave Little Jerusalem." Nimrod waited patiently as Keith tried to absorb the old man's words.

After a lengthy silence Nimrod added, "I know you don't like company, but with the Knights out tonight, we need a place to stay for a bit. If we had more warning, we wouldn't have come here . . . we don't want to bother you and Peggy. It appears that the storm passed, so we'll just stay here outside. And we've brought some food to share, so we won't trouble the two of you."

This was a lot of information at once, and Keith's forehead knotted up. "Trouble," he finally said.

"No," Nimrod responded gently, putting his hand on the young man's arm, "we won't be no trouble."

"Trouble!" Keith shot back. "Trouble, trouble, trouble."

Rossy, her baby on her shoulder, walked forward through the crowd to talk to Keith. "Keith, we grew up together. I promise you . . ."

Keith got a frightened look as he stared at her baby. "Baby. Trouble. Much trouble!" He backed up several steps, limping on his clubfoot.

Rossy was gentle. "What trouble, Keith? How can a baby cause you trouble?"

Keith glanced back anxiously toward his cabin perched on stilts next to the bayou, its windows dark. Even though the sun had set, there was a three-quarters moon rising, visible for now, although shortly it would be obscured by the swift-moving clouds. The wind in the treetops created a low, constant whisper, but as she listened carefully, Rossy could hear, in addition to this, a low moan.

"Is that Peggy? Is she all right?"

A look of anguish overtook Keith's face. "Baby. Trouble. Peggy."

Rossy grasped her child tightly to her shoulder and ran toward the cabin, pushing the door open. Even the clear moonlight could not penetrate the darkness. All Rossy could see was a dark shape on the floor, moaning with unending grief. "Shwadelivbyanj." Over and over a woman's voice wailed, "Shwadelivbyanj."

Above her own anguished voice, Peggy, who was kneeling on the floor, an inert object in the small blanket in front of her, heard the door open and sensed a presence at the threshold. Peggy looked up to see a woman whose features she could not discern standing in the doorway, moonlight streaming behind her. The moon made the woman's outline luminous, and the dust floating through the cabin made the few silvery-blue moonbeams hitting the floor look just like the rays from Mary and Jesus's head on the painting that Peggy used to stare at when she was a little girl in church. Peggy looked up and asked with desperate hope, "Aryuananj?"

"Peggy, it's just me, Rossy." Rossy came into the cabin and went over to Peggy. Clutching her baby in the darkness, Rossy reached out to put one hand on Peggy's shoulder. Just then Rossy's baby woke up and started to gurgle softly.

"Baby? Baby?" Peggy grasped Rossy's knees and started to cry. "Yuhavbrunmenewbaby?"

Chapter 42

Marcus cautiously pushed aside several charred stalks and peered down a trench that ran between the rows of cane. No one was in sight. He listened closely. No noise of horses. Just the crackling of the flames in the field as it swept away behind them and the crinkling of the fire in the uppermost leaves of the trees in the woods ahead of them.

The cane field fire had spread. Although the recent rain had dampened everything, the few crisp dead leaves that had clung on grimly to the high branches were aflame and were drying out the nearby branches, which in turn were smoldering. The top branches of the hardwoods in the distance were a flurry of sparks. The wind stoked the fires and blew flaming leaves from tree to tree, where they ignited others.

"This is not good, not good at all," Marcus whispered. "Gonna drive out the game. Gonna drive out the birds. Gonna make it all the harder in the spring for those who won't or can't go. On the other hand, it's good for us right now."

He motioned for Jake to stay where he was and, remarkably fast for an old man, skittered across the break to the woods on the other side. There he waited behind the trunk of a large hickory. The moonlight illuminated the break, and Marcus, from his hiding place, could now see down the entire length of the gap between the woods and the sugarcane field. Nothing moved in the cleared area, which, for all its width, still had not been wide enough to keep the fire from leaping it.

Marcus signaled for Jake to join him. With the damp, muddy bearskin in his arms, Jake swiftly left the burned sugarcane behind him and entered the safety of the dark woods.

Jake followed Marcus as the old man sure-footedly threaded his way amid the hickory and bay trees, the wet earth squishing under their boots. Jake followed as they walked deeper and deeper into the forest, past the oaks and the scattered mimosa. The ground grew even softer, and now they were often walking ankle deep in water, which penetrated and then filled their leather boots.

Still Marcus pushed on, through stands of gray and brown cypress, their gnarled trunks firmly planted in the swamp. Cypress knees, offshoots of the main trunk, stuck up through the mud and water, evidence of the shallow, spreading roots below that held these ancient trees in place in the heavy clay soil.

They made their way through the swamp without speaking. Although there was no visible path, Marcus did not hesitate. He knew these woods and swamps. He knew each gum and hickory and the drier spots that they signaled. He knew the area where lightning had brought down a huge oak, years ago, now lying like a giant soldier frozen at stiff-backed attention and chopped off at the knee. He knew the stands of palmettos, looking like huge green versions of the elaborate Chinese fans that the Colonel Judge had bought at the Cotton Exposition years ago, long before he married Miss Rebecca. Little Miss used to sit on the veranda in the summer and slowly wave one back and forth to create a little breeze in the hot evenings.

Marcus even knew the areas thick with poison ivy and poison sumac, which they warily skirted. But after they passed yet another heavy growth of them, Marcus stopped on what appeared to be a narrow ridge in the midst of the swamp. The ground was firm. The poison oak and poison sumac, thickly curling around the trunks of trees and reaching up twenty feet or more into their branches, formed almost a veil from the rest of the marsh.

"You can't go back to the road, you know."

Jake nodded.

"They'll be lookin' for you there. But they can't ride no horses into these swamps. You stay in them, you understand?"

Jake nodded his head. He understood all too well. Marcus had put his own life in danger to warn Little Jerusalem. He had helped save Jake as well, but now that the riders had seen Marcus with Jake, Marcus was a marked man, just as he was.

"I got to go my way, and that ain't the way you're goin'. I got to meet up with Sally and Jenny. It's gonna be after midnight 'fore I get to them. But you can't go my way. Ain't no white man can do that. Ain't allowed."

Jake leaned back against a thick tree. The sky was already black, and the stars were twinkling through the overhead branches. "I'll be all right."

Jake had escaped before. Then it was on the train, in that narrow, confined space. Hiding, always hiding, not daring to breathe. He was prepared to fight, but Marcus was right. If he wanted to see them, he would have to escape again, and here he had the whole breadth of the swamp.

The thick veil of poison oak and sumac was like the trees' wardrobe, a vast emerald and olive skirt. He had hidden under women's skirts on the train. Now he was hiding under God's skirts. He would make it to New Orleans, just like he had made it out of Russia.

New Orleans. That reminded him. "You won't forget to tell Jenny about meeting me in the Lafayette Cemetery in New Orleans, will you? It's important."

"I don't forget nothin', Mr. Jake, you know that. Tell her, I will, before the sun rises. But tonight you can't do nothin' 'bout nothin', so you ought to bed down right here. Good thing that Rossy gave you that bearskin. It'll keep you warm, damp or not. Just roll up in it 'gainst this tree, and you'll be all right. Shouldn't be no bears out this late in the season, but I wouldn't sleep too soundly if I was you. Keep your ears and eyes open, and in the mornin' you'll be able to see your way and get to Lamou."

"Just stay south, you said."

"Stay south. We're already long past Little Jerusalem, and you don't want to wander in any other direction. It won't be safe for you, a white man in these woods, until you get near Lamou. South is the only way for you. But believe me, long before you get to Lamou, the folks in Lamou will know you're there. A deer ain't as skittish as them about strangers in the swamp. Them folks in Lamou can read the signs— from the wood ducks' flights to the calls of the geese to the absence of muskrat 'cause it was gettin' out of the way of something unusual— better than you can read a book. They'll find you, even if you're miles away. So, meanwhile, until morning just sit still and enjoy the quiet of the swamp."

The train had been noisy. Constant noise. Constant movement. Marcus was right. Jake would enjoy the quiet of the swamp, at least for one night. He unrolled the bearskin and draped it around his shoulders. He double-checked to see that the Freimer blade that Rossy had given back to him was firmly in his belt, in easy reach.

Leaning back against the tree, Jake murmured, half to himself, "Tonight I'll be *a ganster porits*."

"A what?"

"A whole man of leisure, Marcus."

Marcus shook his head in disbelief. Here Mr. Jake was, being left alone in the woods, and he was thinking of himself as a man of leisure. Then he paused and smiled. "That's a joke, isn't it?"

"*Miten malach hamovess treibt nit kain katovess.* You can't joke with the Angel of Death."

Marcus reached down. The old man's black gnarled fingers encircled Jake's callused white hand and shook it with emotion. The Angel of Death was seeking them both.

Chapter 43

Cooper unwrapped the blanket on the ground. The infant was dead. She looked to be about six months old, a little younger than his and Rossy's daughter.

Cooper had carried the child out of Keith's cabin with Peggy wailing and moaning and leaning on Keith's arm. Tears dampened Keith's cheeks, but he did not have the words to express his emotions.

Nimrod and Rossy gathered around Keith and Peggy, while Esau kept back the rest of the twenty men, women, and children who had trekked into the swamp from Little Jerusalem. One of the young girls standing at the rear of the group was tending to Rossy's baby.

In the moonlight, lying on her blanket, Peggy's child seemed at peace. She had a thick head of curly black hair, and her brown café au lait skin was smooth and perfect. Her little mouth was open, and but for her blue lips and glassy stare, you might have thought that she was in a restful sleep.

"Shwadelivbyanj" Peggy repeated, between sobs.

"An angel," Keith agreed.

Rossy hugged Peggy, who collapsed into her arms. "An angel brought her, Peggy?"

"Ananj," Peggy wailed.

"Angel. Delivered by Angel," Keith said slowly, trying to explain.

Rossy look quizzically at Cooper. They didn't know any midwife named Angel. When a midwife was needed, the folks in Little Jerusalem usually sent word to Cottoncrest, and Sally would come and do the tending and delivery. Who was Angel?

Rossy hadn't even known that Peggy was pregnant. Of course, no one in Little Jerusalem had seen Peggy since she and Keith had moved out of Little Jerusalem and into the swamp more than two years ago. Keith would limp in for supplies, bringing fish and game to trade, but Peggy never came with him.

Rossy's heart went out to Peggy. To lose a child so young, so beautiful.

"Cooper," Rossy said softly, still holding the weeping Peggy in her arms as Keith rocked back and forth on his heels, his arms clasped in silent prayer, "you got to help Keith here give this little girl a proper burial. Nimrod, I know you knows the right words."

Cooper carefully rewrapped the tiny body into the blanket. He went over to the side of Keith's cabin, found the shovel, and, taking Keith by the arm, asked him where he wanted the grave to be dug. Keith pointed to a spot under a large mimosa next to the bayou. "Pink. Summer. Beauty."

Cooper patted Keith on the back. He understood. When the summer came, the mimosa would bloom its feathery pink blossoms so light and delicate that a spider weaving a starburst out of the dew of the first light could not have created something as beautiful. Keith wanted his daughter buried under the mimosa, where beauty would surround her. "I'll dig a grave worthy of her," Cooper said, his powerful arms already pushing the shovel through the layer of leaves that lined the bank and into the soft, dark earth.

Cooper dug quickly, and Keith stood nearby, watching. It did not take Cooper long to excavate a small trench, a few feet long and four and a half feet deep—deep enough so that when the bayou rose, the body would not wash to the surface.

Nimrod was now escorting Peggy over to the graveside, and Rossy bent down to pick up the baby Cooper had wrapped in a blanket. As she gently cradled the dead child and walked toward the grave, Rossy was amazed by the touch of the blanket. It was dark now under the trees, and she couldn't see the blanket clearly, but it felt so smooth. This was not homespun cotton. It was like the finest store-bought linens or like some of the best fabrics that the Peddler Man carried. Rossy didn't know that Peggy and Keith owned anything like this.

Cooper was standing in the grave. He reached up and took the dead child in his arms and tightly tucked the blanket in firmly so that it formed a shroud. Then he placed the baby in the bottom of the grave, arranged some stones over the body to keep it from floating up in high water, and paused for Nimrod to speak.

Nimrod leaned on his cane. Although his legs were weak, his voice was still powerful. "The Lord sent Joseph into Egypt, and when Pharaoh had a dream, Joseph he done interpreted it. Seven fat cows and seven thin cows. Joseph, he knew that meant seven good years and seven bad years, and the people could plan for the bad years by savin' up during the good'uns. Lord, we would be grateful to know when our good years will be. It seems as if we all is havin' seven times seven bad years. But your glory and grace is all-powerful, and you have taken this child to you where she'll have nothin' but goodness for now on, for she was goodness to her mother, and goodness to her father, and goodness seven times over."

When Nimrod mentioned "mother" and "father," Peggy began to wail again. Her piercing cry rose from her heart and extended to the tops of the trees. Keith hugged her tightly.

Over her sad refrain Nimrod continued. "Lord, have mercy on the soul of this child and have mercy on her parents and have mercy on all of us. Jesus and Mary, we ask you to bring comfort to those who know no comfort and healing to those whose hearts is broken. Amen."

The crowd murmured, "Amen," and Cooper silently but swiftly began to shovel dirt into the grave, quickly filling it up.

Peggy's sobbing had begun to subside, but when Cooper finished piling the dirt and patting down the mound on top of the grave, she flung herself out of Keith's arms. She fell to the ground and, hugging the soil, cried out.

"Ainnoanjgwendelivmenomobaby." She repeated the word three times.

Rossy looked sadly at Keith. He was the only one who seemed to understand her. Keith simply stood over Peggy, running his hand through her hair. "Yes," he said slowly, more to himself than to anyone else.

And then, to Rossy's astonishment, Keith said more words at one time than Rossy had heard him say since they were children. "Ain't no angel goin' deliver us any more babies."

Chapter 44

They had drunk all the liquor in Forrest's saddlebags and were ready for more. The Knights were in the Parteblanc bar, laughing and carousing louder than ever. All of them. All of them, that is, except Jimmy Joe, who had ridden out of Little Jerusalem in a huff, not speaking to anyone.

They had gotten so loud that Raifer had been awakened and summoned to make sure things did not get any more out of control than they already were.

Raifer entered the bar and stood to one side, observing, sizing up the crowd and the situation. The men did not notice him or pay the slightest bit of attention. Their focus was on Bucky.

Bucky, his back to the door, was on the top of a table, a bottle in his hand, entertaining a crowd that let out earsplitting whoops at his antics.

"So, I takes this here torch, a torch we done made out of Nimrod's own mattress stuck on his own hoe, and I tried to light the wattle in the walls. But you know what, them darkies' walls was soaked from the rain, and the moss in the wattle wouldn't light, and the wood wouldn't catch. But did that stop me? No."

The Knights egged him on to tell them. "What did you do? How did you do it?" They wanted to hear what he had to say, although all of them had been there with him.

"So, I directed Forrest to take his knife and score the wood in the walls."

The men pointed at Forrest, asleep in his chair, liquored up and limp. They laughed loudly. They would tell Forrest tomorrow how Bucky had claimed he had "directed" Forrest to do anything.

"But Forrest's ol' knife was so dull, it weren't worth as much as a brevet horse to an officer leading a cavalry charge."

The Knights chuckled at the idea of the cavalry being led into battle by someone on a mule.

Bucky continued on. They were being entertained by him, and he wasn't going to let them down. They would all applaud when he was done. He just knew it.

"So," Bucky said, pausing for effect, "I done pulled it out."

"You go ahead and pull it out," Tee Ray yelled back, "pull it out now."

The others whooped, to Bucky's satisfaction, "Pull it out. Pull it out."

With a dramatic flourish Bucky reached inside his filthy shirt and looked around, squinting at the Knights with what he thought was a menacing look. Then he slowly withdrew his arm. Grasped in his dirty hand was a wicked-looking blade.

"Yep. I pulled out this here Jew knife, like the one that done killed the Colonel Judge, and it cut through them log walls like they was made of nothin' more 'stantial than grits. And I flayed that wood and done spent a whole half a bottle of the Colonel Judge's fine rum to make sure it would light good, and before you knew it, that whole darky's cabin was blazin' away."

The Knights didn't applaud.

Instead, individuals hooted out, "Let me see that."

And "Pass 'round that Jew knife."

And "Bucky, let us see how sharp it is."

And "Are you sure you didn't cut somethin' off while keeping that knife in your pants?"

The loud taunting had stirred Forrest. Without lifting his head or taking his beard off his chest, he merely opened one eye and grunted in a deep voice that cut through the commotion, "Cuttin' somethin' off in Bucky's pants? Hell, who would know the difference anyway."

Now they applauded. Now the men laughed. Tee Ray's laugh was loudest of all.

Bucky was angered. How dare they make fun of him! He bent his knees. Crouching in a manner he imagined Indians might have used stalking their prey and grasping the knife more tightly than ever, he sliced the air in what he thought was a vicious manner. "You want to see this?" He slowly turned around, glaring at the Knights from atop the table. "See this here blade? I'll stick it deep in the ribs of the next one of you who . . ."

Forrest, who had roused himself and moved faster than one would have thought possible for a big man, much less one who had drunk as much as he had, snuck up on Bucky. Grabbing him from behind, he held Bucky in his big grasp. Bucky's feet desperately searched for the tabletop as he was hoisted high in the air. Forrest, holding Bucky over his head as easily as if he had been a baby, spun around and around, faster and faster.

Bucky began to get queasy. The ceiling was spinning above him, and his stomach was churning. He could feel the bile flowing. A bitter, thick liquid gurgled up his gullet.

"He's gonna blow, Forrest," warned Tee Ray, reaching up and grabbing the knife from the deputy's hand as the color began to drain from Bucky's face.

Forrest twirled his way to the open door and tossed Bucky onto the rough-planked porch. Bucky hit hard on his back. He groaned and rolled over. Yellow vomit with a bilious smell spewed over his shirt and the porch and dripped through the slats toward the ground below.

Inside, Tee Ray was showing off the knife. He leaped behind the bar, and the bartender rapidly moved away. Tee Ray carved a large X on the surface of the bar, showing the others how deep the gash was and how easily it was made. He borrowed the hat of one of the Knights and sliced a narrow piece off the brim, leaving a cut so clean and straight it looked as if the hatmaker had designed it that way.

Tee Ray was about to demonstrate another wonder of the knife when Raifer walked up and joined him behind the bar that separated the two of them from the rest of the group. In a quiet but firm voice Raifer said, "I'll take that Tee Ray."

Tee Ray glared with fury. No one interrupted him. No one challenged him in front of the Knights. The others grew silent. The room became still.

Tee Ray, his jaw set, his teeth grinding in anger, took the knife and flicked a button on Raifer's shirt. It was just the slightest touch, but the excellent blade cut the button off, and it fell to the floor. Raifer didn't flinch. With a calm, determined manner he simply repeated, "I'll take that."

Tee Ray thought a moment, starting to direct the knife to another button. The Knights were all there. They outnumbered Raifer. They could take him.

Then Tee Ray glanced down at Raifer's hand. Raifer, without any show at all, had pulled out his long Colt pistol and had his finger on the trigger. The others couldn't see this because the bar blocked their view, but Tee Ray could. The barrel was pointed at Tee Ray's groin.

"Hell," said Tee Ray loudly, attempting a smile that turned into a sneer, "if you want to play with this here Jew knife, go right ahead. Go play with it all you want."

Raifer took the knife and tucked it in his belt.

The Knights remained unusually quiet, not understanding why Tee Ray had allowed the Sheriff to order him around. They stared at Raifer through drunken, bloodshot eyes. Raifer effortlessly held their gaze, his features unruffled and confident. They started to go back to the comfort of their drinks.

Raifer spoke to the entire room without raising his voice. "I think it's time you went home to your families. It's late, and you've got to cut cane tomorrow." He came from behind the bar and started for the door.

Tee Ray was fuming. "You tellin' us what to do with our own crops?"

Raifer did not slow down his stride but merely called back over his shoulder, "Do as you please. Drink yourself into a stupor so that you can't bring in your cane and it rots in the field. Just drink quietly, or I'll have to come back and run you all in."

Raifer stepped across the threshold into the cool night air and shut the door behind him. Bucky was still on the porch having the dry heaves. Raifer grabbed him by the collar and hauled him to his feet. "You smell worse than an essence peddler."

Bucky wiped the yellow vomit from the corners of his mouth. "I ain't no skunk," he said indignantly.

" 'Course not. Their smell ain't as bad as yours. Come on. You're coming over to the office to sleep it off in one of the cells. Then, in the morning, you're gonna tell me how it is you stole evidence, and I'm gonna tell you about keeping your mouth shut and how I'm going to lar-rup your sorry frame if you ever do anything like that again."

"You gonna beat me? I don't deserve to be larrupped."

Raifer snorted with disgust and kicked Bucky in the rump, propelling him forward down the street.

Bucky, unsure on his feet from all the liquor and weak from throwing up, stumbled in front of Raifer as they made their way toward the Sheriff's office in the courthouse.

Meanwhile, in the bar, Tee Ray had gathered the Knights around him and was speaking in a low voice. "The rest of you take care of the crops, but tomorrow me and Forrest are gonna ride down to Lamou and catch us that Jew."

"But what," asked one of the men, "if he ain't in Lamou?"

"He's got to be headin' that way. South. That's the only direction he can go. Can't go north. No way to cross the river up here, and no way to get past Parteblanc. No, he's got to go south. He's got to be out there in that woods somewhere or in the swamp. Well, let him spend a damp night out there. It's gettin' cold. Feel it? Let that Jew spend the night freezin' himself. It'll just soften him up for us when we find him."

Forrest smiled. Under his thick beard his mouth was barely visible, but when he grinned, the beard parted and his missing teeth, knocked out in a fight long ago, were like broken pickets in a fence that needed repainting. Dark tobacco stains covered the few good teeth he had left. "We gonna have some more fun, ain't we, Tee Ray. Darkies, Jews, and Catholic Papists. Fun for sure."

Chapter 45

The baby had colic. Maylene was walking around the small house, baby on her shoulder, trying to comfort the child. The cries continued.

"Shut that kid up, Maylene," Jimmy Joe demanded. He sat at the table. His large frame took up almost the entire long wooden bench. His blond hair was askew, his shirt stained with sweat and grime. He took another swig from one of the many bottles he had liberated from Cottoncrest. Some were still in in his saddlebags. The rest were set in a row, two deep, along the mantel over the fireplace.

Maylene didn't respond. She merely patted the baby on the back and jiggled him up and down in her arms.

The baby continued to whine.

Jimmy Joe continued to drink. He looked around the narrow room with disgust. Yesterday he hadn't given the size of his living quarters much thought. He had never considered it an issue. If it was not as large as Tee Ray's house, it was almost as big, and Tee Ray had to have more room 'cause of all them kids. But now, given what Tee Ray was going to have, it bothered him.

Jimmy Joe looked up at the bottles on the mantel. He knew that was all he was ever going to get from Cottoncrest. When those bottles were empty, they'd be tossed away, like Tee Ray had tossed him aside this afternoon.

Before things were different, but now Tee Ray was acting as if he was better. He wasn't that. He wasn't ever gonna be better.

Not better. Only richer. Tee Ray was going to be richer. That was for sure.

Jimmy Joe would show Tee Ray. The Knights all thought Tee Ray was tough. Jimmy Joe would show them. He would be the biggest nigger hater of them all.

The baby's cries got louder.

"I told you, Maylene!" snapped Jimmy Joe. "I ain't gonna warn you again."

Maylene hugged the baby more tightly and prayed that he would stop making noise. She wished her younger sister were here and not living miles away from Parteblanc. Her sister, with all her kids, would know what to do with a crying baby. She would know what to do for colic.

Maylene was at a loss. This was her first child. It would be her only child.

Maylene looked around for something to comfort the infant. A sack of flour. A sack of rice. Salt. Red beans and sausage left in the pot from the night before. Nothing for a baby.

Then she remembered the large jar of molasses. She opened it and dipped a finger in it.

Jimmy Joe, lost in the bottle, did not notice as the baby slowly quieted down, sucking on Maylene's finger.

Maylene, the infant still in her arms, squeezed onto the bench next to Jimmy Joe. Her petite figure contrasted sharply with Jimmy Joe's broad shoulders and bulging arms. Her long dark hair was pinned up, but wisps of it had come loose and framed her face.

Maylene softly broached a subject that had been on her mind. "Have you thought of a name you like yet, Jimmy Joe?"

Jimmy Joe snorted. There was no name she had suggested that he liked, and he had refused to have the baby named after himself. That baby was not going to be a Junior.

Maylene tried again, even more gently. "We got to have a name for him. Whatever you want, Jimmy Joe, is fine with me."

Jimmy Joe looked at her with anger in his eyes. "Always at me, ain't you? First you whine about wantin' to have a kid. Now you have one, and all you can do is whine about havin' a name for it."

It wasn't an "it." It was a "him." A wonderful, darling child. A child she had hoped and prayed for. But Maylene knew the signs. She had said too much. She cuddled the baby and stood up, moving out of reach of Jimmy Joe's fists.

The baby stopped sucking on her finger. He pulled away and hiccupped. Then he started to cry again.

Jimmy Joe jumped up and shoved the bench out of his way, moving across the room. "Maylene! I warned you!"

Maylene retreated to a corner of the room, panicked. In her fear she grasped the baby even more tightly, which only made the infant scream louder. Frantically, Maylene patted the baby, hoping that would help.

Maylene was filled with terror as she looked up at Jimmy Joe towering over her. His hot, liquor breath filled the corner where she and the baby cowered. Anything she said could inflame Jimmy Joe further. She silently said a prayer.

He raised his fist, an anvil of flesh at the end of a muscular arm.

Maylene bent low over the child, hoping to absorb the blows Jimmy Joe would deliver.

Jimmy Joe swung his deadly fist.

Before it even connected with her face, Maylene screamed. Her yell and the child's cries filled the room.

At the last minute Jimmy Joe opened his fist and instead hit her face with his open palm. She fell back into the corner, sobbing, weeping, holding the crying child.

Jimmy Joe was repulsed by it all. By her. By the child. By his house. He turned around, grabbed his coat off the peg on the wall, and stuck the bottle in his pocket. "Ain't nothin' but trouble. That baby's been screaming since he arrived. You ain't had that baby but a day, and all it does is bawl. It's too much. Ain't no baby worth that."

Jimmy Joe slammed the door behind him.

Maylene, still sobbing, pulled off her shawl, spread it on the floor, and laid the child down on it. He flipped over onto his stomach, stopped crying, and started moving as if he were swimming in the shawl.

Drying her tears, Maylene thought proudly that, in a few weeks, he'd be crawling.

Chapter 46

The temperature had dropped precipitously. Sally and Jenny had been walking briskly for hours, but even these exertions were not enough to keep them warm. The cold penetrated through Sally's coat and Jenny's cloak, and the two hurried faster. Their goal was in sight.

Ahead of them, visible in the light of the half-moon, was the tin roof of a home on the edge of Parteblanc. As they neared it, Sally led Jenny off the road. They approached from the back, the tall grass swishing against their ankles.

"Are you sure?" whispered Jenny.

Sally nodded.

Sally came near the back windows and thought a moment. Picking out the window to the left of the door, she softly rapped on the windowpane. Three quick taps, a pause, and then two taps.

There was no response from inside. The house was dark.

Sally waited.

Jenny tugged at her sleeve and put her mouth near Sally's ear. "This is too dangerous. Let's keep walking."

Sally hesitated. Maybe Jenny was right. After all, it had been so long . . .

"One more time, then we'll go," Sally said with more confidence than she felt. She reached up to tap again on the window.

Before her hand touched the pane of glass, the window flew open, and the barrel of a large gun, held by a white man in nightclothes, was thrust in her face.

Sally began to shake, but she held her ground.

A gruff voice demanded, "What do you want?"

"Mr. Ganderson?" Sally's voice was quivery.

"Who wants to know?"

"It's me. Sally. From Cottoncrest. Mr. Ganderson, is the railroad still running?"

Chapter 47

It was still dark outside. It was at least an hour before dawn. The gas lamp cast a flickering glow as Raifer put the cup of steaming coffee on the deputy's desk.

Bucky reached for it. It was so hot he could hardly hold the cup, but he brought it to his lips and sipped slowly, letting the chicory flavor roll around his tongue and rinse away the nasty taste left in his mouth from the night before. Bucky groaned, "I don't feel so well."

"You'll live . . . unfortunately," Dr. Cailleteau said with a dismissive waive of his hand. He had settled his vast bulk into one of the two worn wooden chairs he and Raifer had pulled up near the deputy's desk, which was stuck away in a corner. The chair groaned under his weight.

Shooting a conspiratorial glance at Raifer, Dr. Cailleteau signaled Bucky. "Of course, if you think you have a remittent or bilious fever, I could give you some hog's feet oil or lard heated with mustard or maybe some hickory leaves with pepper and sanguinaria. That'll induce nausea—cleanse you out faster than a twelve-pounder out a straight-muzzle Napoleon cannon."

At the mere thought of these medications, Bucky started to turn green and put his head down on the desk, resting it on his arms.

"Well, maybe you've had too much cleansing nausea already." Dr. Cailleteau reached into his pocket and pulled out a large cigar, cut off the end, and lit it. As he stoked its tip into a fine red ash, the smoke bounded into the corner behind Bucky's desk and then drifted down onto the hapless deputy.

"Bucky, you got no one to blame but yourself for your condition." Raifer was blunt and direct. "Drink the rest of that coffee. You've got a job to do this morning, once the sun's up, and I expect you to do it right."

Bucky didn't respond. He just wanted to be left alone and go back to sleep. He buried his head deeper in his arms atop the hard desk.

Raifer shook his head in disbelief that Bucky was ignoring him. He said loudly, almost yelling across Bucky's sprawling figure, "You heard what happened last night, Doc?"

Bucky didn't move. He kept his eyes shut.

Puffing away on his cigar and blowing the smoke directly at Bucky, Dr. Cailleteau responded. "Are you talking about Bucky getting himself drunker than a blue-belly at a fast house or about how the peddler and Marcus hid from Tee Ray in his own cane field?"

The smoke irritated Bucky's nose, and he stifled a cough. He tried to concentrate on going back to sleep.

"No," Raifer boomed back, "about the accidental fire."

Finally, Bucky stirred. Picking up his head from the desk, Bucky groaned out, " 'Tweren't no accident." His head sank back down to the desk.

Raifer was disgusted. Even though the predawn air was cold and a light October frost covered the yellowed grass in the courthouse square, Raifer opened a window. The frigid air poured in, and the smoke flew away, along with all the warmth in the room. Then Raifer took a ladle and dipped it in the water bucket that only recently had been brought in, breaking the melting layer of ice on top. He poured the water directly on the back of Bucky's head, which was still face down on the desk.

The cold water shocked Bucky into action, and he sat bolt upright so quickly that he knocked the burning coffee into his lap. He leaped to his feet, yelping as the scorching heat penetrated his pants and blistered his groin, "My privates are on fire!"

"I'm glad to see that at least one part of your body is awake," Raifer laughed, as he picked up the bucket and flung the entirety of its frigid contents on Bucky.

Bucky's clothing absorbed the unpleasant chilly water. Goosebumps grew all over. Cold water drained into his boots, and his feet started to become numb. He began to shiver.

Raifer went into one of the cells and returned with a woolen blanket that he handed Bucky, who gratefully wrapped his trembling shoulders.

Raifer refilled the coffee cup. Bucky pulled his damp sleeves over his hands as gloves and used it to pick up the steaming brew. Now he drank it as quickly as he could.

"That fire was an *accident*, Bucky. You understand?"

Bucky did not. He started to protest.

Dr. Cailleteau took the cigar out of his mouth. "Silence, boy! Don't you see the Sheriff is trying to let you keep your job instead of jugging you up for violating the Klan Act?"

"But," Bucky protested, between sips from the cup, "it weren't no Klan. Just the Knights of the White Camellia. So, why would Raifer want to arrest me and lock me up?"

Dr. Cailleteau turned to Raifer. "I don't know why you would want to keep this apple-shaker!"

Bucky, still cold and trembling under his blanket, protested, "I ain't uneducated."

Dr. Cailleteau merely sighed with disbelief and concentrated on his cigar.

"I ain't no doctor, like you, that's for sure, and I ain't got none of that French or Latin or them other weird languages that don't do no one no good, but I got me a whole five years of schoolin'. I can read and write and all. After all," he added proudly, "when Raifer needs someone to send a flimsy, he calls me, and I goes down to the Western Union office and takes care of it."

Raifer pulled up a chair. He was stern. "Listen, Bucky, and listen good. The Ku Klux Klan Act has been in effect more than twenty years. It was passed before you were born. President Ulysses S. Grant got it done. It tries to make certain actions against coloreds a crime, whether you are doing it as a member of the Klan or otherwise."

Raifer drew closer and spoke more softly and urgently. "Bucky, I don't care if Tee Ray busts up some colored's crops or tears up his garden, but I can't have Tee Ray and the Knights going around burning down their cabins. If that happens, then I'll have to act. I won't want to, but I won't have any choice. Why do you think Tee Ray got you to torch the cabin? 'Cause he knows that if I caught him doing that, I'd have to jug him. So, he gets you to do it."

"But I thought . . ." Bucky started to say.

Raifer cut him off. "The problem is, you haven't been thinking at all. Now listen." Raifer spoke quietly but firmly, as if instructing a small child. "The coloreds got scared, thinking that the Knights were coming. They ran. They left their houses quickly and their fires unattended. One of them got out of hand. The fire at old Nimrod's cabin was an accident caused by the coloreds' own carelessness. Do you understand?"

A glimmer of awareness finally penetrated. "I understand," Bucky echoed.

"And I don't want to hear you ever again talk about what you did last night."

"Yes, Raifer. I ain't gonna say no more 'bout it, other than we came across a darky's cabin what done caught on fire by accident."

"Good. Now, you go home and change clothes. I want you to ride out to Cottoncrest with Dr. Cailleteau and me. We've got to check on Little Miss. I'm concerned, having heard Jimmy Joe say last night that none of the coloreds were around. That's not right. They should be there, tending to Cottoncrest and looking after Little Miss. Anyway, I want you to ride on south from there and join up with Tee Ray and Forrest before they get to Lamou. I've got to agree with Tee Ray; the peddler has to be headed in that direction. I'm sending you out there to arrest that peddler for the murder of the Colonel Judge and Rebecca. I can't stop Tee Ray and Forrest from going, but I can send you with them, and you're to bring that peddler back alive and stop Tee Ray and Forrest from doing anything foolish that will cause me to do something I don't want to do. You're a deputy. You act like one, you hear?"

Bucky's head nodded so vigorously in agreement that water cascaded from his damp hair, which made Dr. Cailleteau think that Bucky looked like a scraggly dog shaking itself coming out of a pond. Except that a dog would look better.

Bucky gulped down the last of the coffee and, gathering up the blanket around his damp clothes, dashed out of the courthouse in the moonlight toward his home, his boots squishing and water squirting out of the seams. He was running fast because he wanted to please Raifer, who had given him another chance. And because it was so cold.

Through the window Dr. Cailleteau watched Bucky trot at a good clip across the courthouse lawn. The moon, still in the sky before dawn came, was so bright that he could see Bucky's shadow on the ground as he loped along. "He's putting the licks in, Raifer."

"Sure, he's going to run as fast as he can, even if his head is sometimes as dull as a spinster."

Bucky sprinted across Main Street in Parteblanc, oblivious to the oncoming horse and high hitch wagon, which almost ran him down.

The man violently reined in the horse. It whinnied with pain as the bits jerked taut. The wagon shimmied, and several boxes fell out, tumbling to the ground.

Bucky looked up in surprise. He hadn't expected to see anyone out at this hour. "Sorry, Mr. Ganderson. It's just . . ."

Ganderson, his worn face and gray mustache peeking out from a wide-brimmed hat, climbed down from the seat, easing his way onto the ground from his high perch. The front wheels of the hitch wagon were almost four feet in diameter, and the rear ones were taller. The wooden bed, riding far off the ground, was piled with a towering stack of boxes resting on a thick bed of hay that splayed out over the sides.

Ganderson started loading the fallen boxes back onto the wagon. Although in his late fifties, he was still robust, and he handled the heavy boxes with ease.

Bucky bent down to grab a box to help, and the woolen blanket fell off onto the dirt road. Now he'd have to wash it before bringing it back to Raifer. He slung it back over his cold shoulders and tried to lift the box. It was heavier than Bucky thought, but Ganderson took it from him, holding it as if it were an empty container.

"I got it, Bucky. No harm done." Ganderson stacked it back on top of the other boxes in the wagon and reached down for the next one, lying on its side on the ground.

Chilled by the cold air, Bucky was grateful to be released from any further obligations and trotted on down the road toward his house. No lights were on in any of the homes. The moon was the only illumination. Bucky did not bother to think further about why Ganderson would be traveling with a full wagon before dawn. All Bucky wanted to do was to get home, change into some dry clothes, and get ready to join Raifer and Dr. Cailleteau on the trip to Cottoncrest.

Ganderson put the last two boxes back onto the bed of hay, climbed back up onto the high wooden bench, and flicked the reins. The horse moved slowly north along the road, traveling away from Parteblanc and toward the ferry that crossed the Mississippi River.

Jammed tightly inside the false bottom of the hitch wagon, Jenny, Sally, and Marcus sighed softly with relief.

PART IV

Today

Chapter 48

"So there I was, in New Orleans in 1961, and although it was only May, the heat was already awful. There was no central air-conditioning in those days. In New Orleans you took a bath before you went to bed, just to cool down, but you still went to sleep sweating despite the overhead fan whirling, and all the while hordes of mosquitoes buzzed angrily outside the screened windows. You woke up, and you took a bath, but before you could dry off, you were sweating again. The heat was constant and the humidity pervasive. By the time you had breakfast, the clothes you put on were already damp with your sweat.

"I had left the other boys at the old hotel we had found in the French Quarter and went out exploring. I had given myself permission to be a tourist for a few days until I had to do what I really came down for, until I had to deliver what was hidden in the lining of my suitcase.

"In those days all the hotels were segregated. In fact, all downtown was segregated. You walked down Canal Street, and the differences between blacks and whites could not be more stark, but to the New Orleans' white shoppers, the blacks could just as well have been invisible, for the whites ignored them completely.

"The blacks couldn't use the restrooms in the stores on Canal Street. If they wanted to buy a blouse or a dress or a shirt or a suit there, they couldn't try them on and couldn't use the dressing rooms and couldn't return the items if they didn't fit.

"But I wasn't in New Orleans to shop. I had to conserve my money so I would have enough to rent a car. I was in New Orleans only to try to soak up the atmosphere.

"I walked for hours in the French Quarter. And I tried to find the remnants of Storyville in Faubourg Tremé, but there wasn't much left, just a few old buildings.

"You don't know what Storyville was? Why, it had been the home of jazz, in an area of the city set aside for bars and brothels, in an attempt to stop them from being in every neighborhood. It was the heart where jazz first beat. It was right there, at the edge of the French Quarter, far away from the fancy Canal Street stores.

"Well, if you had brothels, you also got bars and dives and 'dance halls.' And if you had dance halls, you needed musicians.

"That's what I went looking for. Jazz and musicians and Storyville. By 1961, however, Storyville was long gone. It had disappeared almost fifty years before I got there, having been closed in World War I by order of the U.S. Navy to keep our sailors 'safe from sin.'

"For a time I wondered whether your Grandpapa Jake could have walked those same streets. Of course, he passed through New Orleans on his way down and on his way back, and he had business contacts here, but I don't think he ever stayed in the city any length of time or had anything to do with Storyville.

"The more I thought about it, however, the more I realized he couldn't have been there. He left the South for the last time in the winter of 1893 and never returned. That was a few years before Storyville was even created."

1893

Chapter 49

The frost crunched under his boots as Jake made his way through the marshy woods. The sky had cleared as the temperatures had dropped, and now, an hour or so before dawn, the moon cast a bright blue glow. Jake had slept the night only in fits and spurts.

It wasn't that he had been cold. The light October freeze was nothing like the hard winters in Russia. He was used to cold, and the uncured bearskin had kept him pleasantly warm, even if it was muddy, smelly, and itchy.

It was dreams and concerns that disturbed his slumber, not fear. He could live with fear. There was nothing more fearful than escaping Russia under the skirts of women on the train, trying not to breathe when the Cossacks stalked through the cars or when the Czar's militia clattered through in their sharply shined shoes, intimidating everyone. He could live with fear now. But the concerns were something else.

Jake had been on the run so much with Marcus, moving so fast, that he hadn't really had time to think. But once Marcus had gone and Jake had settled under the tree, hidden in the darkness, the impact of the day's events finally struck him fully and caused his thoughts to turn again and again to the Colonel Judge and Rebecca.

He would never see them again.

He would never have another earnest discussion with the Colonel Judge. They would never talk again of religion. Of man's ability to hate those he does not wish to understand and inability to love those he should hold the dearest. Of the things that make us most human and those that cause us to do the most inhuman things.

And Jake would never have Rebecca's beauty and warmth near him again.

Two gone and two lost. That was why he had to speak to Jenny. That was why he had to see her again. He had spent the night wondering if Marcus had found Jenny and Sally and, if he had, how the three of them would get to New Orleans with all the commotion that must be going on in Parteblanc.

And when Jake did drift off, his dreams were disturbing. The girl in New York, with the red spreading across her blouse, had appeared. Before, whenever he had thought of her, it had been with a feeling of yearning. He had contemplated a thousand times her dark eyes and smooth skin, creating a face as perfect as Eve's must have been in the Garden of Eden or as entrancing as Bathsheba's must have been to King David. Although Jake had seen her only once at that party, in his mind was a perfect image of her, one he could recall at a moment's notice— her blouse as white and pure as a Torah cover, her long skirt as blue as a new prayer book in the shul.

But last night, the red spreading across her white blouse was not the wine he had spilled from her glass when he had accidentally bumped into her. In his dreams the red was blood. Endless streams of blood, staining her white blouse crimson, pouring over her dress and onto the floor, and spreading into thick pools that threatened to fill the room. Barrels of blood poured from her slit throat. And behind her, instead of her mother, there was a golem, a creature of mud and evil, shrieking with glee, "*Verem essen toiterhait un deiges lebedikerhait.*" Worms eat you up when dead, and worries eat you up alive.

At Jake's own elbow at the party was not his brother, Moshe, but another golem, who held a long knife in his wicked, oozing fingers. He thrust the blade into the girl's breast, screaming with horrific delight, "*Tsores tsezegen di hartz.*" Troubles cut the heart.

Again and again, the golem shoved the knife into her bosom as blood spurted in rivers. They were now swimming in blood. They were in a sea of blood, and it threatened to drown them, but the golem's laughter only increased, echoing insanely over and over.

Jake had awoken with a start, the cackling of the golem still resounding in his head.

After that he tried to stay awake, for when he closed his eyes for even a minute, the dream returned, and he would again be treading in blood to the golem's incessant mirth. It continued that way throughout the night, sleep enveloping him and the nightmare awakening him.

He couldn't wait for dawn. The only thing to get it off his mind was to start walking. Keep heading south, Marcus had said, for those in Lamou would find you before you found them.

Jake looked up at the moon through the canopy of red bark oaks and hickory and hanging moss and gnarled vines that entwined their way ever higher. The North Star was fading as dawn approached.

It was tough to gauge distances here. He knew how long it took on the road, but now there was no road and no path.

Lamou couldn't be that much farther. At least, that was what he hoped.

Chapter 50

The children had woken before dawn and silently slipped out the door. They knew their tasks.

The older ones went to the lean-to shed, retrieved the scythes, sharpened them on the whetstones, and headed out into the fields to start cutting the cane. The younger ones fetched the water and left the buckets outside the back door for their mother. They brought the wood for the stove from the chopped and split pieces on the woodpile. Then they followed their older siblings out to the fields. Their task was to stack the cane that their brothers and sisters sliced down so that it all could be loaded onto wagons and taken to the Cottoncrest mill to be processed.

All of them worked with the utmost caution while near their house. The oldest wasn't yet fourteen. They didn't dare wake their father. They had seen the bruises on their mother's face, and although she had told them she had just been careless and had slipped and fallen, they knew better. They could see the way she cowered when their father approached. They knew the signs when their mother fell silent whenever their father was in the house. They did not want to anger him and feel his wrath.

The sky had started to brighten when Tee Ray got out of bed and observed, to his satisfaction, that the children had already left. They were good kids, he thought. This would be last season they would ever have to cut cane. This would be the last season they would have to fetch wood. From now on someone else would do it for them. From now on they would be able to go to school, to dress in fine clothes, to live in a house that wasn't tiny, like this cabin, but was magnificent in all its splendor. It was what all of them deserved.

Tee Ray stretched, yawned loudly, and then pulled on his trousers and boots. The anger from the night before was gone. He felt good. He knew exactly what he had to do today.

Mona had heard the children leave but had not dared move in the bed. She had felt Tee Ray get up and pretended to be asleep. Now that he was moving about the cabin, she still kept her eyes closed and tried to maintain the slow and steady breathing of one still deep in slumber.

Tee Ray opened the door to walk to the woodpile and was pleased to see the children had already brought the wood and water. He stoked up the stove and started to prepare coffee, dropping two large scoops of inexpensive chicory blend into the black porcelain pot. They couldn't afford pure coffee now, but soon they would, and he swore to himself they would never drink the chicory blend again.

The aroma filled the small cabin, and Tee Ray went to the side of the bed and softly shook Mona's shoulders. She continued to pretend to be sleeping.

"Wake up, ol' girl," Tee Ray said.

Mona was surprised at the tone in his voice. It was actually gentle.

"Come on, Mona, the coffee'll be ready soon, and I've got to head down to Lamou to catch the Jew Peddler, but when I do, all our troubles'll be over. You'll be able to dress a fine lady. You'll be able to sleep until noon if you want. But we got to get movin' now. The children are already out in the fields, and they'll be comin' back for breakfast before you know it, hungry as a black bear comin' out of hibernatin'."

Mona was amazed. All the anger was gone. He was back to his old self. He was the Tee Ray she had fallen in love with.

She rolled over and pushed the hair out of her eyes, ignoring the bruises and the pain. "You promise?"

"The young ones hungry? No need to promise. You know it to be true."

Mona smiled, "Go on, you. I know that. I mean dressin' like a fine lady and sleepin' 'til noon if I want."

"No need to promise that either. It's as good as done. All I gotta do is give that Jew to Raifer, dead of course, and that'll be it. The Jew killed the Colonel Judge and his wife, and ain't no nigger gonna get Cottoncrest."

"But she didn't look—" Mona stopped. Tee Ray's eyes had retreated into narrow slits. He was clenching his teeth. This was not a good sign. She had said the wrong thing.

"I told you, Mona, how people *look* ain't nothin'. It's what people *is*—that's the thing. She was mulatto through and through. An octoroon. One of her great-grandparents was black. She was a nigger no matter how white she looked. Why do you think the Colonel Judge never had her family down? Why do you think they came up with that story about how she was an 'orphan'? Why do you think some high yellow gal goes and gets some gimpy ol' gray-haired cuss to marry her? She wants to escape and pass for white. That's why. And she could smell his money. If he died and had changed his will and left Cottoncrest to her, why then . . ."

Mona took his hand and softly stroked it. "It's all right, Tee Ray. She didn't get Cottoncrest. I still don't know how you know these things, but I'm so proud of you." If she continued to compliment him, his anger might go away.

"The Knights, Mona, the Knights gotta keep together. As I've told you, I've known for a year. Heard it from a Knight who was passing through on a riverboat who sought me out, knowin' I was head of the Knights here. Knowin' stuff is what gives you power, you see, and I was saving that information for just the right moment."

"You're lucky, then, that you didn't have to confront the Colonel Judge and all about that. Now that the Jew killed the both of them, can't be no one knows the truth but you and me."

Tee Ray withdrew his hands from her grasp and walked over to the stove to pour the coffee. "The truth. You and me. You're right, Mona. Sometimes it's better that the truth be hidden. Just thank Jesus they didn't have no children."

"That ol' man!" Mona giggled. "Can you imagine the two of them spendin' a night of horizontal refreshment?"

Tee Ray walked over to the bed with the coffee.

Mona pulled back the covers. "You sure you don't have time for some horizontal refreshment yourself? We got time if you're quick, and you're always quick."

For the first time in weeks in the house, Tee Ray's unshaven face crinkled into a smile. He put the coffee down on the table. "If they had

had a child, then will or no will, that would have been it. The child would have inherited Cottoncrest. Now there's no one but us."

Tee Ray kicked off his boots and shucked his pants. Climbing back into bed, he reached for her. "Mona, let's celebrate."

Chapter 51

The sun was clearing the horizon and the early-morning light cast long shadows as Dr. Cailleteau hitched up his horse to the buggy. He moved slowly. His joints were stiff, and the cold weather made them ache. He grunted as he cinched the horse into the fittings. When he was younger, he was full of muscle and vigor. But the muscle had turned to fat, and the fat had grown to enormous proportions. He now found himself encased in a body that sometimes even he hardly recognized.

The Colonel Judge had been the last of his old friends, and although the Colonel Judge had grown more distant in the past year, there was something about old friendships that persisted even during the hardest of times. Everyone else in town seemed younger and more energetic but less educated and less interesting.

Raifer rode up on his horse. "You about ready, Doc?"

Dr. Cailleteau climbed up onto the buggy, its wooden joints creaking loudly in sympathy with his own. Dr. Cailleteau flicked the reins, and the horse started to walk slowly down the road. Raifer rode high in his saddle next to the buggy.

They paused in front of Bucky's tiny house. Bucky was waiting for them, sitting on the porch. His horse was saddled and was pawing the ground, its nostrils surrounded by white vapor every time it exhaled in the cold air. Seeing Raifer's impatient look, Bucky swung onto his horse and followed them.

The center of the town was still quiet except for a bear of a man, his blond hair sticking out of his hat, opening the barn door to the black-smith shop.

"Mornin', Jimmy Joe," Bucky called out. "You goin' down to Lamou with Tee Ray and Forrest?" Before Jimmy Joe even had a chance to answer, Bucky added proudly, "You know, I'm goin' down myself as the official presence. Gonna arrest that Jew. Gonna be a grand sight bringing that Jew back, all tied up and ready to face justice."

Jimmy Joe only grunted noncommittally. He threw open the barn door and started to unlatch the long shutters on the wall. Jimmy Joe didn't care about the cold. Once he had the fire lit, it would be hot enough. He had several horseshoes to make today. He wasn't going anyplace where Tee Ray could try to give him commands. Tee Ray was getting too high and mighty. The Colonel Judge's death had done that. Made Tee Ray think he was better than the rest of them.

Bucky pretended to ignore Jimmy Joe's lack of response. He dug the rowels of his spurs gently against his horse's flanks, and the horse broke into a trot as it hurried to pull alongside Raifer and Dr. Cailleteau, who had not stopped as they passed Jimmy Joe's blacksmith shop.

Bucky felt good. Raifer had put him in charge of the Lamou trip, one that was certain to lead to the arrest of the Jew Peddler. "You can come on later and catch up to us if you want," Bucky yelled cheerily over his shoulder. Jimmy Joe ignored him.

"Hold it down!" Raifer snapped, as Bucky slowed his horse and joined the small procession. "You don't have to wake up the whole town."

Dr. Cailleteau turned to Raifer. "Trying to give that boy instructions on how to behave and expecting him to follow them is like shoveling flies across a barnyard."

Bucky bristled. "That's not fair, Doc. Besides, Raifer here tol' me to be ready to go to Cottoncrest with you and then to go on to Lamou, and you see, I was ready when you got to my place. All prepared in every way. Got my gun here. Got my rifle. Got my handcuffs and my rope. I'm ready for whatever happens."

Bucky noticed, for the first time, that the back of Dr. Cailleteau's buggy was filled with more than his black medical bag. "What you got there?" he inquired.

Dr. Cailleteau sighed with exasperation, both at Bucky's ill-mannered insistence and at his grammar. "I do not 'got' anything."

"Sure you do. I see what-all you got there in the wagon—just don't know what it is."

"I *have* everything I need, Bucky. A blanket and shawl for Little Miss. Laudanum, if she needs it, in case she gets too upset by what's happening. Moss bedding for her to lie on for our trip back into town if we need to bring her back. Now, Bucky, you have all the answers you should need until we get to Cottoncrest."

They proceeded along in silence for almost an hour. Finally, around one of the vast curves of the Mississippi River, gleaming a silvery brown in the early-morning rays, they could see the top of the big house at Cottoncrest. They would be there in another thirty minutes or so.

Bucky was several hundred yards ahead of them. When he was out of earshot, Raifer rode up close to Dr. Cailleteau's buggy. "I'm going to leave you with Little Miss. I'll send Bucky on to Tee Ray's cabin to see if he can catch up with him before Tee Ray takes off. Can't have him stirring up any more trouble than necessary."

Raifer urged his horse into a gallop and caught up with Bucky. Raifer made Bucky wait until Dr. Cailleteau's buggy drew alongside, and then the three of them continued on together.

"Bucky, you've got to let Dr. Cailleteau be the first there. If Little Miss is really alone, if the darkies have really abandoned Cottoncrest, I don't know what mood she'll be in. The Doc has to be the one she sees first. Even if she doesn't recognize him, he knows how to handle her."

"It's a shame, Raifer," Dr. Cailleteau said. "If she is aware enough to realize that the darkies have left, then she'll know enough to be heartbroken, for she can't live at Cottoncrest alone, and that's been her home for more than fifty years. It's like her own child, she loves it that much. You know, she's lost the General, she's lost her daughter, she's lost all her sons, and now Cottoncrest may be losing her. But if the coloreds really have left Cottoncrest, there's nothing else to do but bring her back to Parteblanc and get someone to look after her. Then, dammit, I'll have to train someone."

"Train someone?" Bucky perked up. "Could you train me? I learn real good."

Raifer and Dr. Cailleteau gave each other a knowing glance and, unable to restrain themselves, laughed loudly. Dr. Cailleteau's huge bulk jiggled with delight.

"What's so funny?" Bucky demanded. "Dr. Cailleteau said he gots to train someone, and I wants to learn things. You know me, always trying to better myself. So, why can't I be trained?"

"Bucky," Raifer explained, "if the darkies have all left Cottoncrest, that means Sally is gone. She was the only midwife in the area, colored or white."

Chapter 52

Marcus broke off a small portion of the long baguette and handed the remainder to Sally, who in turn broke off a piece and passed the crusty end to Jenny. As they sat in the old cabin, their first stop, they dipped the bread in the wooden bowl of butter that Ganderson had left them.

Marcus and Sally contemplated their newfound freedom. It was intoxicating and scary at the same time. Marcus, of course, had traveled widely when he had been in the Colonel Judge's service during the war, but he had not left Petit Rouge Parish in more than ten years, as the Colonel Judge's world closed in on him. When the Colonel Judge traveled north to Philadelphia, on that fateful trip where he had met and married Miss Rebecca, he pointedly had not taken Marcus along.

But Sally had never left Petit Rouge Parish. She had grown up a slave on a neighboring plantation to Cottoncrest, and the farthest she ever had gone was to the ferry landing that crossed from the west to the east banks of the Mississippi. Now, for the first time in her more than fifty years, she had crossed over. It was like the picture in her small church of the crossing over the Jordan, except this time it wasn't just a hand-painted lithograph. She was really living in the story, heading for better times and better places.

But it wasn't like Sally had expected. She had thought that she would enjoy seeing the broad river flow under the ferry, seeing the old shore and the new shore of freedom approach. But all she could see, crowded into the false bottom of Ganderson's hitch wagon, was the ferry's planking.

Sally, however, could hear the sloshing of the waves as the ferry moved across the current. She could imagine it fully. Like the Hebrew children crossing the Red Sea, leaving Egypt forever, she was crossing the brown sea of the Mississippi away from Petit Rouge, never to return.

"How long do you think we have to stay here before we move on?" Marcus asked, between bites.

"We stay here until it's time we don't stay no more," Sally replied. "The railroad runs on its own time. Ain't nothin' we can do but to wait. Look at all we got, anyway." Sally pointed to the rusty tin that formed a low ceiling over a portion of the rotting wooden structure set far back off the road, surrounded by weeds and a thick hedge of wild ligustrum. "Got a roof over our heads, got food to last a day or two, and got our freedom. We ain't no more house servants. You ain't no more manservant. You and me, ol' man, are gonna be so free we ain't gonna know what to do next 'cept enjoy ourselves. Gonna ride this ol' railroad to freedom as far north as it'll take us, and then we're gonna build ourselves a real life."

"You think Cubit and Jordan are gonna make it?"

"What you gonna worry 'bout them for? 'Course they's gonna make it. We goes east and north. They goes west. Ain't no one can stop any of us."

"What about you, Jenny? Are you goin' north with us from Baton Rouge?"

"No, Marcus." Jenny sat off to one side, lost in her own thoughts. "Not now. I have a few things to do in New Orleans still. Maybe then . . . maybe afterwards."

Marcus and Sally had each other, but Jenny had no one. Of course she would contact Louis when she got to New Orleans, and of course he would help. But could he help enough? Could he act quickly enough?

She dismissed her own worries. Louis always acted discreetly. That's how he had survived so long. That's how he had prospered, carefully treading his way in white society and carefully tending his way in the high Creole culture of New Orleans.

There was everything to look forward to, but Jenny had a terrible sense of loss and sadness. It was the hardest thing she ever did.

It was not Cottoncrest that she would miss. Not the house. Not Little Miss, although she like the old lady, particularly when Little Miss was more alert and would joke with her in French. And she wouldn't miss the Colonel Judge. He had been pleasant but aloof, and he had gotten worse and more angry and silent toward the end.

And although Jenny would miss Rebecca, would miss her every day from now on, would miss her graceful manners and warm smile and the many hours they would spend talking, that was not the hardest thing.

The hardest thing was not losing Rebecca. The hardest thing was leaving the twins.

PART V

Today

Chapter 53

"Anyway, there I was, without a whole lot of money, and I had to rent a car. I knew that if I didn't rent one soon, I'd spend all my money wandering around New Orleans, for I found the city, in all of its crass gaudiness and mildewed decrepitude, endlessly fascinating.

"Back in those days there were lots of little places you could rent cars, mom-and-pop establishments with a half-dozen ancient, battered vehicles. If you were willing to bargain, you could get an even better price.

"Several of the places I went to wanted too much or had a limit on how far you could drive. I knew I had to put a lot of miles on the car just to get from New Orleans out to Cottoncrest, and I needed something cheap but reliable.

"Finally, I found Wings on Wheels off of Elysian Fields Boulevard. The name was far grander than the place or its wares. They had one recent-model Oldsmobile—remember, this was 1961—its hood crumpled from a crash, and the lime-green finish on the passenger side was all scarred up, but the big rounded wings extending backwards from the trunk were still intact.

"I was taken with that Oldsmobile. Mrs. Schexnayder, the owner, could see that. We were eventually able to cut a deal, and I rented the car. I had to pay for a full week, cash up front, but I was to get a portion back if I returned the car early.

"I thought it was appropriate to be in a big car like that. Grandpapa Jake would have loved it. He liked cars. Hated trains but loved cars. He used to tell me about how he and my great-grandmother, Roz, used to drive around on hot summer evenings to keep cool, her long hair blowing out the open windows.

"Grandpapa Jake loved that woman. *A sheyne shidduch*, he would say. It was a beautiful match.

"He loved to tell the story about how they met. He used to say that he never had a glass eye for her, unlike the glass eye she had for Yossel. That was a joke. You see, Roz had been engaged before she married Grandpapa Jake. In fact, they met at the engagement party. Moshe had brought Jake with him to meet the girls who would be there, but after scouting the room, the only girl who appealed to Jake was one with the white blouse and the blue skirt.

"Moshe was shocked. 'Jake,' he explained, 'that's the future bride. She is spoken for. Look at all the other girls in this room. Here in America you don't need a *shadchen*'—that's a marriage broker—'You can almost have your pick of any of them. But not her!'

"Grandpapa Jake was never deterred by anything. '*Ven nit di shainet maidlech, volt men gehat dem yaitzer-horeh in der'erd*,' he told Moshe. If not for pretty girls, temptation would be unheeded. 'What does she see in him, anyway?'

"Moshe tried to explain. Yossel had neither the greatest looks nor the greatest personality. He was moody and temperamental, but he was learned and studious. Already his studies and his commentaries showed that he had the makings of a great rabbi. He was a fine catch for any girl.

"Grandpapa Jake would have none of this. He said love is blind, but I'll open her eyes. Actually, what he said was *chossen-kalen hobn glezerne oygn*. Bride and groom have glass eyes. But that's what it means. Love is blind.

"It was almost too late. The families were making a first toast to the couple as part of the official engagement announcement. The goblets of red wine were lifted high, but Jake forced his way through the throngs toward the front of the room, until he was standing directly in front of Roz. He stared at her intently, as if piercing her soul.

"Grandpapa Jake told me that he did pierce right through her glass eyes and into her heart. Before that moment she had not noticed him at all. But when she saw his handsome face and intent gaze, she stumbled. Just a little, but it was enough. The red wine spilled from her glass all over her white blouse. Grandpapa Jake said it was as if her heart had poured out toward him.

"Yossel's mother screamed. Spilled wine was a terrible sign of disaster. 'Keyn a hore!!' No evil eye, she cried. But it was too late. This was a sign from God that this girl was not fit for her son. The wedding must be canceled.

"Yossel himself was shaken. He did not believe in the superstitions that his mother did, but then he saw Jake rush up to Roz and hand her his handkerchief to cover the stain. She took it gratefully. In a moment of insight Yossel feared the worst—that the veil had been lifted from Roz's eyes.

"Yossel pointed at Jake. 'Mit a nar tor men nit handlen.' With a fool you have no right to do business.

"Jake started to respond, but Roz quietly intervened, turning to Yossel. 'A shveigendiker nar is a halber chocem.' A quiet fool is half a sage.

"Yossel was now doubly taken aback. He was not to be lectured to, not by a mere woman.

"But before Yossel could say anything nasty to Roz, Jake placed himself between the two of them and announced to the entire room, 'A nar ken a mol zogen a gleich vort.' Sometimes a fool can say something clever.

"The crowd erupted angrily at this upstart who dared speak so impertinently to the learned rabbinic student. Moshe quickly rushed Jake out a side door.

"Jake wouldn't see Roz again for almost two years."

1893

Chapter 54

As soon as they reached Cottoncrest, Raifer ordered Bucky to head out immediately to Tee Ray's cabin. Raifer didn't want Tee Ray and Forrest going to Lamou on their own. The Knights hated the Catholics almost as bad as they hated the coloreds. Bucky was to make sure that they got the Jew or found out what the Cajuns knew about the Jew and then leave without causing further troubles.

The Colonel Judge and his family had been staunch Catholics, and although they only attended Our Lady of Mercy in Parteblanc and never went to church in Lamou and wouldn't mingle with the Cajun Catholics, Father Séverin, the Lamou priest, had too many contacts in New Orleans. The last thing Raifer needed was some rich Catholic with influence or, worse yet, some Catholic legislator telling him how to run his business in Petit Rouge. Raifer had made it clear to Bucky that his job, among other things, was to make sure things did not get out of hand in Lamou.

While Dr. Cailleteau went to Little Miss's room to check on her, Raifer inspected the rest of the big house. There was no one there. Up in the attic, where Jenny's quarters were, the room was vacant.

Raifer went out the back door. The kitchen, which was detached from the house as a precaution against fire, was deserted. The fireplace was cold.

The cabins behind the big house where Sally and Marcus and Cubit and Jordan and the others lived were likewise empty. It appeared that everyone had left in a hurry, taking only the barest of necessities. Plates and cups were left on the table. A bag of rice here. A sack of flour there. The coloreds had not taken any of the wagons or the horses, as far as Raifer could tell. They had been careful. They hadn't wanted to be accused of theft.

They hadn't been in Little Jerusalem. They hadn't passed through Parteblanc. They had to be moving through the woods or swamps.

That was all right. He would catch them eventually. He could create some charge that would stick and would bring them back, especially Jenny and Sally and Marcus. There could always be missing silverware or liquor. There could always be theft charged. He'd send out a flimsy when he got back and would telegraph Baton Rouge and New Orleans and all the points in between to be on the lookout for and arrest the fleeing thieves.

He'd make them come back and care for Little Miss. How dare they leave her in her condition? He'd threaten them and tell them they had to stay as long as Little Miss was alive. No need for Little Miss to be a drain on the Petit Rouge Parish budget until someone got the Cottoncrest finances in order, and that might take some time.

Maybe they were just hiding out in the daytime, ready to come back tonight and get the rest of their goods. That made more sense. They had just pretended to run, and then, when they thought it was safe, they would come back and clear out Cottoncrest of all its finery. Raifer might have to post a watch this evening. That would be Bucky's task when he finished in Lamou.

Raifer went over to the barn where the bodies of the Colonel Judge and Rebecca lay. Inside the horses rustled in their stalls. They were hungry. They hadn't been fed. Raifer got the pitchfork and shoveled some fresh hay into each stall. Someone else could clean the stalls out later.

Raifer heard a scraping noise behind him. He knew it. They had come back for the horses. If it was Cubit or Jordan, they'd have a surprise. He pulled out his gun and crouched down behind one of the barrels.

The noise stopped. They must have heard him.

Raifer paused, scarcely breathing. He would catch them.

No sounds could be heard in the barn, just the chirping of birds outside and the distant voices of the sharecroppers in the fields cutting and piling the cane.

Raifer took a scrap of wood from the floor and tossed it toward the barn door, where it made a hollow clatter. That would startle whoever had sneaked into the barn.

Raifer was right. The scraping noise started again. Someone was trying to move quietly but not quietly enough.

Raifer leaped out from behind the barrel, gun extended. "Come on, now. Show yourself or be shot."

The scraping noise continued, but it also took on a wet, slurping sound.

Raifer spun around, looking behind him and glancing up into the loft. The noise stopped again.

Where was he? No one could be seen. Where could he be hiding?

Once more, a scraping sound. It could be someone's boot brushing against the wooden staves of the stall. It could also be a rifle being rested against a post.

Raifer crouched low and focused intensely to determine the place where the sound originated. He heard it again. It was coming from near the boards where the Colonel Judge and Rebecca lay, covered with sheets.

Raifer pressed himself against a post and, resting his finger lightly on the trigger of his Colt pistol, peered out at the corner where the bodies were.

The Colonel Judge was moving his head under his sheet! He wasn't dead.

That was impossible.

Raifer didn't believe in a Cottoncrest curse. Hadn't thought it existed. Not until now.

But if the Colonel Judge was somehow alive, this place was truly cursed.

The Judge's head continued to move. The sheets stirred around his jaw. He was trying to say something.

Raifer's stomach tightened into a mass of knots. He breathed heavily, not seeming to be able to draw enough oxygen into his constricted lungs.

Raifer didn't believe in voodoo and spirits and ghosts. But whatever it was, whatever the Colonel Judge had become, Raifer had to confront it.

Gun cocked and ready to fire, as if bullets could do any harm to one already dead, Raifer took three long, quick strides, yanked the sheet away, flinging it to the barn floor.

A large rat was sitting on the Colonel Judge's chin. It already had chewed off a portion of the Colonel Judge's nose. It had scratched out an eye from its socket. Half of the Colonel Judge's left eye was still in the rat's mouth.

The rat jumped off the Colonel Judge onto the neighboring body, landing on the sheet that covered the headless cadaver. As it hit, three more rats ran out from under Rebecca's sheet and leaped to the floor. Two scurried toward the open barn door, one scampered up the post and into the loft, and the one on Rebecca's chest bared its teeth.

That was too much even for Raifer. He shot.

The bullet pulverized the top part of the rat, and the body fell limp, a bloody furry pool on top of Rebecca's sheet.

Raifer brushed the dead rodent aside and retrieved the Colonel Judge's sheet from the dusty barn floor. The Colonel Judge's body was covered with rat droppings, and his clothes were beginning to be eaten away. Tiny ragged holes marked the locations where the rat had gnawed through the once-fine silk and brocade waistcoat. Raifer didn't bother to look at Rebecca's corpse. It could only be the same, or worse.

What a sad end to a fine gentleman and a beautiful lady.

Raifer went immediately back to the big house. Dr. Cailleteau was sitting on the veranda with Little Miss, still in her nightgown, several blankets draped over her shoulder. Raifer urgently motioned to Dr. Cailleteau, who slowly moved his vast bulk and met Raifer halfway down the elegant front stairs that ran from the columned front porch to the ground below.

Raifer quickly described to Dr. Cailleteau what had happened.

Dr. Cailleteau's face reflected his sadness. "The indignity of it all. I'll get the funereals?"

"Can't do that, Doc. Doesn't matter how badly their clothes are mangled, you can't start scrounging through their bureaus and armoires for funereals. If you get burial clothes for them, then someone will have to dress them, and then they'll see what happened, and the talk will begin. This is just between you and me. We'll get some sheets and wrap them in a shroud. I'll get some of the sharecroppers to dig a grave, right now, next to where the General is buried, and I'll complete the task. You get Little Miss loaded in the wagon and get out of sight of Cottoncrest soon. She can't see any of this."

Raifer went upstairs to get some sheets from an armoire, while Dr. Cailleteau walked back to where Little Miss sat blankly.

Dr. Cailleteau had seen death too often, when lifeless frames, deprived of sepulture, were left to rot openly in battlefields. His old friend should be honored, not dumped unceremoniously into a grave.

But Raifer was right.

It was bad enough, the bullet wound in the Colonel Judge's head.

It was bad enough, his face disfigured by the rats.

No one should see that, just as they shouldn't see the rest of his scarred body bearing his many wounds from the war. The gash of the bullet wound in his shoulder. The shrapnel scars in his left leg, which had shattered the bone and caused him to walk with a cane and a limp since the war. The fact that the shrapnel had cut off his manhood, leaving him with no testicles and only a stump of a penis.

Chapter 55

Bucky proudly rode at the head, followed by Tee Ray, Forrest, and four other Knights, armed with pistols and rifles, who had decided to ride with Tee Ray. The rest had stayed back to harvest the cane fields.

Bucky preened at the way Raifer had treated him once they had gotten to Cottoncrest. Raifer had put him in charge of the posse of sharecroppers. Now the men knew of his importance. They were following him, just as they should.

As they headed toward Lamou, Tee Ray had let Bucky ride at the front. Let him think he's in charge. It didn't matter as long as they got the Jew. Tee Ray had given instructions to the Knights before Bucky got there. They were to kill the Jew the moment they spotted him.

They bore southwest, following the road away from the river and into the swamps. It was just a narrow dirt path barely higher than the surrounding boggy land. Now the hardwoods lined the road. Tall sycamores and oaks and hickory dripping with Spanish moss formed a canopy under which they passed. Thick-leaved vines climbed into the trees on stout brown stalks forming veils that hid the woods beyond. Palmettos, their fan-shaped leaves as wide as a horse's flank, glistened green in the morning sun that filtered through the verdant woods.

The Knights tried to move quietly on their horses, but Étienne, hunting for squirrel, had heard them coming when they were still more than a mile away. By the time they rounded the bend and saw the bayou and the Acadian cottages of Lamou, they were more than expected.

Trosclaire Thibodeaux relaxed in his rocking chair on his porch, smoking a pipe. Aimee stayed inside with the children, but Tante Odille sat in the other rocking chair, calmly shelling peas.

Bucky quickly surveyed the scene. It seemed quiet enough. Trosclaire was sitting with an old lady who was probably as senile as Little

Miss. A young boy and girl—they couldn't be older than fifteen—were loading up a pirogue, probably for a day of fishing or trading with the Cajuns who lived deep in the swamps in houses accessible only by water. They were putting baskets on top of a large muddy bearskin that was undoubtedly covering a stack of other trading items. No one else was in sight. The dozen or so houses in Lamou were dark and empty of life.

Bucky quickly concluded that the rest of the Cajuns were out fishing. These were simple people. They made their living on the water and in the swamps, eating things no one else would eat, doing work no one else would do. This would not take any time at all.

"Trosclaire! I've got to talk to you." Talk to them with authority. That was the way to impress them.

Tante Odille cackled, taking in Bucky's elongated face and gangly limbs. "*Vilain comme les sept péchés mortels.*"

"What did the old lady say?" Bucky demanded.

"She said," Trosclaire explained, "just that you must be an important man to head up such a group."

Bucky straightened up in his saddle. This was going exactly as he had planned.

Jake, hidden beneath the bearskin in the long cypress pirogue that Jeanne Marie and Étienne were loading, smiled to himself. What Tante Odille said was that Bucky was as ugly as the seven mortal sins.

"Well, she's right! I am important. I'm here on official business. I'm looking for the Jew Peddler."

"You mean Monsieur Gold, the peddler? Is he a Jew? This is strange news. Is that now what you do for the law? Hunt Jews?"

Bucky detected a tone of derision in Trosclaire's voice and didn't like it. The way to deal with the ignorant was to show them who was boss. Take control in every way. Bucky squinted his eyes in what he knew Trosclaire would take to be a look of imminent danger. Bucky would show Trosclaire he was not to be trifled with.

"I don't need none of your sass! Has he been here? We know he's traveling in this direction. Tell me where he is, or we're going to execute a writ of habeas corpus and corpus delicti and fieri facias and search each and every one of your houses!" Bucky said all this forcefully. He knew he could scare these illiterate Cajuns with obscure legalistic Latin phrases, even if he himself was unsure of what they meant. They wouldn't know any better. They could not help but be impressed and obey him.

"*Maigre comme un tasso*," Tante Odille said, and whistled.

"She understands that I'm the law, right? And that I have the power to do as I say."

"She does not speak English, but she understands exactly what you are."

Jake, in the bottom of the pirogue, would have enjoyed the banter if the consequences were not potentially deadly. Trosclaire was toying with Bucky. What Tante Odille had said was that Bucky was as skinny as a strip of dried meat.

"Then you and she both know my authority. I demand that you tell me where he is. Or . . ." Bucky dismounted and tied the reins of his horse on the branch of a nearby pine tree. "Or I'll start inspecting each house here. Starting with yours."

Tee Ray and the others sat quietly on their horses, waiting to see what would happen next. They would let Bucky try first, then they would take over.

Bucky had not even taken half a step when Trosclaire whipped out a knife and threw it with deadly accuracy toward the tree next to which Bucky had just been standing. The knife pinned the reins to the branch. "I do not think," said Trosclaire calmly, "that I would like that."

Bucky pulled out his pistol. "You want to oppose the law, Trosclaire?"

"I do not think you have power here to search my house or even stand in my yard. Why, the next thing you'll want to do is to search the church, our blessed Sainte Clotilde sur le Rive." Trosclaire turned to Tante Odille. "*Il est doucement comme le melasse dans janvier.*"

Tante Odille, with a wide, toothless grin, laughed out loud.

Jake, hearing what Trosclaire had said and despite Tante Odille's laughter, could tell they were continuing their dangerous game. Trosclaire had proclaimed that Bucky was slow as molasses in January. Jake reached down and pulled the Freimer blade out of his belt. If Bucky started anything, Jake would be ready.

Bucky, his pistol drawn, started up the steps of Trosclaire's cottage.

Tante Odille put down the bowl of peas and picked up a long knife she had hidden under the bowl, in the folds of her skirt. Holding it in her hands, she stood in the doorway. *"Vous allez en toute probabilité faire une coche mal taille,"* she said firmly.

Jake, under the bearskin, could not see what was happening. Tante Odille had proclaimed that Bucky was about to make a badly carved notch, meaning he was about to make a big mistake. Something was about to happen. To Bucky.

Tee Ray, surprised by what the old lady held, took over. He pulled out his rifle and leveled it at the old lady's head. "I recognize that knife! That's one of the Jew Peddler's blades. Search the church? We'll damn well tear the place apart brick by brick if we have to. We've all heard enough of your French Papist nonsense. Catholics ain't but one step above niggers and two steps above Jews. And Cajuns ain't even a half-step above Jews."

All the Knights now had their rifles out, and they were pointed at Trosclaire and Tante Odille.

Trosclaire didn't get up from his rocker. "Before you do something you may regret, I think you should look around first, no?"

Trosclaire pointed at the other cottages.

The six Knights and Bucky slowly scanned the wooded landscape of Lamou. From every cottage window now protruded a rifle. At least thirty of them were pointing at the Knights. Even the young boy and girl next to the pirogue had rifles in their hands.

"Now," said Trosclaire, very slowly, "I think we shall show you something you may find interesting, yes?"

Trosclaire got up from the rocker, walked up to Bucky, and took Bucky's hat off his head. Trosclaire went over to the tree and, removing the knife from the reins, cut a small hole in the brim and then pinned the hat against the tree so that the bark protruded through the hole, which was not more than an inch in diameter.

"You will not fire," Trosclaire said to Tee Ray and the others as he returned to his rocker. "You will just watch. Then, if you want to fire and take your chances, you may. *Étienne! Jeanne Marie!*"

Jake, underneath the bearskin, relaxed. Trosclaire had things well in control.

The two fifteen-year-olds raised their rifles and pointed toward the tree. The horsemen moved out of the way.

Étienne and Jeanne Marie each fired, almost simultaneously. Then they quickly reloaded and waited, rifles poised.

"Monsieur Bucky, you may now have your hat back."

Bucky strode forcefully to the pine tree, trying not to show how his stomach was quivering and his mouth was dry with fear. He looked at his hat, and his eyes grew wide. He stared with puzzled astonishment. The two bullets were nestled in the trunk of the tree, inside the circle made by the hole in his hat brim. The hat was otherwise untouched.

"*Un front froncé dit pas que la cervelle ap'es travailler; des fois c'est juste un mal de tête,*" Tante Odille commented.

Jake heard the shots. He knew that some fancy shooting had occurred, but he could not understand why Tante Odille had said, "A wrinkled brow does not mean the brain is working; sometimes it's just a bad headache."

Trosclaire now smiled gently and waved at Jeanne Marie and Étienne. "*Au revoir et adieu. Meiux que ça et les prêtrest seraient jaloux!*"

As Trosclaire said good-bye and farewell, any better than this and the priests would be jealous, Jake felt Jeanne Marie and Étienne climb into the pirogue. Étienne began paddling, and Jeanne Marie kept her rifle trained on the men as the flat-bottomed boat moved out into the bayou.

"Bucky!" Tee Ray was furious. "Don't you see what's happening? The Jew is in that canoe! Look at it. It's too weighed down for just two people. Riding too low in the water. Under that bearskin. That's the Jew!"

Bucky looked around helplessly at the many rifles still pointing at them from all the Lamou windows. "What do you want me to do, Tee Ray?"

Tee Ray, in disgust, started to turn his horse around. They could travel farther south and intercept the pirogue as it neared where the bayou narrowed and kill them all before they could make it into the vast marsh where horses could not go.

But Tee Ray's horse whinnied as a man appeared from behind a wide oak. He grabbed the reins of Tee Ray's horse and pointed a rifle directly at Tee Ray's chest.

"I think," said Trosclaire amicably, "that Monsieur Bucky, Monsieur

Tee Ray, and the others of you should be my guests. For lunch and maybe for dinner also, no? We had a *boucherie* the other day, and we now have some fine andouille and tasso, made special by Tante Odille. That, plus some dirty rice and grilled mirliton. We shall share a feast, yes? Maybe my Aimee, she may even make a *tarte à la bouillie*."

"*Andouille y tasso!*" Tante Odille exclaimed unhappily, realizing that Trosclaire was going to feed these ridiculous men the carefully prepared results of the *boucherie*. "*Il y a plus d'une manière d'étouffer un chien à part lui donner une saucisse.*" There's more than one way to choke a dog than giving him sausage.

Chapter 56

"I don't believe it. You got huckleberried by Cajuns! Walked square into it, didn't you. Didn't think about splitting up the men, trying to flank Lamou, did you?"

Bucky slumped dejectedly in his chair behind his desk, trying to disappear into the corner. Trosclaire had kept them in Lamou all day, serving them food and talking constantly but not letting them leave. The rifles had remained trained on them the entire time. Finally, when twilight came, Trosclaire had allowed them to depart. But that wasn't bad enough. Now, all Dr. Cailleteau was doing was jawin' him.

"See you got a hole in your hat. Lucky they didn't put a hole in your head . . . although, come to think about it, if they had, it might have let a little sunlight in there. When, during the Port Hudson siege, a miasma would drift through—and that's about the extent of what's going on inside that skull of yours—the only thing to cure it would be a good day's sunlight and a stiff breeze."

"I don't got no asthma," Bucky pouted under his breath.

"Not asthma, Bucky. Miasma. Poison vapor from decaying corpses." Dr. Cailleteau took another puff on his big cigar and drank down the glass of whiskey that Raifer had put in front of him. "Raifer, a phrenologist could take this boy to Charles Darwin, if he were still alive, and Darwin would have to declare him to be a whole new and inferior species."

Bucky sunk lower into his chair.

"You have to do it now, Raifer. You don't have any choice."

Raifer got up and poured himself another cup of coffee. It was dark outside. Another day lost. "I know, Doc."

"Told you that you should have done it after we came back from Cottoncrest. Should have done it right then, when you sent the flimsy on to Baton Rouge and New Orleans about arresting Marcus and Sally and Jenny for theft and shipping them back here to Petit Rouge."

Raifer didn't want to have the rest of this discussion in Bucky's presence. He turned away from Dr. Cailleteau and said to his deputy, with firm direction in his voice, "Go home."

Bucky just gazed down at his feet, trying to avoid the glare from Raifer's eyes.

"Right now."

Bucky looped two fingers through the hole in the brim of his hat and pulled it off the desk with a scowl. Dr. Cailleteau was behind this. He had pushed Raifer into it. Dr. Cailleteau had just said that Raifer should have done it after they came back from Cottoncrest. Done what? Done did what Raifer just did, firing him and sending him home. Now, with no job, what would he do? People would laugh at him. They would point him out and say that poor Bucky couldn't even catch a Jew and let himself get tricked by Cajuns, of all people. Ain't hardly nothin' worse than Cajuns 'cept darkies and Jews, and yet Marcus has done gone and slipped through his fingers, and the Jew has disappeared into the swamps, and Cajuns got him pinned down all day, feeding him and Tee Ray and Forrest and the other Knights like pigs getting fattened up for the slaughter. And Tee Ray and Forrest would blame him, and they'd kick him out of the Knights. He might just as well die now.

"Get going, Bucky," Raifer commanded. "Can't have you sitting 'round here a moment longer than necessary."

There was no hope. This was it. "Raifer, can't I at least take my stuff from my desk? Just got a few things to clean out. Won't be a minute, then you won't never see me again."

"What are you talking about? I need you here tomorrow morning at dawn. Pack your bag for a three or four days journey. Pack some go-to-town clothes, the best you've got. Clean ones. Understand?"

Bucky looked up, startled.

"Don't sit there like a gin barrel waiting to be emptied. You were right that the peddler had to be in that pirogue. If they were headed south down the bayou, they were making for the swamp. They have to be trying to get him to New Orleans. It's either that or the Gulf of Mexico, and there's no way they can make it into the Gulf with the pirogue.

There's a riverboat coming through at daybreak on its way to New Orleans, and I want you on it. Get moving!"

Bucky rose out of the chair, buoyed by this sudden change of fortune. He wasn't being fired. He not only still had a job, but Raifer was also giving him the ultimate responsibility. Bring back the Jew. And he was going to New Orleans! He was going to ride a riverboat! It had been his dream. For the first time in his life he was going to go outside of the parish. Life could not get better. Bucky loved his job. He almost skipped out of the door into the dark. The sun had set over an hour ago.

With Bucky gone, Raifer could now continue the discussion with Dr. Cailleteau. "I told you why I hadn't wanted to send the telegraph earlier, Doc. Besides, you were dealing with Little Miss."

"Got her settled in for now, though no one in town here speaks French anymore but me. She'll stay at the boardinghouse for a few days—they reluctantly agreed to take her in until we can bring someone else as her caretaker and get her back to Cottoncrest. But you can't delay on the flimsy anymore. Look, I know you're worried that sending an arrest warrant for the peddler down to New Orleans will only flag for them that he's gotten away. Sure, it may cause you to look bad at first, but you've got to do it. Tonight. And you've got to let Tee Ray go after him. The way it is now, if the peddler is caught and brought back, dead or alive, no one will think the worse of you in the long run, and you'll actually be a hero for setting up the capture. But if he escapes, if he slips through and they find out you could have notified them but didn't . . ."

Dr. Cailleteau didn't have to complete the thought. Raifer knew he had no other choice. As long as things were quiet, his job was secure. But the governor and his staff had a lot of power. The governor was anti-lottery and anti-colored. That had been his platform. All against the lottery and all for segregation. It would just take a whisper from the governor, and Raifer wouldn't stand a chance. If it became known that Raifer had let blacks leave Cottoncrest and let a Jew escape, the results of the next election would be a foregone conclusion.

"You were right, Doc. I admit it. And you had the right approach. I'll draft it the way you suggested. I'll send a flimsy tonight to New Orleans seeking the additional arrest of Jake Gold. They already should be following up on my previous flimsy seeking reward for the arrest of Sally and Marcus and Jenny for suspected theft of valuables from Cottoncrest Plantation. Jake Gold will simply be another person to be picked up in connection with missing items following the unfortunate deaths of the Colonel Judge and his wife. No need to mention the cause of those deaths right now."

"That's the way. Once they're caught, it's done, and you're a hero, Raifer. Oh, the four of them are bound to be caught, and if for some strange reason they're not, then it will be Tee Ray's and Bucky's fault, not yours."

"I'll wire ahead to New Orleans to tell them to check with all the Jewish merchants and their Jewish churches—that's where he's sure to head first. I'll tell them I'm sending my deputy and one other. I've got enough funds in the sheriff's account to front the tickets and expenses for Bucky and Tee Ray."

Dr. Cailleteau, puffing on his cigar, nodded his approval. "Tee Ray's got to have blood in his eye after what the Cajuns and the Jew did to him and the Knights. With him and Bucky going down to New Orleans, you can be sure that coming back upriver will be a body in a coffin."

Chapter 57

Ganderson had told them to wait. They had followed his instructions, but the sun had risen and set, and they were still in the broken-down cabin with its partial roof and collapsed walls and no real protection from dropping temperatures. They didn't dare light a fire. The sky was clear, the stars were out, and the glow from the fire would be visible through the open walls for miles. Even the smoke could be seen in the moonlight.

The baguette was long gone. They were hungry and thirsty. Sally had fallen asleep, snoring, on Marcus's shoulder. Jenny was not sure whether Marcus was asleep or not. He was the oldest by far of the trio of traveling companions, but he was the most energetic of them all. Marcus had set the pace, his long legs leading them briskly as they left Ganderson's wagon and made their way through the woods to the cabin. Maybe Marcus was just resting, ears alert for the faintest noise.

Jenny had always been a city girl until she came to Cottoncrest. She still couldn't read the sounds of the night out here in the forest. She couldn't tell which creaks were simply the ancient oaks expanding and contracting with the changes in temperature and humidity and which noises signaled the approach of danger.

She lay her head back for a just a minute against the rotting wooden slats, intending to be like Marcus and close her eyes to better concentrate on the noises that seemed to surround them. The chirping of the crickets. The crunch of a small animal scampering across the crisp leaves fallen thick on the ground. The faint rustle of the pine needles as the wind gently moved through them. The soft, lilting melody of Louis's violin as he sat in his office late at night, taking a break and playing a plaintive gospel, the sadness and longing being drawn from the strings and wafting through the closed door to the back room where Jenny slept. She was careful to wash her hands before she went to bed, to remove any ink that might have gotten on her fingers from her scrivener's work during the day. The legal papers that Louis had her copying were long and complex. Some were in English, some in French. What he had been working on were writs of certiorari to the Louisiana Supreme Court, pleas to the court to hear the passenger car case. She didn't understand all the legal terminology, but she understood the cause. She understood all too well what this case meant to all the Negroes and Creoles, not only in New Orleans but throughout the South, from Secesh land all the way north to the Mason-Dixon Line and beyond.

Louis had said that if and when the passenger car case made it to the Supreme Court, it would fulfill Lincoln's promise. Lincoln had started a speech over the dead by saying, "Four score and seven years ago. . . ." It would be, Louis said, more than one score and seven years from Lincoln's death to get the case to the Supreme Court, but it would be worth it. That was why every word in the briefs that Jenny was copying was important.

The Fourteenth Amendment was the heart of the case, according to Louis. The amendment declared that all persons born in the United States are citizens and that no state could deny any person the equal protection of the laws. Jenny knew those words well. Louis quoted them over and over in his brief. A state could not "deny any person equal protection." Any person! That was the key concept. It applied to any person, former slave or not. It covered any person, regardless of the color of that person's skin. Each and every person was equal in the eyes of the Fourteenth Amendment.

Louis, pacing his office while working on the brief, had tried to figure out how to word it for the maximum effect. Layer upon layer of Jim Crow laws had been enacted since the war, but Washington had grown silent, and a doom descended on the South that hung like a shroud over the once-vibrant hopes of those who had struggled out of slavery only to be legislated back into a status little higher than slavery.

That was why this brief was crucial. The Supreme Court, said Louis, had to take the passenger car case. There was so much at stake.

And for Jenny there was so much to copy. Three sets of the petition for writs had to be filed, and duplicates had to be made for opposing counsel and for co-counsel and to mail to those who were helping with advice from the North. Jenny slept fitfully, thinking of all she had to do for Louis in the morning. Each copy had to be perfect, with every word clearly written. For the printer. For the court. For posterity.

Jenny awoke with a start. Marcus was tapping her shoulder. How long had she been dreaming?

The faintest glow from the east could be seen through the open roof. Dawn was still an hour or more away. Sally was standing next to Marcus. To Sally's right, visible in the light of the setting moon, was a tall white man. Next to him was a short, squat white woman whose height was about four and a half feet and whose width was almost the same.

"Jenny, we got to go now," Marcus said urgently. "There's no time."

Jenny rubbed the sleep from her eyes. "The train's coming to Baton Rouge, and you've got to take it already? At this hour?"

"Ain't gonna be no train for us. Not for Sally and me right now."

The squat woman helped Jenny to her feet and then handed her a large bundle. "You put this on your head, you hear, and follow me."

Jenny was indignant. She hadn't left Cottoncrest and the service of Little Miss to serve any more white women.

Sensing Jenny tense up and fearing she was about to say something she shouldn't, Marcus pulled her to one side and whispered in her ear, "These are Undergrounders too, just like Mr. Ganderson. Seems there is a warrant out for all of us. They're gonna be watchin' the trains and boats goin' north throughout Louisiana, so Sally and I got to follow this man. He's gonna put us on the Underground to Alabama. Once we've passed through Mississippi and over the Alabama line, we can head north from there. But if you're set on gettin' to New Orleans, as you are, then you got to go with this lady. They're lookin' for a high yellow gal like you travelin' alone, not a housegirl followin' a respectful distance behind her mistress, carrying a bundle on her head that shows she knows her place and covers her features at the same time. Understand?"

Jenny nodded and squeezed Marcus's hand.

Marcus leaned over and gave her a grandfatherly kiss on the forehead. "The Lord will protect. Two dead. Two safe. And two on their way to safety. That leaves just you."

Chapter 58

"Monsieur Jake," Jeanne Marie asked in French, "why is it that the Knights hate Catholics and Jews so much?"

Jake sat in the middle of the pirogue wrapped in the bearskin, while Jeanne Marie paddled in front and Étienne steered through the seemingly endless marsh.

After leaving Lamou they had traveled all day in the long, narrow boat, carved from a single piece of cypress, down the curving bayou. The bayou had emptied into the forested swamp. There towering cypress trees had loomed overhead, their gigantic roots poking above the water and forming knees for these ancient sentinels.

Threading the pirogue through the swamp's maze of brackish waters, Étienne had brought them out into the marsh. Once the tops of the trees had almost disappeared over the horizon in the late afternoon, they had paused while Étienne and Jeanne Marie had taken out fishing poles and expertly caught several speckled trout. Then Étienne had located a narrow piece of high ground, where Jeanne Marie built a fire, Étienne prepared the fish, and they had a hot meal before sleeping under the vast sky, secure on the tiny treeless island in the marsh.

Today Étienne and Jeanne Marie had been paddling through the marsh since dawn. The sun was almost directly overhead. The swamp had been confusing enough with its immense trees and canopy of leaves and moss and vines, and Jake did not know how Étienne knew the way through. Here in the marsh, however, it seemed even worse, for from his low perch in the pirogue, Jake could see nothing but still water and thick vegetation. High oyster grass projected five feet above the surface of the marsh and marched to the horizon, broken up only by narrow pathways of water that opened onto hidden lakes from which led more streams and bands, some of which abruptly terminated at dead ends and others of which led to yet more open acres of water. Upon crossing the lakes, they would again be swallowed up by the ocean of grass pushing in on the narrow pirogue. Every so often Jake would see clumps of reeds fifteen feet tall, each stem as slender as Jeanne Marie's little finger, rising above the grasses and casting gently swaying shadows.

Overhead the birds of winter were arriving. Huge flocks of white geese, high in the sky, flapped their wings slowly as they glided along thousands of feet above in precise V-shape formations. Hawks hovered even higher, coasting on the air currents. Flittering ducks, sometimes in groups of twos and threes, sometimes in the hundreds, swooped low over the marsh, settling onto the wide hidden lakes, only to fly off when the pirogue entered, disturbing their feeding. Tiny yellow-throated vireos, darting from the safety of the swamps over the horizon, flew out and then quickly returned to their nests in the hackberry, green ash, sweet gum, and water oaks.

Jeanne Marie knew all the birds and pointed them out to Jake as they passed by, but Étienne never spoke to Jake. He never spoke to anyone, it seemed, except Jeanne Marie and only then when he didn't think Jake was listening. Jeanne Marie had explained that, as Tante Odille liked to say, Étienne kept his tongue in his pocket.

Jake and Jeanne Marie, however, had carried on a running conversation in French. Jeanne Marie did not speak any English.

"Why, Monsieur Jake?" Jeanne Marie asked again. "Father Séverin in Lamou has said that we must all love our neighbors, and I want to love them, but our neighbors do not love us. They hate us, and they seem to hate you more, just because you are a Jew. I could see it in Monsieur Tee Ray's eyes and hear it in his voice, even though I could not understand the words."

"What can I say, Jeanne Marie? People sometimes hate others because they are different. The Cossacks hated us in Russia because we were Jews. We looked different. We acted different."

"But you do not look so different. To me you look like all the others in Petit Rouge. Yes?"

"Jeanne Marie, you are a wonderful girl, and may you always have eyes that see the truth rather than what someone else thinks you should see. In Russia, however, we did look different. My father and uncle wore beards, my mother wore a wig, and even as a little boy, I had long strands of hair that dropped in front of my ears—*pais* we called them. And special hats and special clothes. We looked different. We spoke a different language. Yiddish."

"Yet," Jeanne Marie protested, "today you look like everyone else. You wear the same clothes as everyone else. Your hair looks like everyone else. You even speak English just like everyone else. Your French is so good too, like someone from Paris."

"You are very kind. I hope that someday you will see Paris, Jeanne Marie. You are right. Sometimes even if people look the same, they are still hated because others hate who they are or what they believe."

"I do not understand."

"Sometimes neither do I. There was a war here, you know. The Colonel Judge fought in it. That's how he became a colonel. In that war state fought against state because of beliefs. It was not about looks at all. The soldiers on one side of the line looked like the soldiers on the other side, except for the color of their uniforms. They spoke the same language. They worshipped in the same churches. They had grown up singing the same songs and reading the same books. But they killed each other by the thousands. It was about beliefs. Just like a cheap knife can rust from the inside out—starting with a tiny crack where the blade meets the haft, until there is nothing left of strength in the blade, although the tip of the blade looks shiny and strong—hate can eat away inside a person until there's nothing but the rust of spite and malevolence keeping them alive. That is how I think Tee Ray is. That is how I think some of the Knights are. They hate the Jews because they think we killed Jesus. The Knights hate the Catholics because they think you obey a foreign power, the pope, instead of being American like them."

"How silly. How can Tee Ray and the others believe such things? The *ouaouaron* in the swamp—the bullfrog—has more sense than that."

"I agree. In fact, what makes it all the more strange is that Tee Ray's mother was Catholic."

Chapter 59

Bucky stared out over the railings in wonder. He had imagined what it would be like, but he hadn't imagined half hard enough.

The paddle wheels turned endlessly, water cascading from them as the batons reached the top only to plunge down into the river once more. The boat carved its way through the strong currents of the Mississippi, the brown water swirling around the vessel as it arced slowly port to bypass a sandbar or bore starboard to avoid a huge clump of driftwood half-submerged and drifting downstream.

Port and starboard. Left and right. It was all so miraculous. Bucky was mastering all these new words.

Every part of it was wonderful, even though this was not the riverboat with rooms and actors and a fancy restaurant and rich men and women in elegant clothes with refined manners that Bucky had dreamed about. This was only a cargo transport, its hold filled with hogs and goats and chickens and smelling of animals and manure.

But Bucky didn't care. It was still a real steamboat. It was still taking him away from Parteblanc. It was whisking him, curve by long curve of the river, toward the great city of New Orleans, where he would see sights so fantastic that for the rest of his life he would be able to tell tales to all those who never even left Petit Rouge Parish, whose world never extended beyond the parish lines.

Bucky couldn't bear to be distracted even for a moment. He wanted to remember each and every sight. The vast forests that abruptly bordered even vaster plantations, where the planter's homes, some as large as Cottoncrest, rose up on tall columns like white spectral figures praying to the sky.

Bucky wanted it all to last forever, and at the same time he couldn't wait to get to New Orleans.

Tee Ray couldn't wait to get to New Orleans either. Propped against a rail on the upper deck, he slowly drew his knife across the small whetstone for the hundredth time. Raifer had been clear; if Tee Ray wanted to go get the Jew, he had to go with Bucky. You got to be sure, Raifer had told him, that Bucky is with you when you catch him. That'll make it all legal. Do something to the Jew when Bucky's not there, and then either the sheriff of Orleans Parish or the police chief of New Orleans may get involved, depending what you've done to the peddler, but if Bucky is there with his badge, then they'll let you do what you got to do.

Tee Ray was happy enough to let Bucky continue to stare wide-eyed at everything. For Bucky this was a trip of firsts. His first time away from home. His first time on his own. His first time to experience the sensuous pleasures of New Orleans.

For Tee Ray it was a trip of lasts. This was going to be the last season he would ever be a sharecropper. This was going to be last season his six children would sleep in the crowded two-room cabin instead of each having a separate bedroom with a fine feather mattress and a four-poster bed and a porcelain washbasin and a mahogany armoire filled with new clothes. This was going to be the last time Mona would have to fetch water and cook breakfast rather than ordering a servant to do this and everything else for her.

This was going to be last time Tee Ray's family would ever be just one of many. Soon they would be first above all.

Tee Ray wished his mother were alive to see this day. Would she have rejoiced? Tee Ray was not sure. Even after all the General had done to her, after the bitter rejection and continuing slights, to the day his mother died, she couldn't bring it in her heart to hate him or Little Miss or the Colonel Judge. Every night she said a prayer for them, a prayer for forgiveness.

Those prayers had gnawed on Tee Ray as he had grown up. He had never understood them. Why pray for those who refused to talk to you, who refused to see you, who treated you like you were invisible and worthless? His mother never lost hope, but Tee Ray never found it. If that was the way those folks feel, Tee Ray came to believe, then you should return the feeling ten times over. Love, his mother had said, gave her strength, but Tee Ray knew that, for himself, it was anything but love that gave meaning to his life.

His mother had always done things for love, regardless of the consequences. Now Tee Ray would continue to do things for hate because of the consequences.

PART VI

Today

Chapter 60

"No interstate highways back in those days. No six-lane expressways leading to bridges across the river. No. In those days you took the Airline Highway north out of New Orleans. There wasn't anything for miles and miles. Just cotton fields and sugarcane and hot sun.

"When you got to Luling, you drove your car up the levee, right across the top, and back down onto the ferry. That's how you got across the river. The ferry could fit maybe sixteen cars on it in a squeeze, five on each side next to the railings, lined up like wagons 'round a campfire, and six in the center, parked three and three. You put on the parking brake and got out, 'cause it was far too hot to sit in those cars. You just watched and waited as the muddy water sloshed below, and the diesel engines slowly pushed you across the river.

"I don't know how Grandpapa ever got from Lamou to New Orleans. I know he couldn't take the riverboat; he had said they were watching for that. And he didn't have a horse, and he couldn't take the road. He said they were watching the roads too. Yet somehow he managed to get from Parteblanc to New Orleans.

"In those days that trip took a minimum of three days by horse once you crossed the river. I don't even know where or how he got across the river from the west bank where Cottoncrest was to the east bank where New Orleans sits."

"But there I was, in 1961, crossing the Mississippi on a ferry, having come up from New Orleans in less than an hour.

"And once I was across, there were those strange little cities. It wasn't like it is today, all uniform, with national franchises of everything from gasoline stations to stores to fast food, so every place you go is really like every place you've been.

No, in those days everything was local, and Louisiana was like no place I had ever seen. Little towns like Des Allemands, where lots of people spoke French although it was originally a German settlement. Tiny stores with hand-lettered signs that sold homemade boudin and andouille sausage. Little boys sitting on their haunches next to the ditches on either side of the road—the road having been carved right through the swamp and marsh and built up, leaving deep ditches on either side where the dirt had been dug to pile up so that the road was a few feet higher than the usual water level—a pole in one hand and a net in the other. No, they weren't fishing. They had tied a raw piece of bacon on the end of the line and were hunting for crawfish.

"It was all mighty strange to a northern city boy like me. But what lay ahead, I knew, was going to be even stranger. And much more dangerous than even the Freedom Rides."

1893

Chapter 61

"Now who could be knocking at this hour! Zig, if I've told you once
. . . this isn't a respectable area. We should have bought that house next
to the railway line, right on St. Charles Avenue. But no, you said, this
area is less expensive and would be just as nice. Well, less expensive
gets you this. Knocks at all hours of the night!"

"Leah, shhh. You want the neighbors should hear you?"

"The neighbors! If we lived in the Vieux Carré, with all those houses
with their common walls, then they could hear. Out here in the Garden
District who can hear anything from one garden to the next? Besides,
all our neighbors are asleep. That's what respectable people do."

"Enough! You'll wake the children."

"Who could sleep through this knocking? Go answer the door already. And take a gun. One cannot be too careful." Leah Haber adjusted her green silk dressing gown as she walked out of the handsome
parlor, with its elegant gas lamps flickering a warm glow on pale blue
walls that stretched up past the triple crown molding to the sixteen-
foot-high stark-white ceiling with its carved plaster reliefs.

As she turned the corner, past the tall Chinese vase filled with fresh
flowers, on her way up the wide staircase to the second floor and beyond, up to the third floor where the children slept, Isaac "Zig" Haber
could hear her muttering, "Does he want to live where respectable people live? No. He wants to live where he thinks property will appreciate
faster. What am I going to do with that man?"

Zig reached into a cabinet and, opening an intricately ornamented
oak case, withdrew an expensive revolver. Making sure it was loaded,
he approached the broad double doors that opened onto the front veranda. "Who is it?" he said stoutly. Zig Haber was not a man to be tri-

fled with. Not in business. Not in deal making. And certainly not in his home.

"Please, Zig, open the door. I need your help," a hoarse voice called.

"I don't open the door at this hour for anyone. Go away!" Zig's tone was that of one who was used to getting his way. Since the Italian massacres no one could be too careful. No one, certainly, like Zig Haber, who would always be seen as an immigrant and an outsider by the famously insular French who lived downtown as well as by the brashly proud Catholics and Protestants who populated the uptown Garden District.

"*Siz nito keyn tachlis dorten?*" the voice beyond the door asked.

Zig put down the gun and, unlocking the door, quickly ushered in the young man, who stood shivering on his gallery in the chilly October night air. Jake Gold always began their talks that way. Jake always asked, when he came back from one of his trips to the country, "There's no room for negotiation here?" And of course in their trading there was always room for negotiation.

Hearing the door open and close again quickly, Leah called from the top of the stairs, "Zig! Who is it?"

"It's business, Leah. Go back upstairs."

Leah murmured under her breath as she turned around to complete her way to the top floor of the house to check on the children, "Business. With him it's always business. Even at this hour of the night!"

Chapter 62

"Slow down, Bucky, we've got another full day tomorrow. He's either here already, or he'll be here shortly. He's gonna fall right into our hands, that's for sure. And when he does, remember, you're gonna get all the credit."

Bucky finished off one final mouthful of beer and put the half-filled pint mug back on the counter, next to the two empty ones he had already drained, next to the tumblers of whiskey he and Tee Ray had raced through a half-hour ago. Tee Ray was right. Bucky was going to get all the credit. That's why Raifer had given him this important task.

"But Tee Ray," Bucky asked though the haze of inebriation that was descending over him, "do we really have to start so early tomorrow mornin'? After all, we've been at this four days already. We've been to each of the five Jew churches twice. We've been to most of the Jew stores in town. We done passed out flyers and made it clear that ain't no one should be harboring the peddler and, if they hear about him at all, they've got to let us know. We've been to the Orleans Parish Sheriff's Office, the City of New Orleans Police Department, City Hall, the Cotton Exchange, the Board of Trade, and even the Fire Department. Ain't it time to have some fun yet?"

Tee Ray's face broke into a malicious grin. "Plenty of time for fun when we've caught him, you know that, Bucky. I'll make sure you're gonna have so much fun you ain't never gonna want to stop."

Bucky knew exactly what Tee Ray meant. Bucky could hardly wait. Tee Ray was going to take him into Faubourg Tremé. Before coming to New Orleans, Bucky hadn't known what a Faubourg was, but now, along with *port* and *starboard*, he had added new words to his vocabulary. *Faubourg*, he now knew to his satisfaction, was just a French word for neighborhood. New Orleans was full of strange words. Like *ban-*

quette for sidewalk. Heck, it weren't that hard to be in the big city. It was easy to learn what you had to learn.

But what Bucky really wanted to learn about, firsthand, was Faubourg Tremé. Tee Ray had promised him. Once they caught the Jew Peddler, Tee Ray was going to take him down to one of them fine fast houses in Faubourg Tremé where they got all the good music and all the liquor you can drink and all them girls who dance with you in their silks and some who dance with you without anything on at all and then take you upstairs where you . . .

Bucky couldn't wait. A whole night spent like that. And Tee Ray promised him he could have two gals at one time if he wanted. Who could dream of such a thing? Bucky hadn't even thought of it before, but now that was all he could think about.

"Come on, Bucky, leave the rest of the beer. Tomorrow, first thing, we're going to see Isaac Haber."

"Just another Jew," Bucky complained as he started to pick up the mug again.

Tee Ray grabbed the mug from his hand. "Don't you listen to nothin'?" Tee Ray snapped. "Didn't you hear what they said at the Board of Trade today?"

Bucky was hurt. Why was Tee Ray doubting him? "Sure I heard. Jews like to trade with anyone, but Jews stick together. I ain't surprised. We knew that all the time. It's just like you tell the Knights. Jews get to do special deals, but only among themselves. Secret deals, along with their secret language."

Bucky's hurt feelings now started to turn to anger, fueled by the flush from the liquor. "Heard all of it. Remembered all of it. And I also remember who Raifer put in charge. It's me. You're here to help me, Tee Ray. You remember that, hear? I'm the one with the badge. I get to decide what we do and don't do. So don't go tellin' me what was said at the Board of Trade."

Tee Ray softened his approach. Being stern with Bucky wasn't going to get him where he needed to be. Tee Ray needed Bucky's full cooperation, and Bucky needed to think it was his own idea, not Tee Ray's.

Taking the still half-filled mug, Tee Ray led Bucky to the end of the bar, away from the crowd, and said encouragingly, "That's right, Bucky. No question about it. But I need your help. Maybe I wasn't makin' myself clear. What I need for you to tell me, 'cause I don't remember so well, is exactly what they told us at the Board of Trade this afternoon. You're the one with the good memory. It all kind of slips away from me."

Bucky pulled himself erect. Tee Ray was right. Tee Ray needed him to remember. That's why Bucky was there. To be in control. To make sure Tee Ray didn't make any mistakes.

Bucky squinted and looked at the ceiling, trying to recall the conversation. "Well, as I said, I remember it all. I handed out the flyers and talked about how the Jew Peddler and them darkies, Marcus and Sally and Jenny, were all stealing stuff from Cottoncrest after the Colonel Judge died unexpectedly—I was good, wasn't I, in not mentioning how the Colonel Judge done died? Raifer had said not to say."

"You done real good, Bucky. Go on, what happened next? I'm a little hazy."

"Then, as I recollect, they got real interested because they don't want no Jew stealin' from no one. And then they said that they don't know no peddler named Jake, but they asked what he peddled. And I done told them. He was always wantin', even more than money for his things, skins and hides in exchange. He always was trying to sell or trade a cartload of needles and thread and bolts of fabric and pots and pans and other such stuff. And knives. Real fancy knives."

Bucky's eyes lit up as he uttered these last few words.

"That was it, wasn't it? I remember now. It was my sayin' fancy knives that got them talkin'. Fancy knives to sell. Skins to trade. They done said that while there was lots of pelt traders, there was one Jew place that bought pelts and shipped them upriver to New York, and it also would purchase a supply of fancy knives from time to time. And that was Isaac Haber & Co. Hell, Tee Ray, don't you think we got to see them folks?"

Tee Ray patted Bucky on the back, handing Bucky the mug of beer for him to polish off. "I got to hand it to you, Bucky. You sure know this law business. You keep this up, Raifer gonna have to look out that he don't become your deputy."

As he drank the rest of the beer, Bucky wore a broad, proud smile.

Chapter 63

"You know I'm glad to have you, but it's not safe. Sooner or later they're going to come here asking questions."

Even at this late hour, Louis Martinet was dressed immaculately, his high starched collar in place, his string bowtie perfectly knotted, his suit vest buttoned, his shoes polished, his mustache perfectly trimmed and waxed. He had shut the windows of the small library and had lowered the gas lamp until it barely illuminated the room with a yellowish glow.

Like a caboose on a train, the library was the last room in Louis's law office, a narrow building no more than fifteen feet wide but running forty feet in length. Shotgun buildings were what they were called in New Orleans, because there was not enough width for a hallway. One room opened into another, the doors directly aligned, so that, it was said, you could fire a shotgun through the front door and the pellets would pass through all the rooms and exit through the rear door without scratching the woodwork.

"It's not a matter of whether you did anything wrong. I know you didn't. I know this is just another way to enslave you, to force you back to Cottoncrest. I assume you hadn't been paid in some time."

"Not for months," Jenny replied. "The Colonel Judge was so upset about everything, and it kept getting worse and worse. It was like Rebecca and the Colonel Judge had become hermits. Hermits from the world and from each other. Rebecca retreated to her room. The Colonel Judge couldn't stand being with her and couldn't stand being without her. He almost lived in his study. No, none of us had been paid. Of course, Marcus and Sally and the others expected, at most, room and board and their wages at the end of every planting season, but I was supposed to get paid every month. Not that I was going to complain, not with Rebecca needing me even more than Little Miss."

"You could, of course, bring a lawsuit. You know that, under the Civil Code, those who live in the house who haven't been paid can bring a suit to seize and sell the entire plantation and use the sales proceeds to pay your wages. It's a preferred debt, a privilege under the Civil Code."

"Sure," Jenny said, her voice tinged with irony, "they'll just let a Negro bring a lawsuit to seize the plantation. That's all Tee Ray will need to hear. The Knights will come swooping down with a lynching rope in hand."

"You don't want to take advantage of your rights? Jenny, do you know what it took to add that clause to the 1870 Civil Code over the objection of the white planters and the rich classes? Do you know how P.B.S. Pinchback and C. C. Antoine fought with the Reconstructionists to make sure that this law was enacted? Do you realize how Pinchback and Antoine suffered for pushing this proposal? They stood up for our rights. Your rights and mine. Jenny, if we don't stand up for our rights today, no one else will. If we don't, Pinchback and Antoine, the first two Negro governors of this state, will be the last two Negro governors as well. We have to use the law as a sword. We're going to cut a swath through the fields of hate and slice open the swollen belly of the wounded beast of prejudice."

"It's all well and good for you to talk about the law, Louis. What good has it done you? You've lost the passenger car case, and now things are worse than ever."

"Worse than ever, and yet there is still hope. Hope because everyone now knows what's at stake. Hope because I believe the U.S. Supreme Court will do what the Louisiana Supreme Court refused to do. We must keep up the pressure to vindicate our rights at every turn. Here . . ."

Louis reached behind him and pulled a stack of papers off the shelf. He rifled through them and smoothed out five pages. Even in the dim light, Jenny could see he was reading from the printed slip opinion of a court decision.

"Listen. Here's what the Louisiana Supreme Court wrote a few months ago, upholding the Separate Car Law. First, the opinion quotes from a case handed down by the Massachusetts Supreme Court upholding segregated schools. There Massachusetts had noted that while this might stem from prejudice, 'this prejudice, if it exists, is not created by law, and cannot be changed by law.'"

Louis paused, shaking his head in dismay. "It gets worse. Then the Louisiana Supreme Court quotes from an opinion by the Pennsylvania Supreme Court, which wrote:

> Whether there is such a difference between the white and the black races in this state, resulting from nature, law, and custom, as makes it a reasonable ground of separation.
>
> To assert separateness is not to declare inferiority in either. It is simply to say that, following the order of Divine Providence, human authority ought not to compel these widely separated races to intermix. Law and custom having sanctioned a separation of races, it is not the province of the judiciary to legislate it away. We are compelled to declare that at the time of the alleged injury there was that natural, legal, and customary difference between the white and black races in this state which made their separation, as passengers in a public conveyance, the subject of a sound regulation to secure order, promote comfort, preserve the peace, and maintain the rights both of the carriers and passengers.

"Doesn't that language destroy your case, Louis? Doesn't it mean you can't ever win this?"

"Don't you see, Jenny? Listen, the Louisiana Supreme Court realizes that these cases were decided before the Fourteenth Amendment was passed. They realize that . . ."

Louis held the opinion up so he could see it better in the dim light. He read slowly and dramatically:

> To hold that the requirement of separate, though equal, accommodations in public conveyances, violated the fourteenth amendment, would, on the same principles, necessarily entail the nullity of statutes establishing separate schools, and of others, existing in many states, prohibiting intermarriage between the races. All are regulations based upon difference of race; and, if such difference cannot furnish a basis for such legislation in one of these cases, it cannot in any.

"That's terrible," Jenny said sadly. "There really is no hope."

"No. It's what gives me hope. This reflects a perfect understanding of the issues. If the Fourteenth Amendment means what it says on its face and not what this court misconstrues it to mean, then not only can there be no separate railway cars for the races; there can be no separate schools. No laws against intermarriage. No distinction of any kind based on race. No more discrimination because you're 100 percent African or 50 percent or a quadroon or an octoroon or because you have one hundredth of a drop of African blood. No more need to 'pass for white' if you're light enough. No more discrimination based on what you look like on the outside or what racial mixture of blood flows beneath your skin. This is truly the test case, and it is perfectly framed. And, most importantly, Homer wants to see it through to the end."

"Homer may want to see it through, and you may want to see it through, but all I want to do is to stay long enough to get my business done with Jake and then get away from this city and this state. Get away and get as far north as possible."

"Jenny, I'm going to help you. You know that. I still don't understand why you want to help this Jew so much that you risk your own safety by coming to New Orleans."

Jenny said nothing in response. How could she explain it to Louis without endangering the others? Marcus and Sally knew, but they were on their way out of state, never to return. They would never say anything. That just left her and Jake. The two of them had to protect the secret. And she had already done so much. She couldn't fail them now. It was a matter of life or death. It always had been.

Chapter 64

"And the Acadians brought you all the way here in a pirogue?"

"No, Zig. They got me to Des Allemands. I gave the bearskin to those two young people as compensation for their getting me that far, and there I met up with Otto Schexnayder. He and I have been doing trading a while, and he owes me three more installments on two knives and some goods. I forgave the balance in exchange for him ferrying me across the river here to New Orleans."

Jake, wrapped in a blanket, sat on a velvet ottoman in front of the fireplace. He stroked the thick stubble on his cheeks and chin. He hadn't shaved in almost a week. At this rate, he thought, he would start looking like his father or Uncle Avram. They wore their beards long, never shaving.

Jake had finally stopped shivering from the cold. Still, he was not warm. He started to sip the cup of steaming coffee that Zig had now refilled for the third time.

"You can't stay here, you know. There have already been flyers distributed at the shul about you and three Negroes. The Rabbi says that a scrawny fellow from Cottoncrest with a big badge accompanied by an evil-looking man have been around twice to ask questions. It just isn't safe. I can't have you here with Leah and the children."

"I'm not asking for that, Zig. There's someone I must meet here, however, before I can head north. There's something I have to know. What I need from you is just time."

"Time? How can I give you time?"

"Time to repay you."

"But you don't owe me anything. We're square from your last trip to town when you brought in all those fine furs."

"We may be square until this minute, but I'm soon going to owe you a lot. I need cash, and I need it now. When I get to New York, I'll repay you. It may take a while, but I'll repay you. With double interest."

Zig trusted Jake. For over two years Jake had always been as good as his word. Zig walked over to the wall and moved aside a huge portrait of Leah and the children that hung in its gilded frame from wires attached to a track in the molding near the ceiling. Behind the picture was a safe. Zig opened the safe and withdrew a wad of bills.

Zig reached in again and pulled out a Freimer knife with a six-inch blade and, turning to Jake, said "This I give you as a gift. I don't know why you are in trouble, and I don't want to know, but I'm sure you can use this."

Jake reached behind his back and withdrew from his belt the ten-inch Freimer blade, the one Rossy had given back to him. "Thanks, Zig, but I'm prepared already for whatever might await me. *Hof oif nissim un farloz zich nit oif a nes,*" Jake said, meaning hope for miracles, but don't rely on one.

Zig smiled. Jake would be fine. "Since you'll need a place to stay while you're here where no one will dare bother you, doing whatever it is you need to do, go down to the Red Chair on Customhouse Street, next to Faubourg Tremé, and ask for Antonio. It's a two-dollar house. For seventy-five dollars he'll be happy to help. Just keep the rest of this money in your shoe and keep your shoes on, if you know what I mean. And be strong. Very strong. They will take advantage of you if you don't. *Az me est chazzer, zol rinnen fun bord.*"

Jake knew what Zig had said in Yiddish was right. If you're going to do something wrong, enjoy it.

Chapter 65

Dr. Cailleteau ignored the woman who was still screaming. His attention was elsewhere. "Hold that lamp up higher," he commanded.

The man—his shirt in tatters, his skin black as polished ebony, his face turned away from the woman—extended his arm holding the lantern as high as it would go.

Dr. Cailleteau, holding the baby upside down by the ankles, hit him again on the buttocks. The infant's lungs filled with air, and the grayish-blue tint disappeared from its face as its tiny yells filled the room.

The woman stopped screaming and started to weep. A big smile broke across the man's face, and he placed the lamp down on the table and hugged the woman lying on the bed.

"You got yourself one fine baby boy," Dr. Cailleteau said, handing the still-wailing newborn to the woman, who gently moved the man aside so she could clutch her baby to her breast.

Dr. Cailleteau finished up with the afterbirth, wiped his hands on his apron, and packed his bag. These people could not pay him. Maybe one day, in the spring, he would find outside his back door a bushel of corn or a few loaves of bread or a dripping basket of still-flopping catfish or sacolet freshly caught from the bayou. That would be payment enough.

Dr. Cailleteau wished, however, that Sally hadn't left Cottoncrest. For years she had taken care of all the births for the blacks not only on the plantation and not only in Parteblanc but also at Little Jerusalem and wherever else in Petit Rouge Parish she was needed. Dr. Cailleteau had trained her well, but given what the Knights had done to Nimrod's cabin in Lamou and with the gossip about Sally and Marcus and Jenny's disappearance having already spread, no Negress would want to take her place, traveling alone across the parish in these dangerous times.

Dr. Cailleteau pulled his pocket watch out, flipped open the top, noted the time, and then wound it again before putting it back into his vest. It was long past midnight. He was getting too old for this.

Sighing as he left the tiny cabin, Dr. Cailleteau climbed back into his buggy for the fifteen-minute ride south to Parteblanc. It was a good thing that man had come to get him. His woman might not have made it. As the baby's head emerged, Dr. Cailleteau had seen that the umbilical cord was entangled around its neck, and it was only by the barest that Dr. Cailleteau had been able to save the child.

Dr. Cailleteau still liked to deliver babies. White babies, who emerged almost crimson. Black babies as dark as coal. Babies the color of mahogany or the color of brown Mississippi mud or with skin like darkened copper or yellow-brown like pine or light tan like a fine palomino or so pale and sallow they could pass for white.

Assisting with a birth was still the most satisfying thing he did. Unfortunately, too many woman died in childbirth, and too many babies did not make it to their first birthday. It was another mystery of life and death.

During the war Dr. Cailleteau had been able to make snap decisions on care. He could look at a dozen bloody soldiers lined up on the ground outside his tent, with limbs missing and organs protruding through holes in their abdomens, and tell at a glance which ones would not make it through the night, which ones would survive even without immediate care, and which ones' very existence depended upon his skill, if he acted in time.

But childbirth was not like that. It was one woman at a time. It was much better to bring a new life into the world, one full of promise, than to salvage a soldier so that he could savage another living being when he was able to fight again.

Often, despite his skill, however, Dr. Cailleteau couldn't predict beforehand which young woman would have a child who would live and which one would have a child born sickly. Then there were the women who seemed to be fine but would die during the birth or soon afterward. Some of these girls were barely women at all.

In one out of every ten to fifteen births, despite his best efforts, all was lost. Dr. Cailleteau would then give what consolation he could. As he would take his leave, the grieving husband and the wife's parents would stare in disbelief at the dead baby and dead mother. Some sobbed inconsolably. Some maintained a stunned silence. Others prayed to God for strength, while still others cursed God for permitting such tragedy to occur.

And then there were the stillbirths and the miscarriages. A dead baby but a live woman. Dr. Cailleteau had thought for a moment earlier this evening that he might have just such a situation here. As the woman pushed and the child emerged, he was not sure whether he would be able to save even one of the two.

Sometimes, even when he was able to save the mother although she lost the baby, something happened to her insides. Sometimes, in these cases, she could never have children again. It was like that with Maylene, Jimmy Joe's wife. But Dr. Cailleteau had honored her and Jimmy Joe's wishes. He hadn't told anyone about it.

Dr. Cailleteau knew how to keep secrets. After all, he had kept the Colonel Judge's problem a secret for the more than two decades since the war ended. How the Colonel Judge dealt with Rebecca when he had no manhood left was something Dr. Cailleteau knew was another secret he would never fathom.

Chapter 66

By the time Jake had walked the few blocks from Zig's house to the Lafayette Cemetery, the gates had long since been locked. Zig had told him they were shut down at 11:30 p.m. every evening to keep the voodoo priestesses out and to prevent this uptown cemetery, several blocks from St. Charles Avenue, from becoming home to the kind of rites and rituals that occurred almost nightly at the St. Louis cemetery near the French Quarter.

Jake had tried the gates, just to be sure. The heavy chain was secured firmly with a large padlock. He would have to come again tomorrow night, at dusk, to see if Jenny would show up as he had asked. He had to talk with her. He had to know about their survival.

It was almost three in the morning before Jake reached Customhouse Street. He cut a strange figure in the long black coat and wide-brimmed black hat that Zig had given him but no stranger than many others whom he passed. Sailors from foreign ships so drunk they lay in the gutter, clutching bottles of whiskey. Soldiers stripped to their waist, carrying their shirts and coats in their hands, looking dazed. Men from the North with bowler hats and canes peering in the doorways and deciding which establishment to frequent. Black men counting out their pennies to see how much they had left, to see if they could afford another round of drinks. Or women. Or both. Men of all races and sizes.

A babel of languages surrounded Jake. It was like being back in New York. English. French. Spanish. Italian. German. Chinese. And languages he could not even identify.

While the rest of the city slept at this hour, Customhouse Street and the entire nearby neighborhood of Faubourg Tremé was alive. Gas lamps blazed away through open windows. Music came from every doorway, most of which were ajar to welcome anyone who passed by.

Laughter drifted from second- and third-story balconies and galleries. Laughter from women, high and seductive. Laughter from men, deep and desirous.

"Hey," a siren's voice called down, almost directly overhead.

Jake looked up. On a wrought-iron balcony right above him, a woman lowered the strap of her dress, revealing a brown breast with a dark-brown nipple. "Yes, you. You want to see more? Come inside and ask for Lulu."

Next to her, a pale white girl, looking no older than fourteen, if that, swirled her skirts so that Jake could see she had nothing on underneath. "You ask for Betsy, now, sugar, and I'll show you a good time."

Lulu laughed, and her mouth opened into a wide grin revealing three missing teeth. "Hell, if you got enough in your pants—your pants' pockets, that is—" she cackled, "you can have both of us."

Jake planned to keep moving on down the street, but he stopped. Lulu and Betsy gave each other a knowing glance.

But it wasn't Lulu and Betsy that made Jake pause. It was the sign hanging from the balcony, visible in the glow coming through the open door next to it.

There was no writing on the sign. It was merely a picture of a large chair with a wide seat. On the wide seat was a crude picture of a tiny naked lady holding a large bottle with XXX on the label.

The chair was red.

PART VII

Today

Chapter 67

"I was planning it all out, you see. I knew it was dangerous to go to Petit Rouge Parish. I didn't know whether he would meet with me when I got there or, if he did, what might happen.

"It wasn't just that there had been beatings during my trip down on the bus from Washington with the Freedom Riders. There were a lot of us, and if we were going to pursue a non-violent approach in the face of violence, at least we had the strength of numbers and the ability to get word to the press and to our families.

"But now I was on my own. If I got into trouble, there was no one to send out a call for help. We didn't have cell phones in those days, and making a collect long-distance call was a time-consuming and expensive proposition, even if you got to a phone and even if your mother up north could afford to pay the charges, which mine couldn't.

"But this was something I had to do. Now that my father was dead and now that Grandpapa Jake had died, I was the only one who knew.

"Of course, Grandpapa Jake had never told me about him, and I'm sure my father and his mother never knew either. I had found it out by going through Grandpapa's papers. It was only right that this be done now, now that all of them—Grandmama Roz and my father and Great Uncle Moshe—were all dead and there was no one left to hurt. Grandpapa Jake would have wanted it this way, I was sure.

"I stopped in Des Allemands at a gas station and bought a Rebel flag, which I propped up on the dashboard. I bought a couple of bags of cracklins. Although I had stopped keeping kosher when I went away to college, I couldn't bring myself to taste fried pork skin, but I hadn't bought the cracklins to eat. I dumped part of the contents down the toilet at the gas station and put the half-empty bags on the seat. I bought a bottle opener, a couple of bottles of Jax beer, and a few Dixie beers and left them on the back seat as well.

"I also bought two MoonPies and an RC Cola. Now, those I did consume, leaving the empty bottle and the MoonPie bags on the floor of the front seat. If anyone stopped me, if anyone looked in my car wherever I might park it, I wanted it to look ordinary. Messy. Southern. I wanted it to fit in.

"'Course, while I could try to make my rented Oldsmobile look like it was being driven by a good ol' boy, with its Louisiana plates and the flag and the other stuff, I couldn't make myself look like I belonged here. I stuck out like a geisha at a bar mitzvah, like someone dropped in from another world. Which I was.

"It was almost an hour-drive from Des Allemands up the west bank River Road to Parteblanc. I knew I was there when I saw the signs at the city limits. There were trees set off the road where someone had tacked up a hand-lettered placard: PARTEBLANC FEED STORE. YES, WE HAVE CRICKETS, WORMS, SHINERS, RAT POISON, AND ROACH SPRAY. There was a big wooden railway tie set upright in concrete with the emblems of Kiwanis and the Rotary International and the Elks Club and Woodmen of the World stacked one on top of each other, like a totem pole for white men's clubs. There was a rusted steel shaft with a sign covered with mildew, reading, PARTEBLANC, PARISH SEAT OF PETIT ROUGE PARISH.

"But towering over the Parteblanc sign and above the railway tie with the club emblems, there was a huge billboard on a cleared field behind a fence. It read: 'IMPEACH EARL WARREN. Join the Citizens' Council and stand up for your rights.'"

1893

Chapter 68

Inside, facing the entrance to the Red Chair, was a wide bar behind
which stood a giant of a man with olive-colored skin and jet-black hair.
He was at least seven feet tall. A scar ran from his left ear across his
cheekbone to the corner of his mouth. Where his left eye should be,
there was nothing but a mass of scar tissue, evidence of some terrible
battle. His nose was flattened, further proof of a history of rough fights.
His hairy arms and barrel chest were barely contained by the washed-
out red shirt that he wore.

To the right of the bar there was an upright piano where a black man
played at a furious pace, accompanied by a lighter-colored black man
on guitar and a short man of middle age and indiscriminate race on
the saxophone. Next to them a young black boy sat, coronet in hand,
and every so often the piano player would signal to the boy, who would
raise the coronet to his lips and blow out a string of dizzying notes that
somehow meshed with what the others were playing.

The floor of the bar was filled with a half-dozen couples. Women
clung to men as they drifted around, some in time with the music, others completely ignoring it.

Two of the women wore loose-fitting dresses. Three were clad only
in their slips. And one had on only a beaded necklace. The men and
women kissed and rubbed each other.

As Jake stood in the doorway, one of the women in a slip led her man
by the hand up the staircase, passing Lulu coming down with a naked
drunk stumbling behind her. Lulu called to the bartender. Her voice
had a sharp and angry edge. "Coso, he woke up. He ain't got nothin'
left, and he wants some more."

Coming from behind the bar, Coso grabbed the naked drunken man by the arm, pulling him over the banister. "You want more and no pay? Out!"

Coso pointed to the door. The naked man lay on the floor where he had fallen when Coso had pulled him off the stairs. He appeared dazed. He didn't move.

Reaching down, Coso grabbed the man's left ankle. Although the man was not small, Coso's hand was so large that it completely enveloped the man's limb. Coso dragged him easily to the door, the man yelling as splinters from the wooden floor dug into his back. Jake moved out of the way.

Coso kicked the man out onto the street, where he lay in chilly October air without anything on.

Jake could see someone toss down, from an upper floor, a pile of clothes that landed near the man. He rolled over with a groan, sorted them out, and started to get dressed.

As Coso started back toward the bar, working his way through the dancers, Jake followed him.

Coso spun around. He was at least a foot and a half taller than Jake and twice as wide. "What you want?" he growled.

Jake smiled, his teeth white against his dark stubble of a beard. "What do I want? A good question in such a friendly place. A drink would be good for a start."

Coso nodded and went behind the bar. He put a tumbler on the counter and poured two inches of whiskey into it. "You pay."

Jake smiled again. Smiling, said Uncle Avram, was always the way to begin a conversation where you wanted something from the other side. "Gladly." He laid a two dollar bill next to the tumbler.

Coso looked at the bill and examined more closely this strange man with the long black coat and black hat with its broad felt brim. Without taking his eyes off of Jake, Coso called out, "New one."

The listless woman on the dance floor did not pay any attention. Jake heard a rustle from the staircase. He looked up and saw the skinny fourteen-year-old white girl he had seen on the balcony sashaying down the stairs. She came over to the bar and put her arms around him. "I tol' you, sugar, ask for Betsy, and I'll show you a good time."

Jake uncurled her arm from around his waist. "No thank you."

"What's the matter, sugar? A little shy maybe?" Betsy rubbed his crotch with her hand, and Jake jumped back with a start.

"You no like?" Coso grinned. "You want something else? We have lots. Lulu maybe?"

Lulu, her chocolate-brown skin glowing in the gas lamp's illumination, insinuated herself between Betsy and Jake. Gone was the anger in her voice about the naked man who wanted more and wouldn't pay. Now she just purred, "You want some sugar, maybe, from a woman with more on the upper shelves than this one?" Lulu pointed to Betsy, pulling the shift off the young girl's shoulders while at the same time dropping the straps of her own dress. Where Betsy had tiny breasts like miniature pink-tipped funnels, Lulu's were large rounded mounds of toffee topped with coffee nipples.

"I think you misunderstand. I want only a drink and one other thing."

"Two dollar. That get you drink and girl. You no like girl?" Coso asked, his eyes narrowing in curiosity at a man who would pay the proper price and then refuse what he had bought.

"Here," Jake said, pushing the tumbler back toward Coso. "You can have this too. I just need some information on where I can find Antonio. Two dollars should buy me that, no?"

The olive complexion of Coso's broad face turned red with anger as Coso reached under the bar and then emerged from behind it carrying a large wooden club. His scarred-over left eye was the only part above his neck that was not crimson.

Betsy and Lulu, the tops of their bodies still exposed, moved away from Jake and retreated to the far corner of the bar.

Coso's face was a scowl. "You come in and no want drink? You come and no want girl? You come in and want Antonio? Who be you?"

Coso put his big hand on Jake's shoulder, where it rested like a slab of olive-colored beef. "You be law? Maybe you be friend of Hennessy? But I no see you before. You no be friend of Mr. Micelli, I think."

Coso's fingers started to tighten on Jake's shoulder.

Jake forced himself to smile again. "Two dollars is not enough? I can maybe go to three. That's a lot of money. All I want to do is see Antonio."

The band members saw Coso's expression and knew that a fight was about to begin. They played louder and faster. It would be over in a minute.

"You no see anything no more," Coso snarled, raising his club and starting to swing it toward Jake.

That was it for Jake. He couldn't reason with this giant of a man.

Jake had been chased by Cossacks. He had hidden and escaped. Jake had been chased by Tee Ray and the Knights. He had run and escaped. It seemed to Jake that he had been running for his life for half his life. But now there were the lives of others at stake, and he was through running. Zig had refused to give him shelter and had sent him to ask for Antonio. Zig had said that Tee Ray and Bucky were here in town looking for him. Until Jake found Jenny, until he found out what he needed to know, where else could he go but to Antonio? Zig said the Red Chair was the place to find Antonio. This was the Red Chair. Jake had to make a stand.

As the club started to descend, Jake twisted out of Coso's grasp and darted for the bar.

Coso moved toward him, swinging the club back and forth like a scythe. It made an angry sound as it sliced through the air.

Coso was between Jake and the door. There was no way to get past.

Coso approached, taking large steps, his club coming closer and closer.

Jake dropped to the floor.

"You fall? I squash you like bug!" Coso took a wide stance and, raising the club above his head, prepared to pound it down on Jake's head.

But Jake was too fast. Jake scooted between Coso's legs and then, whirling around, his black coat flaring out, leaped up on Coso's back while at the same time pulling the Freimer knife from his belt.

Jake wrapped his legs around Coso's wide waist, crocked an elbow around Coso's broad neck, and put the point of the blade directly under Coso's right eye.

Coso could feel the cool metal pressed against his flesh, threatening to plunge into his eye socket, depriving him completely of his sight. He had lost the left eye years ago. If he lost the right eye, what good would he be to anyone? He stood very still, the club in his hands but now held motionless in midair.

The band stopped playing. No one had ever challenged Coso before.

Most of the dancers halted, although some, oblivious to the music, continued to sway back and forth.

"Now," said Jake, calmly and softly, "should I remove your eye? If I do, should I also take an ear? The slightest twitch of this blade will be enough. It is so sharp you won't even feel the pain. At first."

Coso tried not to move any part of his body. He relaxed, breathing slowly, waiting for the man on his back to make the slightest mistake, to loosen his grip even the smallest amount. Then Coso would act.

"Even if I took your eye and ear as souvenirs," Jake whispered, his mouth so close that Coso could feel on his ear the stubble on Jake's chin, "you wouldn't look so bad. The scars I leave behind with this sharp blade will be tiny in contrast to the scars you already have. I shall gladly let you keep your sight and this misshapen ear, however, if I can only get the information I seek. So, you see, I think you should listen carefully to my questions. I've come a long way. A very long way. I've been told to ask for Antonio. I have paid more than enough for this information. I have asked politely once, and I will now ask politely again."

Jake, still clinging to Coso's back, raised his head from Coso's ear and, tightening his grip and holding the blade more firmly, ready to plunge it deep into Coso's eye, spoke loudly enough for all to hear. "So, why don't you tell me where I can find Antonio."

From a dark corner of the room a swarthy man in his thirties stepped out of the shadows. He wore a red vest over a blue-and-white striped shirt with a high starched collar and carried a double-barreled shotgun. His black hair was pomaded down into a glowing shine. A part as straight as a surveyor's line ran through the center of it. Beneath the careful coiffure he had a baby face, but his eyes were as black and cold as a snake's.

The musicians retreated to behind the piano. The few women who had still been dancing stopped and led their men to the sides of the room. Lulu and Betsy crouched down on the other side of the bar.

While outside the Red Chair, music could be heard filtering through from other establishments and while the noise of the street crowd continued its drone, inside it was deadly silent.

The man with the red vest pointed. Extending his index finger, he gestured first to the side of the room and then to the point directly in front of Coso.

Jake drew the blade with the slightest degree of pressure across the bottom of the eye socket. A thin line of blood appeared and started to drip down Coso's cheek. Coso didn't dare move.

Red Vest pointed again, and his dark eyes sent an angry gaze toward the naked dancer who had huddled at the foot of the staircase. Quivering with fear, the woman pulled a table to the center of the room and then ran back to the wall.

Red Vest held up his index finger again, this time tapping his nose as if thinking. He put the shotgun down on the table and reached under his coat, behind his back.

Jake moved the blade to Coso's neck, ready to cut his jugular vein if necessary.

"Coso," said the man with the red vest. "I think . . ."

Coso got ready.

Jake, feeling the giant tense up, held the knife firmly to Coso's neck.

Jake knew he could kill Coso with a single swift stroke across the neck. If he did, Jake knew that Red Vest would reach down for the shotgun, pump it, and fire. If Coso fell forward, dead, Jake thought he might have time to leap off his back in time to make it up the stairs or out the side door. If Coso fell backward, however, there might be no chance to escape the shotgun blast.

Jake and Red Vest locked eyes, Jake from his perch on Coso's back, Red Vest from behind the table on which rested the shotgun.

Why had Red Vest put the shotgun on the table? Jake couldn't figure it out.

Red Vest moved slowly and deliberately, all the while seeming to drill into Jake with his dark eyes. Red Vest reached under his vest and withdrew an item from his waistband.

"I think, Coso . . . ," said Red Vest, holding an eight-inch Freimer blade in his hand and then putting it on the table next to the shotgun. "I think this is a friend of Zig's. No?"

PART VIII

Today

Chapter 69

"Off to my right, behind the big IMPEACH EARL WARREN sign, was Cottoncrest.

"What? You don't know who Earl Warren was? He was the chief justice of the Supreme Court when *Brown versus the Board of Education* was decided. He had taken a divided court and had fashioned a unanimous decision reversing *Plessy versus Ferguson,* the old separate-but-equal case.

"And what credit did he get for all that? For changing the course of race relations in the United States? For uniting the Supreme Court in a way that it has seldom been united before or since on a critical issue of national importance? For fashioning a decision that was as revolutionary in its effect as it was reactionary in harking back to the original meaning of the Fourteenth Amendment when it was enacted in the heady days after the Civil War? What credit did he get? In the South, none. He was hated. It was an intense, personal hatred. On our Freedom Ride we had seen IMPEACH EARL WARREN signs alongside of the roads from Virginia southwards.

"You know, to get the unanimous decision, Chief Justice Warren had to agree to the infamous language of having integration 'with all deliberate speed.' What was that? How can speed be deliberate? If the decision was a watershed, the language was a dam against change. *Brown* came out in 1954, and here it was 1961, and the schools still weren't integrated, and the transportation system still was segregated.

"That's why I had gone on the Freedom Ride. I believed it was the dawn of a new time in the country. We had a new young president, and JFK had inspired all of us in college. 'Ask not what your country can do for you, ask what you can do for your country.' We believed him. I had done something for my country with the Freedom Ride, and now I was doing something for grandfather. And for myself.

"So, I steered that big Oldsmobile to the right and headed down the dirt road for Cottoncrest. You could see it in the distance across the fields. It was a narrow dirt road in those days, not the fine paved one the tourist buses travel now.

"Cottoncrest back then wasn't anything like you see it today. Now it's all pristine and nice, restored with bright white paint. Now the vegetable garden is filled with tomatoes and eggplant and onions and squash and okra and mirliton that they serve you at the Cottoncrest restaurant for the plate lunches and fancy candlelight dinners. Now it's got the rose garden with its neat paths and the masses of azaleas and hedges of ligustrum and honeysuckle twined around the picket fence from the parking lot to the gift shop.

"But back in '61, when I first saw it, Cottoncrest was in a state of advanced decay. Those wide columns, which run up three stories, were mildewed and worn. Some portions had just rotted away. The veranda was sagging, and parts of the galleries on the upper levels had gaps so large that they looked unsafe to walk on. Thick vines had climbed up the sides of the house and had spread across most of the roof so that the house looked as if it was being slowly covered with a ratty green carpet.

"It was a house that had more pride than prestige. Like its owner."

1893

Chapter 70

"The minute I saw the Freimer blade, I knew that Zig must have sent you here. No one in New Orleans—that is, no one who's not working for me—has such a blade. I know that Zig only wholesales them to one other person. The Jew Peddler who told him about the Freimers in the first place."

Antonio Micelli, in his red vest, was sitting with Jake at a table in a dimly lit corner of the room where Antonio could see everything but few people could see him. The band was playing again. Coso was back behind the bar. Lulu was back upstairs with a new customer. Betsy was dancing with a man at the bar, the top of her dress still around her waist. Other girls in various stages of undress were dancing with each other, whiling away these late after-midnight hours until the dawn came and they could finally go off duty.

Jake and Antonio had already reached a deal. Jake had offered $35 for sanctuary for up to two weeks. Antonio had countered at $200. They had settled for $75, which Jake had just paid.

"You knew," Jake asked, "that I told Zig about the Freimers?"

Even in the dim light, Jake could see Antonio's broad smile and white teeth as Antonio said, with satisfaction, "Information is something valuable, is it not?"

Jake marveled at how Antonio had known that it was Jake who had convinced Zig to import Freimers from Germany. Jake had seen them while he had worked on the docks in Hamburg, after he left Russia and before he came to America, and Jake knew that no American knife could match the keen edge and precision of a Freimer.

Jake took a small sip of the whiskey in his tumbler. "A Freimer is my protection. I'm just glad you recognized the one I carried. Your double-barreled shotgun, however," Jake said, pointing to the weapon that was propped on the side of Antonio's chair, "seems protection enough."

"Protection? You can never have too much protection." Antonio rolled up the sleeves of his blue-and-white stripped shirt, revealing long red scars on both arms. "You see these? I have them on my back as well. Lucky to escape the massacres with just these. But they're so ugly, I have to keep them covered all the time."

"My people have a saying," said Jake. "The ugliest life is better than the nicest death." Jake silently thought it sounded better in Yiddish. *Der miesteh leben iz besser fun shesten toit.*

"No death is nice," Antonio declared, raising the mug of coffee to his lips. His work was more important than drinking liquor. He had to keep a clear head at all times. "You know about the massacre? No. I can see it in your eyes. You have been out of the city too long. Three months ago two Italians were accused of murdering Hennessy, a policeman. They didn't do it. We expected them to hang, nonetheless. What would a New Orleans jury do but to agree with the police and convict Italians of murdering an Irishman. But a miracle. The jury found them not guilty."

Antonio paused, scanning the room, watching the customers. Satisfied, he poured more whiskey into Jake's tumbler.

"Tears of joy, however, turned to tears for which there was no consolation. The Irish and the Americans in the city became furious. They stormed the police station and killed the two men who had been acquitted. A few days later a boat landed with eighteen hundred Sicilians coming to this country for a better life. They knew nothing of what had happened. How could they know? But the Irish and Americans swarmed the docks, and they massacred fifteen hundred men, women, and children. Do you know what that means? Babies were flung into the harbor to drown. Women were beaten to death, their bodies so badly mangled that we couldn't identify many of them. The men were shot time and again. It was only by the barest that those of us who had gone down to the dock to greet the arrival were able to save ourselves and a few of the passengers."

Antonio paused a moment, refastening his shirtsleeves and covering his scars.

"Our best efforts were not enough. My sister, her three children, her husband and two cousins—all were on that boat. All dead.

"Where was the protection of the police? Nowhere. The police let the massacre occur. They encouraged it. So, protection is only where you create it for yourself. La Famiglia was not something I had wanted or needed before the massacre. But now La Famiglia is all that there is. We stick together. We make our own protection. I have Coso. I have my shotgun. I have a Freimer. And I now have hired many men to work for me to protect my business. I have built up my business, and I shall not lose it. No. I have a family. A wife and eight children—seven daughters and one son—and no harm shall befall my business or my family or me."

"My people," said Jake, "have another saying. If I am not for myself, who am I for?"

"Your people seem to be full of sayings. I do not have time for sayings. I have time only for action. It is not enough to be for yourself. You must have the support of others. And the only ones you can trust are your family. We Italians know this. This city is too full of people who are either too proud of what they are or want to pass for something that they are not. Here, look at me. I have the skin of an Italian and the hair of an Italian and the accent of an Italian. What can I do but be what I am? My cousin Roberto Micelli, he passes for black Irish. Bobby McKelly they call him. As an Italian Catholic, there are no jobs, but as an Irish Catholic, he can be a conductor on the railroad. That's where he is now. Conductor McKelly. And you, Jew, you could pass if you wanted. You speak English with no accent. You could be almost anyone. You could pass for someone who is not a Jew, and yet you are known as the Jew Peddler."

Jake said nothing. He could not tell where this conversation was leading. What could he say? As Uncle Avram used to admonish, *Far dem emes shlogt men.* For the truth you get beaten up.

"I think you do not know New Orleans, even after your two years here in this state," Antonio warned. "Look, over at the bar, the young girl dancing with the man. What do you see?" Antonio pointed to Betsy.

"A girl. Too pale. Too young as well."

"What else?"

"Straight black hair. Narrow lips. Tiny nose. Tiny breasts. Slim hips."

"And white?"

"If you say so."

"If I say so? To every customer she's white. She passes. But she's an octoroon. One eighth black. You know there are lots of octoroons out there. Roberto Micelli—Bobby McKelly—had to arrest an octoroon. Did you know that? An Italian passing for Irish had to arrest an octoroon who could have passed for white but insisted he was black. This Homer Plessy, white as Betsy here, got on a train bound for Covington, a two-hour trip, and went to the first-class Whites Only car. It had been arranged in advance with the railroad. They knew what Plessy wanted to have happen, for he had told them what he was planning to do. So, the railroad told Roberto and gave him instructions. Roberto didn't want to do it, but he had to follow orders to keep his job. When Roberto asked him for a ticket, this Plessy said, 'I have to tell you that, according to Louisiana law, I am a colored man.'

"Roberto asked him to move to the cars for Negroes and drunks, but, as planned, Plessy refused. So Roberto arrested him, as planned, which was what Plessy wanted so he could sue the railroad. The 'Irish' conductor arrested someone who insisted he was colored although his skin was lighter than the conductor's. Plessy's skin was as light as Betsy's."

Jake looked again at Betsy, dancing with her pale white breasts exposed. So Plessy was as light as Betsy. Both of them were darker than Rebecca, and all three of them were of mixed blood.

Chapter 71

Where the Mississippi River makes the huge curve that gives the Crescent City its name, it curls back northward in an eight-mile loop as if it wants to take one last look at the vast continent through which it has flowed, and then, at the foot of Canal Street, at the very place where the French Quarter begins, it abruptly dips south to empty into the Gulf of Mexico more than eighty miles away.

As Bucky and Tee Ray walked upriver from the foot of Canal Street into the Tchoupitoulas Wharf area, Bucky gazed around him in wonderment.

The street was crowded, although it was just shortly after dawn. The October sun that was casting its glow upon them rose over the west bank of the river, which, because of the Mississippi's serpentine path, was east of them at this point.

There were more people here in this one spot than lived in the entire town of Parteblanc. Bucky couldn't believe the variety of occupations, of dress, and of skin colors. Black women balancing baskets on their heads. Mulattoes hauling carts of goods. Strong-limbed sailors on the decks of massive steamships were directing crews of men carrying one armload of goods after the next up gangplanks and stowing them into immense holds below decks. Gangs of ruddy Irishmen were unloading roomfuls of furniture newly arrived from abroad—heavy armoires, intricate cabinets, inlaid tables, stout chairs, and fine linen. Scurrying pods of Chinese peddled tea and cakes alongside Negroes hawking winter vegetables. And in the doorways of the back alleys were women raising their skirts to their thighs, even at this early hour, seeking to lure the passing men inside.

"Come on, Bucky, keep up!" Tee Ray plowed ahead through the crowd.

Almost trotting to keep abreast of Tee Ray as they wove their way down the packed street, Bucky pointed out excitedly, "Look at that over there. A darky and a Chinaman, shoulder to shoulder, like it was natural. And them women in the doorways—white and black and all colors in between—showin' themselves all over. And the sun comin' up in over what they call west bank! Well, back at Parteblanc they ain't never gonna believe me when I tell them what I done saw. They just ain't. Have you ever seen such wonderment?"

"Once we catch the Jew and take care of him—and I got the feelin' we're real near to doin' that—we'll go down to a fast house, you and me. Then you're gonna see and experience some real wonderment."

"Can't we go tonight, Tee Ray? Just once?"

"Afterwards, Bucky. Look, we're here."

Tee Ray had stopped in front of a wooden building where there were two sets of shutters, one stacked on top of the other. The lower ones were closed, but the upper ones had been opened, and through them Bucky and Tee Ray could see that the ceiling was at least fifteen feet high. A sign hung over the door: ISAAC HABER & CO.

"Remember, Tee Ray, I'm the one with the badge. I'm in charge, just like Raifer said."

Tee Ray held his tongue and pushed open the door. Inside, a small, compact man with wiry hair was writing in a large ledger at a desk piled high with papers. The warehouse stretched out behind him. Above him, draped from the rafters, hung long ropes and coils of wire and huge nets. On the wooden floor were crates and boxes stacked high. Along one wall were skins. Long planks of rattlesnake and cottonmouth, stretched out in taut lines. Muskrat and rabbit in furry mounds. Bobcat and bear with their heads still attached.

Zig quickly took stock of the two who had just walked in. They were not buyers, traders, or trappers.

"You Mr. Haber?" asked the disheveled young man, almost a boy still, with a greasy face and stained shirt.

"Certainly." Zig stood up, closed his ledger, and walked around the desk to shake their hands. "What can I do for two fine gentlemen this morning?"

Bucky reached into his pants pocket. He pulled out some twine, then some cigarette paper.

Tee Ray stewed while Bucky fumbled.

Finally, Bucky located his badge and showed it proudly. "I am Deputy Bucky Starner from Petit Rouge Parish, and I got some questions for you."

"For an officer of the law, I have all the time in the world."

"We don't need no time, Mr. Haber. There are really just a few things we got to know. First, do you sell fancy Jew knives?"

Zig remained calm and showed no emotion. This young man was both impertinent and foolish. "I am, as you can see, but a poor merchant. I buy skins and furs. I sell supplies wholesale. You need traps for wolves or bears? Traps I have. You need nets for shrimp or fishing? Nets I have. You need chandlery? That, too, I have."

"We don't need no candle-ree. We got more than enough candles in Petit Rouge, and pretty soon we might even have gas lamps on the street corners and 'lectricity!"

Zig hid a smile. "Mr. Deputy, I am sure you have abundant lighting in Petit Rouge. Perhaps I was overexpansive and excessively indirect. You see, in addition to operating a wholesale and brokerage operation, I sell goods for use on ships, both those that are oceangoing and those that ply the Mississippi. That's what's called a ship's chandler. I apologize if I was being obtuse."

Bucky wasn't sure he understood all the words Mr. Haber had just used, but he wasn't going to let on. "No, you were 'tuse enough with your 'ply. But what I want to know is about them fancy Jew knives what that Jew Peddler carries with him and done hid out at Cottoncrest."

Zig shrugged his shoulders. "A Jew knife? Who knew knives had a religion? You know, Mr. Deputy, I learn something new every day. They just built a big Protestant church up on St. Charles Avenue. Maybe I can talk to them about what kind of Protestant knives they use. With all the Catholic churches in town, I must find out about Catholic knives as well."

"We ain't lookin' for a Catholic knife used by Papists. We're lookin' for . . ."

Bucky stopped because Tee Ray had grabbed his arm. "He's joshin' you, Bucky."

Tee Ray stood up and, reaching into his coat pocket, pulled out a flyer and handed it to Zig, saying coldly. "We're looking for four criminals. Two niggers—Marcus and Sally—a mulatto named Jenny, and a Jew peddler. They are wanted in Petit Rouge for theft, and the Jew Peddler carried a special kind of knife. Extra sharp. Ain't any kind of knife none of us have seen before. We heard that you sell fancy knives. Do you got that kind of knife, and do you know a peddler named Jake Gold?"

Zig studied the flyer. "Jake Gold, you say? Never heard of him."

PART IX

Today

Chapter 72

"When I saw that big Rebel flag hanging from the porch on the second floor, I was glad that I had bought the little Rebel flag in Des Allemands and had stuck it on the dashboard.

"There was no one in sight when I drove up. The house looked deserted, all empty of feeling, like a place that had lost its soul. If he wasn't home now, I would sit in the car and wait, but the house was so huge, someone could be far in the back and you wouldn't know it.

"I walked up the front steps. They weren't the sturdy concrete structure you see today. The old pine boards were sagging badly, and the brick foundations on which they rested to keep them elevated above the moist soil had cracked.

"I walked across the splintered veranda and got to the big front door. Mildew had turned the corners of the double-wide entry a brownish green. There was no doorbell. The metal knocker was broken off its hinges, so I used my knuckles.

"I rapped several times, but there was no answer. I called out to see if anyone was home. No response.

"I walked around the house on the veranda under those huge columns. You saw for yourself during the first part of the tour; the view from there is a fine one. Of course, back in '61 there wasn't the fancy housing development that's there now over where the sharecroppers' cabins used to be or the petrochemical refinery and its city of metal and lights over there where the sugar mill was or even that grove of pecan trees where it used to be just fields. No, none of that was there then.

"So, I sat down, my back propped up against the front door, with my file folder on my lap, planning to wait. I tried to imagine what it had been like for Grandpapa Jake when he had spent long evenings here with the Colonel Judge. I tried to visualize Grandpapa and the Colonel Judge sitting right here on the veranda, talking about who knows what.

"They might have sat right up there, where those white wicker rocking chairs are now, whiling away an evening. Maybe Rebecca would come out and sit with them as twilight descended and the shadows stretched out from the oak trees to cover the lawn. Perhaps the Colonel Judge and Grandpapa had been speaking in French and switched to English while Rebecca was there.

"The world was changing around them. A new century was less than seven years away. A Jew from Russia in his twenties, a white-haired Catholic planter of Confederate aristocracy, and his beautiful young wife—somehow, in some way, the souls of those three were touched by each other.

"You know, though, I still find it strange that Grandpapa, who had escaped from Russia to avoid prejudice, could become friends with someone who had led troops in a war to keep people in slavery. I once asked him about that, and Grandpapa said that the Colonel Judge was a learned man with a tortured soul. That didn't make any sense to me and didn't answer my question. Then he told me something in Yiddish that the older I get, the more I understand: *Der ligen iz in di oigen, der emess iz hinter di oigen.* The lie is before your eyes, the truth is behind them. That's why I was at Cottoncrest. To get the truth. To reveal it as well.

"I must have started to doze off on that warm afternoon late in May because I don't recall hearing any footsteps or the latch turning.

"All I remember is that I was completely startled when the door opened abruptly from the inside. I fell backwards into the dark hallway.

"There was a shotgun pointed in my face and a man bellowing, 'Who the hell are you, and what are you doing trespassing on my property?'"

1893

Chapter 73

"You got your badge out?"

Bucky showed Tee Ray that he had it in his hand.

"Don't want you diggin' in your pocket again. You're a deputy. Got to act like you're in charge at all times, understand?"

Bucky nodded.

"Got to get information carefully. You got to ask questions in such a way that don't set them off from the start."

Bucky didn't respond this time. He was upset. Since the meeting this morning at the Jew store, Tee Ray had been jawing at him, just like Dr. Cailleteau. Tee Ray wouldn't stop breezing him, lecturing away at him like he was stupid. Complaining about what he did. About what he didn't do.

Bucky felt that Tee Ray was getting to be too carpetbagger, too high and mighty, especially on this trip where Bucky was to be in charge. Tee Ray kept on digging at him, and it was like picking away at a scabrous wound, just more and more irritating the longer it went on.

"Jew knife! You can't get no information from a Jew, Bucky, askin' about a Jew knife. Got to be more indirect with Jews. You opened up your mouth, and all that Jew merchant gone and done was make fun of you."

Bucky and Tee Ray walked a ways in tense silence, finally turning off Canal Street, the Mississippi River almost a mile behind them. They turned right onto Rampart Street, the far edge of the French Quarter. The sun would set in a couple of hours.

Here there were no white businesses. No white homes. No white people on the streets. But the place was abustle.

Narrow two-story brick buildings stood shoulder to shoulder, sharing common walls. Each had tall shutters hiding the windows and trying to keep in the warmth on this crisp October afternoon. Small shops crowded the sidewalks, their wares on makeshift wooden tables. Voodoo stores, with strange vials filled with dried things and wicker cages with tiny live reptiles and bugs and spiders and cloudy liquids in glass containers. Stores with bright calicoes and pastel cottons, cheap silk and used taffeta. Bars. Cobblers. Dry goods.

It was all there. A little city unto itself. Tee Ray and Bucky were the only white people on the street. Negroes of every hue filled the area, their voices loud and boisterous, not soft and respectful as they were when they were around white people.

The Negroes made way for them as Bucky and Tee Ray passed, but they stared with a hard look, not with the downcast eyes of those in Parteblanc. They pointed at Bucky and Tee Ray. Some even laughed behind their backs.

Bucky was uncomfortable with their attitude, but Tee Ray was simply mad. He glared back at them, which only made the young men laugh louder.

Tee Ray whispered to Bucky under his breath, "You let me handle the nigger lawyer, you understand. I know the way to talk to niggers. They're not like Jews, trying to be clever and all. Approach 'em right. Show 'em who's boss. The sooner we get the information, the sooner we can leave."

Bucky gritted his teeth. He knew it was going to come to this. Tee Ray was taking over. Well, if Tee Ray thought he was so smart, let him. Bucky had other plans. When they were finished here, Bucky would put them into effect.

They stopped before a door where the sign read "L. MARTINET," neatly printed underneath a picture of the scales of justice.

Tee Ray didn't knock. He simply opened up the door and stalked inside with a firm stride. Bucky followed.

The only person in the room was a black man with closely cropped hair and spectacles above a thin, waxed mustache. He wore a nicely tailored dark suit and vest, a white shirt with a high, starched white collar, and was quietly working at a desk. In front of him a large law book was open. The man ignored them and dipped his pen into the inkwell and continued writing out a legal pleading in a careful, neat hand.

"Lawyer Martinet?" Tee Ray demanded. The black man at the desk didn't know his place enough to stand when whites entered the room!

The man at the desk put the pen down and looked up calmly. "And who is inquiring?"

Before Tee Ray could respond, Bucky interrupted. "The law! That's who!" Bucky thrust out his badge.

"Now, isn't that interesting. May I examine it?" Louis Martinet, without leaving his seat, reached across the desk and took the badge out of Bucky's hand. Adjusting his spectacles, he read out loud, "Petit Rouge Parish."

Louis Martinet leaned back in his chair. "How unusual. Aren't you jurisdictionally impaired in these environs?"

Bucky stared blankly at the question.

Tee Ray, however, snapped back. "We don't need none of your put-on airs. Just answer our questions, and we'll leave. You know a Negress named Jenny. She used to work here before she went to Petit Rouge to work for Colonel Judge Chastaine. Right?"

Louis Martinet didn't flinch in the slightest at Tee Ray's offensive tone of voice. He looped his fingers calmly in the lapels of his vest. "And the basis for your authority to start this interrogation is what, exactly? I note that you, sir, do not carry a badge, even one from a distant parish. I note that your attire does not contain the usual accoutrements of a duly appointed official. I am curious, therefore, of the precise nature of the legal authority that gives you the right to act as my interrogator."

Tee Ray snarled, "When I come back with—"

Bucky interrupted again. "He don't have to come with no 'gator or any other kind of creature. We got the law on our side. That badge proves it!"

Tee Ray shoved Bucky aside. "You don't got no right to stall. We're gonna be back first thing tomorrow morning. And when I come with a gun and an Orleans Parish sheriff, you're gonna answer my question. Ain't no nigger lawyer gonna put on airs with me!"

Louis Martinet just smiled gracefully. "You know, language can be an interesting tool. Nouns can be subjects or objects. Verbs can be active or passive. And adjectives? They can be descriptive, or they can be decorative, or they can be derogatory. I think, if I were you, I would be cautious in using imprecations in the issuance of purported legal threats."

Tee Ray, his face crimson, strode out the door, calling back over his shoulder, "Gonna be sorry, nigger. Real sorry."

Bucky snatched his badge from Martinet's desk and left quickly as well.

As Bucky and Tee Ray were winding their way down the crowded street, Louis Martinet finally got out of his chair. Standing in his doorway, he called out after them, in a loud voice that all could hear, "Remember, I'm a believer in equal protection for all. So, if you two of the Caucasian persuasion need effective legal counsel to protect your rights, you just come right on back."

The crowd's cascading laughter followed Tee Ray and Bucky as they quickened their pace on their journey back to Canal Street.

Jenny, her ear pressed against the library door in the back of Louis's office, sighed. She had to get to the cemetery tonight. They would come back. It wasn't safe.

Jenny hoped Jake would be at the cemetery. Regardless, she could not return here in the morning. She could not put Louis in that kind of danger.

She had to find Jake and tell him what she knew. Then the two of them would have to leave Louisiana as soon as possible.

Chapter 74

"You want me to get Sooley to fetch you a fix-up, sugar? You give me another four dollars, and I'll get you anything you want. And then," she said, spreading her legs wide, "I'll give you anything you want, sugar."

Bucky sat on the bed, his eyes taking in the sight. Outside the third-floor window of the tiny room, it was dark. The candle in the dirty lantern cast a dim glow over the room, but it was more than enough.

"What's your thirst, sugar? Coso's got monogahela. He got whiskey. He got rifle knock-knee and vinum and copus cup. Any kind of bracer you want. It'll send you over the bay and get you squiffed for sure."

Other than whiskey, Bucky didn't recognize any of the terms she was using, but he felt sure it was all about alcohol. He felt squiffed already. He had given two dollars to the Italian downstairs who ran the Red Chair. For his money Bucky had been given a drink and a choice of the girls. He didn't want any of the blacks or mulattoes. He wanted only a white girl. He took the whitest one in the room, the young skinny one with straight black hair and a pale expression. They had come upstairs, and it was over before he knew it. Back they went downstairs again. Another two dollars, another drink, and up they went.

Bucky was beginning to get the hang of this. They had made a third trip downstairs, and the Italian said he could have the skinny girl for the rest of the night for five dollars, but all the drinks after the next one would be extra. Bucky had dug the fiver out of his pocket and paid it right then and there. He had flung back the whiskey as he had seen the other men at the bar do, choked on it but kept it down, and then had taken the girl back upstairs.

They had done it again. She was now lying on her back. Her tiny breasts glowed in the candlelight, and the soft hair between her legs glistened.

"Come on, sugar. You gonna look or you gonna do it? You paid for it. Might as well get your money's worth. But, hell, the least you can do is buy me a drink."

"I'll buy you anything you want." Bucky walked over to spot on the floor where he had flung his clothes and picked up his pants. Reaching in his pocket, he pulled out a wad of money. "See, I got lots. Raifer done give it to me, and I'm in charge. Ain't nobody, Tee Ray or no one else, gonna tell me what to do and when to do it. Ain't no one gonna tell me I got to wait until the job is over to come here to Faubourg Tremé. Right?"

"Whatever you say, sugar."

"My name is Bucky. You can call me Bucky if you want. And what's your name?"

The skinny girl on the bed giggled, her naked body twitching as the giggles turned into a laugh. " 'Bout time you asked, sugar. They call me Betsy."

"Betsy. That's a beautiful name."

"Come on, sugar, you got a roll there. Gimme four, and I'll get us both enough monogahela to last us until dawn." She slid out of bed and sidled up next to him, grabbing him firmly in the crotch. "I can see that you're ready. A little bracer, and we'll both go strong for hours."

Bucky had imagined what this night would be like. He had imagined it for years. But it was better than he had dreamt. It was better than the riverboat ride down the Mississippi from Parteblanc. It was better than anything.

He let her stroke his naked crotch while he unfurled four dollars from the roll. He could hardly pay attention to what he was doing because what Betsy was doing to him was so wonderfully distracting. The roll of money was getting smaller and smaller, but he didn't care. Other parts of him were getting larger and larger.

As soon as the bills were freed, however, Betsy snatched them from his hand and stopped fondling him. She went over to the door quickly and walked into the hall without a stitch on.

"Sooley," Bucky could hear her calling out. "Sooley girl, where are you?"

"Here Miz Betsy," a young child's voice responded.

"You go take this threefer down to Coso and have him bring me back a bottle of that stuff I done like. He knows what it is."

"Yes, Miz Betsy," the young child replied and scuffled away.

So what, thought Bucky, if Betsy sent only three dollars down for the liquor and kept a dollar for herself. It was worth it.

Bucky turned to gaze out the window. He wanted to remember every part of this night. He wanted to remember every curve on Betsy's body, every corner of the room, and even the view out onto the street below.

A gas lamp on the corner showed groups of men in twos and threes drunkenly weaving deeper into Faubourg Tremé, stumbling from bar to bar. A couple of them had passed out already in the street, mere dark shadows on the ground.

But there was one man moving in the opposite direction. He wore a long black coat and carried a broad-brimmed black hat in his hand. As the man passed under the street lamp, Bucky got a good look at his face and gasped.

Bucky grabbed the window and flung it open. "Hey, you! The Jew Peddler! You stop right there. You're under arrest!"

Jake looked up to see a naked Bucky yelling at him from the window.

It had been a foolish mistake not to keep Zig's hat on. Jake had been so careful until now. He had stayed in the room Antonio had given him all throughout the day, leaving only after it was good and dark. He had gone down the back stairs and out the back entrance to avoiding running into anyone.

To be spotted now by Bucky meant he didn't have much time. If Bucky was upstairs, Tee Ray had to be somewhere near.

Jake pulled his hat down tightly on his head and started to run as fast as he could.

Bucky was screaming at the men on the street to stop the runner, that he was a criminal.

No one on the street below paid Bucky the slightest bit of attention.

With his body half out the window and his attention on the street, Bucky didn't notice that, inside the room, Betsy was going through his pockets. She took almost all of his money and, wrapping the remaining bills around a scrap of fabric so it looked like a full roll of cash, stuffed it back into the pocket of Bucky's pants and let the trousers fall to the floor next to his shirt.

She put the money under the mattress and then lay back on the bed, legs wide open, and cooed, "Sugar, you gonna spend your night sticking your thing out the window or sticking it in me?"

Chapter 75

Bucky's feet hurt inside the rough boots. He hadn't had time to put on his socks as he dashed out of the bedroom and down the steps of the Red Chair and out onto the street. He ran at a gallop, trying to button up his shirt as he went, holding his coat in his teeth. His belt buckle was still unfastened and it flapped with each step, slapping against his bare stomach.

The Jew Peddler was a good two blocks ahead of him.

Bucky redoubled his efforts. He let his coat drop and tried to lengthen his stride, ignoring for the moment the way the boots chaffed his toes, raising blisters that Bucky was sure would be bloody before he had finished.

Bucky felt he was starting to gain on the Jew.

Jake took a moment to glance behind him as he turned a corner down a narrow alleyway. He could see Bucky panting heavily as he ran.

Several blocks away the customers and ladies of the Red Chair, in various stages of undress, who had leaned out the windows and watched the spectacle, now turned back to their other activities as the figures disappeared from view and promptly forgot about them.

The alleyway that Jake had entered was paved with broken and uneven bricks. Running was difficult here, but Jake moved swiftly. Any hesitation would be disastrous.

Nearing the last thirty feet of dark alley, Jake prepared to slow down slightly so he could turn right at the corner and head uptown. One more block, he figured, then take another right, go a block, and then turn left uptown once more. Uptown, away from Faubourg Tremé and away from the French Quarter. Uptown, toward the Garden District and Lafayette Cemetery.

Bucky saw the Jew duck into the alley. Between his gasps for breath as he ran, Bucky felt confident. That black hat and long black coat can't disguise the Jew. This Jew can't disappear by wearing black at night. Bucky knew what he looked like and now knew what the Jew was wearing.

Bucky ignored the pain in his feet and toes as well as the pain in his lungs. He was running faster than he ever had run before. He would capture the Jew.

Bucky could see it all. He would be a hero. He would be on his way to having Raifer's job. No one would ever laugh at him again. No one would make fun of him. Respect. He would get all of their respect. He would have earned it.

Making the turn into the narrow, dark, alley, Bucky saw the outline of the Jew at the other end, his wide-brimmed hat on his head, the ends of his long coat flaring out as he started to bear right down the next street. The Jew was slowing down.

Bucky knew he could overtake him. He had never taken such wide steps. He had never sprinted as quickly as he did now. His boots seemed to bound over the uneven bricks.

There was a fire in his chest with each breath. Bucky ignored it.

There was a squishing in his boots each time they hit the ground. The blood was coating his feet. Bucky ignored it.

His right foot was turning numb. Bucky ignored it.

His thigh muscles ached, his calves started to knot up, and he could hear his pulse rapidly throbbing like loud drums in his ears. Bucky ignored all of this.

Hearing the sound of pursuit getting nearer—Bucky's heavy panting and the hollow ricocheting of his thick heels on the bricks—Jake pushed himself harder, picking up speed. From his years of pulling the heavy cart for miles around the countryside, Jake had built up vast endurance. He could run like this for several hours if he had to. And he had to do it now. Jake ran faster. He could outrun and outlast Bucky.

Bucky saw the Jew turn the corner.

The wind rushing through his wild hair, Bucky gave it all he had and veered right as he neared the corner.

There was a strange sensation in Bucky's rapidly numbing right foot. It wouldn't seem to obey him. As his body turned right, his foot did not. The toe of the boot had caught in one of the broken bricks.

Bucky heard, before he felt it, a crunching sound from his right ankle.

The boot stayed wedged in the brick as Bucky's foot pulled free of it.

Bucky was in mid-stride, and his momentum carried him forward. He couldn't avoid coming down on his now shoeless right foot.

Now the pain came.

Bucky collapsed onto the ground as his ankle gave way, and he screamed in agony.

Hearing a yell behind him, Jake continued running, further quickening his pace.

PART X

Today

Chapter 76

"So, there I was, flat on my back, shotgun in my face.

"The man at the other end of the gun had a full head of white hair and a gray stubble of a beard. His belly strained against the buttons of his shirt and poured over his belt.

"His blustery face was lined with wrinkles, his thin, angry mouth carved beneath dour jowls. Kind of like the energy of his life had been spent on envy and hate, and these emotions had been etched permanently on his features.

"'Course, it's strange to think about it. Back then he seemed to me to be so elderly. Yet he was younger than I am now. I guess I look elderly to you.

"Anyway, while on the floor, I kept talking. You know, I can talk about almost anything. Like to talk.

"Oh, you noticed that, did you? Well, some people are afraid to talk. It's as if they don't think people will care what they have to say, or maybe they think they'll embarrass themselves, or maybe they're just shy. But I don't think you can really live if you don't talk. You can't find out about people if you don't talk to them.

"I told the man I was a student. That was true. I told the man I had come from up north. True also, and I couldn't hide that. Told the man I was working on a research project about the South. That was close enough to the truth.

"Told him that that I had done research on Cottoncrest and that I was trying to complete my research. Definitely true.

"Told him I wanted to meet Hank Matthews, who owned Cottoncrest, and that I wanted to ask him a few questions and show him the results of my research and get his reaction. True. True. True.

"The man didn't take the shotgun away, but he did ask if I was really a student, if I was really doing research, and if all I wanted to do was ask a few questions.

"You know, telling the truth has a remarkable effect on people. When you tell the truth, you connect with them. The man could see I was telling the truth.

"He finally moved the shotgun from my face and helped me to my feet. Told me, in his own sour way, that he was Hank Matthews and that if I wanted to get the real facts about Cottoncrest and the South, I had come to the right place. Said that the rest of the country didn't understand the South, and all he wanted was a fair hearing and fair treatment for the southern way of life that had been so distorted by 'them damn northern liberals.'

"I thanked him and told him I was pleased to meet him. Which I was. True again. Told him I only wanted to get to the truth, that 'heaven and earth have sworn that the truth shall be disclosed.' He liked that.

"Of course, I didn't tell him that this phrase was a literal translation of a great Yiddish phrase, *Himmel un erb hoben geshvoren az kain zach zol nit zein farloren.*

"That's what I was there for. To get the truth and to disclose it as well."

1893

Chapter 77

Lafayette Cemetery had many more crypts in it than the last time Jake had been there. It was dark, and Jake could not read the inscriptions, but he could see the newly built ones that were laid out with mathematical precision on the grid of pathways. Line after line of diminutive homes for the deceased. Given the high water table, where buried coffins would rise to the surface in every rainstorm, aboveground crypts were the only solution possible.

Death continued to stalk New Orleans, and the cemeteries were ever expanding. Waves of yellow fever came and went, an army of destruction, leaving behind hundreds of jaundiced victims whose bodies had to be quickly removed from homes. Death by childbirth for women. Death in childbirth for infants. Death by malaria and influenza and pneumonia. Death by cholera in the hovels that lined brackish drainage canals. Death by bilious fevers and pleurisy and catarrhal fevers. Death by French fever—syphilis—and by internal hemorrhages and by mysterious growths in the glands. Death by infections and gunshot wounds and stabbings. And even, occasionally, death by old age.

All of this required an industry of death. Crypt builders. Stone masons. Plasterers. Artisans. Makers of funereal wear and the somber black attire that many wore for years after the loss of a spouse or a child.

Those who survived used the design of the crypts as a strange combination of both competition for permanent social status among the deceased and proof of the wealth of their spouses, siblings, and descendants. A hoped-for eternal monument to those who, a few generations hence, would be beyond the memory of the living except in this place where their names were inscribed in stone or marble or plaster.

Some of the crypts had peaked roofs and spires. Others had embellished designs in the limned plaster that coated thick red bricks. Some had tiny doorways and steps and even stone windows. Some were miniature churches. Some had stone flowers and stone plants. Some had imported marble and others smooth granite. Some even had a statue of the deceased or their likeness carved in bas-relief.

Then there were the unadorned boxy structures, seven feet high or more, that held thirty or more burial slots in high, medium, and low rows in their brick walls. Called "ovens," these crypts were reusable. The heat and the humidity so quickly decayed the bodies that the next internment in the same narrow slot could occur within seven weeks.

Jake had thought, when he had left word with Marcus for Jenny to meet him here, that Lafayette Cemetery would be the easiest and safest place to convene. Jake had assumed he would be staying with Zig Haber; Zig's house was only a few blocks away from Lafayette Cemetery. Jake had not wanted to meet in the French Quarter—it was too public—or in Faubourg Tremé, for the same reason. The St. Louis Cemeteries were not suitable, for voodoo rites were still going on there secretly late at night.

Lafayette Cemetery, in the still-developing Garden District, with its big homes and large lots, would be away from prying eyes and chance encounters from night wanderers. There should be no one lingering on the streets of the Garden District late at night.

The chill of the evening had descended. Jake was barely out of breath from running. He had lost Bucky more than two miles back, and he had not seen anyone as he slowed to a casual walk while traversing the last few blocks into the cemetery.

Jake sat on the steps of one of the crypts far back from the main cemetery entrance on Washington Street. Here he could see anyone who came in either that way or from the Prytania Street gate. The cemetery occupied an entire block, bounded on the north by Prytania Street and on the east by Washington.

Jake hoped that Jenny would come tonight. It was not safe to go back to the Red Chair or anywhere in Faubourg Tremé. It was not safe to go to Zig's house.

Whether or not Jenny came, Jake would have to leave New Orleans. Jake had been pondering how to do so. The more he thought about it, the more he realized that Antonio Micelli, back at the Red Chair, had given him the perfect solution.

Too bad it involved a train. Jake did not like to travel by train. He hadn't liked trains since his escape from Russia. And yet now he might have to use a train to escape from Louisiana.

Escaping Russia, he had become invisible hiding under the hoop-skirts of women. But that was when he was twelve.

Now that he was grown, thanks to what Antonio had said, Jake had figured out how to become invisible on a train traveling north from the Crescent City.

Chapter 78

"You sound like an old woman with that yelpin'. Just hold on, and I'll be done in a moment. Don't be such a flicker."

"Don't call me a flicker, Tee Ray. I ain't no coward. I done proved it to— OUCH!—night, didn't I?"

Tee Ray kept on wrapping the long gauze bandage around Bucky's ankle, pulling it tighter. "What you proved tonight is that you're a fool. Snuck out to go to a parlor house. Couldn't wait, could you, until we had caught the Jew? Couldn't wait to go to a place I know where they wouldn't roll you? Went to some Dago's fast house. Spent your money like a fool. Then got almost all the rest of it taken by a whore. You'll be lucky if she didn't give you the French fever."

Tee Ray finished, cutting off the end of the gauze with his knife and tossing it up on the table next to the few bills that still curled forlornly around the linen scrap.

"You were gonna hold onto the money 'cause you were in charge. You couldn't lead a charge up the banks of a shallow bayou without falling down on your face in the mud and gettin' snakebit to boot!"

Tee Ray sat back in the chair that faced the horsehair sofa where Bucky lay. He had been hauled back to the boarding house by a couple of drunken men, and Tee Ray had given them each a dollar and sent them back to Faubourg Tremé so they could buy some more drinks and keep on being squiffed the rest of the night.

"But I spotted the Jew, Tee Ray. I gave chase. I almost caught him."

Tee Ray just glared, his eyes cold and heartless. "You gave chase! Did you have a gun to shoot him? No. Did you have a knife on you? No, and you know what he done did at Cottoncrest with his Jew knife. You just ran out without thinkin'. Assumin' you caught him, what was you gonna do? Ask him polite to walk with you to the Orleans Parish Sheriff's Office where they have handcuffs and can throw him in a jug?

Don't you think he might have a Jew knife on him and could slice you up quicker than Greek fire?"

Bucky's expression showed that he hadn't considered any of these things. "But," he said quietly, "it ain't a matter no more of wonderin' *if* he is here in New Orleans. We now know that he *is* here."

Tee Ray shot back, "And he knows that we're here. Do you think he's gonna go back to anywhere near Faubourg Tremé at this point? Not likely. He's gonna make himself scarce as hens' teeth."

Tee Ray went over to the closet and pulled out a rifle. He checked to make sure it was loaded.

Bucky raised himself up on one elbow, "Where'd you get that?"

Tee Ray was pointing the rifle out the window, checking the sight at the end of the barrel. "Knew you was up to no good when you said you wanted to go get some dinner on your own. What you want wanderin' around lookin' for dinner when we paid good money for room and board here? Now I see your appetite weren't for no food."

Satisfied that the rifle was ready, Tee Ray rested it on top of the dresser. "Ain't gonna let no nigger lawyer make fun of me. No sir. Ain't gonna let no Jew storekeeper lie to my face. I gone and seen one of the Knights who works for the Orleans Parish Sheriff's Office. Tol' him what had happened, and he lent me this here rifle so I could prod compliance. Don't you like that? I was gonna stick this rifle up in the face of the Jew storekeeper and prod him to tell us where the peddler was. I was gonna prod this rifle up the black nostril of that nigger lawyer to answer my questions. But you gone and ruined all that now, Bucky. That Jew is on the run for sure, and wherever that high yellow girl Jenny was, she ain't no more use to us 'til we catch the peddler."

"I'm sorry I done messed it up, Tee Ray. I thought I was doin' the right thing. I was tryin' my hardest." Bucky brightened for a moment. "You know, I never done run as fast as I did tonight."

Tee Ray snarled, " 'Tweren't half-fast enough."

Bucky was deflated again. He asked dejectedly, "So, what we gonna do, Tee Ray?"

"We? 'We' ain't gonna do nothin'. You ain't goin' anywheres on that ankle, even if I wanted you to, which I don't. You gonna stay right here on the sofa in this here roomin' house, and I'm takin' the badge and the rest of the money. You do what I say, and I won't tell Raifer how you lost the parish's money and how you lost the Jew. Don't think you'd have a job anymore if I tol' Raifer these things, do you?"

Bucky was torn between feeling grateful to Tee Ray for helping him keep his job and hating Tee Ray for the way he continually talked to him like he was a child who didn't understand anything. Bucky responded simply, "No."

"Good. Don't you leave this room, then. I'm goin' out now to find all the Knights on the Sheriff's staff—they're a bunch of 'em—and get their help. You know, they would have found a way to get rid of the Dagos that the court done let loose for murdering Hennessey if the Vigilance Committee hadn't organized a mob to go get them and the other Dagos who had just come in on the boat. They don't want no more Dagos in this city, and they don't want no Jew gettin' away. When I tell the Vigilance Committee that the Jew was at the Dago's Red Chair place in Faubourg Tremé—something I got out of that Betsy when I went back to fetch the rest of your clothes—they're all gonna help. All them Knights gonna watch the river. Ain't no chance of any Jew man gettin' on a boat headin' north or south from this point on without them checkin' each of them out. If he tries to go by river, we'll have him. Gonna get them to watch the road north to Baton Rouge. Ain't no chance of a Jew man goin' up River Road or out toward Lake Pontchartrain or headin' to Chalmette without some Knight with a badge or some member of the Vigilance Committee spottin' him."

Bucky understood all of this, except one thing. "What's the Vigilance Committee?"

Tee Ray sneered at Bucky's ignorance. "There's time when the Sheriff won't act—or can't act. In that case the Vigilance Committee is there. Most of them are Knights. Can't stand niggers or Jews or Papists or Dagos. 'Specially Papist Dagos."

"But if the Sheriff and the Vigilance Committee are watchin' the docks and the roads, what are you gonna do?"

For the first time this evening Tee Ray smiled. His lips pulled back, and his crooked teeth made the grin all the more sinister. "There're two trains scheduled to leave tomorrow, one in the mornin' for Chicago and one in the afternoon for New York. I'm gonna be at the station. I feel it in my bones. By tomorrow at this time there's gonna be a coffin goin' back upriver to Parteblanc."

Chapter 79

Jake saw a shadowy figure slip through the Poydras Street gate of the Lafayette Cemetery. Jake looked up at the stars. It was, he judged, almost midnight.

The figure, wrapped in a cloak, moved cautiously through the cemetery. As it got closer, he could tell that it was a woman. She wore a tignon. Even in the dim moonlight, he could see the brightly colored kerchief covering her head. A cloak draped from her shoulders and shielded her from the chilly night air.

When she was two rows away, Jake called out, softly *"Une alliance."* An alliance of two. It was also a Cajun term for a wedding ring.

The woman lifted her head, startled at the sound.

Jake could see it was Jenny. *"C'est bon."*

Jenny ran and gave him a hug. "I knew it was you."

Leading her gently by the arm, Jake pulled her back down one of the rows where the tall crypts shielded out even the moonlight. She uncinched the blanket with her few belongings from around her waist and joined him on the steps of a crypt shaped like a small church. The miniature steeple rose seven feet above the ground, the stone cross on top a pale icon against the star-dotted sky.

"I've got to leave New Orleans as soon as the sun comes up, Mr. Jake. Do you know that Tee Ray and Bucky are in town?"

Even in the dim light, Jenny could see from Jake's expression that this was not news to him.

"Mr. Jake, both of them came to Louis's earlier today. I'm sure they're coming back tomorrow. I can't stay around. It will only hurt Louis and put him in danger if I do. He's done more than enough already."

"I'm sure he has. There are many people who will be in danger if either of us stay." Jake paused. This was the moment. "You've got to tell me. I've got to know."

271

Jenny took his hand and said in the softest of voices, "Don't worry, Mr. Jake."

If there had been anyone in the cemetery at this hour, even a few feet away, they could not have heard Jenny. Although there was no one, Jenny took no chances.

She put her mouth next to Jake's ear and whispered, "The Colonel Judge's and Rebecca's babies are alive. Their twins are safe."

PART XI

Today

Chapter 80

"Matthews and I sat under that big oak tree, right over there. At the time it was right next to the IMPEACH EARL WARREN sign that he had put up on old telephone poles. The top of that sign was almost as high as the third-story roofline of Cottoncrest.

"He had poured some bourbon for both of us, although he was on his third glass while I was still working on my first. I was taking notes as fast as I could.

"'Tell me, if you don't mind,' I asked, to keep him talking, 'how it was you acquired Cottoncrest. So many of these old plantation homes have been lost. Some have burned, some have sloughed off into the Mississippi River as it changed course, and others have been lost when the original owners simply abandoned them as being too expensive to keep up. And yet you managed to purchase this place in the midst of the Depression.'

"'It was a real coup,' he said. 'Old Widow Brady had let this place run right down into the ground. Boll weevil had got the cotton crop. Sharecroppers had taken off; they couldn't even raise enough to feed themselves. Widow Brady's kids had all left for Baton Rouge and New Orleans to find work, but there wasn't much of it, and what little they could scrape together to send home to her wasn't enough to even pay the taxes on the plantation. She was about to lose everything to the tax sale. So, I just offered her a thousand for the entire thing. Hell, she cried something awful. But I didn't care. Served her right.'

"'A thousand dollars for all of Cottoncrest? That was a remarkable deal.' I said.

"I ignored what he said about Mrs. Brady crying. He seemed to be proud that she did, and I wasn't about to do anything to antagonize him. All I wanted to do at this point was to encourage him. People like nothing better than to talk about themselves, especially to someone who listens to them with interest. Nothing is more interesting to someone than his own life story.

"'Ain't nothin' remarkable about it,' he told me, after taking another sip of bourbon. 'Had to scrape together every dime I could. Had to put a mortgage on my house and my business—couldn't sell my house in those days, what with the Depression and all. The 1930s were a rough time, a very rough time. Sylvia, my wife, thought I was crazy. Here I was, in my midforties, and I was taking on so much debt she thought that we'd lose the little we had built up, and with two young boys and all, not even eight yet—she worried 'bout those twins. But I told her, 'Sylvia, I've been waiting for this all my life.'

"'My Daddy had told me time and time again that the only man he hated more than niggers was Widow Brady's husband. Tee Ray.

"'So, you see, I was doing this for my dead Daddy.'"

1893

Chapter 81

"They're both safe, Mr. Jake. Rebecca and the Colonel Judge's children will grow up separated. The boy and the girl won't know who their real parents were. Won't even know they were one of two. But the twins will be alive, and that's the most important thing."

"You've accomplished a miracle, Jenny. When Rebecca began to show, she stopped going out. The Colonel Judge didn't want to tell anyone until they were born. He had to be sure they didn't die in childbirth, that they were born alive and could survive and inherit Cottoncrest. And yet, once they were born . . ."

"I know, Mr. Jake. He never recovered, did he? Just withdrew more and more into himself. I sometimes think he aged more in the six months after the twins were born than he had aged in the last ten years. When I got to Cottoncrest, the Colonel Judge and Rebecca were so happy. He was like a young man again. And after the twins were born, whatever was young in him dropped away, never to return."

Jenny and Jake sat in the cemetery. Jenny wrapped her cloak around her more tightly. The damp chill from the October night air and the cold from the crypt's stone steps penetrated deep under her skin.

"The problem was, he didn't know, Mr. Jake—not until the twins were born."

"Did you?"

"'Course. From the moment I got there. But I was not going to tell anyone. That was her secret. But once the twins came, he knew. It broke his heart, I think. He wanted to love them, but he couldn't. He wanted to hate her, but he couldn't do that either. He was so torn."

Jake thought back to all his conversations with the Colonel Judge. On the lower veranda. On the upper gallery. In the library. The Colonel

Judge often said he would do anything to keep his nephew from getting Cottoncrest. He would honor the General's wishes.

Maybe that was why, when the Colonel Judge met Rebecca in Philadelphia, he had fallen in love with her so quickly and had married her before leaving Pennsylvania. He was both in love with her and in love with what she represented—a way to save Cottoncrest. But the longer they were married, the more concerned he became. Without children, when Little Miss was gone, what if something happened to both Rebecca and him? Tee Ray would then inherit Cottoncrest, despite the fact that the General had tried to disinherit Tee Ray's mother.

"Mr. Jake, until those children were born, the Colonel Judge, he didn't know she was passing for white. But once they came out, once he saw the boy, white as Rebecca, and the girl, darker than me with kinky black hair, he knew. It destroyed him, didn't it? A colonel of the Confederacy with a mulatto wife and mulatto children. His own flesh and blood."

Jake didn't say anything. How could he tell Jenny what the Colonel Judge had confided to him that fateful night, more than a year ago? That, because of his war wound, the Colonel Judge would never be able to have any children.

Today

Chapter 82

"Since Hank Matthews said he had bought Cottoncrest for his dead daddy, I told him he must have loved his father very much.

"'Loved him? Don't know if you could call it that. He was a tough man. Big in every way. Big beard. Big arms. Big voice. Big strap of a belt that he'd whip me with. Blacksmith he was, until there weren't any enough need for blacksmiths to make a living. He refused to go back to sharecropping. Said he'd rather die than sharecrop on Widow Brady's plantation.'

"You know, some people get misty-eyed talking about their fathers, but not Matthews. It was almost as if he had distanced himself from both the man and the memory.

"He leaned over to refill my glass, which was less than half-empty. 'What's the matter, boy? Can't hold your liquor? If you're going to sit here, drink with me, unless you're too proud to do that.'

"What could I do? I picked up the glass and drank deeply. It wasn't time yet to show him what I had brought. Not yet.

"So, I asked him what was it like, growing up in Parteblanc. That was a way to get into the subject.

"'You know what it's like to be poor—really poor?' he asked me. Then he just leaned back in that chair, staring up at the big oak. 'I saw at a glance from your clothes and your manner that you have no idea. Being dirt-poor—if you don't know any better—is not that bad. When you're young, you just think that's the way things are. You have nothing to compare it to. Except for the really rich—and you know you'll never be like them—you're surrounded by people in your same condition. What you have, they have, and what you don't have, none of your friends have. But worse than being poor, you see, is getting a whole lot poorer. Then you see the difference. Then you remember what it used to be like. And that's the worst.'

"'That's what happened to us. Just getting poorer and poorer. And nothing that my Daddy did changed anything. That man seemed to have the worst luck. Wouldn't talk to his old friends because of some grudge he had about something they did to him years before when he was a member of the Knights of the White Camellia. Wouldn't ask for help. Just took it out on me. He'd get angry at the slightest thing, and he'd pull off his belt. Never hit me with all his strength, that I know. If he had, he'd have cut me in half. I've seen him pick up an anvil by himself. You know how heavy that is?'

"'I knew better than to mess with my Daddy. I just took those beatings, even though they were most undeserved.'

"Here he was, an old man, and the scars of his childhood were still with him. I had put down my pen, and I was just listening. I was trying to be empathetic, not saying anything but trying to nod my head in the appropriate places to let him know I was paying close attention.

"He finally fell silent. But I needed him to continue. We had to get further before I pulled out my folder. I needed to steer the topic to his relationship with Ganderson. I just was unsure about how to do it in a subtle enough way.

"I tried a different approach. I asked him whether all these beatings gave him less respect for his father in any way.

"'Hell no,' he told me. 'I respected the hell out of him. I mean, after all, he was doing the best he could do, and yet the best was not enough. What I wanted to do more than anything else was to please him. He hated niggers. I would show him that I hated them more, as was only right. He hated Tee Ray Brady's widow and all of that family. I would hate them more and get revenge for whatever Tee Ray had done to him, which I did. He hated ol' man Ganderson, despite, or maybe because of, what Ganderson did for me. So, I grew to hate Ganderson too. Spit on his grave the day he died, I did.'

"Ganderson! He had gone and mentioned the name all on his own! And yet he talked about spitting on his grave in such a self-satisfied way. I hadn't expected that. I had thought he would have loved—no, that's too strong a word—maybe respected, or at least missed, Ganderson. Yet hatred was what poured through Hank Matthews. Pure, mean old hatred. You know what they say. *Siz nit mit vemen tsu geyn tsum tish.*

"Okay. Yes, yes. You don't know Yiddish. I forget more and more these days of what happened recently and dwell more and more on the past. It's a Yiddish expression—he wasn't someone you would want to sit down to dinner with. But the morsel I had brought with me was going to give him plenty of food for thought.

"And now that he had mentioned Kenneth Ganderson, I had the opening I had been waiting for."

Chapter 83

"Do you think it will work, Mr. Jake?"

"I don't see why not. Have you ever taken a train?"

"No. Never."

"But it's true what Antonio told me, isn't it?"

"Sure is, Mr. Jake. That's what Louis has been spending all his time on. He was working on it before I left to go to Cottoncrest, and he's still working on it now. He's trying to get the passenger car case heard in the Supreme Court. I've seen the pleadings he's going to file. Homer's name is right there, right on papers going to the U.S. Supreme Court. Homer Adolph Plessy versus J. H. Ferguson. Of course, Louis can't argue the case. Can't even put his name on the briefs if it is going to have any chance to be heard. Two white lawyers, Al Tourgee and Jim Walker, have their names on the briefs, but it's Louis who's behind it all."

Jake didn't care about the lawsuit. He didn't care about the legal issues. The important thing was that Jenny had confirmed what Antonio had said.

Jenny began to shiver with the cold, despite her cloak.

Jake opened up his long black coat and held out his arm. Jenny snuggled into the warmth of his coat, into the warmth of his embrace. She rested her head on his shoulder and drifted into sleep.

Jake stayed watchful, his eyes continually scanning the two entrances to the cemetery.

There was no time for any carelessness. There was no time for any mistake. There was no time for any lapse in attentiveness.

Dawn would be here shortly.

Today

Chapter 84

"I pretended at first not to know anything about Kenneth Ganderson. I asked Hank Matthews who Ganderson was and why he spit on Ganderson's grave.

"'A meddler,' he said. 'My Daddy didn't want any handouts. He didn't want any sympathy. All he wanted was to do a day's work for a day's pay, but although he worked from almost dawn 'til twilight, the pay wasn't there. The century had turned. We passed through ought-six and ought-seven, and the blacksmith business kept dropping off. And yet there was still old man Ganderson coming by once every six months or so. Bringing a basket of food. Paying too much to get his horse shod. Slipping me candy and, as I got older, sometimes slipping me money. He would see me on the street and stick out his arm. Put 'er there, little fella, he'd say, and when I reached out to shake his hand, in his palm would be a quarter.

"'Made the mistake of telling Daddy about it one day. Do you know what he did? Went over to Ganderson's house and told him to stop it. My Daddy told Ganderson that he could take care of his own family without the help of anyone.'

"'Without the help of anyone,' I repeated as I wrote that down in my notebook. 'So Ganderson stopped?' I asked.

"'No. It kind of became our secret. As I got older, the handshake I received contained four bits, then it contained a dollar bill. A real dollar bill. My Daddy sometimes had to work three days or more for that, and I got it only for a handshake.

"'Do you know what found money does to you? Makes you lazy. Makes you fail to appreciate hard work. Makes you forget how difficult earning money can be. Also makes you think like you deserve it for doing nothing.

"'It was when I turned sixteen that it ended.'

"'Why?' I asked.

"'My Daddy was reduced to taking odd jobs. No better than nigger work. I had dropped out of school years before. I pretended to work, but I was living off the money that Ganderson slipped me. Gave half of it to my Daddy—my mother was dead by then—letting him think I was earning it across the river. But I was really spending it like I owned the world. Spent the week drinking and whoring in Baton Rouge. Came back on the weekend, saw Ganderson, and then gave half of what I got to Daddy and saved the other half for my trip out on Monday. Enough to last the rest of that week, and then it would start again.

"'I got to the point where I think my Daddy was embarrassed to talk to me. We didn't talk much, the older and the bigger I got, and when he did talk, it was about niggers and Jews and Papists and Tee Ray Brady. He kind of lumped them all together.

"'The Friday of the week I turned sixteen, I showed up at Ganderson's, expecting the usual handshake. What did he do? He handed me one hundred dollars. That was more money than I had ever seen. My Daddy, I don't think, ever saw that much in his lifetime. I know he never had that much, ever.

"'Did I thank Ganderson? Did I say anything? No. I just took it, like it was my right. My Daddy wasn't home. I left twenty on the table. That would take care of him for a long time.

"'As for me, I took the ferry to Baton Rouge and from there got on a train to New York. Lived like a king. And when the money ran out, I joined the army. It was just a few weeks before the First World War broke out.

"'Didn't make it back in time to see my Daddy before he died. Didn't write him. He couldn't read anyway.

"'Daddy died hating Jews and niggers and the high and mighty on plantations and all. And Ganderson. That's why, when I got back, I spit on Ganderson's grave.'

"And then, as Matthews finished off his glass of bourbon and poured himself a fourth one, he said something I'll always remember. 'Crazy old Ganderson. Thought he was trying to help me. But all he did by giving me money was make me ashamed of my Daddy. Can you imagine that? Ashamed of your own father.'"

PART XII

1893

Chapter 85

The railway station was crowded. On the engine a worker was stoking up the coal-fed fire. As a head of steam was being built up, sparks drifted down in the early morning, a light snowfall of red and black ashes.

Tee Ray, badge pinned on his coat, rifle at his side, scanned the swarm. Bucky had described the peddler's outfit. Big black hat with a broad brim. Long black coat.

If the Jew were here, Tee Ray had no doubt he would find him. Despite the horde of people, the Jew would stand out.

Tee Ray climbed upon the big wooden luggage cart, its wheels chest high. From here his view would be unobstructed.

The front cars were for whites. That's where the Jew would go. That's where any white man would go. Those were the cars to watch. Scores of women, children, and men boarded. First-class passengers. Others in less-fancy apparel. They stood their turn in line.

Porters loaded luggage, hauling it through the entry doors between the cars or grunting as they lifted heavy bags onto boxcars.

Children let loose high-pitched yells as steam hissed and descended in clouds onto the platform.

The conductor was blowing his whistle. Last call.

The remaining passengers pushed forward on the platform, calling out over their shoulders to their families a final good-bye as they climbed up the steep steps into the entranceways between the cars.

The white passengers were all aboard. There was no sign of the Jew.

Tee Ray looked in disgust as the last of the Negroes moved onto the train. Slow. No hurry. As if they had all the time in the world.

Tee Ray climbed down from the luggage cart, rifle in hand. There was no need to wait here all day. He would come back an hour before the afternoon train.

At the far end of the platform, one last pair of Negroes was getting on. A young woman and an older one. The younger one in a dress and a brightly covered tignon was adjusting the thin cloak over her shoulders. She then helped the older one up the stairs into the Jim Crow car. The old lady wore a shawl over her blouse; it draped down almost to her skirt. Walking with a cane in one hand, she carried a large black bundle under her other arm. The old lady had an unusual, misshapen black bonnet covered with wilted green leaves pulled low over her face. Tee Ray thought that the old lady was probably as ugly as her bonnet.

Tee Ray paused one more moment to look closely at the old lady. No, he was sure. The older one was not Sally. And no sign of Marcus. Sally would not travel without Marcus.

The younger one, though, looked familiar.

The door closed.

The train started to pull out.

Tee Ray realized it was Jenny, her long hair hidden beneath the tignon.

As the train moved slowly down the tracks, gathering up speed as it left the station, Tee Ray ran, clasping the rifle tightly. He hoped that the small Derringer he had stuck in his belt, the one the Orleans Parish Sheriff had lent him, the one he had not told Bucky about, wouldn't slip out.

As the train cleared the station, Tee Ray was holding onto a handle, pounding on a door with his rifle as the tracks rushed by below his feet.

The conductor, spotting the badge on this wild man's coat, opened it.

Tee Ray entered the train.

Chapter 86

Outside the train's windows to their left, the marsh that curved around the northwestern edge of New Orleans stretched out to the horizon, and to their right was a vast expanse of water. The tracks, atop miles upon miles of wooden pilings, skirted along the edge of Lake Pontchartrain. Then the rails bore north, nestling the narrow spit of land that ran through woody swamps.

The engine pulled six passenger cars followed by more than a dozen boxcars, several flatbeds, and a caboose. The conductor was working his way down the train, collecting tickets, starting with the first-class cars.

Back in the two Jim Crow cars, right before the boxcars, a number of passengers had unpacked their breakfasts. They had spread on their laps the old newspapers in which they had wrapped a biscuit or a scrap of ham or a piece of French bread and ate slowly, savoring the taste. They had to make the food last the entire trip. It was all they could do to afford the ticket. There was almost no money left to purchase the expensive items at the stations at the numerous stops along the way to Chicago.

Near the back row of the last Jim Crow car, Jake, dressed in Jenny's spare blouse and skirt, sat demurely next to the window. "Is it still straight?"

Jenny fiddled with the silver hairpins that held the broad felt brim of Jake's hat in a curled, decorative edge on one side and the thick, drooping greenery that hid the edges of the folded brim on the other. With the strange shape and the wilted leaves, it was unsightly, but, pulled down enough, it helped to hide Jake's face and stubbly beard.

It was the beard, not the color of Jake's skin, that was the problem. If passengers, no matter how white they looked, boarded the Jim Crow cars, no one looked twice. They were simply mulattoes who, unlike Homer Plessy, knew their place.

The front door of the car opened. The conductor entered, asking for tickets. He folded each into three parts and punched a hole through the thick paper. One part he put in the pocket of his coat, one part he gave back to the passenger, and one part he put into the metal holder that stuck up on the back of each seat.

Jake pulled the folded blanket that he hoped others would mistake for a poor woman's shawl more tightly around his neck and raised its frayed edges high on his cheeks.

Jenny glanced over. Jake's stubble of a mustache was clearly visible.

The conductor was still taking tickets at the front of the car. Before he could look up and observe them, Jenny pulled out a kerchief and pretended to wipe Jake's nose, helping an old lady suffering from an October cold. Jake took the kerchief and, bending forward in his seat and leaning on the stout branch he had picked up outside the cemetery to use as a lame old lady's cane, continued to wipe his face.

The conductor finally came to their seat. Jenny, as obsequious as she could be, handed over the tickets they had bought with Zig's money. The conductor, without giving these two women any thought at all, punched the tickets. There was no point in spending any energy on coloreds or spending any more time than necessary in the Jim Crow cars.

Finishing with his task, the conductor headed back toward the front of the train.

Jenny sighed with relief.

Jake put down the kerchief, but he kept his face to the window. Jake did not want to take any chances, even though Jenny had assured him that no one in this Jim Crow car would say anything, no matter how strange a bearded lady might appear to them. They were not about to complain to—or seek help from—a white conductor.

It was curious, he thought. All his life, when he had sought protection, he had found it, and women always seemed to be involved. He had found safety by hiding beneath the skirts of women leaving Russia. Jeanne Marie had helped him escape from Lamou. Now he was seeking to safely leave Louisiana by hiding, with the help of a woman, in the skirt of a woman.

Jenny leaned over and said, just loud enough so that Jake could hear her over the rumble of the wheels, the creaking of the wooden passenger car, and the metallic groans of the couplings of the train. "Taking a final look at Louisiana? I think it will be the last time either of us see this state."

In the front of the car the door opened. A murmur rose from the passengers.

Mothers hugged their children and shushed for them to be quiet. Old men, former slaves all, quickly cast their eyes down to the floor; they didn't want to be mistaken for being uppity. Strong young men turned and looked out the windows, trying to avoid the glare of the angry white man who had just entered, a lawman's badge prominently pinned on his coat.

Jake kept his face turned against the window, the back of his head facing into the car. He wondered whether he had conquered all his fears pertaining to trains. The fear of the Cossacks discovering him on the train in Russia. The fear as he hid beneath the women's skirts, hearing the tread of boots passing by, separated from him only by an opaque veil of petticoats and linen.

But that was then. This was now. But the fear was still there. He didn't turn.

The intruder was looking for him, no doubt, and the dress wouldn't hide his stubbly beard and mustache, and he couldn't pull the blanket up at this point without being noticed.

Looking at the man's reflection in the window, Jake hoped that the intruder was scanning faces and bodies, not windows.

If Jake could see the man, the man could see him. Floating over the images of the moss-laden cypress trees and palmetto-filled marsh that rushed by the window outside hovered the ghostly, transparent figure of Tee Ray holding a rifle.

Jake immediately pressed his face as close as he could to the window so that his hat would hide his features and his own reflection would not be seen.

Tee Ray spotted Jenny and strode forward, pointing a rifle at her. "Nigger, you ain't leavin' Louisiana. You're under arrest. I know you gotta know something about the Jew. You don't do as I say, I'm gonna shoot you dead right here."

Chapter 87

"Get up, nigger!" Tee Ray commanded Jenny, approaching her, rifle held level at his waist, its barrel pointing directly at her chest. Tee Ray ignored the woman in the seat next to Jenny, obviously so terrified of him that she wouldn't turn around. That was as it should be. Let them all keep to themselves.

Jake remained motionless, his face frozen against the window. He forced himself to be still. There was nothing he could do at this moment. He had to wait, as difficult as that was.

"The rest of you," Tee Ray called out as he moved through the car, "stay seated."

The passengers did as they were told. The white man had a badge and a gun. He was angry and upset. None of them moved. They awaited his instructions.

Tee Ray prodded Jenny with the barrel of his rifle. "You heard me, nigger. Up!"

Jenny slowly rose to her feet.

Jake still did not remove his face from the cold window. He could not turn around without endangering both Jenny and himself.

Tee Ray pointed to the rear door of the carriage. Jenny walked ahead of him, his rifle in her back. There was only one more row of seats between the rear door and the spot where Jenny had been seated.

"Now," Tee Ray called out loudly so everyone could hear him, "this is law business. You ain't seen nothin', and you ain't gonna say nothin'."

Jake heard the rustle of Jenny's dress and the scuffling of Tee Ray's boots as they moved toward the back of the car. Now it was time to put an end to his fears. Now was the time to act, while Tee Ray's back was to him.

Jenny reached the rear door.

"Open it!" Tee Ray commanded.

At the same moment that Jenny complied, pulling the door open and filling the compartment with the loud rush of wind and the roaring clatter of the wheels on the track as the train speeded through the woody marsh, Tee Ray felt a sharp object in his lower back and heard a man's voice say firmly, "Drop the rifle, or I'll slice your spinal cord in half. You'll be crippled for life."

The passengers remained frozen in place, puzzled by what was now clearly a bearded man in a woman's outfit and terrified by what the white lawman might do.

Tee Ray held the rifle firmly in his grasp, its barrel now pointed at Jenny's head, and tightened his finger around the trigger. Without taking his eyes off Jenny, Tee Ray spoke in a loud voice to the man behind him. "I don't know what kind of jackass nigger you are, but if you don't back off right now, I'm gonna kill this one first and then you."

Jenny stood motionless, holding the door open, the wind blowing in her face. The passengers tried not to make a sound. The slightest noise or movement could set the white man with the rifle off and be fatal to the woman at the door and to others in the car.

Tee Ray felt the pointed object withdraw from his lower back. The stupid man behind him had listened. Now it was time to teach them all a lesson.

Tee Ray jerked the rifle backward as he whirled around, aiming to hit the man behind him in the stomach with the butt of the rifle. As he did, he inadvertently pulled the trigger and the rifle fired. The bullet whizzed by Jenny's ear and shattered the window of the passenger car door she was holding open. It plowed through the cheap wooden panel and lodged in the metal structure of the car.

As Tee Ray spun around, he was surprised that, despite his quick and vicious thrust with the rifle, it did not connect with anything. He felt a throbbing behind his right thigh, and before he had turned halfway around, he found himself falling. He caught, out of the corner of his eye, a figure of a woman bent down low and moving toward the door.

Tee Ray tried to maintain his balance, but he could not stand up.

A warmth emanated from his leg. First warmth, then pain. Horrible pain. Tee Ray dropped the rifle and reached out to the nearby seat for support.

Jake, knees bent and moving close to the ground, squeezed by Tee Ray as he fell. Ignoring the blood pouring from Tee Ray's thigh, blood that was turning Tee Ray's right trouser leg a dark crimson, Jake pushed Jenny out the door onto the narrow metal platform at the end of the car.

Jake then grabbed Tee Ray, who was leaning on the edge of a seat, around the waist. Kicking the rifle away, Jake hauled Tee Ray out the back door of the carriage and onto the metal platform.

PART XIII

Today

Chapter 88

"'So,' I said, 'you got Cottoncrest. And yet your father was not around to see it happen. What about Ganderson? Did he live to see you get this place?'

"Hank Matthews just sat in his chair and stared at me with the most unusual expression. Couldn't figure out what it was. I was too young to know then what I know now. When you get to a certain age, your past is sometimes more real than your present. When you think back on what happened to you long ago, your memory is like a sieve, constantly sifting through events. You relive them as you think you remember them. You relive them as you wished they had been. You relive them as you ponder what you might have done differently. And you wonder how strange it is that things that seemed inconsequential or even accidental had such a big effect on you that you remember them so well that they are always with you, a theme with endless variations.

"Before you know it, minutes have flown by. You were somewhere far in the past, and then you snap back, and you're here in the present.

"That's kind of what happened. I didn't say anything, and after a few minutes, maybe five, he just looked at me as if he were waiting for me to speak. 'Mr. Ganderson,' I reminded him, 'did he ever know you got Cottoncrest? Did you get a chance to show him that you made a success of yourself without his money?'

"Now Matthews was his old gruff self. 'Hell no,' he said. 'Ganderson was long dead. They all were dead. Ganderson. My Momma. My Daddy. All gone. Don't make no difference, though, because I know what I am, and I know what I got. And I got Cottoncrest. They can talk all they want to about curses and things on this place, but it ain't cursed. It's blessed.'

"He looked up at that big Rebel flag hanging from the long pole nailed to the frieze above the second floor. 'The South shall rise again,' he said, 'and this will be the place it rises. Ain't no one gonna take Cottoncrest away from me, 'cause it's my blessing, just as no one ain't gonna take the South from the white man. My Daddy was right about that. No one has ever done it, and no court can do it now. No Earl Warren, sitting in his black robes—and ain't that a kick, a white man in black robes—sitting in his black robes up in Washington, D.C., is gonna tell us who we have to associate with or go to school with or eat with. Hell, boy, if this thing don't come to a halt, no telling where it's gonna end. Might as well have blacks marrying whites before it's all over, with their little mixed-race pickaninnies running 'round everywhere. Well, it's not gonna happen. No sir. Not here. Not ever. Cotton is white, and that's why Cottoncrest is painted white, and that's why Cottoncrest is gonna stay white.'

"How he got from Ganderson off onto something about the South rising again didn't make any sense to me, but before he got away from Ganderson completely, I had to finish what I had come for. Ganderson was the key to the truth about his past. He just didn't know it yet."

1893

Chapter 89

The trees whipped by, and the soot from the engine's smoke, seven cars ahead, swirled in their faces.

"You cut me!" Tee Ray screamed, swinging his fist into Jake's face and breaking his nose. As soon as Jake released his grip, Tee Ray fell to the metal platform, unable to stand. His right leg was useless now.

Even though Jake's knife had sliced clean through the thigh muscles to the bone, severing all feeling in Tee Ray's right leg, Tee Ray retained a remarkable amount of strength. The blow caused Jake to stagger backward, and blood from his nostrils dripped down onto his stubble of a mustache and beard.

"Now you die, Jew!" Lying on his left side on the metal platform, blood now pouring out of his wounded thigh, Tee Ray reached inside his coat and started to pull out the small Derringer stuck in his belt. It was an over-and-under model with two barrels. He had two shots, but he needed only one.

The knuckle joint holding the first boxcar to the last passenger car gave off metallic groans as the train swayed on the tracks. Jenny, holding onto the railing, saw the small pistol emerge and stomped on Tee Ray's bloody right thigh as hard as she could.

Tee Ray roared with pain and reached out to grab Jenny's leg. Although still lying on the metal platform, he held Jenny's ankle in an iron grip. Jenny could feel her hands slipping off the railing as the train went into a curve.

Jake's vision was blurred. His head was ringing, and his entire face was afire with pain from Tee Ray's blow.

Tee Ray, not letting his left hand loosen its grip on Jenny's leg, raised the Derringer in his right hand.

Jenny let go of the railing and, with her free foot, kicked Tee Ray once again in the spot where Jake had cut up his thigh.

Tee Ray swung the Derringer from Jake to Jenny.

Jake leaped on top of Tee Ray's right arm. Using his knee, he pinned Tee Ray's arm to the platform, but he couldn't wrest the Derringer from Tee Ray's grasp.

Taking the Freimer blade, Jake made a long slice across Tee Ray's right hand. He cut through the muscles and nerves. With a sawing motion, he pushed the blade deeper. He could feel beneath his blade the joints of two fingers separating. The Derringer dropped to the platform. Jake tossed it into the marsh through which the train hurled.

Tee Ray yowled and bared his teeth, but still he held onto Jenny's leg with his left hand. Jake took the Freimer blade and sliced through Tee Ray's left bicep. The muscle separated. The grip on Jenny's leg loosened.

With all of his strength Jake pushed Tee Ray off the platform.

The last that Jenny and Jake saw of Tee Ray was his face, contorted with a yell, screaming at them as he fell off the train and tumbled into the marshy water.

Chapter 90

Long after the train had rumbled out of sight, Tee Ray dragged himself, with great effort, out of the now blood-filled marsh and onto the raised mound of earth the railroad had built for the tracks.

Tee Ray was in pain, but he was alive. He was losing blood, but he didn't feel despair. He was confident. He would live. Even if the peddler escaped now, there was proof that the peddler was guilty of the murders of the Colonel Judge and Rebecca, for who else but a guilty Jew would attack a man with a badge and cut him up and throw him off a train?

Tee Ray had planned it so carefully. Bucky had already proclaimed to the whole parish that it was the Curse and that the Colonel Judge had shot himself after killing Rebecca, which was exactly what Tee Ray had hoped everyone would think. That was supposed to be the end of it. With Rebecca dead and the Colonel Judge gone, and with it just being a matter of time before Little Miss passed, Cottoncrest would fall to the Colonel Judge and Little Miss's lawful heirs.

Tee Ray was in too much pain to smile, but he was satisfied to be the sole lawful heir. How his Momma would have loved to see this day when her son regained Cottoncrest, when her son took over the plantation. Momma could pray all she wanted to for God to forgive her father, the General, for kicking her out and disinheriting her for running off and marrying a Baptist. Momma could bow to what she believed to be God's will that she was poor while her mother and brother were rich. Momma could worship at the little Baptist church every Sunday—never praying for vengeance—while her mother and brother went to the big, fancy Catholic church and returned to their big, fancy home, never speaking to her or acknowledging her presence.

It was so perfect. The Cottoncrest curse had overtaken the Colonel Judge. It was the hand of a vengeful God come to reap justice.

But Raifer started causing problems, raising questions about how the Colonel Judge could have shot himself. There was still an option, however. Tee Ray had figured it out in a flash. The Jew. Jews could always be blamed, and no one would give a Jew any benefit of the doubt.

With the two usable fingers of his right hand, Tee Ray ripped the shredded trousers and formed a makeshift tourniquet for both his left arm and injured leg. He then wrapped the remainder around the stumps of the two fingers on his right hand that the Jew had cut off. This would stem the flow of blood.

Tee Ray knew he was safe here, on the mounded earth and limestone that rose a few feet above the marsh, forming the railroad bed. He was out of the water. He could spot any alligators or snakes from up here. He was alive.

A train would pass by later today. The engineer would spot him.

The train would halt.

He would be rescued, and then the Jew would be caught.

But what if the train was late? What if, before it arrived, he passed out from the constant pain and loss of blood? He had to make sure that those who found him knew the truth. He had to leave written evidence.

What could he write on?

Tee Ray pulled himself up on top of the tracks, each movement now agony. He lay there, stretched across the railings, writing, "The Jew did it," with his own blood on the crosstie.

Tee Ray hadn't realized how exhausted he was. He closed his eyes for just a minute. He would rest a minute, and then he would crawl off the tracks onto the limestone siding and wait.

Tee Ray was still there, unconscious, when the cattle guard of the four o'clock train from New Orleans hit him, unable to stop. The impact cut Tee Ray's body in half, spewing blood everywhere and tossing his now-lifeless torso into the marsh.

The railroad sent a crew out to retrieve it, and if it hadn't had been for the crumpled Petit Rouge deputy's badge pinned to the mangled corpse, they never would have been able to identify him.

Chapter 91

"I don't know where he is. When I woke up, he was gone. I assumed he was at the train station." Bucky sat in the chair, his wrapped foot propped up on a big pillow.

"He wasn't at the train station. And he didn't come back to check with us," the man said. He hadn't given Bucky his name. He had just said he was from the Vigilance Committee.

"Tee Ray must be onto somethin', like a thousand of brick. It's just a matter of time. He's gonna find that Jew if it's the last thing he does. He and I are gonna go home to Parteblanc a-glory. Ol' Cottoncrest ain't never gonna be the same after he and I get back."

✦ ✦ ✦

The passengers in the Jim Crow car said nothing when Jenny and Jake came through the door.

It was not that they lacked anything to talk about. Jenny's cloak was missing, and the woman's clothing that Jake had worn was now gone. Jake's nose was a bloody mess, his face was beginning to swell, and dark circles were beginning to form under his eyes. But the passengers averted their eyes. The white lawman was no longer around. Whatever had happened, they had seen nothing and knew nothing. Ignorance was the safest path.

Jake had used the blanket he had folded as a shawl, as well as the blouse and skirt that Jenny had lent him, to try to wipe up the excess blood off the metal platform. Their other clothes had been tossed into the marsh.

They took their seats as the train continued northward toward the first stop, Hammond, still more than a half-hour away. Jenny rested her head on Jake's shoulder, just like the night before. She was so tired.

Jake put his arm out and held Jenny. He remembered holding Rebecca that one night. At the Colonel Judge's request. Help me have an heir, the Colonel Judge had pleaded. An heir to save Cottoncrest.

By doing what the Colonel Judge had wanted, it had destroyed everything.

The Colonel Judge hadn't known who Rebecca really was. And even after he found out, he still loved her, although that love tore him apart.

Now there were only the children left. Children that the Colonel Judge couldn't bring himself to love and couldn't bring himself to abandon. But in death he had abandoned them anyway.

Chapter 92

The coffin was still on the wagon.

Bucky had not left Tee Ray's body since it had been loaded on the riverboat for the ride upriver to Parteblanc. Bucky had sat in a chair in the hold, next to the coffin, the whole trip, not once going on deck to view the river or the sights. The odors of the hold were now imprinted in his memory. The combined stench of human sweat and dead fish. The grainy smells of the sacks of flour and wheat. The smell of old nets and rope, of muddy water and salted meat, of old barrels of wine and newly made pine crates. And of death.

Now that they were outside of Tee Ray's sharecropper's cabin, Bucky remained next to the wagon, as if guarding the body was the most important thing he could do. He could hear the voices from inside the cabin, voices of Tee Ray's wife and of Raifer and Dr. Cailleteau, but Bucky could not make out the words.

Inside, Mona Brady sat on the bed, surrounded by the children. She daubed her eyes with her kerchief. She had cried so much in the last few days, since the Sheriff had come out with the telegram, that she hadn't thought she had any more tears left. In unexpected moments, however, grief would overwhelm her. Like now.

Raifer handed her a small package. "This was Tee Ray's things. Most of it was pretty badly damaged, as you can imagine, but they salvaged what they could, and this is what they sent."

Mona unwrapped it on her lap. There was not much. The buttons from Tee Ray's coat. A small wad of bills and some loose coins. Tee Ray's suspenders, a set of worn leather braces.

Mona looked up, her eyes starting to water again, and her lower lip quivered with grief. "That's it? That's all there is?"

"That's all they sent," Raifer said kindly, putting his hand on her shoulder.

Mona shrunk back from his touch. "What about his daddy's revolver? Where is his daddy's other revolver? Tee Ray had taken down the second one a while back, and I know he must have had it with him. He wouldn't let his daddy's other revolver ever leave his hand. It was too precious to him."

Raifer pulled up a chair so he could be at eye level with Mona, who was perched on the edge of the bed, the children hugging her and each other and weeping loudly as their mother's emotion spread to them. Raifer spoke softly and gently. "I didn't see Tee Ray carrying any pistol when I saw him and Bucky depart on the riverboat, Mrs. Brady."

Mona pointed to the fireplace. Above the mantel were four nails. Two were empty, the wood behind them stained red with rust in the shape of a pistol. On the other two nails hung a rusty revolver with a large cylinder, an extended handle, and two barrels—a longer one on top and a short, fatter one underneath.

Dr. Cailleteau and Raifer both recognized it right away. It was a LeMat. Just like the rusty one found in the Colonel Judge's hand.

Chapter 93

"We've got to do it, Doc."

Raifer and Dr. Cailleteau were sitting in Dr. Cailleteau's parlor in front of a low fire. The twilight outside was giving way to the cloudy dark of the October evening.

The funeral had been a long one. Mona Brady and the children had wept loudly from before the start of the service at the Baptist church until after the body had been put in the graveyard behind the church and they had been led away by the preacher.

The Knights had been there, filling up the pews and swearing to get revenge. On coloreds. On Jews. On Catholics. On everyone they hated. It didn't matter to the Knights who was really responsible—the coloreds and the Jews and the Catholics all deserved whatever was coming to them.

The rest of the sharecroppers had been there as well as a smattering of folks from town.

At the back of the church Jimmy Joe had taken a seat in the last row, away from everyone else. It appeared to Raifer that, when Tee Ray's coffin was lowered into the grave, a strange and bitter smile momentarily had passed over the blacksmith's features.

Raifer reached out and poured himself another shot of bourbon and passed the bottle to Dr. Cailleteau. "If we don't, it will only hurt the family even more. They've suffered. Let them have their peace. Let them move into Cottoncrest next week believing that Tee Ray died in the pursuit of a Jew and a thief."

"But not a murderer."

"You know that's the way it's got to be, Doc. There can't be a killer of the Colonel Judge if he was the one who killed Rebecca and then turned the gun on himself. And there can't be a murderer if the bullet that the Colonel Judge used to shoot himself was found deep in Rebecca's back in a place under her dress we hadn't examined when Bucky was with us."

Raifer reached into his pocket and pulled out the mashed metal bullet he had dug out of the floorboards at the landing on the second floor of Cottoncrest. Raifer tossed it on the table.

"Raifer, you know what Bucky is going to say, don't you? That he had it right all along. He's going to be acting out that scene of the Colonel Judge and Rebecca until he's eighty years old."

"Doc, just write up the death certificates as Rebecca being killed by the Colonel Judge and the Colonel Judge then committing suicide lying across her back. I've already taken care of the LeMat that was in the Colonel Judge's hand. It will never be found. Let Bucky do all the talking he wants. By the time he's finished, everyone in Parteblanc will believe that the Cottoncrest curse got the Colonel Judge. And who knows, maybe that place really is cursed."

PART XIV

Today

Chapter 94

"Hank Matthews was starting to turn the conversation away from Ganderson, but I stopped him. I had that file folder with me, and now I opened it. 'Mr. Matthews,' I said. 'I think I have something you might be interested in. It's a letter.'

"He asked me why the hell he should be interested in any letter that I had, and I explained that there was a connection between my family and this part of the country. I asked him to take just a moment to read it. I told him if he would just look at it, it might mean something to him.

"He took it from me with suspicion. I told him that the letter was addressed to Jake Gold, who was my grandfather. He got even more suspicious, but he adjusted his glasses, and he read it.

"As he perused it quickly, his face turned red as blood.

"I don't know if he read it carefully, but he clearly had read enough.

"I had not really thought carefully about what his reaction would be. Maybe it was because I was so young. Surprise I expected. Shock, yes. Chagrin? Perhaps. Sorrow? Certainly a possibility.

"But it was none of those things. He exploded into unmitigated anger. Fury. Rage. Resentment. A hostility so palpable it was as if he were possessed.

"Matthews crumpled up the letter into a ball and angrily tossed it in my face. Picking up his rifle and prodding me with its barrel, he forced me off the porch, down the stairs, and onto the driveway, quick-walking me to my car, cursing all the time. I moved as rapidly as I could, stumbling along with the rifle barrel now in my back. I was afraid that even if didn't intend to shoot me, the gun would go off by accident if he tripped.

"I jumped in my rental car and gunned the engine. As I pulled out, the Oldsmobile's tires squealing, I could see him in my rearview mirror, just daring me to turn around so that he could shoot up the car. Or me.

"As I drove away, he yelled at me to get off Cottoncrest and never come back.

"I did as he said. I never returned to Louisiana at all and never came back to Cottoncrest . . . that is, until I came here today with you, more than fifty years later.

"You know, if I thought it would have had that effect on him, I never would have gone in the first place.

"What was in the letter? Is that what you're asking? I have it here. Yes, with me today.

"Look, it's in the inside breast pocket of my coat. Behind you. On the bench. Yes, that's it. In the envelope.

"Open it carefully. It's so old, and the paper is a little brittle. Look, you can still see all the wrinkles on the pages; this is the very letter that I had with me more than forty years ago.

"You're right. It's a copy. The old-fashioned kind, the kind that looks like a negative of a picture, with the background all black and the hand-writing all white. I only brought with me a copy the first time I came; the original was too valuable. I still have that one, the original, in the bank safety deposit box back home, next to my will.

"Just in case anyone needs to get into that box, you know I keep the key to the box in the desk drawer, don't you?

"Okay, don't complain. If you say I've told you that fifteen times before, you're right. It's just sometimes I forget. When you get old, you'll see.

"Look how neat that handwriting is, with old-fashioned flourishes on the letters. I always liked that. It seems to match the old-fashioned flourishes in the language.

"Go ahead. Read it out loud."

> *Dear Mr. Gold:*
>
> *It is with regret that I must inform you, with this epistle, that you should not send any more money. I fear that it is for naught and that, despite all of your best efforts and intentions, all you have sent for the*

past sixteen years not only has had little salutary effect but, rather, has had deleterious consequences.

I have tried, with increasing vigor, to instill in young Hank the need to educate himself and to learn about the world. I have urged him to use his money to further his education and to accumulate a portion of it for future use. You can be sure that I have not revealed to him the source of the funds. He continues to believe that this largesse is entirely my own and that it is a purely eleemosynary effort of one who has taken a liking to a young man.

Despite all my efforts, the mechanisms of his mind have become altered. I fear they will not be righted in the foreseeable future. I would hope, as he ages and grows in maturity, that wisdom will accrue and that one day he will be in a position to comprehend the truth and appreciate all you have done for him and his dearly departed sister.

Even sixteen years later, I know how deeply you still must feel about the loss of his sibling. That she did not live even a week after Jenny brought her to Little Jerusalem is not to blame Jenny or anyone else.

"Who is Jenny? That's an excellent question. You know that I did not find this letter until after Grandpapa Jake had died, so I never had a chance to ask him. It's one of those mysterious things about the past that we never will know.

"Go ahead. Read on."

I have never doubted the correctness of the urgent decision that had been made that awful night at Cottoncrest. I have always believed that saving the lives of both children was an angel's act of mercy and that separating them was the only way to spare both of their lives. Certainly, to protect their safety, they could not know the truth. Even had they each possessed some small memento and proof of their heredity and parentage, such as a small intaglio of their mother, it would have doomed them, for since the Cottoncrest curse struck that night, the rumors persist in Parteblanc and throughout Petit Rouge Parish that Rebecca Chastaine was of mixed blood.

It is better, of course, that young Hank not know at this time that these rumors were true. It is far safer for him not to have any aware-

ness that his twin sister could not pass for white. He does not believe that he is passing, and certainly Jimmy Joe and Maylene do not know. They have held him out to the world as their son. They have never had another child, and I have long suspected that Maylene was unable to bear and thus convinced Jimmy Joe to treat Hank as his son once the baby had been brought to her by Jenny, who must have known of Maylene's plight and hoped that she would accept this child.

Maylene, as I have written to you previously, died egregiously estranged from her sister, Mona. One wonders whether there is some power at Cottoncrest, whether it be curse or otherwise, that destroys families and burrows deep into the minds of those whose lineage lies in Cottoncrest. It seems as if that power has ensnared young Hank's mind at present.

The one hundred dollars you sent for his sixteenth birthday I presented to him, as you desired, but he displayed not an iota of gratitude for this munificence. He is not only ill prepared to use your money wisely, but he has now absented himself and has not been seen or heard from in months. It is said by some that he has gone north and joined the army, but as you can appreciate, this is not something about which I can inquire without raising potential curiosity about my motives and subsequent disquiet and suspicion.

Therefore, I remit to you the money you sent in the hopes that, at some time in this new century in which we now live, young Hank will develop his moral compass and reject the rage of racism that seems to have infected his being for the moment. Perhaps he is merely reflecting Jimmy Joe's attitudes, although I fear it is more than that. This move to separate the races here in the South grows stronger by the moment. No doubt you have read in the papers about the rise of the Klan again and the pillages upon the Negro communities and the lynchings that have occurred. I assure you that what you read is but a thin veneer of the truth and that viciousness and hatred grow as segregation has become part of every aspect of life.

One day, it is hoped, Hank will no longer be so young and naive and will comprehend that the epidermis that cloaks us is but a mere envelope for the blood flowing in our veins and that the envelope's color reflects nothing about its contents.

Mr. Gold, you are a kind and generous man to have, all these years, *been the unseen, unknown, and invisible godfather of young Hank. It is my hope that we will all live to see the day when this young man reaches maturity and is prepared to accept the truth about his parentage and to be thankful to you, a Jew, for protecting and supporting the son of a Catholic of the old Confederacy and his Octoroon spouse through the meager, and as it appears for now, insufficient efforts of your humble agent.*

Sincerely,

Kenneth Ganderson

"So, you see, that's it. They're all dead now, everyone who knew the truth. The Colonel Judge. Rebecca. Grandpapa Jake. Ganderson. Matthews. Maybe that's the real curse of Cottoncrest—that we can never know the complete truth, that each of us bears witness only to our own version of the truth, and that this incomplete vision blinds us in some way that we can never comprehend.

"Tears? Yes, those are tears in my eyes. Tears are a wonderful human trait. We cry at sad and tragic occasions. We cry at joyous ones as well. This whole trip with you has been one of pleasure. And today, especially, being here at Cottoncrest with you, has given me nothing but *nachas*—nothing but happiness and delight and fulfilled contentment. To have been able to share with you all of these memories. You have grown into such a beautiful young woman, and I am so proud of you!

"Give me your handkerchief, will you, to wipe away these tears.

"Yes. *Altsding lozt zich ois mit a gevain.* Everything ends in weeping."